ALSO BY P.G. STURGES

Shortcut Man

Tribulations of the Shortcut Man

ANGEL'S GATE

A Shortcut Man Novel

p.g. sturges

SCRIBNER

New York   London   Toronto   Sydney   New Delhi

SCRIBNER
A Division of Simon & Schuster, Inc.
1230 Avenue of the Americas
New York, NY 10020

First Scribner hardcover edition February 2013

For information about special discounts for bulk purchases,
please contact Simon & Schuster Special Sales at 1-866-506-1949
or business@simonandschuster.com.

The Simon & Schuster Speakers Bureau can bring authors to your live event.
For more information or to book an event contact the Simon & Schuster Speakers Bureau at
1-866-248-3049 or visit our website at www.simonspeakers.com.

Manufactured in the United States of America

1   3   5   7   9   10   8   6   4   2

Library of Congress Cataloging-in-Publication Data is available.

ISBN 978-1-4767-1297-0
ISBN 978-1-4767-1465-3 (ebook)

To Alison Paige Ferguson, my darling girl

&

All of my little people, some of whom are not so little:

Mac, Kelly, Taka, Thomas, Sam, Kian, and Daisy Faye

A Note from the Author

It is not the author's intention to amend, emend, reduce, ameliorate, or redress any wrongs, misfortunes, tragedies, or perditious conditions known to exist in this world or the next. You will depart the premises no wiser than you arrived. However, it is hoped you will be entertained in the meantime.

p.g.sturges

Contents

CONTENTS

CONTENTS

PART THREE

A Sentence

CONTENTS

Epilogues

PART ONE

A Gift

ONE

Justice in the Morning

Nevil Jonson had been giving Jack Hathaway the long, cold screw but I would put an end to it. Daydreaming in my cumulus-ride 1969 Cadillac Coupe de Ville convertible, headed west on Wilshire Boulevard, a section called the Miracle Mile, A. W. Ross's gift to the world of urban planning, only when I passed the La Brea Tar Pits did I realize I'd gone too far.

I reversed course, passed the tar pits again. A million fossils had been extracted from the site, but only one human being. Before stoplights, plumbing, algebra, electricity, and lotto tickets, a young woman had met her demise hereabouts, blunt force trauma to the head.

A body then was as inconvenient as a body today. She had been tossed into the tar pits where her murderer watched until she sank. Nine thousand years later a team of Hancock Park amateur paleontologists had recovered her. Piece by piece.

It set me thinking. Somewhere back there must have been a man like me. A man the grieving family came to, looking for answers about their disappeared kinswoman. What had he told them? Tales of jealous gods? Tales of saber-tooth tigers?

Perhaps, back then, as now, justice did not absolutely require a body. Maybe common sense, circumstantial evidence, would have sufficed. My predecessor would have studied her friends, her family, her lovers. Because, mostly, only those who loved were capable of hate. Then he would draw a conclusion. And then—then, who knows? She might have been inconvenient.

I wondered what they called that man. They call me the Shortcut Man.

I found my destination, the old Desmond's building. I parked on Dunsmuir, walked up to the once-grand stretch of boulevard.

The building directory was aged, too, the white plastic letters crooked. Nevil Jonson, Esq. was on the fourth floor. Suite 404.

Jonson practiced a narrow subspecialty at the periphery of the profession. The DA called it UPL—the unauthorized practice of law.

A blatant violation of a client's trust, most frequently by keeping his money and doing nothing, the usual result was a pablum letter from the State Bar. If the guy did it fifty times he might be prosecuted for a misdemeanor and fined a thousand bucks.

Sometimes, rarely, the lawyer was actually disbarred and ordered to cease practice. In fact, Nevil Jonson had been so ordered. Of course, a practiced bureaucrat, Jonson ignored the order. He then managed to ensnare one Jack Hathaway as a client; that's where I came in.

The elevator grumbled to a stop. I exited into a lobby serving four offices and a restroom. Jonson's office was off to my right. I opened the door and stepped inside.

Suite 404 smelled like a case of diminishing returns, musty, dusty, humid. Out-of-date moderne furniture sagged brownly around the waiting area. A fluorescent overhead flickered intermittently.

"How can I help you?" inquired a woman behind a glass partition. A small vase held plastic flowers.

"I'm Dick Henry." I demonstrated my Mr. Affable smile. "Here to see Mr. Jonson."

Linda Hart looked up at the man in front of her. He wasn't among the usual run of customer. He didn't look worried, rabid, or defeated. Maybe he was another alkie running on a fresh tank of early-morning resolve.

It had taken Linda just a few weeks to realize her boss was a cheat, a thief, and a tartuffle. A man who did nothing for his clients but accept their retainers. Not that the look of the office wouldn't warn a prudent customer. She always took her paycheck directly to the bank. "Is Mr. Jonson expecting you?"

"You told me he would be. Yesterday."

"Have a seat, Mr.—uh . . ."

"Henry."

"Mr. Henry."

The magazines on the table were as stale as the air. I thumbed through a few, learned about cold fusion, pagers, and quadraphonic sound. At least they had come to exist. I still relied on the promise of flying automobiles.

"Mr. Jonson will see you now."

I followed the woman down a short hall, lined with cardboard boxes, to the door at the end.

Jonson's private office had long, narrow windows affording little light. Buildings along the Miracle Mile had actually been designed *to be seen through a windshield* at thirty-five miles per hour. Not lived in and looked out of.

A tall, bony man with a rubicund complexion rose from a disorderly desk. Thin hair, enhanced to a shade of wiry Gouda, fluffed for volume, shaded his scalp. A red tie was the final touch. Matching his face. He approached me solemnly, hand extended. He had perfected a grave, funereal tone. "I'm Nevil Jonson."

We shook hands. "Dick Henry."

He gestured me into a seat. "Coffee?"

As a rule, office coffee will be no better than the lobby magazines.

"No, thanks." I looked around. Nine or ten certificates hung from the walls. There was one sign of life. A vigorous ficus tree rose gracefully from a big, bright, Chinese-yellow ceramic pot three feet high, three feet in diameter.

Jonson took a sharpened pencil from a jar and a fresh legal pad from a credenza behind him. "How may I be of service, Mr. Henry?"

"I'm here for a little advice."

Jonson smiled in neutral. "You're prepared to pay for a little advice?"

"Of course."

"Please continue," said Jonson, pencil point to tongue.

"I have a friend who spent a good deal of money on a certain matter. Now, months and months have gone by, eleven months, and my friend can't get any work done, and the man he hired to do it can't seem to be reached."

Jonson nodded, made bullet points. "A compliance issue. Perhaps fraud. What's the sum involved?"

"Thirty-three hundred dollars."

Jack Hathaway, my old friend at World Book & News, the newsstand, had fallen in love with a Filipina bar girl. All that stood in the way was another bar girl he had married fifty years ago near an air force base in Manila. He had no paper from the event, just an indelible memory of an incredible act she had performed on their wedding night. A feat, even.

"I just want to set things right," Jack had explained, raising his shoulders sheepishly.

What was wrong with bigamy? In this case.

"I want to die a proper married man," said Jack.

In other words he wanted to go down screwed.

"Thirty-three hundred dollars." Jonson did some more scribbling on the legal pad. "Which means we're still in small claims territory."

"It's a lot to him."

Jonson smiled with his teeth. "Now, look. There's no reason to be embarrassed. But I have to know what's what. To help in this matter. Is this friend you're talking about *you*?"

"No, it isn't."

Jonson set pad and pencil aside. "Then I'm a little perplexed. There're going to be fees, here. I don't work for nothing. I'm going to need to know who's who and who's going to pay. Who is this friend you're talking about?"

"His name is Jack Hathaway."

Jonson's eyes narrowed for a second.

"By the way, Mr. Jonson, where's your restroom?"

"Out by the elevators," said Jonson. He was suspicious. "Who's Jack Hathaway?"

"Jack Hathaway is your client." I rose from my chair. "This is a ficus, right?"

Jonson was on his feet, suspicious. "Yes, it is a ficus. What are you trying to pull?"

Pull was, indeed, the word. With a zzzip I emancipated the Love Captain, directed its attention to the dry leaves in the yellow pot.

Jonson's eyes saucered in horror.

I pointed a finger from my free hand at him before he got any bright ideas. "Don't make me piss on your loafers, Nevil, because I'd be happy to." His thin-soled, tasseled lawyer-shoes wouldn't handle it all that well. They weren't built for complications.

"You owe Mr. Hathaway thirty-three hundred dollars. You've had his money for eleven months. Including my fee, the total comes to four thousand nine hundred ninety-nine dollars. Which keeps us, as luck will have it, in small claims territory."

Jonson finally found his voice. "G-get the f-fuck out of my office. I don't respond to blackmail."

I finished off, shook, reeled in, zzziped.

Jonson pointed at the yellow ficus pot. "You're going to pay for that. I'm calling the police."

"Call anybody you want, Nevil. What I'm talking about is your specialty, UPL. The unauthorized practice of law? You're lucky I don't represent all the people you've been screwing. Though I do have your client list." No, I didn't.

I walked up to him, nose to nose. "I'm only interested in Mr. Hathaway. He wants his money back and I want my fee."

I saw his degree on the wall. "That your degree?"

7

He looked at it, perhaps recalling earlier hopes and jubilations.

"Have your secretary write the check I asked for, Mr. Jonson. Right now. And don't make me come back. Or I'll wipe my ass with your certificate."

See how my business works? My efficient arbor service made my final ultimatum a credible threat.

Three minutes later, check in hand, I rolled up La Brea, Chase Bank up ahead on my left. I passed the La Brea Bakery, loving the smell of freshly baked bread.

In my opinion, the baking of bread was the line of demarcation between civilized and uncivilized man. *Homo bakens*. Before I died, I promised myself, I would learn to bake bread. Sourdough.

I took a deep breath. Even more satisfying than the smell of fresh bread—was the smell of justice in the morning.

TWO

Kneepads

If there were a worse dancer in the universe than Amberlyn d'Solay, Mark Markham of the Mark Markham School of Dance had never seen her. She was the size of a linebacker but moved like a lineman.

Everything in proportion, but huge. Dancers' breasts were supposed to be suggestions of femininity, not impediments to motion. Counterweights to that ass. An ass only a breeder could love.

But the money tendered on her behalf was real and the bottom line was all that counted in the end.

Peter was late but entered now with the promised sandwiches from Greenblatt's. His face was smooth and unlined. Peter would break his heart one day. Just as he himself had broken Lawrence's. Just as Lawrence, in his day, had broken a string of older men's hearts. That was the price one paid for a short lease in heaven in this corner of the universe. Soon he would see young men and they would look right past him. And he would have to smile.

Peter kissed him on the cheek, Mark closed his mind, lived in the moment.

Peter turned to the flock of females practicing their entrechats. "Good God, that cow is back."

"Amberlyn d'Solay."

Amberlyn galumphed her way across the studio, giant arms high in the air. She could probably lift a Subaru and throw it across the room.

Peter smirked. "What do you think her real name is?"

Mark shook his head. "Colonel Sanders, I don't know. I have three of them."

"Three?"

"A new one last week. Same exact body type. All blondes. All on scholarship."

"Who pays?"

Markham had wondered that himself. Devi Stanton was the girl who visited, wrote the checks, but she was obviously someone's employee. Never once inquired about progress. *Progress*. Not with that trio of elsies.

Well, speak of the devil. Mark waved at the girl walking in, glanced at Peter. "That's who pays."

Devi was a pretty girl, late twenties. Black hair, hazel eyes, one arm fully sleeved in vibrant Asian tattoos. Cresting waves and dragons.

"Hi, Mark," she said. She pulled out a checkbook, tore out a completed check, handed it to Markham. "For Amberlyn, Stacy, and Michelle."

Markham looked at it, the figure was correct. A hundred per session, three sessions per week, three cows. Nine hundred dollars.

Peter stepped forward, extended a hand to the tattooed woman. "I'm Peter."

"Devi."

They shook. Devi sized him up. A beautiful boy who knew he was beautiful.

"You pay for Amberlyn," said Peter.

"I do. Why?" Devi wondered where he was going with this. Kid looked like a smartass.

"That's was what I was going to ask you."

Amberlyn pirouetted, miscalculated, fell with a thud. Rattled the windows. Markham moved in her direction but Amberlyn waved him off. Devi restrained a smile, turned back to Peter.

"Amberlyn is being specially groomed."

"Groomed?" inquired Smartass.

Amberlyn got to her feet.

"Yeah, groomed," said Devi. "What of it?"

Peter grinned at Mark, then back at Debbie or whatever her name was. "Why don't you just cut to the chase and buy her some kneepads?"

Markham watched Devi, who had not been humorized. He kept a straight face, glared at Peter, shocked, shocked.

Devi glared at Markham. "Hey, Mark, your boyfriend is an asshole."

She turned on her heel. Out she went.

Markham turned to Peter. "What the fuck?"

But Peter was laughing, bent at that supple waist, holding his sides.

"I'm serious," said Markham. "Don't fuck up my good thing, bitch." But he couldn't be mad at Peter. He loved him too much. And then they both were laughing.

Behind the Desmond's building, chest heaving, Nevil Jonson stood with hands on hips, perspiring. That Dick Henry son-of-a-bitch had ruined his ficus. His office had smelled like the men's room in the park after the illegal aliens played soccer and drank beer all afternoon. Now, yellow pot and all, forlorn, the ficus stood crookedly by the Dumpster. Henry would get his. Wait and see.

Motivation

Howard Hogue had loved once and that had proved sufficient. Angela, coincident with his first million, had taken the first exit. Brokenhearted, eager to prove her apprehension of his character in error, he had given her everything in a spasm of generosity.

His lawyer had called him an ass. In his weaker moments he had agreed with his lawyer. But the wording of his generosity clause, an ultimatum of sorts, precluded her from ever coming back for more. It didn't mean much back then. But now, a billion dollars later, the Hogue clause was the stuff of legal legend.

However, with his acquisition of fortune came the realization he could never trust again. Was he the object of affection or was it his wallet? He knew he would never be wise enough to be certain.

His solution was to buy people, wholly and completely. Then there were no misunderstandings. He never went cheap and the purchased persons clearly knew he or she had been purchased. When he tired of their services, sexual, psychological, monetary, or even automotive, he tossed them aside without guilt.

He had women all over Hollywood. Twenty-eight, he believed, but he had to count. From the rear of Soundstage 13, where he stood with his assistant, the fully purchased Melvin Shea, he watched Heather Hill and wondered if she might be number twenty-nine. Or was it thirty?

On the set, under the lights, was a detective's drastically untidy office. Papers haphazard on every horizontal surface, and on the desk, on top of more paper, a revolver and bullets.

Night. Rain beat against the window, view occluded by damaged Venetian blinds hanging at angle.

Behind the desk Smokin' Jack Wilton, heartthrob of the moment, played his biggest part yet, Johnny Marion, hard-boiled private dick up to his ass in trouble. Across his desk was the traditional damsel in distress, Angela. Known to her parents as Ann-Heather Ballogler, to her agent and Howard Hogue she was Heather Hill.

Sidestage, director Eli Nazarian leaned forward. "And . . . action."

"Speed," said the cameraman's runner, letting everyone know the camera was working properly.

Angela, blond and very busty, sat up straight, thrusting her bosom forward. "How can I ever repay you, Johnny?"

Johnny ran his eyes over her frame. "I think you know how, doll."

"That's all you want from me? I have a lot more to give."

"Sorry, babe. My heart ain't workin' right."

Angela rose from her chair, looked down at Johnny. "Well, if that's what Johnny wants, that's what Johnny gets."

Lightning flickered, thunder crashed.

Angela walked around the desk, Johnny spun his chair around to face the window. Angela trailed her fingers on his knee, then knelt down, disappearing from the camera's view.

ZZZip.

Johnny rested a hand on her head. "That's it, darling." From below desk level came a deep moan. "Mmmmm."

Johnny closed his eyes in rapture—one, one thousand, two, one thousand, three—but suddenly hands were waved widely from behind the desk and Heather stood up. "Wait! Wait! Hold on a minute. What's my motivation at this point?"

Nazarian the director, famous for his vile temper, leapt to his feet, threw his script to the floor. "Cut! Cut!" He pulled on his long black wavy hair in furious incredulity. "Heather. You fucking *moron*. Your motivation? What are you talking about, motivation? You're giving Johnny a blow job. That's your motivation. *Blow job*."

Melvin Shea eyed his boss.

"I like this girl," said Hogue.

Melvin nodded. The dumber the better. "Yes, sir, Mr. Hogue." Number thirty. Actually, number twenty-nine. After he dispatched Bambi back to the minor leagues.

You couldn't eat a Pink's hot dog everyday, it just couldn't be done. Like Mark Twain's report about eating quail thirty days in a row. An implacable revulsion set in. But every once in while a Pink's chili dog was the only thing that could satisfy.

Pink's was an LA institution, architecturally unique as add-ons accreted over the years. Ancient, greasy, B- and C-list framed celebrity headshots lined the walls of the dining salon.

Keep cookin', Pinks! Pitt Wheadon
Dog me, Dude! Shep Archer

I preferred the tables out back.

It was there I waited for a new client, referred by Jack Hathaway. Mrs. Clendenon was from Tacoma. Paper mills came to mind. The aroma of Tacoma. Probably all those jobs were gone now. Exported way south, where no one complained about odor.

I looked up to see a nice-looking strawberry blonde staring at me. She wasn't Hollywood thin, she looked like a mom. Which reminded me that Georgette, my ex, had been calling. Couldn't figure out why. I was up to date on all payments and the washing machine was working. Maybe the tank was leaking again in the upstairs bathroom. Or, worse yet, bowl seepage.

I stood up, visored my eyes. "Mrs. Clendenon?"

She came forward. "Mr. Henry?"

She had a strong, unpretentious handshake. I pulled out one of the white plastic chairs for her.

"Thank you, Mr. Henry."

No one called me Mr. Henry for very long. Pretty soon we were both two dogs down.

"That was a good dick, dog."

She couldn't have meant that. *"What did you say?"*

Mrs. Clendenon was horribly embarrassed. "Please forgive me, Mr. Henry."

"Of course."

"What I meant to say was, *that was a good dog, Dick.*" She waved her hands, shook her head. "That doesn't sound all that much better." Her face was crimson.

I came swiftly to the rescue. "You're right. These are the best dogs in L.A." I studied her. "Now what's on your mind?"

Mrs. Clendenon breathed deep, looked at me. "It's my sister."

She reached into her big purse, pulled out an envelope, took out a picture. She slid it across the table.

It was an old photo. A high school yearbook shot. "How old is this?"

"Ten years ago," she said.

"That's quite a while."

"For a long time I thought I didn't care."

"I take it she came here."

Mrs. Clendenon nodded.

"To Hollywood or L.A.?"

"Is there a difference?"

"Big difference."

"She wanted to be in show business."

"Hollywood, then."

"I guess so."

I looked at the picture again. She was pretty. But not Ava Gardner pretty, not Jennifer Connolly pretty. "She get any work?"

"Little things, you know. Here and there. But I don't know any titles." Then she remembered something. "I do remember something. Ivanhoe."

"The movie Ivanhoe? Or the production company, Ivanhoe?"

She thought a moment. "Maybe it *was* Ivanhoe Productions."

"Ivanhoe Productions, Howard Hogue."

"Hogue. I've heard that name. He invented the paper clip."

"Then he must be about a hundred and fifty years old."

"*Someone* invented the paper clip."

"Maybe it *was* Hogue. Right after he finished up the wheel."

We had a good laugh. I liked Mrs. Clendenon. "When was the last time you spoke with your sister?"

"Six years ago."

"That's quite a while. Why now?"

She hesitated for just a second. "Dad is sick."

"Did she have a stage name?"

"She liked her own name. Ellen Arden."

FOUR

Little Melvin Prevails

I took care of few smaller matters, then headed up into Hollywood proper. I parked on Cahuenga, crossed the street to World Book & News. Jack Hathaway worked the afternoon shift.

He looked up at me with his crooked grin and pirate squint. "Hey, Dick."

I peeled a honeybee off my moneyclip, put it into his shirt pocket.

Aside from his morbid interest in matrimony, Jack was a decent, optimistic human being. He studied the picture of Benjamin Franklin with honest gratitude. "What's this for?"

"That's for referring Mrs. Clendenon."

He nodded. "Glad that worked out."

"It sure did." Mrs. Clendenon had left me a thousand-dollar retainer. "And . . . I got some news for you."

"News? You're getting married, too?"

I snorted. As if. "Been there, done that. Lost sixty percent of my worldly goods." I smiled. "I've been to see Mr. Jonson."

"My lawyer?"

"The very man."

Jack shook his head. "Look. Maybe I was a little hard on him. Maybe he just works a little slow."

"Actually, he felt pretty bad after I talked to him. He wanted to give you a full refund."

"He did?"

"He did. Said he was sorry for all the trouble."

Jack shook his head. "Wow. And I thought he was a prick."

I handed Jack a substantial envelope. Thirty-three Benjamins. He didn't count them.

I had other matters to attend to, had to push on. "Don't get married, Jack."

"Why not, Dick? Why not?"

What a sweet soul he was. "Because you're *already* married."

Jack reflected. Sadly. "You're right, Dick. I am. Delia." As I drove for Laurel Canyon I couldn't help wondering. What feat had Delia performed?

Melvin Shea remembered listening to a late-night, sci-fi radio show. The genial but credulous host entertained all scenarios as possible. Aliens, astral projection, possession by evil spirit, death by cosmic ray, sludgification of all rivers, failure of genetically engineered vegetables to maintain human sustenance.

This particular evening was devoted to the horrors of overpopulation. What if there were fifty billion people on earth? Why, we'd run out of room! We'd be standing in the sea!

No, you ass, thought Melvin. There is only a finite amount of water on earth. It could be in the seas and glaciers, or it could be contained, fifty kilograms at a time, in a human body. That's where the water would be. Fifty billion people meant that the Big Apple would be inland. People were just big bags of water.

And sometimes no more intelligent than a big bag of water. Heather Hill. What did Hogue see in them all? Aside from the obvious.

Heather Hill. Full of ridiculous ambition. Unattached to the real world. Hadn't understood the concepts they'd discussed after she was thrown off the set of *Gumshoe.* The Ivanhoe talent program. Use of her talents. Gratitude. You could lead a horse to water but you couldn't make it see it would have to fuck the boss.

Well, if she got with the program, he knew where'd he'd put her. The vacancy on Harper Avenue. Which was slightly in the future.

He parked his Beemer on De Longpre, a thirty-second walk from Bambi Benton's Harper Avenue, West Hollywood apartment. He could see her windows, spread wide for the sunshine and the breeze.

Bambi Benton was a bag of water, too. But at least she knew it. In fact, she was a little too smart for her own good.

Her digs were top class, for her station in life. Nice flagstone courtyard, flowers, trellises, a fountain. She buzzed him in. He walked up to the third floor, knocked.

He was tapping his foot by the time she opened up. Bambi was casual, black capris, blue chambray shirt, sandals. She was close to six feet tall, with the de rigueur blond hair and big chest. Big wasn't quite the word. Heroic.

She also would know by now that her free ride had likely come to an end.

She looked at Melvin with sad baby-doll eyes. "Hi, Melvin," she said in a tiny voice, "come on in."

He looked around. He always had liked this particular apartment, big windows facing west, wide-planked wooden floors, nice comfortable leather furniture.

"You don't have great news," said Bambi.

Good. She'd read the tea leaves. "No, I don't. Sorry."

"I've been writing," she volunteered. "I just need a little more time. I'm on to a really good thing. Real money. Then I'll move out."

"Don't bullshit me about real money. The only kind that counts is cash money."

"I need thirty days, Melvin."

"I think we had that discussion last month. What can I do? You know what's up."

"I tried really hard."

"Trying doesn't count. You never established a good thing with Howard."

"After a while, Howard just didn't like me."

He shrugged. "What can I say? You wanted Howard to read your screenplay."

"I spoke my mind."

"You don't have a mind. And Howard didn't hire you to speak it."

"You . . . I liked." Bambi undid a button on her chambray shirt.

Melvin absorbed a lengthening jot of adrenaline. "What do you have in mind?"

Bambi loosed another button. "I don't have a mind."

Not much of one, he had to agree. But those tits. "Maybe you're of two minds," he reasoned.

Bambi allowed her tongue to visit the corners of her mouth.

"Why don't I talk . . . to Little Melvin. Maybe he could help me."

"Maybe he could. Little Melvin always appreciates a consult."

She sat down on the arm of the big black leather recliner.

He walked toward her. Seven steps to heaven. Well, five steps.

Now he was hurrying to his car. A lamp had just crashed behind him on the steps. Then an ashtray.

"You lowdown son-of-a-bitch," shrieked Bambi. She'd been used like a Kleenex.

Melvin reached the sidewalk. Bambi threw like a girl. He was probably safe. He looked up. "Like I said. You've got twenty-four hours to vacate your ass outa there. Get me?"

"Fuck you, you weasel."

Ha! A weasel who just plastered your tonsils. Her rage filled him with a golden ebullience. He was Melvin Shea! Melvin Shea, Hollywood producer! Melvin Shea drove a BMW, knew everyone in town. And he had just whitewashed the epiglottis of a beautiful potted plant! Which reminded him . . . what about a remake of *Tom Sawyer*?

Or was he thinking of her uvula? Whatever that thing was. In her throat.

He pointed at her. "Twenty-four hours, outa there, or I send in G
nady to help you."

Gennady, the drunken, dentally deprived potbellied unshaven Mus
vite handyman, God's gift to the women of the world.

The Beemer started right up with a powerful growl. Life in the f
lane, baby.

Surely make you lose your mind. Ha!

FIVE

The Horizontal Mambo

I got home just in time to think of Myron Ealing and head back to Hollywood.

I loved Hollywood. The lights, the sounds, the dreams, the schemes, the schemers. You could win the world, you could lose your soul. And I guess you could do both at the same time.

Myron had an office in the Hollywood Professional Building at Hollywood and Cahuenga. He'd been a very heavy mathematician but had blown his mind on string theory.

String theory said that everything in the universe was composed entirely of tiny strings—vibrating like guitar strings—that different pitches produced different phenomena—neutrons, electrons, quarks, and—and the rest of them. More every year. The only problem with the theory, said Myron, was that bullshit also vibrated.

Now Myron was compiling the definitive encyclopedia of pornography. In the process, he had learned everything about everybody in Hollywood. They didn't call Chuck Connors the Rifleman for nothing.

I entered off Hollywood and climbed the stairs to the fourth floor. Somewhere someone was singing opera on the second floor. Loud and not English.

Myron met me at the door. "Hello, Brother Dick. Come on in." He extended one of his huge hands.

Myron weighed four hundred twenty pounds. The weight had come years earlier, on the heels of an excruciating personal tragedy. He had since abjured the company of women. I had never known him during the days of his movie-star looks and unshadowed laughter.

We went back to the inner sanctum and Myron sought the refuge of his desk and the ever-present barrel of stale Christmas popcorn.

Again I heard cut-rate Pavarotti yodeling in the distance. "What's up with that? The Three Tenors move into the building?"

Myron laughed. A big, low hoot. To hear it was to like him. "The One Tenor. He gives singing lessons, I guess."

"You guess?"

"Well, none of his student's seem to be able to sing." Myron spread his hands, grinned. "But he gets paid. So Phil doesn't mind."

"Maybe Phil hasn't heard him."

The low hoot again.

Phil was a drummer who'd inherited the Hollywood Professional Building from his father. He ran a tight ship, business wise. Legend had it he'd played drums for Blue Cheer. Albeit for ten minutes. Then he'd quit. But too late. The damage had been done. His hearing had never recovered.

Myron slid the popcorn across the desk to me. "So what's up?"

"I've come to question the sage. Ever heard of an actress named Ellen Arden?"

Myron leaned back, studied the ceiling, put his prodigious mind to work. "Heard the name. Five or six years ago, maybe. I think she did a few little things."

"She may have been associated with Ivanhoe."

Myron gave him a squint. "Not good. Ivanhoe had a two-track system."

"What's that mean?"

Myron searched for words of the proper piquancy, found them. "Lemme put it this way. One track was on screen, the other track was on your back."

"Ahh. The horizontal mambo."

"You're a Little Feat fan?"

"Shouldn't everyone be?" Little Feat was a legendary L.A. band that had suffered the slings and arrows of outrageous fortune. Side one of *The Last Record Album* equaled anything by the Stones or the Beatles or anybody else. Right up there. Self-assured, comfortable in their own skin, sublime tunes, recorded beautifully. The sudden sadness of "Long Distance Love" entered my mind. I'd had some of that.

Little Feat continued its sojourn round the planet to this day. Minus their wonderful drummer, Richie Hayward, whose contributions to the universe did not qualify him for health insurance. If only he'd made keys or cut lumber at Home Depot. God bless the Feat, every one.

Ealing reached for a fat, tattered address book, dug through it. "I'm going to call Connie Daniels. Think she used to be a housemother at Ivanhoe."

"Sounds like the Girl Scouts."

"With the Sodom and Gomorrah Merit Badges." Ealing found what he was looking for. "Here she is."

I looked at Myron's dilapidated compendium of friends, enemies, acquaintances, and contacts. "You haven't gone digital?"

Ealing winked, shook his head. "I like my secrets on paper, Dick. When I throw them away, they're gone."

On the second floor of Hollywood Professional, in Suite 212, Andrea Montefiori was wondering how he, a musical genius from Padua, had come to be here. Of course, he was happy for the work. Any work. But to teach those who did not possess the ability to learn, that was another thing.

Michelle d'Orsay was such a person. He remembered an admonition about teaching a pig to sing. *Don't do it*. It can't—and it won't like it.

Montefiore's task was to teach this woman to sing. Yet something down deep was wrong. He'd had many students over the years. Rich, poor, richly talented, or threadbare, all partook of the desire to express themselves more fully. In a musical manner.

This woman, built like a '58 Cadillac, was a puzzle. He could discern no inclination to song. Yet she had convinced someone to pay for lessons. Obviously, there was some aspect of a sugar-daddy involvement. Maybe daddy was deaf as well as stuffed with Viagra.

She stared into her compact mirror, mouth in an o, picking at her eyelashes.

Everything about her was staggeringly, stupendously artificial; an amalgamation of inserts, implants, and implausibilities. From those green eyes to those blinding teeth, to those grapefruits on a plank. Even her name. Michelle d'Orsay.

The name intimated an association with the fragrant rosewater of Paris. But no. He'd looked through her purse when she'd tottered down the hall to the ladies' room on those spindly high heels. She was eight feet tall. Her driver's license said Plurpkin. Eloise Plurpkin. From Centralia, Washington. A famous hotbed of culture and creativity.

And he, the great Montefiore, was tasked with teaching Plurpkin to sing.

"Okay," he said, "let's try it again. Push—from the diaphragm."

Eloise snapped her compact shut. "I've never used a diaphragm."

He was confused. English was a second language. They didn't teach context in books. "What? What do you mean?"

"I got a Depo shot."

He grasped for meaning. "What is a Depo shot?"

"Gun control."

"*Gun control?*"

"I meant birth control."

Montefiore felt his temper beginning a slow boil. "Look," he said, grinding a molar, patting his abdomen, "push, push from down here." He tightened up beneath his belt, relaxed his throat, let sound rise out. Like a fountain. "La, la, la, la, laaaaa." He looked at her. "Like that. Okay?"

"Okay."

He walked over to the computer. "Ready?"

She nodded. He pressed the start key and the music resumed.

He put a hand to his diaphragm, gestured her to begin.

She opened her mouth—and why the fuck was he surprised? In a dreadful, thin, quavering, off-key bleating came the lyrics. "People, people who need people—"

Montefiore felt an eye start to bulge and then he vesuviated. "No, no, no, no, NO!"

SIX

The Golden Gun

Howard Hogue's office was huge. A hundred twenty feet by a hundred fifty, fourteen foot ceiling. Every day, from behind his mahogany desk, he took pleasure in its expanse. The world at large pressed in upon a person, pushing to swallow them up. The size of your office was a measure of how hard you pushed back.

His office was divided into sections, so that he might accommodate his guests in various ways.

The desk area, directly across from the entryway, conferred a measure of formality. From his desk he might commend, negotiate, or reprimand. Behind his desk was a twenty-foot width of floor-to-ceiling windows that gave out on the lot. With a touch of a button, the glass could go dark.

To his right, with various small hills, lay the three-hole putting green. The green terminated in a thick stand of ficus trees.

On the far side of the ficus grove, a koi pond and a Japanese sand garden summoned a visitor's subtle sense of *wa*. Harmony, peace, and balance. Around the pond was informal seating, used to greet friends, such as they were, and to woo new people into his life as necessary for new projects.

Every day, Sensei Odo Kinichi precisely raked the sand garden and inscribed the day's symbols. Supposedly, Kinichi took his patron's astrological sign and the I Ching into consideration before setting implement to sand. Kinichi had long since perfected the solemn Japanese wise man routine. Bowing, muttering, gazing inward. Probably a callus where each thumb met forefinger. OMMMMM. With a sushi chef's bandana to boot. On the lot it was whispered that wise Sensei Kinichi could levitate.

Hogue laughed. Kinichi liked redheads with big Western racks. But visitors expected a successful producer to be extravagant and arcane, and the black-sand semiotic humbuggery seemed to satisfy them. Though the epigram that had fomented the greatest comment had been done by Demosthenes. An odd corollary to crop circles. Demosthenes was a cat. Before his hurried expulsion from paradise, Demosthenes had buried a souvenir in the imported sand.

The last section of the office was a conference area, the long table brought in through the big windows. It could seat twenty-two ass-kissers at a time. That was another of the troubles with money, no one ever told you the truth again—just words carefully fashioned to impress your money.

He looked at his watch. It was time for another move in the endless chess game of life. He pushed the bar on the intercom.

"Yes, Mr. Hogue?"

"Send them in, Helena."

"Right away, sir."

In the waiting room six people waited. Melvin Shea held his face neutral. The five searched his face for clues, nervous and uncertain. He possessed a factotum's power of access and influence. But once in Hogue's office, that power evaporated. Soon they would look past him. And he would hate them.

Shea had entered Hogue's gravitational sphere as a new face in town, a hot young producer. They'd made a few things, more than broken even, but not much more, had created nothing that changed lives. Then, some-where along the line, in proving to Hogue his access to the menu of the hidden and forbidden, he had moved from associate to employee. The smoothest of lines to cross.

The money was unbelievable. Intoxicating. Glorious. Irresistible. Then, one day, he realized he couldn't do without it.

Hogue had changed as well. Oh had he? Peremptory. A brusque edge, was that it?

And the power of Melvin's office, almost Caesaric. *Almost*. That was the rub. His sure knowledge of its limits fostered a cruelty in its use. The starlet who attempted to use him for access to Hogue was well used in the process. He would casually explore her limits of humiliation and self-abasement. Then, depending on Melvin's mood, Howard would be busy. Or not.

Chrissie Volanta, executive producer, was studying him. "How are you, Melvin? Lost in your thoughts?"

The other four peered at him. Nazarian, the golden boy, successful director, prince of Hollywood. Arnie Mannheim, producer, Hud Fisher, his partner, Anne Hall Black, principal writer.

Melvin was their living barometer. The face of Hogue's mind. He shrugged. "Oh, I'm alright, Chrissie." The movie had been a big success. They'd be fine. Bastards.

The door opened, Helena Richards put her head in. "Mr. Hogue will see you now."

Without thinking, the five rushed ahead of him. With a pang, Melvin readjusted his face. Bastards.

Six chairs had been positioned around Hogue's desk. Melvin took the one at the extreme right.

Hogue leaned back, savored the hunger of his guests. He twirled a pencil, dawdled. This was his moment to play, he could stretch it out as long as he wanted. He looked solemnly from face to face. Finally, he grinned and everyone relaxed. "Well, the final numbers are in for *Terminal Velocity*. We've done very well. Ivanhoe's biggest ever, domestic. Two hundred eighty-seven million."

Producers Mannheim, Fisher, and Volanta cheered, hi-fived. Anne Hall

Black concentrated her *ki,* breathed deeply. She would be rich. Which was a relative term. And she'd forgotten the DVD market! The rule of thumb stated that DVD sales would equal domestic box office. She *was* rich.

Hogue regarded them all. "In addendum to my last, let my just say that *Terminal Velocity* has done two hundred eighty-seven mil *so far.* Now come the discount houses, and foreign should be significant. Especially Japan. In lieu of all this good news, I've asked Helena to prepare a few documents." He turned to Helena, standing to the side. "Helena?"

Helena stepped forward, passed a manila envelope to Hogue.

He took it, looked inside, grinned. Then pulled out a sheaf of checks. He slipped on his spectacles, opened one of the checks. He looked up at Anne, the writer. "Anne, this is for you."

Anne watched herself accept the check. Watched herself unfold it. *$1,000,000.* She was numb. "Th-thank you, Howard."

Hogue nodded. "You're welcome." He opened another. "Arnie?" Mannheim took his check.

As did Hud and Chrissie.

Melvin tried to maintain nonchalance in the presence of others' extreme good fortune. "Congratulations, folks," he croaked, parched with envy.

Everyone had been gifted except him and Nazarian.

In case there were nothing, which couldn't be, Nazarian effected a cool nonchalance. Something was coming. Or why was Shea visibly leaking jaundice and spite? Nazarian breathed deep, channeled patience. How many times had he come in second at award ceremonies? Forced to cheer for others? For the talentless and the undeserving.

Hogue examined them all. It was a game of many dimensions. Centered around money, of course. His money. He'd left Nazarian till last, so he could watch him pretend nothing mattered. And Shea—Shea was wearing out his teeth suppressing his covetousness. He'd give Shea a taste—but only a taste. It was all that was required. "And now for our director, Eli Nazarian."

Nazarian sat up straight, smiling, bashful, like a puppy. A vicious puppy. But a puppy that shat gold. He'd just have to make sure there were plenty of newspapers. "Helena, the box."

All eyes turned to view a finely crafted wooden box Helena picked up from a table off to the side.

"Eli, this is for you," said Hogue. "With my thanks and congratulations." He smiled. "And I know this is only the beginning."

"*Gumshoe* will be just as good," said Nazarian.

"I have no doubt." Hogue gestured that Helena might give it to Nazarian. She passed it into his outstretched hands.

Shea watched the Asshole from Armenia spread anticipatory delight over his fashionably unshaven countenance. *A gift from Howard Hogue!* Nazarian would rejoice over anything he found. A comic book. A dog bone. A dog turd.

Nazarian opened the box and drew a quick breath. In the box, on a bed of rich burgundy velvet, was a gold-plated revolver and silencer. A Smith & Wesson Model 500. Fully loaded, with five .50-caliber bullets, it weighed five pounds. Bullets would fly from this thing at 1,625 feet per second, if he remembered correctly. Engraved perfectly on the barrel: *Terminal Velocity—Eli Nazarian—from Howard Hogue.*

Nazarian reached in and picked it up. Then reached for the silencer, screwed it on. With two hands he hefted it, pointed it in the direction of the ficus grove.

"Biggest handgun in the world," said Shea.

Nazarian turned, pointed it at Shea. "I think you may be right."

"Be careful with that thing," said Hogue. "It's gold plated, but it's real."

Melvin felt an increased gravity in his testicles, hoped he wasn't trembling. "Put it right here," he said, placing the tip of his index finger between his eyes. Hogue's remonstrance of Nazarian had not come from a real concern for his well-being. Midas didn't want a mess.

Nazarian winked at Shea, lowered the pistol. "Melvin knows I love him."

Nazarian again examined the weapon, looked up to Hogue. "Howard, thank you so much. I don't know what to say." He paused. "Almost."

There was a general bray of laughter.

The Asshole from Armenia, over time, had secured a reputation for having the last word on any subject. Disagree, on the set, and whack—you were fired. So different from the time Melvin had first met him—met him and brought him into the fold. Then he was diffident, polite, obliging. Melvin had misread the *calculating* part.

"Oh," said Hogue, patting down his pockets in pretended confusion, "I almost forgot." From his inside jacket pocket he brought another envelope. "Eli . . ."

The Grateful Armenian took the proffered envelope, a flash of humility passing through his body language.

Melvin watched the scenario, pushing his feelings down. He would be careful. As always. But Nazarian would rue the day he had thrust Melvin aside. Because, inside any organization, all projects required an uncle—an inside man *committed* to the matter at hand—the man who would assure that even a sure thing would not accidentally run off the tracks. Because eventually, in the production process, all projects got wobbly. Well, Asshole no longer had such an uncle. Which was why *Gumshoe* was subtly running into difficulties. Scheduling, craft services, minor casting. Case in point, that imbecile, Heather Hill. *Motivation.*

"Open that envelope when you're sitting down, Eli," counseled Hogue, grinning, surveying the scene. Melvin didn't much care for Eli, that much was clear.

Hogue patted himself down again. "Wait a second, what's this?" Then, with a smile, he pulled the last envelope out, handed it to Melvin. "Don't spend it all in one place, Melvin."

Nazarian sat, looked into the envelope. *Christ Jesus Mary and Joseph.* "Howard," he said, shocked into real emotion, "thank you. Thanks for everything." His future had arrived. Like he had known it would. Now what would he do with it?

• • •

In the privacy of his office, across the lot, Melvin tore open his envelope. A hundred grand. What the fuck. Pitiful. A taste, a whim, a subtle insult. Because Helena's assistant owed him, he knew what the others had received. At a minimum, each of them had made ten times as much. And that *fucking* Armenian.

Once upon a time, a hundred thousand dollars in hand would have been a stupefying sum. But then he had met rich men. Consorted with them. They could drop that much in Vegas in a night. Every night. Whores and coke. Bread and circuses.

Christ. He had to start producing again. Really producing. Finding good scripts, attaching talent, spreading some risk around. He had to get off the Hogue train. Because it would kill him.

SEVEN

Devi

I had been tempted, over the years, to get rid of my Caddy. My '69 Cadillac Coupe de Ville convertible. But then, cruising down one of the big boulevards, Wilshire, Sunset, Hollywood, lounging back, driving with just a finger, a feeling of well-being would come over me. Those men from Detroit knew what they were doing. At least for a while. Before the Yellow Peril ate their bento box.

Myron Ealing had called me. Connie Daniels, housemother at Ivanhoe, was long gone. Her replacement, Devi Stanton, had been there going on four years. But she's heard of the Shortcut Man, said Myron, grinning. She'll meet with you tonight, if you're interested.

I called her. She was terse, not too friendly. We'd decided on Canter's. I figured if she had nothing at least I could get a good Reuben.

As far as Reubens were concerned, Canter's had the best in L.A. Sixty years of practice. Canter's was open 24/7, rain, shine, or earthquake. A million years ago the place had been a theater. The Esquire. Preston Sturges movies had probably played there. Sending the populace back into the streets, weary hearts lifted, able to slog on for another day. Now the bakery did Sturges's job.

Lot of stars at Canter's, too. I'd seen Brian Wilson, Tom Waits, David

Lee Roth. And lots of people you'd only recognize during their fifteen minutes. Which took only ten minutes these days.

I parked in their lot, down on the corner, got my ticket, and walked up Fairfax.

The familiar smells greeted my nose. They knew me here and the greeting lady welcomed me personally. "Hi, Jack," she said. "Howya been?"

"Fine, thank you." *Jack.* Guess it was better than Dick-Dave. The hayseed.

I looked past her into the lower seating area, saw a likely suspect. I pointed and greeting lady nodded, *go ahead.*

In the middle aisle on the left, underneath the autumnal ceiling squares, sat a pretty woman, black-haired, hard-looking. One arm was fully sleeved in well-executed oriental tattoos.

She reminded me of Eileen Klasky, but younger. Eileen, who had famously married a dead man, now emptied bedpans in a minimum-security lockup.

Tattoo-lady looked up.

"Are you Debbie?" I asked.

"I'm *Devi.* You the Shortcut Man?"

"That's what they call me."

"Sit."

I sat. "Have you ordered?"

"Not yet. I thought you might want to buy me dinner."

I liked her immediately. "It so happens, I do."

"You and I could get along."

"We just might."

Our waitress, Pat, a disagreeable old crab, whom I enjoyed very much, arrived. "What'll it be?" she inquired gruffly, tapping a sneakered foot. She'd given up on humanity several decades earlier. Just my style. I extended an open hand toward Devi.

"Reuben, pastrami, well-done, so the cheese melts, fries, and a Heineken," said Oriental Arm.

A woman who knew exactly what she wanted. Wow!

"And you, sir?" asked Pat.

"I'm going to have exactly the same thing, including the Heineken. And can we have a plate of pickles?"

"Plate of pickles." Noted. "Is that it?"

"It's a start."

With a grunt, Old Gruff snapped her little book shut, made for the deli counter in a resigned trudge. The deli counter was where it all began.

I looked at Devi. On second look, a lot prettier than Eileen. "I love this place."

"So do I."

"The best Reubens in L.A."

"Hands down." She studied me. "You didn't order just what I did to make me comfortable, did you?"

Her question could have been considered a fastball right down the middle. I swung for the fences. "I don't care if you're comfortable. Yet." I smiled an oily smile.

"Touché!" Devi put up a high five and we banged palms. "How long have you known Myron?"

"Fifteen years, around there."

"He likes you a lot."

And why not? There's only one Dick Henry in this world and that's me, baby. "Myron's a good man."

"That's what I think."

The Heinekens arrived on scene with the pickles. "Glasses?"

I looked at Devi, she shook her head.

"No glasses, thank you."

Pat sighed, departed.

Devi and I clinked bottles. "Good day today?"

She thought about it, nodded. "You betcha, Red Rider."

"You're an optimist."

"Four days out of seven."

Which was what an optimist was all about. A preponderance. We sat in a comfortable silence for a bit. I took a bite of a crisp pickle. She set her bottle down. "So what did you want to know?"

"I'm looking for somebody. Somebody who may have been part of the Ivanhoe system."

"Actress or a mattress-thrasher?"

"Is there a difference?"

"Occasionally." Her eyes had a sharp, perceptive glitter. "So she was a mattress-thrasher."

I spread my hands. "Well, probably. Maybe. She came down ten years ago."

"That's an eternity around here. I've only been at Ivanhoe four years."

"I'm just taking a shot in the dark."

"Shoot. What was her name?"

"Ellen Arden."

Devi put some beer down the wrong pipe, choked. Finally she recovered. "Ex-excuse me. *Jesus.*"

"You alright?"

"I'm okay." She massaged her throat. "I know I'm going to die. One day." She sipped her water. "But I don't want to die in public. At Canter's." She sipped more water, sat back. "Ellen Arden. You can't mean the lady from *Our Miss Brooks*?"

"That was *Eve* Arden. And she'd be a hundred and three by now. This woman would be about . . . about thirty."

Devi cleared her throat again, shook her head. "Sorry. Never heard of her."

EIGHT

King Sunny, Considered

Devi was a liar. She'd heard the name Ellen Arden before. Dick Henry may be stupid but he isn't blind. I reevaluated her reaction. She'd been surprised . . . surprised but not frightened. Not freighted with guilt. My gut said Ellen Arden was at least alive. And Devi's recall was instantaneous. Ellen Arden was probably not too far off. In space, in time, or both. Then why lie? I didn't know, but there was nothing further I could deduce. I'd let the question roll around, let my subconscious work on it.

I hadn't questioned her further at Canter's. There was no point in making her an adversary. I liked her and could always go back. Using our first conversation as a basis, calling on her reasonableness, her obvious knowledge. As it was, I'd had a good time.

We talked movies and music. Was I familiar with King Sunny Adé? Of course I was. Juju music, Nigeria.

In fact, I'd been to one of King Sunny's early concerts in America. At the Music Box in Seattle. I'd gotten to the venue very, very early. So early, everyone assumed I was with someone else. No one asked for a ticket. They were still setting up and I sat close. The band was huge, nineteen pieces or so. Trap drums, congas, percussion, talking drum, bass or basses, two or three guitars, a steel guitar, various keyboards, singers.

They talked easily, laughing and joking in whatever language Nigerians spoke in. Some black Americans walked in from the street, same as I had. They, too, took positions stageside, silently watched the setup.

I watched both sets of people, the great-grandchildren of American slavery and the great-grandchildren of the free peoples of Africa. I wondered what each thought of each other.

I'd heard many variations on the *get-over-it, it-was-a-hundred-fifty-years-ago* argument advanced by current white America. Intellectually, that argument held water. But emotionally, if my family members had been ruthlessly destroyed, sold, and exploited by your family members, I would be carrying around a cold, lethal spike of pure hatred. Right next to my heart. *Today. This moment.*

That my country had condoned slavery, the absolute rejection of another's humanity, and by extension my own, shamed me deeply. To this day. That various churches condoned and blessed that evil made me want to burn them all down. *Burn them today.* In beautiful, raging, avenging flames.

So I watched the Americans checking out the Nigerians.

That's why the most important aspect of humanity is the ability to forgive, said Devi.

That's hard to do.

Yes. But it must be done. It *must* be done.

She was right.

But was there anything more flawed than a human being? Craven, selfish, greedy, self-important, oblivious. But then there was Beethoven, Newton, Curie, Ellington, Holiday, Rembrandt, Shakespeare, Didion, Picasso, Kahlo. Muddy Waters, John Coltrane, Django Reinhardt, Etta James, Nina Simone.

So, yes, there's potential for heaven, along with my personal expectation of hell. It's all a bloody mess.

Which is where the Shortcut Man comes in.

• • •

Devi and I had yakked for a good while that night. We saw Mick Jagger. We saw Hale Montgomery. Then we parted. I gave her my card, told her to call if the need arose. Even just a need for a Reuben.

I crossed Sunset at Crescent Heights, headed up into the canyon. It was late and quiet and I reached up into the passing airflow. Cool and hopeful.

My house was quiet and dark. Through the screens crickets held their rhythmic sway. I flopped down on the couch in the living room. Just for a second.

Next thing I knew . . .

NINE

A Call in the Night

The house sagged out of square, you could tell in any room, up in the corners. Sky-blue paint, faded, blistered here and there, gave evidence that the walls had once been very wet, that the underlying plasterboard had swollen, though now it was dry and chalky.

She was going up a crudely framed staircase, every step a different size and a different height from the previous. The top step was two and a half feet wide, a normal height from the one before, but only three inches deep. There was no door after the last step; one pushed up, then turned a hundred eighty degrees and stepped a long step into a dim, hot room over the staircase itself. It was an attic. Old furniture, cobwebby lamps, cardboard boxes left open. It smelled hot and forgotten.

She walked across the plank floor to a highboy with a mirror on top. In the mirror her face was very long and high, grossly misshapen, very white. Slick and sweaty like old turkey. She had no eyes, just sockets puffed to slits. Around and depending from her neck were thick ropes of darker flesh. She grasped the loose flesh, it filled her grip. She watched herself pull on the ropes of flesh. She was not afraid. A bell began to ring . . .

Devi woke up from her dream. *Uggghh,* disgusting. The cell phone on her bedside table was playing its rising tone. She looked over at the clock. 2:09. Who in hell would be calling this time of night?

41

She ran a hand over her face as the dream fell to shards, then to dust. She picked up the phone. "Hello?"

An unintelligible voice, breathing with difficulty, said unintelligible things.

"Who is this?" Some creep. She'd known a few.

"Wronga. Ith Wronga."

"I'm not understanding you. Who is this?"

"Wronga."

Wrong-uh. Who was wrong? Or what was wrong?

"I'm sorry, I'm not understanding you. Who is this?"

"Wronga. Wronga Carlin."

Wronga Carlin . . . wait, *Rhonda Carling*? "Is this Rhonda?"

"Yeth. Help me."

"Are you at home, Rhonda?"

"Yeth. Help me. Pleathe."

Then the call clicked off. Rhonda Carling. Where did she live? On Wilshire? On Rossmore? Yes, Rossmore. The El Royale.

Devi threw herself into the clothes she'd just taken off. What was with Rhonda? Please, not too many downers and a broken heart. Though she'd journeyed out in the middle of the night for lesser things.

In the garage, her copper Lexus LS started right up. As it should. You don't sell your soul for nothing. She was backing out when she realized she hadn't brought the keys. She slammed the car into Park, ran back into the kitchen, opened the drawer by the refrigerator. There they were. A big, heavy, jangly ring of keys. Twenty-eight of them.

South on Canyon Drive, right on Franklin, past Scientology, south on Gower. What had Dick Henry said earlier about Scientology? Something about its quintessential American charm. The can-do spirit. Like the race to the moon. Based on the writings of a writer who couldn't write. Could things be more divine?

Objective: *God*. Method: *Technology*. Result: *Scientology*.

And, like god-systems anywhere, when you got to the nitty-gritty, God insisted on a hefty fee. In this case, a fortune. And somewhere, she had to agree with Dick, probably in that very building, Scientological altar boys were lifting their skirts for the One. The Big One. Yay, God!

Right on Yucca. Left on Vine. Pedal to the metal.

She had no sooner crossed Hollywood Boulevard on the yellow when a bum stepped directly into her path. She slammed on the brakes and things went slo-mo.

The old man turned his head to see her car and halted his forward progress. Devi wrenched the wheel to the left as tires screeched. The man passed on her right, went down. Something thumped against her car. The car stopped.

She was out of the Lexus in a second. No one was on the street except the old man, getting to his feet. She ran to help him. "I'm so sorry. Are you alright?"

The old man brushed himself off. "I'm okay. I think."

"Did I hit you? What's your name?"

"Dave."

"Did I hit you, Dave?"

"No." The old man shook his head, pointed at a dirty white shape thirty feet in front of the Lexus. "You didn't hit me. You hit my dog."

Devi was filled with horror and remorse. This old man had nothing, probably lived nowhere, ate out of garbage cans. Had nothing but the love of his faithful companion. And wasn't that the thing? Regardless of position in life, queen of England or laundry queen, all humans were flattered and ennobled by the affection of animals. Like her cat, Felonius Monk, had made her a better human being.

Devi looked toward the shape on the pavement. Large, flattish, yet lumpy. Dirty gray. What had she done? *Ohh*. A blanket. The old man carried his dog in a blanket. A filthy blanket. She lifted the edge. The dog was clearly dead. A Chihuahua. Smelled as bad as his master. She picked up dog and blanket, carried it, albeit at arm's length, to the old man. She placed the bundle in his waiting arms.

"I'm so, so sorry. Your dog . . . it's dead."

Dave sorrowfully nodded his head.

"I'm really sorry."

"That's okay, lady."

She should give him something. Taking away a boon companion. *Ripping away* a boon companion. For eternity. From someone who had nothing. She glanced at her copper Lexus. He probably thought she was a rich lady. "Can I give you something, Dave? And I know that no amount of money will make up for—for him."

"Little Dave."

Little Dave. Her eyes filled with tears. "Can I give you something, Dave? For Little Dave? I'd like to."

Dave shrugged.

It was the shrug, so nonaccusatory, yet so decently human, so honest, that made her change a twenty to a fifty. Hell, she'd give him a hundred. She opened up her Coach bag, *Christ, the bag cost six hundred at Barney's,* dug around, found her wallet. She opened it up, reached in to count, then thought *why am I counting,* his dog is dead. She proffered the entire wad of bills.

The old man didn't even put out his hand. She reached for his wrist, pulled it toward her, put the bills in his palm. "I'm sorry, Dave."

"That's okay."

"I mean it. I'm really, really sorry."

"That's okay," said Dave. "Little Dave died last Thursday."

Devi shrieked in disgust.

Dave just stood there, blanket in his arms, blinking.

Devi turned, strode for her car, her hands high in the air. What horrible loathsomeness was all over her hands? She wiped her hands on the pavement of Vine Street, climbed into the Lexus, then climbed right back out.

Dave was still looking at her.

"Bury that fucking dog, mister."

PART TWO

A Crime

TEN

An Evening
at the El Royale

Winston Peckham was thirty-seven years old and didn't want trouble. He'd come to Hollywood thirteen years ago joy-riding an enthusiastic theatrical review in the *Seattle Times*. *Winston Peckham was superb.* His narrow, ascetic face with piercing dark eyes shouted Character Actor. He'd been the night man at the El Royale for three years now. He maintained a neat and tidy OxyContin habit. Never used a needle. Well . . . rarely.

When he told the lady with the one arm full of tattoos that she couldn't park out front for longer than ten minutes, she told him to fuck off. He watched her disappear into the elevator.

Pride suggested he follow her up and kick her ass. OxyContin suggested a little more OxyContin. He ground up half a tab and snorted it. *Bitch*.

Devi stepped out of the elevator on the fourteenth floor and turned left. At 1414 she stopped, knocked softly.

No response.

She knocked again. Nothing. She turned the handle, it opened. She shut it silently behind her.

The lights were dim. After a moment she remembered the layout of the apartment. The entry passageway, in which she now stood, extended both right and left, to the kitchen, to the den and the bedrooms. But each arm of the entryway also gave into the very large living room, with golden parquet flooring, with a wide stone fireplace. She took ten quiet steps and turned to peer into the living room.

"Rhonda?" she whispered, "Rhonda?"

There was a moan from the couch. Devi's eyes grew accustomed to the light. A solitary candle burned on a low table. Devi tiptoed over.

Rhonda sat huddled at the end of the couch, knees drawn up to her chest, hands over her face, turned away from the light. Fetal.

"Rhonda?"

Rhonda moaned but didn't move.

"Honey, are you alright?" Devi reached for the lamp, pulled the little brass chain. Rhonda turned toward her, removed her hands from her face.

Jesus H. Christ. She barely recognized the girl. Matted blond hair surrounded a face battered and swollen, nose pushed to one side, eyes puffy slits. Blood had run down from her mouth, open to breathe, stertorously, and had soaked the pink fleece bathrobe. The bathrobe hung open. There were cigarette burns on her nipples.

Devi felt an animal rage rise within her. "Jesus Christ, Rhonda, who did this to you?"

Rhonda whimpered, shook her head.

On the table was a huge gun. A handgun. It was gold. The barrel was covered with blood. *Terminal Velocity—Eli Nazarian—from Howard Hogue.* She reached for it, then drew back her hand. Maybe it would be evidence.

She looked at Rhonda. "You're going to be alright. I'm going to call the doctor."

Rhonda moaned again. Devi pulled her bathrobe closed.

In the thirteen hundred block of N. Alta Avenue, Beverly Hills, in his seven-thousand-square-foot home, Dr. Ulbrect Wolf lay sleeping in his blue silk pajamas. The window behind his bedside table was open, exactly ten inches, as he prescribed, and crickets could be heard. A cool breeze, but not too cool, blew over him. Half-conscious, he adjusted the light blanket and linen sheet to just past his doughy waistline.

Then the phone rang. His dream dismantled itself gently, like a dandelion in wind. He realized who he was, where he was, that the phone was ringing. With a grunt he pushed himself up.

"Hello?"

"Dr. Wolf? This is Devi Stanton. We have a problem."

Devi Stanton. Devi Stanton. Oh, the smartass girl with the tattoos. Gradually his mind was coming online. That girl. He checked the bedside clock. 2:42, the middle of the night. "Can't this wait until morning?"

"No," said tattoo smartass. "I need you over here *right now*. I'm at the Royale. The El Royale. On Rossmore. Apartment 1414. Come *now*. Somebody's been hurt."

"Can you describe the injuries?"

"Broken bones, burns. Who knows what else. Get over here. I didn't call you for nothing."

"Alright, alright." Three in the damn morning. He swung his legs out of bed.

Gretchen, his wife, rolled over. "Ulli?"

Dr. Wolf shook his head. "Girls Club emergency."

The doctor was fully awake a minute later, driving his big Bentley east on Sunset.

After he had killed the young girl in Florida during the abortion, he almost killed himself. The hospital review board had to blame somebody, better the new foreign surgeon than the alcoholic, politically connected elderly physician, senior doctor on the floor.

It had been a little of them both, Wolf had always protested, to the mirror, Dr. Whitfield leaving him to finish up, and then—and then he had just plain fucked up, had been too afraid of showing ignorance to ask on-the-spot advice from the nurse. And before they all knew the fuckup was a *fuckup,* her blood pressure dropped off the chart and then she was dead.

Dead. How could something be dead that was alive a moment ago? *A moment ago?* What tiny switch in the brain had been thrown? Irrevocably and forever. They'd paddled and paddled, pushed and shoved, but nothing. The girl was gone. Wolf had bargained with God, his every hope on the table, his every expectation offered in exchange.

"She's dead, Doctor," said the nurse. Was she accusing him with that look?

He had gone home late. Gretchen was asleep. A meal ready to be reheated in the refrigerator. Shamefully, he found himself hungry. He ate.

He partially explained the situation to Gretchen the next day. "Don't blame yourself," she said, aware of half the facts, certain of her conclusion.

"Why not?"

"People live and people die. It's the will of God."

Maybe it was. Perhaps everything really was the will of God. Though sometimes God didn't seem to have his mind in the game. Buchenwald. Hiroshima.

Rationalizations aside, the sick, wrenching feeling that fingered his heart told him the death of Olivia Counts was entirely his fault. He had killed her as certainly as the poor father in the newspaper. Who'd run over his daughter in his own driveway. On his way to the liquor store.

He found a little place where he could buy a gun. "What are you going to use this for?" inquired the salesman.

He found he couldn't speak.

The salesman smelled commerce. "Going to do some target shooting?"

"Yes," said Wolf. He bought all the stuff. Goggles, gloves, boxes of rounds, a cleaning kit, a leather case.

As the sun sank into the gulf, Wolf prepared the weapon. At the exact moment the sun dropped below the horizon, sometimes a brilliant green flash was seen. He had read why that occurred but that was unimportant now. The green flash was very rare. It would be a sign from God. Of his forgiveness.

The sun moved swiftly, you could see it move. A hemisphere, an arc, a line, a point. Then it was gone. No green flash. God had maintained His strategic silence.

He picked up the gun. Then his phone rang.

On the other end of the line was a Hollywood producer. His name was Hogue. He'd heard Dr. Wolf was at loose ends. Would Dr. Wolf come west?

The Bentley passed into West Hollywood. The lights. All that neon. He'd always liked the lights. Cal-eee-fornya.

As Devi disconnected with Wolf she heard a toilet flush. *A third person in the house?*

She was on her feet in an instant, backing away from the couch toward the deeper shadows of the room.

A door shut somewhere. She heard footsteps and then a dark-headed man with long hair, in Japanese-dragon boxer shorts, walked into the room, came over, calmly looked down at Rhonda.

Devi held her breath. She recognized him from the trades. Nazarian. Director. It was his gun on the table.

The man looked around, sensing something. Then he found the woman in the far corner. He did not appear to be shocked, angry, or ashamed. "Want to party, bitch?"

"The police want to party, you degenerate fuck," said Devi, coming forward.

That didn't go down so well.

"Who do you think you are, talking to me like that?"

"I'm your worst enemy, Mr. Eli Nazarian." A red mist, rage rising, was forming before her eyes. She pointed at Rhonda. "You responsible for this?"

"I don't know who you are, bitch . . . but if you're smart, you'll realize this is none of your business."

"Wrong, *asshole*. This is exactly my business."

"Fine." He moved forward quickly. The powders and elixirs in his system had narrowed his rational choices down to one: *shut her up*.

Devi judged his approach, let him commit, stepped to the left, threw a hard overhand right, twisting her fist in delivery, catching him beneath his right eye, catching him coming in. Standing him up like a Sears manikin at an in-store picnic.

The left uppercut following was all instinct. It struck him on the right underside of his jaw and knocked him out on his feet. He stood there like a pillar of salt, vacant, then fell over backward.

He didn't fold at the waist and sit down, he fell like a tree. His head hit the flagstone flat of the fireplace with a terrible sound.

Devi was over him in a second.

She'd seen that look. Once a Marine, always a Marine. That look. On the dusty streets of Baghdad. The man was dead.

The phone was ringing. I didn't know where I was for a second. Must have fallen asleep in my clothes. Here in the living room. The phone.

There it was. "Hello?"

"Dick," said an urgent voice. Female.

"Yeah?" Still hazy.

"Dick."

"Who is this?"

"It's Devi."

"Who?"

"Devi. From Canter's."

"You. What do you want?"

I let the Caddy roll down the canyon, turned left at Hollywood for a ride over to Vine.

I'd told a lot of people to call me anytime. Usually I never heard from them again. That's generally why I told them to call me.

What did I know about Devi?

She was the latest in a line of Ivanhoe housemothers. She took care of the Ivanhoe contract starlets.

Devi was also a liar. She knew something about Ellen Arden. But what was worth hiding?

Devi wanted me to meet her at the El Royale. One of those grand old apartment hotels right past where Vine crossed Melrose and turned into Rossmore. Whatever had gone down wasn't good. I wasn't to come directly up. Could I wait at Dunkin' Donuts? Corner of Vine and Melrose?

Fine. There was a mystery brewing. I had that fubar feeling. The bohica premonition. Which usually meant someone was dead. I'd have to watch my step.

A mystery wrapped in an enigma wrapped in a riddle. Turducken.

Nazarian was dead. She peeled back an eyelid. Gone. She'd've snuck out the back door and called the police from a pay phone, but she'd made a scene with that *Addams Family* reject at the front desk. He was on something. But he'd remember her.

She breathed deep, tried to think. Her mind was a small, shallow, shiny purse full of nothing. Not even bus fare. *Jesus.* The asshole was dead. What had Rhonda seen? And Dr. Wolf! Her heart thudded, she'd called Wolf how long ago? What about the body? She'd have to move it.

Where to put it? In the closet in the entryway near the front door. She dragged him by his feet. He was heavy. Finally she got him in there. Crumpled amongst all the shoes, staring up at the bottom of the coats and jackets.

She shut the door. There was a long smear of blood that led back to the living room. The back of his head. Smashed against the stone. Probably flat as a pancake. *Ms. Stanton, how was the decedent's head flattened? I don't rightly know, Your Honor, I think he did it himself.* Christ, they'd rip her to shreds and feed her to the hyenas.

In the kitchen, on top of the refrigerator, she found some paper towels. Some Formula 409 under the sink. The fight between Nazarian and Rhonda had gone on here as well. Blood splatter on the wall.

In the living room, she got down on her hands and knees and cleaned up the trail of blood. She needed more towels. On the plastic wrap that contained what was left of the package of eight rolls, she saw Brawny Man, the cheerful can-do problem-solver. Her next thought was *Dick Henry.*

She stepped on something. A tooth. *Call Dick Henry.*

She asked Dick to wait at Dunkin' Donuts. So he wouldn't meet Dr. Wolf. The less crossing of wires the better.

A knock at the door. Was everything where it had to be? NO! The golden gun was still where it had been, on top of the coffee table. Covered in blood and other, more private, liquids. There was no time to hide it. But . . . but she would put it on the bottom shelf of the table. Cover it with a magazine.

A second knock at the door. With some impatience. She took a last look around. Things would have to do.

She answered the door. Dr. Wolf entered, black bag in hand. She'd interacted with the doctor in their paths of duty, but seldom.

"Whose place is this?" asked the doctor.

"Rhonda Carling's. Thanks for coming so quickly."

The doctor grunted. He was tall and had been handsome in that pale, eerie, gas-chamber way. He had secrets. Devi could see them behind his eyes. Behind those efficient frameless spectacles.

She led him to Rhonda. He sat down beside her, rolled her over in the light, looked at her. Then up at Devi. "I've seen worse. Get me some hot water and some towels."

Devi just stood there. Dr. Wolf seemed unmoved by the damage. "Water and some towels!" he barked. "Right now."

She was half-startled. "Okay, okay." Don't get your swastikas in a twist.

When saucy-bitch left the living room, Wolf moved the magazine on the lower shelf of the coffee table. Something had glinted, caught his eye.

Vell, vell, vell. A golden pistol. Crusted with blood and who knew what else? *Terminal Velocity—Eli Nazarian—from Howard Hogue.*

He wondered how he would play this. Hollywood, on one level, was a game of secrets. The young ingenue storming the gates with pure talent was a myth. Had never happened. The young ingenue who knew how to rip her little white panties off, drop to her knees, and suck—well, *that* young ingenue was on a million screens, playing a virgin in fear for her life.

He replaced the magazine, filed the incident for later exploitation. Just in time.

Devi entered with towels.

"About time," said Wolf.

"She also said she had something put up her vagina." Had he seen the gun? She could almost see it now. But she knew it was there.

Something up her vagina. Yes, indeed. He knew what that was. "Something was put up her *vagina*?"

"That's what she said."

Wolf washed her face, carefully, without kindness. In the right legal hands, here was a gold mine. Broken nose; exfoliation of several teeth, the upper-right canine and incisor; lacerations of the interior of the mouth. Various facial abrasions, probably where she'd been slapped by someone with a ring. Contusions around the orbit of the left eye.

The neck, some abrasions, some contusions. Burns to the nipples, to the breasts. Some bite marks. He looked quickly at the wrists. No signs of ligature, no defense wounds on the hands and arms. Which implied concussion. She must have been knocked out and then burned. You don't sit there and take a burning. A cigarette combusted at 760 degrees Celsius.

He gestured to Devi to help stretch her out. He donned a fresh pair of gloves, spread her legs.

Nice, neat carpet trim. Piercing through the clitoral hood. Some blood, maybe from tension on the piercing? Yes. And some vaginal bleeding. Not copious. A gun up there, maybe the sighting device could have caused some abrasions, possibly some lacerations. Nothing major.

She'd need a good rinse. When the medicated douche ran clear into the stainless steel bowl, he was finished. He stood up and stretched.

Her life as a starlet had ended. Her face would never perfectly heal. And healing would take time. No starlet ever had enough of that.

He'd have to set up a convalescent situation. Fairfax Convalescent.

The girl moaned. His first shot of Dilaudid hadn't been quite enough. He dug in his bag's special pocket, got some more.

He showed tattoo-girl the vial and the syringe. "This is how you do it." He wiped off the top of the vial with an alcohol wipe, then held the vial upside-down, put the needle in, drew the plunger out slowly. The syringe began to fill with the viscous, clear solution. When it was near fifty cc's he stopped, withdrew it from the vial. He held it upside down, tapped it so the bubbles would rise to the top. Then a little spritz. "No bubbles," he said, looking at Devi. "She'll be alright," he continued, "like I said, a little bleeding down there but nothing major. Her nose—she's going to need reconstructive surgery. A rhinoplasty. And we're going to need Dr. Tasman, as well."

Devi watched as he gathered the meat of her thigh, put the needle in. He refilled the syringe and repeated the process in the other leg. "Who's Dr. Tasman?" she asked.

"A reconstructive dentist."

Wolf left her two vials of the Dilaudid and a handful of syringes. "Keep her hydrated. If she's in too much pain, give her a shot. Just like I just did. In the fat of the thigh. You'll know when. When the whimpering starts to get on your nerves."

Vimpering. She loathed the pale Nazi.

He zipped up his black bag. "Any idea who did this?"

"No."

"No?"

"No. What's your problem?"

"No problem here." Just checking, tattoo-girl. Of course, you know who did this. You're dirty on this one. And so is Melvin. And so is Eli Nazarian. There was a pleasant odor in the air. The smell of money.

She walked him to the door past the coat closet. Blood had just run under the door. The doctor put one foot in it and walked on.

At the front door he turned back to her. "I'll be back tomorrow noon. I'll arrange a convalescent situation." How much cash could be squeezed out of tattoo-girl? Or would she be sword-swallowing on his behalf? Why not both? Yes, both. "Goodbye, Devi."

She shut the door behind him. She didn't like the way her pronounced her name. There was something filthy about it. She shuddered.

Call Dick Henry.

I bought two small cups of coffee, one regular, one decaf, poured them both together in a large cup. Half-caf. I polished off half the half-caf as I watched the creatures of the night come and go. Nothing truly healthy began after two o'clock in the morning.

A shabby man held a sleeping dog inside his coat. A little white nose peaked out. The man looked over at me. It looked like he'd been crying. Or maybe it was conjunctivitis. Or bubonic plague. "My dog hasn't eaten in days," he said.

"Some shit you just *can't* eat," I replied, early morning philosopher that I was.

I must have hit a nerve. Shabby Man started crying for real. I caught a whiff of him. Eeee. It wasn't good.

Dr. Wolf had driven south on Rossmore, turned right on Wilshire. A sheet of melancholy had fallen over him. A minute later he approached the eastern end of the Miracle Mile. The streets were deserted, dreams in abeyance. He saw the buildings and cars as facts but could not summon reasons for their existence. They loomed hollowly, empty of significance.

Literally, it was true. On an atomic level, most matter was empty space. If a basketball were an atom's nucleus, the electron in orbit was a pebble half a mile away. Only because the eyes and brain were crude interpreters of certain wave phenomena did he perceive things as solid objects.

He was made of nothing, driving down a street made of nothing, in a vehicle made of nothing, past buildings made of nothing. Yet he lived and thought. *Cogito, ergo sum.*

Suddenly, with vividness, he recalled the situation that had propelled him to his eventual, his current, success. He'd been in Los Angeles about three months when the call had come.

At that time Howard Hogue had a large, three-story house in Hancock Park. In the maid's quarters lay the girl. She had been violated everywhere it had been possible. Then she had been cut.

Hogue had paced back and forth. There'd been a party. A certain movie star had taken some LSD. More LSD than he'd been accustomed to. Or maybe it was better. Everything seemed alright. Then the movie star had wandered into the party at large. He was covered with blood and giggling. The soiree ended immediately. People did not want to learn things they did not want to know. The girl was discovered.

Betty Ann Fowler was a special girl. She had nobody. That's what made her special. She'd arrived months ago at Union Station in Los Angeles, her entire universe in a small black suitcase. She had found occasional work. People found her attractive.

The movie star was known around the planet. As a good man. As a Christian man. A family man. He contributed money where he was directed to, he jogged for breast cancer. It came down to this. Could a man be considered guilty of a crime he did not realize he had committed?

"I need your help, doctor," said Hogue, upon his arrival.

Wolf looked down upon her recumbent figure. Her face was ruined. The tip of her nose had been sliced off. One ear was gone. Half her lower lip had been ripped off. Other knife wounds radiated from the mouth like cat whiskers.

The doctor looked over at Hogue. "You say she is alone in the world."

"Yes, Doctor," said Hogue.

He had gone back into the girl's room. She could live. A disfigured life. An object of astonishment and pity. Where could she go? What would she do?

His decision was made.

I found a spot on the street, walked into the El Royale. Devi had called. *Come on up now.* The night man knew something was up; his curiosity signaled that he didn't know exactly what. The man looked like he'd walked out of a Tim Burton movie.

"Can I help you, sir?"

He looked a little toasted. I shook my head. "No, thanks. I know my way."

"Fourteenth floor," he volunteered, "that's where all the action is." He was Winston Peckham. Winston Peckham knew where shit was packed.

I nodded. Rode up to twelve, walked up the rest of the way. The place was old, with thick walls. I didn't hear a sound from anywhere. I knocked at 1414.

Devi opened up. "Thanks for coming."

"No problem." I looked over my shoulder, right and left, entered. She took me down the entryway into a big living room. "Whose place is this?"

"Rhonda Carling's."

"Have I heard of her?"

"If you saw *Police Academy 9*."

"Missed it."

"So did everyone else."

Devi looked freaked out, but not frightened. Maybe I would be surprised. Someone was *not* dead.

"What's the problem?"

She led me to the couch. It had been made up as a bed, sheets, blanket, pillows. A woman lay on her back. Was she breathing?

"She's alive, right?"

Devi nodded.

"What happened?"

"She had an evening caller. Beat the shit out of her. Shoved a gun up inside her."

"Nice." Not unheard of, but nice just the same. "You know who?"

"Eli Nazarian."

"I've heard that name."

"He directed *Terminal Velocity*."

"That made money, right?"

"Three hundred mil."

"You call the police?"

"No." She took a deep breath. "There's a situation." She exhaled.

Things were hooking up in a general way. Devi worked for Ivanhoe. Terminal Velocity was an Ivanhoe picture. Eli Nazarian was Ivanhoe property.

"You know where Nazarian is?"

"Yes."

"Are you *going* to call the police?"

"No."

No. Because this was Hollywood, after all. "Where is Nazarian?"

"He's in the closet."

"In the closet?"

"Yes," said Devi. "He's dead."

Goddammit. I'd *known* somebody was dead.

She led me to the closet. There he was. Curled up for eternity in a disorderly nest of boots and shoes.

"How'd he die?"

"A left uppercut."

Obviously I was going to get fed one crumb at a time. "How'd he get in the closet?"

"I dragged him."

One fucking crumb at a time. "How do you know it was a left uppercut?"

"I threw it. He went down, hit his head on the fireplace." She pointed at the wide stone fireplace.

I waggled my fingers, beckoning. "Just tell me the whole story, okay?"

"I got a call from Rhonda. A little after two. I came over here, thought we were alone. I called the doctor. Then I heard the toilet flush and asshole came in here. Then he saw me, saw what I'd seen, decided to kick my ass."

"Then he caught the streetcar."

"All the way to the beach."

I looked at Rhonda. Battered, but cleaned up, bandaged. "And I waited at the Dunkin' while the doctor was here."

"Exactly."

Then someone knocked on the door.

A wave of involuntary fright chicken-skinned me. And I'd known better. I'd *known* someone was dead. Why was I here? Why? Because Dick Henry was stupid.

I gestured at Devi—*where do I go?*

She put a finger across her lips, grabbed my shoulder, led me to Nazarian's closet.

I'm supposed to go in there? I mimed.

Devi spread her hands. *What else?*

Another knock sounded on the heavy wooden door. It was insistent, authoritative.

I stepped into the closet. She shut the door behind me. I heard her walk to the front door.

"Who is it?" she asked quietly.

I heard the mumble of a male voice, heard Devi draw the door back.

Devi admitted Melvin Shea. Devi carefully shut the door behind him.

"What the fuck is going on here?" Melvin walked toward the light, toward the living room.

"How did you know to come here?"

Melvin looked around. This place was nicer than Bambi's on Harper. "Our favorite Nazi called."

"Someone was here and beat the shit out of Rhonda."

Melvin walked over, inspected her. She was messed up, yeah. But the ramifications of the situation. He'd have to be careful.

He looked over at Devi. "I've seen worse. Any idea who was over?"

"Don't play innocent with me, Melvin."

"What does that mean?"

In the closet, I could hear everything pretty clearly. I listened as if my life depended on it. Because it did.

"You know who was here. Your end was probably a grand or two."

Melvin felt the slow, hard squeeze of the situation; his stress turned to anger. "I do a favor for a girl every now and then. Works for her, works for me. Every girl who goes out knows the game."

"Rhonda didn't know the Nazarian game."

"I thought he'd been for the cure."

"You don't cure psychopaths. He put a gun up inside her." Melvin said nothing. There were levels of danger here.

First, Howard. He wouldn't dig someone fooling around with what was his. And Rhonda. Though she was owned, what would she want?

He couldn't let that happen. Rhonda must be placated. With some restoration, some vacation, some money. And—ahh, yes—promised a part in a forthcoming movie. A horror movie. That wasn't funny.

Then the Nazi doctor. No doubt he'd submit an extortionary bill. And his bill would have to be paid. Or he might leak to Howard.

What was it about the Nazi doctor? On his high horse. The bills he submitted to Howard, that Melvin had seen, were extraordinary. But never questioned.

The doctor obviously knew the ways of power. He'd been stuffing Stephanie Waters.

Starlet-stuffing. An art in Hollywood. At least a science. And in order to keep stuffing her, he'd trolled out a small part in a Hale Montgomery movie. Melvin had laughed upon hearing rumor of the doctor's tactic. But America's favorite granddad had acceded to the doctor's request. Stephanie, as stiffly implastic as Pinocchio, was cast in a Mideast oil thriller as a doomed spy/prostitute. Cruelly drowned in a vat of hummus.

Devi stood with hands on hips. Obviously, Melvin-the-scum was trying to figure out how to save his own rancid bacon.

"Melvin, did you hear me? He put a gun up inside her."

"Yeah. I heard you. Did he pull the trigger?"

Devi was incredulous.

Melvin spread his hands. "Did. He. Pull the trigger. Yes or no?"

"No."

"No. He didn't pull the trigger."

"Are you excusing his behavior, Melvin?"

"No. I'm parsing it."

"This is a police matter."

Melvin sniffed the air. "Something stinks around here."

"Stinks?" *Was Nazarian rotting already?* Or had he voided his sphincter?

Melvin faced her, coldly angry. "Yeah. It's the smell you smell when assholes get religion, when they start developing a conscience." He pointed at her. "That's dangerous at your age." Police matter. Was she nuts? Had she not seen that she was in as much shit as he was?

"If this isn't a police matter there aren't any."

She couldn't be serious. This was a bluff. She was playing an obtuse extortion angle. Fuck her. Greedy bitch. He'd play stupid. "Are you insane? Howard gets wind of this we're both out on the tiles. This is classic Hollywood under-the-covers."

"Your friend's got to pay."

"That's something different and he's not my friend. And I'll figure something out. We're both in this mess."

"How am I in this mess?" Besides sending your animal friend directly to hell. If there were a God, Nazarian's eternal torment had already begun.

"How are you in this mess? Don't play fucking innocent lamb, Devi. Shit goes down. And you know it goes down. This is the Hollywood Christmas parade. And you just got a turd for Christmas, *house-mommy*. You're in this just like me. Sorry this shit isn't your flavor."

Meanwhile, in the closet, I listened to strangers argue. I didn't know this woman any better than a sandwich at Canter's. And it seemed that her housemother position was a little more involved than she had made it seem.

A murderous housemother, an evil pimp, a sociopathic director, a woman severely beaten. All I needed was the police, slavering at the opportunity to put me away for a while. I thought of that horrible picture on my driver's license. Yet, right now, one might legitimately conclude I was as stupid as I looked.

Devi and Melvin, whoever he was, started in again. I was trying to find who was the good guy. Maybe there wasn't one. Like Lynette.

Not for a day had I forgotten her. Broken doll on the rocks. I paid for a little patch of grass in Holy Cross off Sepulveda with some of Artie's money. There was no one to claim her ashes, or at least no one did, so I pulled some strings and the small, greenish, reinforced cardboard box, containing a heterogeneous mixture of bone fragment and gray sand in a tied-off plastic bag was given to me. Now she was planted with the Catholics. Who knows, might do her some good.

I didn't visit often but I knew where she was. After a while, all the bad shit had dropped away and I was left with recollections of happiness. Hello, darling, I would say. And then I would see those green eyes, brimming with love for me, hear her laugh, feel her holding my hand as we walked the streets of Ojai. If only I had known those few hours were the apogee of my joy on this earth.

"Lemme make a call," said Melvin.

"Who?" returned Devi.

"None of your business, bitch."

There was a silence. I imagined him thumbing the tiny keyboard. Then we waited. All three of us, both of them, and me, the half-secret sharer. Then, in the darkness of the closet, a phone rang. Melvin, whoever he was, had called the man at my feet.

Well, I was about to meet Melvin face-to-face. Like a jack-in-the-box. Or did I mean pop-goes-the-weasel?

"What the fuck?" I heard Melvin say. A voice of gathering incredulity and outrage.

In the living room, Melvin looked at Devi. "Is there something I don't know?"

Yes, there is, I thought. And I think you're about to find out.

I heard the tread of angry feet and I saw two shadows occlude the light coming under the closet door. I felt that tingle in my fist. I crouched for action. He was right outside. Then one shadow withdrew and I heard a kamikaze shout and the door was ripped open.

I had aimed my overhand right straight out at shoulder level and planted my right foot. Force was transferred from right to left foot as I pivoted and I caught him right on the point of the chin.

The punch was picture perfect. He flew back, unconscious in the air, landed with a bang, on his head.

"Jesus," said Devi, looking down on the prostrate form, then up at me. "You know how to throw a punch."

I shrugged. I guessed she'd never been to the Thirteenth Naval District when I'd been in my prime.

Devi was trying to put all the pieces together, I could see it on her face. "Jesus. *Jesus.*" She looked up at me. "Have I fucked you up totally."

"Yeah. I guess knocking your friend out kinda puts me at the scene of the crime."

She looked at me. "You're awfully calm about it." She paced in a tight circle. "I'm going to *have to* call the police. Which means this is going to be a huge fucking mess. You don't know. This whole thing is a house of cards. Going way high."

She looked in the direction of the closet. "You think I could go justifiable homicide?"

"No."

"Manslaughter?"

"No."

She looked at me, the future looming blackly. "I didn't commit *murder*, Dick. That wasn't murder."

"You're getting ahead of yourself."

"What else is left?"

I pointed to the closet. "He isn't dead yet."

Seldom had I been the bearer of better news. Her eyes went wide, filled with tears. Deliverance.

She pounced on Nazarian, dragged him out of the closet by his shoulders, laid him beside Melvin. She put two fingers to Nazarian's carotid artery.

She looked up to me, eyes still full, full of joy. "He's alive. He's really alive."

I'd already leapfrogged to the next problem. "Yeah. Now what do we do with 'em?"

But I knew she would have no answers. When you're in a dangerous nest of snakes you don't need an ophiologist. You need the Shortcut Man.

I reached for my phone. Time to call Rojas.

Over on the 700 block of Gage Street, in downtown L.A., in a small house, in the kitchen, six Hispanic men played poker. Enrique Rojas was winning, enjoying himself. Winning meant one had sized up one's opponents accurately. And the luck of the gods was with you.

Beto was a novice, Sleepy had been cooking the tar, Popeye squinted every time he had a hand. Basically the game came down to himself, Kiko, and Little Franky. And Little Franky was betting wild, trying to catch up.

The last card was turned over. Little Franky threw his hand in, disgusted. Kiko displayed a full house, taking the pot after Rojas's two pair came up short.

Then a phone rang. Rojas looked at the display, *Dick Henry*, picked up. "*Buenos noches,* motherfucker."

Actually, Rojas loved Dick. Dick was a friend and a stand-up guy. Who paid in cash. A call from Dick, aside from beer, barbecue, or a covey of loose women, usually meant cash money. And Dick didn't mind if Rojas did his own thing. In fact, Dick had even set up independent actions for him a few times. Like that dickhead chapel-crier. What was his name? Morton Cockey. Cock*ley.* Brown-shoe crybaby motherfucker. He'd have to give Ravenich a call one of these days, jiggle his handle. And that one gig had led to others.

Rojas listened as Dick explained what he needed. He was required immediately. Good. End of the poker game. With the best excuse in the world, paid employment. Rojas disconnected, rose to his feet. "*Hasta la vista,* my brothers, duty calls."

Losers grumbled, but not too vociferously. Sleepy was on the nod. Rojas said his goodbyes, split.

Once he reached the sidewalk, Rojas called Tavo.

Tavo didn't mind. A call from Rojas meant business. Estella tried to pull him back but he shook her off. Always leave 'em wanting more. That's the ticket.

The battered green Dodge van, the perfect anonymous vehicle, proceeded east on Wilshire passing MacArthur Park. Tavo Gonzales took a long hit on the blunt, passed it over to Rojas. "What the fuck he want with a refrigerator box?"

"*Shit.*" Rojas shook his head. He'd pondered that question himself. A refrigerator box and a bag of plastic ties. A refrigerator box by itself meant the disguised transport of unknown items. Like bodies. But the ties . . . the ties meant something was to be restrained. Kidnapping. Well, there were special kidnapping fees.

The pair drove for a while and there was Rossmore. Rojas made a right and soon passed Beverly Boulevard, where down the street Jews had not been allowed to play golf.

What was it with the fuckin' white man? Not allowing Jews to play golf? Segregated drinking fountains? What sense did it make? The bullshit over illegal immigration. Pretending to surprised by the numbers. Everyone knew they were coming across. By the millions. To work. To support their families. To bus dishes, to mow lawns, to frame up buildings. At least for a generation or two. Till they went to school and wised up and America hired newer immigrants.

Man, if they wanted the Jews not to play golf, make it mandatory that they do. Then the greens would be clean as a whistle, as clean as illegal immigrants could make them. Every once in a while, here and there, a red-faced, potbellied, white-headed Methodist in plaid pants shouting oh shit in the wilderness.

But it wasn't the Methodists that fucked things up. It was the effect of breathing that rarefied air at the top of the heap. You got to the top, whatever color you were, then you breathed your own farts and declared them indispensable for others. Human nature was the problem. Whatever brand of humans was on top—*bingo*—the will of God had, at long last, been achieved. Here was the El Royale.

"Here we are," said Rojas. "Right on," said Tavo, slowly.

Winston Peckham eyed the two *cholos* with the refrigerator box. Maybe the planets were in negative alignment or something. Whatever. Something was going on the fourteenth floor and he was getting left out. Yes, the doctor had slipped him a Grant. But that was because he'd known the doctor's name. Dr. Wolf. Underground doctor to moneyed Hollywood. The fifty wasn't given him for remembering, it was given him to forget. To forget the doctor had ever been here. What doctor?

Peckham had looked over the fourteenth-floor tenant list. An author, an actress, some agents, an ancient songwriter who didn't talk right, an insurance dude, a gay couple. But who would need a doctor? He'd bet on Rhonda Carling. Actress. Starlet.

Starlets were trouble. Nobody treated them right. They were always on the cusp of a fame explosion and of course it never happened. After a while, they got to be bitches.

The *cholos* reached the desk with the box. Peckham indicated the clock over his shoulder with his thumb. "Sorry. No deliveries after hours." This approach usually resulted in retreat or a twenty.

The older man stepped forward, his eyes cold. He tapped the counter. "That's why we're here *before* hours, *ese.*"

The second man just stared at him.

The standoff continued for about ten seconds. Fuck it, thought Peckham, I'm not going to lose my teeth over a fucking box. "Up to the fourteenth floor, turn left."

"Right on," said the second man.

Peckham watched them go. He'd squeeze the starlet later. *Something was going on.*

Rojas looked down on the two bodies on the floor. At least they were breathing. He turned to me, shook his head. "Do I want to know, dude?"

I shrugged. "Couple of assholes on dream street. I need a delivery."

Rojas looked closer. "They're going to be lumpy tomorrow."

"*Grumoso,*" said Tavo, with a smile. He'd heard of Dick Henry from Rojas and a few other sources. But he'd never met him. Looked like a dude who could handle himself.

"What does *grumoso* mean?" asked Devi.

Rojas grinned. "Lumpy. It means lumpy." Rojas gestured toward Tavo. "This is Tavo."

"Hi, Tavo." I reached out, we shook hands. His hand was small but hard. If Rojas had brought him, that was enough for me. The kid was okay.

"*Grumoso.*" Devi grinned. Ever since Nazarian had returned from the dead she had been filled with a sunny delight. Her calamity was now a situation. "I like that word."

Tavo, encouraged, tossed a compliment into the mix. Meant for the Shortcut Man. "Someone throws a mean right hand."

Devi slipped into her stance, threw a lightning left-right-left. "Actually," she allowed, "it was a left uppercut."

"You box, *chica?*" Rojas hadn't seen this coming.

"Keep calling me *chica* maybe you'll find out." But then Devi's eyes twinkled.

I grinned, spread my hands. She could move. "You heard the lady."

Everyone was nodding and smiling.

"So," said Rojas, back to the business at hand. "Where're they going?"

Winston Peckham watched the little indicator lights. Someone coming down from fourteen. An economic opportunity coming down from fourteen. If he could figure how to play it.

The elevator doors slid back, the two Eastsiders stepped out with the box. This time it looked like it weighed something, some lateral distension at the bottom.

He tossed out a soft interrogatory. "Things all figured out up there?" Maybe their upstairs success would engender some downstairs generosity.

The older of the gangsters, Porkpie, paused, stared at Peckham. *Gangsters?* It suddenly occurred to Peckham that he was entirely uninterested in the activities of these Aztec gentlemen.

Porkpie leaned in at him. "Hey, buddy," he said, "they need you up there."

"Th-they d-do?" Peckham's tongue had involuntarily flopped into double duty.

"Yeah," said Rojas, ladling in some Eastside menace, "they need you to put your head between your knees."

"B-between m-my kn-nees?"

"And kiss your ass goodbye."

70

There was a long silence. Tavo, charmed and educated, maintained poker face.

"Mind your own business," finished Rojas, whispering. Finishing quiet imparted its own message.

Peckham, whose diaphragm had been frozen, nodded his head and drew in a great draft of replenishing air. *"Adiós, amigos,"* said his lips, talking on their own. From Olvera Street.

Rojas touched the brim of his hat in salute. He turned to Tavo. Tavo got moving.

Devi looked up at me. She was frightened. "You're not having them whacked, are you?"

"No." What a night. "I'm not a murderer." I was having them dumped. "I'm having them deposited."

"What does that mean?"

"They're going to get a ride up to the Mulholland Drive Overlook, then, attached wrist and ankle, they'll be left in the brush. They'll find their way from there. Come morning. If the coyotes don't get them first."

Devi shook her head. It was now a situation, true, but either way, over-look or no overlook, she was half-screwed. She didn't work *for* Melvin; he was more of an associate, a loose associate at a higher level. Maybe he wouldn't remember anything. If he did, Nazarian was a debit to *his* account, not hers. Whew. Still, he'd be furious. Waking up in the bushes.

It was complicated.

The green van crossed Melrose, Rossmore turned into Vine. There, on the right, was Stein on Vine, the pro drum shop.

Rojas had played drums for a while. Tito Puente, Alex Acuña, Hora-cio Hernandez—and *Enrique Montalvo Rojas*. One day, he'd been positive, the greats would welcome him as one of their own. But first came the day he overheard some acquaintances discussing his talent. He's okay, said one classmate, damning with faint praise. He sucks, said a second, unvarnished and direct. He sound like a horse with three legs said a chortling Paco Ruelas, smartass, rival for Marisol.

Rojas grinned. The memory still stung a little. But they'd been right. His was to listen, not to play. Then he'd discovered Eric Dolphy and Thelonius Monk and everything was alright.

And Marisol. God bless her. Not quite the virgin he'd waited so long for. The power of *cerveza*.

Tavo looked over at Rojas. "So who are these guys again?" Rojas had gotten the particulars from Dick. In the blood-splattered kitchen. "The little fuck is a pimp. The other dude beat the shit out of the girl, stuffed a .357 up her *coño*."

"The big guy is a movie director?"

"I guess." A distasteful incident rolled into Rojas's mind. "You know, something like that happened to a cousin of mine. Back when I was a kid. Twelve and shit."

"Gun in the *coño*?"

"Yeah."

"What happened?"

"Not enough. Not nearly enough."

Tavo sparked his blunt, looked at the big box in the back. "What are you thinking?"

Rojas was thinking that he was tired, that he didn't feel like a ride up to Mulholland. Plus these assholes didn't deserve it, didn't deserve so soft a fate. Too bad they couldn't be smoothly paved into an extension of the 710 freeway. Except that community activists in ritzy Pasadena shot down the extension. Which had already been forced on the brown people of South Pasadena.

Then he remembered Gloria's cousin, Consuelo. Consuelo worked for the *Hollywood TattleTale. Wouldn't that be something?* The *TattleTale* was a gossipmonger, a dirt collector. No, a *filth* collector. Always hungry for a turd. How about a couple of turds?

At Yucca, Rojas turned right, with another right on Argyle. That put him back to Hollywood Boulevard. Then left on Vine, south, back the way they had come.

Tavo was confused. "You got a plan, brother?"

Rojas grinned, ear to ear. Oh, yes. He had a plan.

It was plain that Devi wasn't safe at Rhonda Carling's.

Events were like rocks in a pond. If forceful enough, the vibrations returned, flowed back over their point of origin. Once Nazarian and Shea were free, shit would hit the fan. Revenge, cover-up, the works. Devi wouldn't be safe. Rhonda needed a better babysitter. We needed the doctor back.

"He's not going to come back," said Devi. "I know him."

I thought about the flow of events. I saw a way. "We'll call on his sense of duty."

I explained how it could go down. Devi picked up the phone, dialed.

Wolf's nocturnal journey had shaken forth a cascade of old memories, dark and heavy. Didn't want to go there. Rather than think, he'd eat.

Ahh. Here were some cubes of blue cheese in rosemary olive oil. Some prosciutto. And a little wine, yes. Then, on the sideboard, under glass, a reasonably fresh sourdough baguette.

He sat with a grunt at the stout, oaken kitchen table. It was foolish to regret what was impossible to change. Irrevocable choices had led, with the irrevocable choices of others, to outcomes written in the stars. For a second he smelled the salt water, heard the ocean lap at the sides of the vessel.

Then that splash in the great enormity, the ghostly flare of phosphorescence, the watery clink of descending chain. And then—then nothing.

Fractured light upon dark water.

Moonlight.

Gretchen padded into the kitchen, sleep all over her face. "Ulli? Is everything alright?"

He speared a cube of cheese, put it in his mouth. "Everything's fine. The usual. A bloody nose."

"They should know better than to call you for that stuff." Wolf nodded, tore off a hunk of bread, pushed it into his mouth. "They'll be charged, don't worry."

Gretchen poured herself a drink of water, drank half, dumped the rest down the drain. "I'm going back to bed," she said.

He watched her go. Thank God he didn't have X-ray vision. Though in a way he did. Underneath that bathrobe would be those grandmotherly undergarments. Capacious, voluminous, accommodatory, as big as home plate at Dodger Stadium and just as white. And shaped like home plate! Not that it mattered, he hadn't been there in a long time. And she hadn't mentioned it.

But there had to be that point. When a woman said to herself these things are just too small. And ridiculous. The discrete moment a woman decided to throw away the blacks, the reds, the greens, the pinks, the lace. Throw them into the can, purchase a parachute, breathe a sigh of relief.

Luckily, there was Paulita. His cock twitched. Alive and kicking down there. Sildenafil citrate, and away!

After he finished eating, he sat there in the quiet kitchen, not moving. From outside came the distant rush of Sunset Boulevard—lapsing into the contented silence of Beverly Hills. A dog barked. The universe, calm and serene, did not reward those undeserving. The yin and the yang were in balance. He exhaled. He would sleep well now.

Then the phone rang.

"Yes?"

"Dr. Wolf, this is Devi. At the El Royale."

Again? At this hour? Cut to the chase. "If she's whimpering, just give her another shot of Dilaudid."

Vimpering. "Listen, Dr. Wolf, thank you for sending Melvin over."

Melvin the pimp. He'd gone over there? What had he said? "I just thought that—"

Devi cut him off. "It doesn't matter what you thought. Now that he's here, Melvin doesn't want me playing doctor. He wants you over here right now."

Melvin *wants*? He would skin Melvin. "Let me talk to Melvin."

"No. Just get over here. Right now. You assholes are driving me crazy. If you're not here in ten minutes I'm calling the goddamn police."

He felt his heartbeat surging in his temples. "Call whoever you like, nothing connects me there."

"Except the vials of that shit with your fingerprints all over them. And fifteen other things. Get over here. Melvin says."

Devi snapped the phone shut. Dick grinned. "That oughta do it."

Three seconds later a phone rang on the coffee table. Melvin's phone. After four rings it went to message. *"You've reached Melvin Shea. Leave time and date and I'll get back to you."*

On came Dr. Wolf. "Hey, Melvin, pick up this goddamn phone." After a bit, where Wolf's breathing could be heard, the phone disconnected.

Ten seconds later it rang again. *"You've reached Melvin Shea. Leave time and date and I'll get back to you."*

Wolf was steamed. I grinned at Devi. "This is Dr. Wolf. I don't know what you told that little bitch. I am a medical doctor, not a serving boy. I'm on my way. This will be expensive, Melvin. Count on it." Wolf clicked off.

"I think we punctured his pride, Dick."

"And it's leaking all over the place." I rose from the couch. I had bagged the golden gun in a freezer bag. It lay on the table, all evidence, such fluids as there were, undisturbed. In my coat was a small document I'd plucked from the unconscious Nazarian's coat when we shared closet space. He'd have five million reasons to want it back.

"Okay, then," I said to Devi, "don't argue with the doctor when he gets here. Once he's in, you split immediately. He won't be going anywhere. He may be really pissed, but just go."

"And don't go home."

"If it were me, I wouldn't. There're going to be some very angry people running around. Maybe sooner than we think. You gotta see how things are going to play out."

I handed her a paper with my address on it. "I'll see you in about forty minutes. Alright?"

"Okay, Colonel."

I picked up the gun, slipped it under my coat, split.

"Can I help you?" Peckham wanted to sleep, but habit demanded he cast a last fly on the water. The man who had just walked out of the elevator was one of the fourteenth-floor crew.

Didn't look like a pleasant dude. Fuck him.

Fuck him. The great, unconsulted Winston Peckham would go home, grind up a half tab of Oxy, enjoy the rush, and obliviate till noon. Fuck 'em all.

I walked out of the El Royale. A light rain was falling. Dawn would come soon.

ELEVEN

A Very Dead Dog

In Stage 13 at CBS, it was almost time for the eight-o'clock morning news.

Edwin Nueves and his dark good looks had come to Hollywood to kiss the girls and make them cry, but chance had intervened and a career had been born.

Intrinsically, he did not possess the slightest curiosity in news of any kind. He liked history. News was all a bunch of wide-eyed, breathless, artificial earnestness over events only interesting until the next baby drowned in a washing machine. Better yet in a laundromat. Where love of money intersected with bad luck on the field of shoddy maintenance.

He looked over at Carlita Jimenez. She was pretty, peppy, busty, and could read English. A home run, in other words. And then that cute little Maybelline Marilyn mole. Salsa!

Eddie George, producer, counted them in. "Five, four, three," then two fingers, one finger . . . and *in*.

"Good morning, Los Angeles," said Nueves, flashing his celebrated teeth. "I'm Edwin Nueves."

"And I'm Carlita Jimenez. It's raining in Los Angeles and this is the eight-o'clock morning news. Our top story comes from Hollywood, where we have another disturbing tale courtesy of the *Hollywood TattleTale*."

"That's right, Carlita. We've been informed that very early this morning, on a seedy corner in south Hollywood, two Tinseltown bigwigs were found unconscious in a soggy refrigerator box."

"Not only unconscious, Edwin. Witnesses at Dunkin' Donuts, at Melrose and Vine, reported both men reeked of gin, and both had been physically battered."

"It gets better, Carlita. The men were attached at the ankle with plastic tie locks and both men had no pants on. Also in the box, in a filthy white blanket, was a very dead dog."

Carlita shook her head in disgust. "The names are currently being withheld until the circumstances become clear. We'll be right back." She concluded the segment with the fatigued cluck of a professional scold.

Commercial up.

She smiled winningly at the three cameramen. *They'd* never get a taste of what she was sitting on. She was Carlita Jimenez. Life was good and it would only get better. She would leave Edwin Nueves in the dust.

TWELVE

Exposure and Intensity

I'd gone home, made myself a sandwich, waited for Devi. She was right on time, forty minutes later. Now she lay asleep in my living room.

I studied her as she slept. Ultimately, she wasn't as starkly beautiful as Lynette had been, but she was very pretty, and she threw a mean left hook. And I just liked her.

The depth of any relationship is the product of exposure and intensity. You say "hi" to the doorman in your building every day for ten years. You don't know him from Adam.

But save a person from drowning, or you and a stranger pull someone from a burning car—you've met these people once, but there's a connection.

Devi sighed, turned over on her side. I'd only known Devi for—for twelve hours.

The rain started to come a little harder.

THIRTEEN

Bad Law

The cosmetically perfect metal-flake cardinal-red 2012 Cadillac Sedan de Ville with gold trim pulled up at Hollywood Precinct and oozed to a stop in the no-parking zone. Huntington Derian, Esq. had arrived.

Derian watched as the media, scavengers that they were, gathered around his automobile. When a sufficient number had metastasized, he opened up, spread his umbrella, and made exit.

Derian was of average height, portly but graceful. His red suit, cardinal-red like his Cadillac, was exquisitely cut and hung perfectly. His New & Lingwood Russian calf loafers now suffered the brutal assault of rain. He hoisted and waved a beringed hand with a simple twist of the wrist; in all things he demonstrated the unhurried demeanor of Massachusetts aristocracy. To which he was distant cousin. Vanishingly distant perhaps. For those who calibrated such things. But he was a cousin who'd done very well for himself. He was Howard Hogue's personal counsel-at-large and his word was money.

Head and shoulders draped in a torn plastic trash bag, a reporter asked if he'd come to bail out Eli Nazarian and Melvin Shea.

Derian exuded calm and reason. "Gentlemen, excuse me. I am here to discover the truth. If the truth *can* be discovered. Though, I must say, those putting stock in the vaporous utterances of Edwin Nueves and Carlita Jimenez have only themselves to blame."

With that, he climbed the stairs and entered into Hollywood Precinct.

Of course, Huntington Derian's visit to Captain Dempsey's office was a formality. But formalities were necessary and one might take pleasure in their proper execution. The men knew each other, both had consummated business of this nature before.

Indeed, as the *Hollywood TattleTale* had hinted, two Hollywood big-wigs *were* in the can. As rumored, the two men were Melvin Shea and Eli Nazarian.

Derian coughed quietly and began. What had been the nature of their offenses?

Dempsey smiled to himself. A conversation with Huntington Derian resembled a dance. A stately waltz of shared values.

Dempsey tapped his pencil to signify his engagement. The offenses. Indecent exposure, public intoxication, and, in obvious violation of Penal Code Statute 374d, placing a dead animal within a hundred feet of a street, public highway, or road.

Where *had* the animal been placed?

Between the men as they recreated, unconscious, in the box.

Derian raised his eyebrows as he considered the possibilities. Certainly, he reasoned, aloud, the destruction of reputation would not benefit the men in question, would not benefit Ivanhoe Studios, ultimately would not benefit the great state of California—as far as tax receipts might be concerned.

Captain Dempsey was of similar mind. For the most part, boys would be boys. As for the unfortunate creature, at some point, weren't animals in that condition called *meat*?

Derian removed a fat, unsealed envelope from his inside pocket, placed it on the table, its contents visible to the captain.

The captain assumed a thoughtful posture, rubbed his chin. Unique cases made bad law. And this, indeed, was a unique case. To impede the flow of commerce would be fruitful to no one. Why belabor the stumbling legal system with the straw that might break the camel's back? Creating meat. Of course, rightly, one would have to take incidental expenses into consideration . . .

Huntington Derian beamed. There was nothing wrong with peace, love, and understanding. He pushed the envelope across the desk, studied the stained ceiling of Dempsey's office. When he looked back down, the envelope had disappeared. The captain stood up. Derian stood up. Hands were extended and shaken.

That was that.

It was still raining when Derian reached his car. Apologetically, he raised his finely manicured hand. "I'm sorry to disappoint everyone. What we have here is a case of mistaken identity. Both Eli Nazarian and Melvin Shea are comfortably resting in their own homes. This is just a big hoo-doo on a slow news day. Thank you very much."

The reporters clustered. What about the dead dog?

Is it true the men had no pants on?

Was the dog wearing pants?

Derian rolled off with a wave.

The reporters turned to themselves. Y'ever hear the one about the pig with three legs?

Yeah. You don't eat a pig like that all at once.

Fuck you.

What a town, baby, what a town.

FOURTEEN

With a Pan

Heather Hill woke with a start. It was a new day, but the events of yesterday rushed immediately to mind, filling it.

On the set. Firmly in the land of opportunity. *Gumshoe*, an Eli Nazarian film. Eli Nazarian! Her future before her like the yellow brick road. Centerstage with *Vanity Fair*'s hot actor of the year, Smokin' Jack Wilton. In a speaking part. And there, in the middle of her golden moment, she had applied the advice of Mary Mortensen.

Mary Mortensen, actress. Mary Mortensen, afternoon waitress at Denny's in East Hollywood.

Mary Mortensen had told her yes, Heather was in a movie, but Heather's real thrust was to get herself noticed. To parlay her moment in the sun into lasting exposure. How do I do that, Mary? Simple, said the waitress. In the middle of the first take, when everyone's expecting things to go wrong one way or another, that's when you turn to the director and ask him about your motivation. It shows them you're really serious about your character.

So, summoning all her courage, she had risen from her knees, from the unseen foam pad, waved her arms largely and inquired about her motivation.

She realized instantly she had miscalculated. Eli Nazarian's outraged face was now burned into her mind. Like a brand.

The director had thrown his script to the floor, the veins in his forehead creeping and crawling. "*Heather!* You fucking *moron.* What are you talking about, motivation? You're giving Johnny a blow job. That's your motivation. *Blow job."*

Blow job. Motivation: blow job. Heather remembered the amazed and delighted looks on the faces of the crew. True entertainment on the set. A rare bird. From forty directions she saw pantomimed blow jobs. This is how you do it!

There was no retake. The assistant director came over, said *we're breaking for lunch.* And one other thing.

What's that?

Eli's decided to go with someone else.

She'd gone numb. Various conversations swirled around her. But didn't include her. She was now a leper. A red-faced leper. One of the laughing lepers of Lewiston, Pennsylvania. Where she'd be returning shortly. The brilliant camaraderie that she had enjoyed was no more. She'd been expelled and the merry company had closed ranks.

Then her phone rang. Bob Herbert. Her agent. She explained they were breaking for lunch but he didn't go for it. Someone had already gotten to him. Did she know how much the production was costing per day?

"No. A lot."

"That's right, a lot. Half a million dollars a day."

"That is a lot."

"Roughly twenty thousand dollars an hour."

"Wow."

"Yeah, wow. You wasted ten thousand dollars in an instant. *Motivation?* You're off *Gumshoe,* Heather. That's final. And they'll spend another ten replacing you. Which means I won't be representing you any longer." Herbert clicked off.

She was not escorted off the set. No one said goodbye. She just realized she didn't belong. She radiated bad luck. Like a wolverine in the pantry.

She wandered around the back lot, fuddled, found herself at the cafeteria, sat down in the corner with a wilted salad, eyes full.

Then she saw a man she thought she recognized. He was coming toward her table. He *would* escort her off the lot. Into Rite Aid, discount graveyard of broken actors. Before they crawled back to Lewiston.

Yes, he did know her. "Excuse me, Heather," he said softly. "I'm Melvin Shea. Could we talk a moment?"

His unexpectedly kind manner set her tears loose. He handed her a paper napkin.

"D-do I know you?" she asked after a while, breathing with that wretched hitch, wiping her eyes.

"Rough day, I suppose."

"Yes." The tears came back. "Worst day of my life."

The man nodded. "Well, you know what they say about the Lord, he shuts one door in order to open another."

Shut the door to Oz. Open the door to Rite Aid. "What's your name again?"

"My name is Melvin Shea."

"Hi, Melvin."

"Hi."

"They told me Howard Hogue was going to be there today. I hope he wasn't."

"He *was* there. He saw you."

Her face sunk into her hands.

"I work for Howard Hogue."

"Oh, *God*. You were there, too."

"Yes."

"Oh, God." In her mind's eye, she rose from behind the desk, waved her arms widely and kicked her career into the toilet where it gurgled and drowned. She thought of how she would kill Mary Mortensen. Slowly. With a pan.

"Mr. Nazarian didn't seem pleased."

Didn't seem pleased? Maybe this guy was a jerk, living on the second-hand grief of failed actresses. "What do you want, mister?"

The man looked into her eyes. "I have news for you, Heather. Howard liked what he saw."

For a second, she didn't understand. "He, he—"

"He liked what he saw, Heather." The man paused. "He liked *you*."

Liked *me*? Here, on the edge of nothingness and despair and stupidity and murder and suicide? "He *liked* me?"

The man, Melvin, he smiled. "Yeah, he did. And he sent me to see about you."

See about *me*?

"Howard wondered if you'd ever heard of the Ivanhoe Special Talent Program?"

"Are you for *real*?"

"We're for real. Every now and then, Howard, or one of his top scouts, sees someone whose talent is felt to be unique and compelling. That man or woman is offered a place in the Ivanhoe Special Talent Program."

Heather could barely breathe. Had merciful angels rescued her, in air, falling, and returned her to bliss? *"Are you offering me a place in the Special Talent Program?"*

The man smiled. He was pretty cute. Brutal acne when he was a kid. "Yes, I am. The program provides you with a suitable luxury apartment, a monthly stipend—"

"What's a stipend?"

"A salary."

"A salary???"

Nice Mr. Melvin counted his fingers. "An apartment, a salary, singing and dancing lessons, either or both, and the chance to advance your career at your own pace." Melvin sat back. "What do you say?"

Joy surged through every cell of her being. He shuts one door only that He may open another. What had been the worst day of her life had been transformed into the best day ever.

She left the cafeteria on an endorphin cloud. Strolled to her car in the visitor's lot. She called Vince to tell him the news but had only managed to explain the bad part when she was overcome by happy tears. She hung up. She'd tell him later. In person.

FIFTEEN

Ficus in Focus

Vince Furnatato, one of the Edison second-shift crew in Mid-City, had received Heather's incomprehensible message. As a fellow actor, day-jobbing at night, he understood her distress. But what could she have done to get tossed off *Gumshoe*? As Heather had described it, it was a plum. Walk into the detective's office, shake your tits, hand Smokin' Jack a pack of gum. What could go wrong?

Meanwhile, a transformer had blown in the 5300 block of Wilshire and 2,500 customers were affected. Soon all their digitals would be flashing 12:00 12:00 12:00 12:00. It was when he was up the pole that he looked down and saw something. Wow. Big. Cool. And then it hit him: the perfect gift for Heather.

There was a knock at the door. It would be Vince. It was. For some reason there was dirt all over his chest. She brushed it off. "Are you a lineman or a gardener?"

He looked down. Christ, he *was* dirty. He hated being dirty. Years ago he'd promised himself that when his star finally rose, cleanliness next to godliness would be his byword. He'd be manicured and pedicured daily. He'd purchase underwear by the boxcar, wear them only once, when they were truly white and hadn't yet passed pizza gas, then throw them away.

A true luxury. That's what Sylvester Stallone did. According to the *Hollywood TattleTale.*

Heather, surprisingly, appeared happy. They sat in the breakfast nook.

"So, what happened with *Gumshoe*, hon?" Had that happened to him he'd be broke-dick broke up.

"You know what I learned, Vince?"

"What?"

"That He closes one door but that He may open another." Joseph, her large mixed-breed dog, wandered under her hand. She scratched his head. His big black eyes stared coldly at Vince.

Vince didn't like Joseph. Those eyes. Mutts were unpredictable. Jump across the table and rip your face off. "You didn't say hello to Joseph, Vince," said Heather brightly.

"Hello, Joseph," said Vince, feigning open-minded enthusiasm. With two tentative fingers he leaned over and rubbed the groove between Joseph's eyes. Joseph made no indication he'd been pleased. Why was he trying to please a dog? Fuck you, Joseph.

"So what happened on the set?" continued Vince, withdrawing his hand slowly.

"Creative differences," said Heather, suddenly certain that had been what happened. "But it's what happened later that's really important."

"For the fifth time, what happened?"

"Someone noticed me."

"Someone noticed you?" A flame of suspicion rose up, complicating his breakfast burrito. Heather was five-ten, blond, with Cadillac breasts. The most beautiful woman he'd ever been with. "W-who noticed you?"

Heather smiled at him sweetly, enjoyed his jealousy, patted her legs. "I've been invited to join the Ivanhoe Special Talent Program."

Wow. "Wow. What's that about?"

"It's for people the scouts at Ivanhoe think have *compelling* talent. If I enroll, they'll provide me, *listen to this*—they'll provide me with a luxury apartment, career opportunities, singing or dancing lessons, or both, *and* a salary." Reciting these benefits aloud thrilled her again.

Vince mounted a smile. They'd rip her away from him in a second. "That sounds great." She'd be off in the arms of some Hollywood smoothie, high-lifin'. He'd be up the pole. Soldering. Crying into his toolbag.

Sweet Vince. He was upset, trying to hide it. "The program isn't just for girls, Vince. There're guys, too. I bet your talent is compelling, too." Maybe it was.

Maybe it was. Though *Backdoor Bust-In,* produced by the late Artie Benjamin, hadn't utilized his higher talents. "So, you *are* going to enroll, right?"

"I think so. I was waiting to talk to you." Not that a lineman's appraisal of her career would really matter. Not now. Like Mary Mortensen's ideas. Never trust amateurs.

"I say go ahead. You should do it."

"I knew you'd say that, honey." He'd better.

Suddenly he remembered the consolation gift in the back of his F-150. Now it represented something different. Not to console, but to celebrate. How selfless was that? He smiled. "I have something for you."

"You do?"

"Sure do. Let me go get it. It's in my truck."

"Uh, okay." It sounded big. You didn't leave jewelry in your truck. You put it in your pocket.

Five minutes later he was back. Dirt all over his shirt again.

"Close your eyes," was his request, "until I tell you to open them."

She heard something big coming in. She heard it grind across the threshold, bang against her hollow front door. Then something was set down with a grunt and a thud.

Her eyes were still closed, good. He brushed himself off again, straightened his back, let his gold chain refall into the manly fur. He took a deep breath, looked around, then shut the front door, got her up from the kitchen table, led her to the middle of the living room. "Okay, baby, open your eyes."

Jeez. It was big. It was a *tree*. A ficus tree. In a gigantic yellow pot. It dwarfed everything in the apartment. The pot itself was almost as big as a washing machine.

Vince spread his hands. "I searched all over town, baby. For something special. Something that says I love you. For something that says I'm sorry 'bout you getting fired from *Gumshoe*, but congratulations for getting into the special talent program." How could she resist? "So, whaddaya say, Heat?"

Heat was Vince's diminutive of Heather, recognizing her *hotness*.

"Wow, Vince. It's big." A slightly acrid odor had become apparent. At her side, Joseph looked up at her, moaned. She gazed at her big, boyish Italian stallion. "Thank you, Vince."

He turned to her, opened his arms. "Gimme a kiss, doll."

Her kiss was deep and long and sweet. He felt those Cadillac boobs against his chest. Maybe things would work out. Maybe he would get into the Ivanhoe talent program, too. Then, slowly, a sound that didn't fit disassembled his reverie.

It was the sound of a stream of liquid. On dry leaves. He opened one eye. *What the hell?*

Joseph, eyes black, cold, and expressionless, stood atop the coffee table, left leg cocked high in delivery.

SIXTEEN

What Pussy Said

She woke up to the rain and for a second wondered where she was. Then she remembered. She'd woken up in worse places. Much worse. But she'd forgiven herself.

Lots of books. She rose, pulled the blanket around her, perused the shelves. A long series of books by Patrick O'Brian.

She pulled out one in the middle. Well thumbed. Another toward the end. It also bore the signs of readership. Must be good books.

She moved on to some paintings. A de Chirico print, *Girl with a Hoop.* It had an odd, creepy feel. She liked it. Then some Robert Barrere paintings. Whoever he was. But he was good. The figures in the bright, vibrant pictures had no facial features, yet their moods were clearly apparent from body language. Neat.

Lots of CDs. Stones, Beatles, Little Feat, Muddy Waters, Johnny Winter, Aaron Neville, Pearly King. Never heard of Pearly King. Pearly King and the Temple Thieves. Some jazz. Art Pepper, Thelonius Monk, Miles Davis. Arcade Fire. He listened to new stuff, too.

Some family pictures. There was Dick. And a wife, must be. Big girl. Like Howard Hogue's girls. Ha! Probably gave him more than he could handle.

She'd heard somewhere that whatever attribute drew you into a relationship, the same attribute drove you out. The concept seemed human and possible. You were attracted by her freedom and spontaneity. You left because of her disorganization. You were attracted by his sense of silence. You left when you realized he was a moron.

Dick had some kids. The little girl looked belligerent and lovable. The boy looked like he played third base. Freckles. She glanced around. No kids lived in this house. No woman, either. But the house was clean. Well, pretty clean. For a guy.

The kitchen was relatively clean, too. She got herself a drink of water from the tap. Rain drizzled into the bushes behind the house. She thought she detected a plan in the green abundance. But long since grown over.

She remembered last night at Canter's. Before everything went upside-down. Her housemother gig had some distasteful aspects, true, but it had never been a cesspool. Now it was dark and dangerous. Everybody's interests conflicted. She had a little money put away. Thank God.

A strange man's house.

But she felt comfortable and unthreatened. Dick had made no demands or suggestions. She hadn't laughed like they'd laughed in a long time. She finished off the water, set the glass down.

A hallway led out of the kitchen. Must be Dick's bedroom down there. She proceeded on tiptoe. That would be the bathroom, yes, it was. Dick's room was open.

She stood in the doorway. Nice-sized room. More books. Clothes on the floor. His clothes from last night. His nightstand. A little thrill went through her. A lamp, a clock-radio. And a gun. It wasn't as big as Nazarian's, it certainly wasn't gold. A workingman's weapon. Scuffed and unshiny in morning's half-light.

Then, the answer to the question she'd been asking herself entered her mind. As soon as Myron Ealing had mentioned his name, she knew she'd heard about him from somewhere. A smile broke out across her face.

• • •

Before I opened an eye I knew someone was looking at me. Someone was in the doorway. It was the girl. "Everything alright?" I asked.

She grinned at me. "You know, I have heard of you. Before yesterday."

"Yeah? Don't believe everything you hear."

She grinned again. "Oh, yes. Now I *do* remember."

Something in her manner rang that little gong in my brain. I was going to end up in bed with this girl. Sooner or later. I looked over at the clock. Later. I needed more than four hours' sleep to think correctly. But the gong reverberated down a long and pleasant corridor and I couldn't help myself. "What exactly do you remember?"

"I remember who I was talking to."

I didn't feel like pulling teeth. "Look. I didn't get a lot of sleep last night. I don't want to play twenty questions."

"I was talking to Puss."

"*Puss?*" Had I heard correctly? For fuck's sake, oh, dear.

"Pussy Grace," Devi replied.

"Well, Pussy Peach."

They say it's a small world. And it is small, like Steven Wright said, as long as you don't have to paint it. But I guess Devi *did* know Puss. Penelope Peach. "I don't know what Pussy told you, but, as you must know, Pussy is a famous liar."

"I recognize the truth when I hear it."

"Do you."

"Yes. Puss said you were an ass man." She paused for deliciousness. "Is that true?"

Gong.

Yes. I was an ass man. Dyed in the rut. I pointed a finger at her. "Don't fool around with me, girl."

Instead she turned away, but looked back at me over her shoulder. The blanket wrapped around her was suddenly captured by gravity. It slipped to the floor with a sigh.

What I saw thickened my vision, set my pulse thudding in my neck. A black thong delineated superior geometry at the corner of attitude and intention.

"I love rainy mornings, Dick." A velvet whisper.

Sleep? I'll sleep when I'm dead. I looked into her eyes and I smiled, lifted up the sheet in welcome. "Come here, girl. Come talk to Papa."

SEVENTEEN

Monopsony

Huntington Derian had been shown into Dempsey's back room. He gazed upon the expensive fools, Nazarian and Shea. They'd been whacked around pretty good. Like they'd gone a few rounds with Iron Mike. When he'd been Iron Mike. Served them right. But they were each a little ripe to go public. Not with the *Hollywood TattleTale* already on their tail.

He would cut a check to the *TattleTale* for $5,000 as it was. Because *TattleTale* had restrained itself from naming names. Of course, the *Tattle-Tale* had done so in the hopes of reward. Any further mistakes, however, on his part, or the fools' part, would be fair game.

The director stared up at him with swollen, purple malevolence. "What happened to me?"

"You were found naked in a soggy refrigerator box behind Dunkin' Donuts, attached to Mr. Shea, both of you stinking of gin. With a dead dog lying between the both of you in a dirty blanket."

"Attached?" The director spoke through clenched teeth.

Derian had considered medicine in his college years but had reconsidered. He knew his bedside manner would be found insufficient. But he could see Nazarian's jaw was broken or dislocated. Painful. "You were attached with tie wraps. Those plastic things. To Mr. Shea. Ankle to ankle."

Nazarian turned to Melvin. "Where the fuck did you come from?"

Melvin shook his head. This was delicate ground. He didn't know how he got to Dunkin' Donuts, but he remembered the initial scenes at Rhonda Carling's. "Where the fuck did you come from, Eli?"

Derian watched both of them. Shea knew more than he was pretending. Hmmm. There was a story here. Maybe he'd lean on Shea later.

Shea was a pimp and drug dealer. Among other things. With one client. Hogue. There was a word for that . . . the opposite of monopoly . . . uh, uh, *monopsony*. That was it. A business that relied on a single client.

Shea had shown up on the scene as a fast-talking producer. Gotten a few things made. His name in the trades. Boinking starlets. Then, smoothly, Hogue had transformed him into a Stepin Fetchit. Very well paid, but on the hook, on the book. Yes, he'd lean on Mr. Shea for his answers if need be.

The only thing that honestly bothered him was the dog. Cruelty to animals. People, generally, could take care of themselves. But animals? Though the dog in question was long dead. Ants. "So which of you gentlemen killed the dog?"

Both men were suitably, if blearily, outraged. Assholes, the both of them. Hope it ruffled their feathers. Their stinking feathers.

Derian checked his watch. "There're two large towels behind you, gentlemen. Put them over your heads, and Officer Gundy will lead you to the van that will take you to see Dr. Wolf."

"Who's Dr. Wolf?" asked the Hollywood golden boy, teeth clenched.

"Dr. Wolf is one of Howard Hogue's personal physicians." An off-duty officer poked his head in. "Everybody ready?"

EIGHTEEN

Redolent of Nature

Dr. Wolf had struggled beneath a thick blanket of fatigue but the Modafinil had finally kicked in. Once the body got used to eight or nine hours of sound sleep, three or four wouldn't do. Fuck Melvin Shea and tattoo-girl. The little bitch walking out and leaving him with punching-bag girl bad telling him to give Shea's phone back to him. Shea leaving him orders! Dr. Ulbrecht Wolf didn't take orders from pimps.

But actually, he felt pretty good. Pretty darn good. His mind was clicking like an abacus. The golden gun. It had been moved. Which meant Devi or scum-Shea had moved it. The magazine on top of the gun on his first visit. He was the first visitor after the attack. The gun was not hidden by the perpetrator. Therefore, Devi, at least, was cognizant of its being moved from where he had seen it.

He had searched the entire apartment while Rhonda lay sedated. The gun was gone. Unless there was some secret hiding place that Rhonda's guests would know. Not probable.

No. The gun was gone. But he had discovered Rhonda's underwear drawer. She liked green silk. So did he. He reached in the pocket of his suit. There they were. Crumpled up alongside the ones he'd plucked from beside the bed. Black and redolent of nature and an expensive scent. Barely enough material to cover the palm of his hand. His cock twitched. One saved and savored one's erotic experiences. For recall and use later.

• • •

The one good thing had been the time to arrange the convalescent situation. Moncrief at Fairfax Convalescent was reliably incurious. Had maintained his indifference as he, Luis, and Ernesto trundled Rhonda out of the anonymous van and into Moncrief's shadowy back entrance.

Then the call from Derian this morning. Wolf had been on the verge of complaining about long hours when he realized Derian did not know the full scope of last evening's events.

Vell, vell, vell. A tangled veb ve veave. When first we practice to deceive. And now weasel Shea and psychopath Nazarian were being delivered to him. After their mysterious midnight misadventures. Fees. Fees! There were going to be fees involved.

Wolf exited his kitchen into the garage, and through the garage, into the private office/urgent care facility he operated on his property. Not that the county zoning commission was any the wiser. None of their business, anyway.

Besides Hogue's people, he served a wide celebrity clientele. Actors, musicians, athletes, the rich and private. The Hollywood elite. Those who wished to avoid the scrutiny of the *TattleTale*. Knife fights, acts of battery, overdoses, sexual assault. Even the Tattletale's son had paid a visit. He had broken an arm illicitly entering a pharmacy after hours. Radial fracture.

He found Carol Stanleigh at the autoclave.

"Good morning, Carol."

"Good morning, Doctor."

Carol had become too fond of pain medication when she had worked for Kaiser years ago. He had made her an offer she did not refuse.

"Two visitors will arrive shortly, Carol. A Mr. Shea and a Mr. Nazarian. I'm told they've been battered quite severely. So, possible X-rays, extensive first aid. Then they're going to need clothes. And probably makeup."

Carol nodded. This was the usual, give or take a contusion or a laceration. She reflected. "Do you mean Nazarian the director?"

Only the director who'd rammed a pistol up the vagina of a battered woman. Wolf shrugged, *don't know*. What he knew was useful. He wouldn't squander it. "I don't know the name."

"I bet it's him," said Carol. "He's got a reputation."

"Reputation for what?"

"For partying pretty heavy. Hurting people. How long until they arrive?"

Wolf checked his watch. Patek Philippe. White gold. Twenty grand. "Fifteen minutes." He'd often wondered how accurate the watch was. The fact that it was called a *chronometer,* not a watch, quintupled its price immediately. But, as far as time was concerned, how could he check it? A watch that counted the same seconds could be had at Burger King for $1.99. And it came with a sandwich.

The police van bounced and jounced. Which made everything hurt. Nazarian stared at weasel-pimp with hate. "I still can't figure it, Melvin. How did you and I end up together?"

Melvin had spent the journey thinking about that exact circumstance. It wouldn't be prudent to level with this out-of-control asshole. "Dr. Wolf called me. So I got there, saw you lying on the floor, on your back, and then something hit me. Then Dunkin' Donuts in that fuckin' box."

"Did you see the bitch?"

"Who are you talking about?"

"Who are *you* talking about?" returned Nazarian, peering at him.

Melvin realized he'd fucked up. Talking about Rhonda, implying Devi. Then he saw a way out. "I didn't see any bitches at all."

"The coked-up whore made me lose my temper."

"She made *you* lose *your* temper?"

"That's what she did."

Melvin was incredulous. "Made *you* lose *your* temper."

Nazarian was furious. His face was screaming, spikes of jagged glass. "Fuck you . . . and fuck her."

• • •

Officer Gundy pulled into the driveway on Alta Drive. As he approached the garage the door went up. The garage was empty—neat and clean to a nosy neighbor's squint. The door shut behind him.

Shit rolled downhill. Fine with him. He'd made these runs for Captain Dempsey before. His cut would be five hundred dollars. Protecting and serving had its rational limits.

And those assholes in the back. Hollywood shitheads. In the box with the dead dog. There was a story here. But he'd learned nothing of value. The two shitbirds hadn't exchanged fifty words the entire journey. They didn't like one another. He'd settle for his five clams and be done with it. Curiosity and greed got you in trouble.

Gundy watched a nurse take the men through the garage's back door. He peered after them, saw nothing. The door shut, and behind him the garage door rose. Dismissed. Fuck it. He'd gotten his five.

Wolf studied Nazarian's jaw. It wasn't supposed to look like that. Carol had cleaned him up, given him fifteen stitches in the back of his head, but there was only so much you could do at a clinic. "How did this happen, Mr. Nazarian?" he queried innocently, Hippocrates himself.

"I don't know," said Nazarian. He remembered that initial long rail from the first eightball of coke. As if Roman trumpets, grand and deserved, were introducing him, Eli Nazarian, to the feast. The Feast of Nazarian.

Then what had happened?

He'd fucked the whore. Unremarkable. Big tits. Black panties. Then he'd played around with that—had he brought that golden gun? To the whore's house? Why? He couldn't have. And then—then when his blood, viscous with chemicals, then—came that *other girl*. Was there another girl? Yes . . . there *was*.

You responsible for this? This is my business. That's what she'd said. Something like that. He'd moved forward, to give the bitch a swift kick in the cunt—then nothing. Nothing until that stinking, wet blackness, the pain all around his head, then light, rain, cops snickering, and a bunch of gawking low-lifes. Derian said there'd been a dog. A dead dog. That had to be bullshit.

But this was no time to tell this doctor anything. Who knew what side he was on? "I don't know what happened, Doctor. I went out for a few drinks—that's all I remember. Now, what have you found?"

"You've broken your jaw, first thing. It's going to have to be reset. A taxi will take you to Century City Hospital. Dr. Merritt will see you. He's part of the team and your privacy will be taken care of. Secondly, you've suffered a concussion, and a good-sized laceration on the back of your head. And I see you asked Carol to shave your head."

"May as well." He was beyond personal vanity. He didn't need it. He had power. Moths to flame, starlets to cock.

"Thirdly, you've got various scratches and bruises. All over, and all attended to. And, finally, it appears someone has plucked a patch of your pubic hair. And you remember nothing?"

"Nothing," said Nazarian.

Wolf nodded. His hand settled into the pocket of his white smock. Something silky.

Panties!

Meanwhile, behind the parking garage of the Hillside BonContempo Luxury Apartments, near the Dumpsters, Tavo Gonzales studied the ficus tree in the large yellow pot. Estella had become unenchanted with Rojas and the midnight adventures in which Rojas had invited Tavo to participate. It was a case of ruffled feathers. Jealous feathers. And nothing unruffled feathers like a gift. Especially if it looked expensive.

Tavo turned to Osvado, who worked for the Tavares Gardening Service and had seen a sweating Italian stallion heave it where it now leaned. "What kind of tree is this?"

"A ficus," said Osvado.

"Are they expensive?"

"The pot is expensive."

Tavo nodded. He needed an adjective. El Dorado. The Seven Cities of Gold. That might work. It would have to. Estella would be charmed. She better be. Tavo looked over at Osvado.

"Let's do it."

NINETEEN

Nine Ball

Wolf now examined Shea's face. Circumstances dictated he could be more forthright with the *liddle veasel*. "You're going to be in pain for a while. Who hit you?"

"I'm not sure." Melvin's head felt like a bell that had been rung by a gorilla with a sore dick. "But I'm going to find out." Other primates didn't have big dicks. "Devi Stanton knows." Only humans did. There must be a reason.

"But you ended up, without pants, at a doughnut shop——"

Melvin pointed a warning finger at the doctor.

"——with your finger up a dead dog's ass." The doctor allowed himself a giggle. Fuck the pimp.

Melvin glared. His recollections of the box had been from the outside looking back. Against the wall, near the water meter. Soggy. The rain, the pain, the looky-loos, the grinning cops.

"The situation is delicate, Mr. Shea. It needs to be contained. And tattoo-girl must be handled as well."

Suddenly Melvin remembered standing in front of that closet. Then the closet had burst open . . . and a man had come out like a jack-in-the-box ninja. Why was he standing in front of the closet . . . his phone, his phone, no . . . he'd called someone and it was ringing—from the closet. That's right! He'd called asshole Nazarian, author of all this fucking mess.

Where was his phone? He patted himself down, it wasn't there. Had he left it at Rhonda's? That could be trouble.

The doctor was grinning at him.

"What's so funny?"

"You looked like you were looking for your phone."

Melvin patted himself down again, then looked up at the Nazi. "You have it?"

Wolf handed it to him.

"Where was it?"

"Up the dog's ass."

"That's real funny, Doc."

"You left it over there."

Melvin went to the all-calls register. "What's your number, doc?"

Wolf handed him his card. From a tray.

There it was. "You called at 3:38." And the next call. At 4:17. Eli Nazarian. *Yes.* Meaning that at 4:18 the guy stepped out of the closet and clocked him. That asshole would pay.

Was it possible that Devi didn't know someone was in the closet? Possible. But not fucking probable. He'd lean on her. She'd give.

"What about your friend?" How does he fit into the occasion?"

"I'm not sure. And he's not my friend." He'd have to be careful around the doctor. Always snooping for a payday.

"Well, whatever he is. I just put him in a taxi. To Century City Hospital. He's going to have his jaw wired shut."

"Serves him right. But it's his mind that's the problem."

"We must be careful. Let's hope this whole thing does not attract . . . official curiosity."

The doctor was fishing. With his little needle Nazi-hooks. "This *whole* thing." Melvin stared at him. "What are you talking about?"

"You think I'm stupid, Mr. Shea?"

"Listen, here. The El Royale and me and him have nothing to do with one another."

"Nothing."

"I mean it. Nothing to do with each other."

"Nothing. Fine. I just hope Howard's position is not threatened."

Where was Mengele Jr. going with this? "What are you saying, exactly?"

To clarify a threat is to limit its power. The doctor strategically retreated. "Well, if your friend had nothing to do with the girl—then—then he had nothing to do with the girl. But I would hate Howard to get the wrong idea." Then, a stiff jab to the pimp's face. "Should I send her bill to you?"

"Are you suggesting you might send it to *Howard*?" The doctor was playing games with him. It was time to root him out. From behind that chilly platinum facade. "That sounds like a threat, *Ulbrecht*. Of course, you send that bill to me. To my office. You threatening me?"

"No. *Melvin*. I'm just apprising you of the situation. I live a comfortable life. As you do. I don't want anything interrupted."

There. The sound of truth. Enlightened self-interest. The Nazi probably had a closet full of thousand-dollar suits. With shoes to match. "What do you suggest, Doctor?"

"Settle the matter quickly." Wolf picked up a scalpel, fresh from the autoclave. He moved a step closer to the pimp. "The second thing I suggest is that you never . . . ever . . . ever *summon* me anywhere again. I'm a medical doctor, not a serving boy. Or a delivery boy."

The doctor *was* threatening him. Melvin tamped down a strand of red anger. Things were complicated enough. Too fucking complicated. Otherwise he'd take his index finger and plunge it right through the doctor's eye. Then we'd see who Mengele might threaten.

"Put that thing away, Doctor. You might cut yourself." He looked neutrally into the Nazi's eyes. "But the word *summon*. What are you talking about? Did someone summon you? Who summoned you? You called *me*."

"You didn't have that Devi bitch call me last night?"

Aha. The doctor's carefully tailored pride had been pricked. Good to know. He'd make use of that button when the time was right. "Devi called you again, *Doctor*?" Touching. The way Mr. Fatherland *loved* being called Doctor.

"Yes, she did. She said you'd asked her to bring me back."

"Never did."

"So I went back over there and babysat until the people came to get her." Melvin was filled with terror. "What people?"

"My people. To take her to Fairfax Convalescent."

"She's at Fairfax now . . ."

"Yes." Oh, yes. The little pimp was afraid. Afraid of getting mixed up in the mess. Because he was already mixed up. And thought that no one knew. No doubt, he'd provided Rhonda for Nazarian. He looked at the pimp's bruised face. "Would you like codeine with the Tylenol?"

"Fuck, yes."

Fatigue had moved into Melvin's bones like mercury, heavily rolling, finding the lowest point in his body. He felt like he weighed four hundred pounds. And his day would last until nightfall, relentless, and only then could he wash off the thick makeup and toss away the cheap sunglasses and sleep. Sleep. But not now. What he needed was a fat rail of coke. Waiting for him in his office. Like a friendly serpent. Two fat rails.

The taxi would have him there in twenty minutes. He had to think. Devi, Nazarian, the Nazi doctor, the man in the closet, Howard Hogue. He'd have to play them like a fine round of nine-ball.

He'd just seen a nine-ball tournament on cable. A frigidly beautiful Asian woman had cleaned up, leaning over the table, showing her rack, standing on one leg to make those impossible shots. In Melvinworld, where his imagination was law, he would come up behind her, rip that black skirt down, bury his cock in her ass, press her face flat against the felt.

He reached for his phone, punched up Devi. Bitch wasn't answering. It went to message.

"Thank you, Devi, for giving the Nazi my phone. And, since you're not answering your phone, you fucking bitch, lemme just clue you in on a few things. I don't know who hit me, but he's fucking dead. Dead man walking.

"So I'm going to need his name. So I can have his coffin made up. Or you're fucking dead, too.

"And I don't know what you pulled with our Nazi doctor last night, getting him to come back and shit. But I smell something dirty. I pray to God, for your sake, that you didn't mention Nazarian's name to him.

"And how *I* ended up, all tied up in a fucking box at Dunkin' Donuts, then meeting the cops—you better have some answers. Or I'll peel your skin. When you get this message call me. *Bitch*."

TWENTY

The Sins
of Howard Hogue

Sometimes two people making love just don't fit together. Uncomfortable with each other, uncomfortable with their own bodies, uncomfortable with the situation. It could be a million things. But Devi and I flowed together like the ten rivers that flowed into the mighty Mississippi.

No embarrassment, no shame, no hesitation. Her body was supple and trim, mine less so but filled with hunger and flame. She laughed, coaxed, pleaded, denied, and finally succumbed fiercely to pleasure. I felt like God Himself. She took all I could give her and I gave her everything I had. Then, as the rain fell, we slept.

We woke hours later, having drifted softly to consciousness together. "Shortcut Man," she smiled, stretching, "that's so wrong."

She rolled over so I could again appreciate her austral architecture.

Forms in nature are repeated, because they are successful. The spiral of a nautilus shell; the outgassing of binary stars. The lilt of a descending willow branch; the mathematical graph of diminishing return.

Here's what I'm getting at. Take the perfect apple. Not round. Tall, fluted. From the stem end, the top, flowing widely, laterally over the side, into a descent that pushes outward to maximum, roundly, before tapering in, to a lesser circumference than the top had been, then the last, swift downward arc until terminus.

Take that apple, turn it upside-down. Voilà! The shape of the perfect rear end revealed. Nature repeating its success.

I've studied. Like dear old Puss said, I'm an ass man.

Early afternoon found us famished. Where to go. Superstitiously, I wanted to avoid Hollywood, so we went the other way, over Laurel Canyon into Studio City.

Twain's at Ventura and Coldwater seemed a good fit. She had the appetite of a crocodile but the waist of a debutante. I watched her eat in bemused wonder. Then we ordered coffees to talk over and I asked her about her housemother position.

She shrugged with a studied nonchalance. This was a conversation she'd had more than once. With herself.

"The long and short of it," she began, "is Howard Hogue. He likes young blondes, tall and vacant, with huge tits. When he finds one that tickles his fancy, he has Ivanhoe set them up. A nice apartment, an allowance, singing and dancing lessons. And, once in a while, maybe, he gets them little parts in little things."

"The Ivanhoe Special Talent Program."

"Exactly." Devi reached into her purse, took out a big ring of keys, dropped it onto the table. It landed heavily. "At the moment, he has twenty-eight of these girls."

"Twenty-eight?"

"It's been as high as thirty-three."

Thirty-three girlfriends. My marriage had foundered for many reasons, one of them the fact that love is seldom divisible by three. *Thirty-three.* I couldn't remember thirty-three names. I guess that was where *darling* was useful.

I did some quick devil's math. Rent, lessons, allowance, uh, $7,500 per month. Times thirty. $225,000 a month, round that up, for drill, to a quarter million, for a year, that makes $3,000,000. "I guess Hogue can do anything he wants. What does he want?"

"You mean what *exactly* does he want?"

"I'm curious."

"Well, once or twice a week, any night, he might choose any of them. Then he drops by for a dance."

"A dance?"

"Let me start at the beginning."

"Please."

"Well, first he chooses one of the twenty-eight. Then he calls up Melvin. Melvin ensures she's ready for business on the evening in question. Melvin also ensures Howard's chauffeur knows where he's going."

Devi sipped her coffee. "The chauffeur drops him off and waits. Howard goes to the girl's place. She'll be ready. The lights will be low. Music will be playing softly. No country music, no heavy rock. She'll greet him like she missed him. She'll thank him for his patronage, his generosity. She'll fix him an Old-Fashioned."

"She's taught how to do that?"

"I teach them. Dissolve a lump of sugar in two dashes of bitters and a little water. Add ice, some lemon peel, a jigger of bourbon. Mix with a spoon, leave the spoon in the glass. Give to him with a napkin underneath."

"He's a spontaneous fellow."

"Isn't he. Then they'll sit and he'll ask how things are going for her. Nothing personal, of course, just what's happening career-wise. After a few minutes of this preamble he asks them to dance."

"And they're thrilled."

"Thrilled. They dance to 'Love Letters in the Sand' by Andy Williams. Three or four times."

"No other song?"

"No. Just that one. Every girl has her Andy Williams CD."

"You see to that."

"I see to that."

"Then what happens?"

"At that point he steps away from her, goes to the bar, takes out his little leather case, opens it up."

"This is pretty amazing."

"He knows what he wants."

"Then?"

"Then he takes out this little vial, shakes out a little mound on the mirror in the case. With a platinum razor blade he chops it up. Makes it into two lines."

"Two equal lines."

Devi smiled. "You're getting the drift."

"Cocaine?"

"The finest shit in the world, mixed with a tiny bump of triple-A Persian heroin. To take the edge off."

"This guy knows exactly what he wants."

"Then he huffs one line, appreciates, then the other. Then another dance."

"'Love Letters in the Sand'?"

"Yes. But about halfway through this spin, he whispers in her ear. Then she moves to one of the bar stools, which just happens to be the perfect height—"

"You're kidding."

"No. Every girl has a set."

"Go on."

"She goes to the bar stool, lays down over it. He comes up behind her, lifts up her little black dress. She'll be wearing green silk panties."

"No!"

"Little green panties."

"Green is a requirement?"

"Always green.

I found myself amazed and repelled. This was not human interaction. It was playing with dolls. "And then?"

Devi sipped her coffee again, her eyes seeking the tabletop. "Then, usually . . . usually he bangs 'em in the can." She looked up at me.

I shrugged. "That's very special."

"Then he goes to the bathroom, where he cleans up with refreshing iced cotton towels, ready and waiting, then takes a piss."

"The antiseptic piss. That he's been saving."

"I guess so." She looked at me. "You do that?"

"That's what they taught us in the Navy. Blow out the pipes before anything bad swims upstream."

"Gross."

"Smart."

"Then he leaves her a nice tip, a thousand bucks, splits. His chauffeur takes him home."

I shook my head. "So what does he do for fun?" We both laughed. "I don't see the humanity in all this."

"I didn't think sailors were into humanity."

"We're deeply into humanity." But I'd met young sailors, when I was a young sailor, who didn't seem to have a clue. Getting married, they said, to assure themselves a steady supply of pussy. Which made it seem curiously independent of the person attached. Where had they learned to think like that? What was the point?

"So. You're the housemother."

"You better not be judging me."

"I'm older than that."

There was a silence. "Yeah," she said. "I'm the housemother."

TWENTY-ONE

Yawning of the Pit

As his liver gradually cleared his mind, Melvin fully realized the trouble he was in. What had appeared to him earlier as a web of relationships now had resolved into a singularity. Howard Hogue.

Hogue paid him $6,250 a week. That fat miracle had taken place when fifteen hundred had been a godsend. The extra money seemed barely believable. Too much to possibly spend.

But, like a fucking fool, he'd grown used to it. The Beemer. The condo. Sluts. Drugs. Clothes he'd never wear twice. Shit he'd bought to stave off those horrible cocaine depressions. Expensive restaurants where they'd Mr. Shea'd him right, left, and center. Where prices were large, portions were small, artfully arranged over vast peasant plates.

Now he needed every penny. Had run up balances on all seven graciously offered credit cards. Stupid Mr. Shea had succumbed to every temptation.

But if Hogue actually discovered that Melvin Shea had pimped out one of his thirty girlfriends—actually, eight or nine—well, the ramifications of that would be overwhelming, a monstrous thunderclap of retribution. Hogue's blood-red rage would mean the end of everything. Certainly everything in Hollywood.

Could he survive that? Physically, he could. But he would never move again in the circles to which he had become accustomed. *Welcome to The*

Palm, Mr. Shea. He would eke out a smaller life, telling stories to small-time, small-town losers about shit they'd never believe he'd had or had done. *Welcome to The Grill, Mr. Shea. Your usual table?*

What he needed this minute was heavy money. To make Rhonda a good offer. Not that good. Good enough for her to accept. Above the threshold of first refusal. Where she'd get the whiff of fortune and avarice would set in, like dry rot, shutting her fucking mouth.

And Nazarian. Well, Nazarian wouldn't want trouble either. That's where he'd get Rhonda's bread. The asshole from Armenia. Nazarian had better come across. Pointing that golden gun at him in Hogue's office. Who the fuck did he think he was? Didn't matter. Asshole had a lot to lose. Probably had already made sure that the Hollywood Boulevard star committee could spell his name correctly.

His face hurt. Bad. He'd kill that closet mystery man. Devi would give him right up. She couldn't stand a break in the income river either. Driving a Lexus, living up Beachwood.

He took a deep breath. His mind was working. Priorities were in order. Rhonda, Nazarian.

He opened the big drawer in his desk. In the back corner, in a wooden box, was a quarter ounce of cocaine. Almost Merck quality.

He would break a rule of his own making. Don't mess with the shit at work. The separation of business and pleasure. But this wasn't pleasure. He coughed. A jagged, tributaried skein of lightning passed downward through his face, between his teeth, through his teeth, into the marrow of his jawbone. Then faded. Like a retina flash. Something was fucking broken. Had to be.

One line.

Okay. Two lines.

No. One line.

The phone rang. In-house call. "Yes?"

It was Mary, his secretary. Who knew nothing and imagined less. Brave new world. The rise of the morons. "Helena called from Mr. Hogue's office."

"And?"

"Your meeting is in half an hour."

Two lines.

TWENTY-TWO

A Million Dollars

The waitress at Twain's had just disappeared with my credit card when Devi's phone rang. She picked it up, checked. "Melvin."

"Let it go to message."

Devi set the phone down. "This is going to get ugly."

"Don't go home."

"Till when?"

"Till I tell you."

Her eyes narrowed. "You just want me in your bed."

I grinned. "There're worse places."

"So what happened between you and Puss?"

"Lots of stuff. Thankfully under the bridge."

"You can tell me."

"No, I can't."

"Why not?"

"Maybe you'd lose respect for me."

She laughed, drained her coffee. "I should visit Rhonda."

"You know where she is?"

"We usually send them to the same place. I mean, Dr. Wolf does."

"This happens *frequently*?"

She interpreted my question more harshly than I'd asked it. "No. I'm not a criminal, Dick. Jeez."

I didn't think she was. On the other hand, there was no such thing as moral neutrality. Every human action, at its core, was either good or bad. "Wolf is the house doc?"

"Yes. He's the guy I call." She paused. "You think it's safe to visit?"

"If we do it quickly. Those guys are going to be pissed when they get their act together."

"Where did Rojas take them?"

"Up to the Mulholland Overlook. And over it."

"Why?"

"Thought I'd buy a little time. Let 'em wake up slow, cold, and sore this morning. In the bushes. Then a difficult, tandem climb back to Mulholland. Give 'em time to think." Maybe scare them. "So where's Rhonda?"

"Fairfax Convalescent. Block and a half above Canter's. Want to go with me?"

Devi wasn't all that much worse than I was. I feasted on a lot of Hollywood crumbs, just not as close to the table. As they say, if you're going to dine with the devil, find a long spoon.

Like everybody else, it seemed, she'd gotten used to the gravy train. Where was my end out of all this? Somewhere in the vicinity of Nazarian's gun, crusted with various liquids. And a bloodstained check for $5,000,000.

Did I care about Rhonda Carling? Sure. Abstractly. Like I cared about hurricane victims in Haiti. Rhonda had walked the delicate edge. Meaning part of her accepted the fall. Welcomed it. The fall she told herself would never come.

Did anyone care about Rhonda Carling? Her mother. Maybe. But probably no one in Hollywood, California. But she'd make her current circle care. Battered, violated, unconscious, and anonymous, she held the cards.

"Let's go see Rhonda," I said. It was the only pragmatic thing to do.

My Caddy crossed Fountain at Fairfax, Methodists on one side, Catholics on the other, Jews down the street. What a mess. Of course, that was why, every now and then, someone needed me, the Shortcut Man. To get to what was real.

"Dick?" Devi looked over at me. "Thank you. For everything."

"You've already thanked me."

"I don't mean that."

"Neither do I."

"Want to hear Melvin's message?"

I nodded. "Let's hear it."

I detected pain in his voice. "Thank you, Devi, for giving the Nazi my phone. And, since you're not answering your phone, you fucking bitch, lemme just clue you in on a few things. I don't know who hit me, but he's fucking dead. Dead man walking.

"So I'm going to need his name. So I can have his coffin made up. Or you're fucking dead, too.

"And I don't know what you pulled with our Nazi doctor last night, calling him back and shit, but I smell something dirty. I pray to God, for your sake, that you didn't mention Nazarian's name to him.

"And how *I* ended up, all tied up in a fucking box at Dunkin' Donuts, then meeting the cops—you better have some answers. Or I'll peel your skin. When you get this message call me. *Bitch*."

I looked at Devi. "That's quite a message."

"That's Melvin."

"What is he talking about, tied up in a box at Dunkin' Donuts, then meeting the cops?"

"I have no idea. I thought he was spending the night on Mulholland."

I found a spot up the street from Fairfax Convalescent, parked, told Devi to wait a minute, immediately called Amanda Stewart.

Amanda was a friend of long standing. Back from the old days. She was an archivist at the LAPD. A pretty brunette with a cheerful smile for everyone, she had solved more cold cases from behind her desk than most detectives in the field. Her memory was elephantine and encyclopedic.

"What can I do for you, Dick?" she inquired brightly.

"I need you to trace a name. See if he crossed paths with the department. Would have been this morning."

"What's the name?"

"Melvin Shea."

Amanda's laugh bubbled over the phone. "Melvin Shea. Everybody knows about him. He's the case of the day."

"Case of the day? Tell me."

And she did. Dunkin' Donuts, refrigerator box, physical attachment to director Eli Nazarian, the reek of gin, swollen faces, dead dog. Was that the Melvin Shea I'd been talking about?

"I think so, and thank you, Amanda."

"You're welcome. But one day, you know, you'll have to explain your part in this. Just for me."

I told her to expect a honeybee. She disconnected, laughing. I called Rojas. He wasn't picking up.

Fairfax Convalescent was a one-story sprawl of outdated sixties modernity. I opened the door and the smell hit me. And the memories. The unholy mixture of urine and disinfectant. An odor you never forgot.

Georgette's aunt Nan had Alzheimer's and had lived out the last year and a half of her life in a place in Studio City. Not all that far from Twain's.

Alzheimer's was a horrible and degrading disease, stripping away from its victims both memory and personality. Leaving a cantankerous shell of confusion, loss, bitterness, and rage. And that was the good part. A downward slide without possibility of recovery, visiting Aunt Nan was to visit a suspicious, sulking stranger who thought she had been secretly and unjustly confined in Mexico. Mexico. Because the majority of the nurses were brown-skinned Filipinas.

Georgette would leave in tears, and I would beg her never to return, remind her that Aunt Nan wasn't there. Just not there. After a while Aunt Nan lost all humanity and then she forgot how to swallow. The loss of that ability was the last fork in the road. One choice, a merciful death of hydration and morphine; the other path, the hopeless, long-term main-tenance of a human vegetable. You'd think that the Methodists, the Cath-olics, and the Jews would come to agreement on this one. No.

Aunt Nan went on water and morphine and slipped gently away in a week's time. God bless you, Aunt Nan.

Devi spoke to the Filipina at the front desk and inquired about Rhonda Carling. We were directed to Room 156.

At least the place was clean. We walked through the human ware-house, finally reaching our destination near the end of the north wing.

Rhonda was the lone occupant of 156. Her breathing was long and slow. We looked down on her.

Jesus. I guess I'd seen her before the blackening and the swelling set in. With the black now were yellow, plum, and green, the skin swollen tight. Her nose was off to one side. Her ingenue days were over. To wher-ever she returned, she'd be one more liar from Tinseltown. One eye was swollen shut.

"Rhonda," said Devi, softly. "Rhonda, it's Devi."

One bloodred eye opened, wheeled around, found us. Or didn't find us. "Who's there?"

"Rhonda, it's Devi."

Rhonda's lips were grotesquely swollen obstacles to speech. "Where am I?" she managed, thickly.

"You're in Fairfax Convalescent."

The red eye rolled my way. "Who's he?"

"I'm Dick Henry, Rhonda."

"Fuck you," said Rhonda. The eye found Devi again. "He really fucked me up good, didn't he?"

"You're going to be better," Devi lied. "How are they treating you here?"

"How the fuck should I know? I'm here and I hurt all over. He put a gun up my cunt."

"I know he did. You told me. He won't get away with it."

"Yeah? What are you going to do about it?"

"We'll do the right thing."

"I don't give a shit about the right thing. I want a million dollars."

Devi nodded.

"I want a million dollars, Devi," repeated Rhonda.

"I heard you," Devi returned.

"A million dollars."

Devi nodded again.

"Did you hear me, Devi?"

"Yes, I heard you. A million dollars. That's a lot of money."

"Whose side are you on?"

"I'm on your side."

"I want a million dollars."

"I get the figure, Rhonda. But I don't think this is the proper time for a real discussion. I think that—"

"*Fuck you,* Devi."

"Fine. But no one's going to pay you a million dollars. Let's be realistic."

"Howard will pay."

"*Howard?*"

"Look at me. *Look at my face!* I want a million dollars. And I'll get it. Or I call the police and CNN and Fox News and the *L.A. Times.* And I'll tell them all about the Ivanhoe talent program. I'm no fool. He's probably got eight or ten other girls like me. You remember Tricia?"

Red-eye kept up her barrage. "I visited Tricia. Jesus Christ, I visited her *right here*! Right here!"

"Rhonda, calm down. You've got to—"

"I don't have to do anything. Ivanhoe is a criminal operation." She pointed a finger at Devi. "And you're part of it! You tell fucking Melvin I want my million dollars or I pull down his evil house. *Tell him!* Let him put that in his pipe and smoke it."

Devi looked over to me with a slight shake of her head. "Alright, Rhonda, I'll tell him."

Rhonda's bloodshot eye rolled back over to me. "You know what, mister?"

Well, I knew it wouldn't be salutary. "What?"

"Fuck you," said Rhonda, summing up neatly.

Devi's cell phone rang.

"Oh, perfect," said Rhonda. "There's the boss man now! You suck Melvin's dick to keep your low-ass job? I did. And I know that's him now. Checking on your progress. Seeing how far you'll jew me down. Well, you won't! I want a million fucking dollars or I bring the house down. Now get out!"

"Rhonda, listen," began Devi, but Rhonda steamrollered her. "GET OUT!"

We left.

TWENTY-THREE

Mr. Hogue Will
See You Now

Just yesterday he'd been in this very room, this antechamber, awaiting good news and waxing fortunes. Now it was all on the line. Thankfully, three lines of coke had done him well. He felt a little bit human. He looked over at the Asshole from Armenia. Asshole's jaw was wired shut. And his head was shaved. A ball cap perched on painful territory. The Nazi told him he'd put fifteen stitches back there. Served him right.

Of course, with Nazarian's big case of director's dick, he'd have to be handled carefully. Don't ruffle the feathers of the great creator. What old movie had he seen? There'd been a great line. Something about the people most in need of a beating were enormous.

Nazarian looked at him balefully. "Talk to him yet?"

"No."

"We're here about Dunkin' Donuts, *only*."

"That's all, Eli. He doesn't know about anything else."

The door opened. Helena stuck her head in. "Mr. Hogue will see you now."

Hogue watched the assholes walk toward his desk. Eager as kids walking to the woodshed for a dialogue with Daddy. And Melvin didn't like

Nazarian, that much was obvious. But few people did. Nazarian was a cold fish.

He could fire both at will. And he would, if it came to serious collateral damage to Ivanhoe. If America demanded it. Who was he to stand against the will of the people? Of course, the rabble would have to wait until Nazarian finished *Gumshoe*.

In the final twenty feet of the penitent's march, Hogue turned his chair to look out the grand window behind him. He heard them sit. Outside the window a tall strawberry blonde with a nice chest sat down on a bench in the Merry-Olde-England village set. A very nice chest. Very, very nice. Maybe he'd send Melvin after her. Later.

He turned to regard the pair. "Well. The two Hollywood-refrigerator-box bigwigs. No pants. Gordon's gin. Dead dog.

Where was I, gentlemen, where was I?"

A silence held until Nazarian broke it. "I don't know what happened. I woke up in that box, connected to Melvin."

The director was talking funny. "What's with your mouth, Eli?"

"My jaw's been wired shut. It's broken."

"How?"

"Don't know."

"You do know you're in the middle of shooting an Ivanhoe picture."

"Yes, I do."

"Then you have taken into consideration that your absence today has cost me five hundred thousand dollars."

"I'm aware of that."

"And you, Melvin?"

Melvin shrugged. He'd decided on the fuck-me-blind-I-don't-know-shit ticket. He spread his hands, shook his head, painfully. Hogue was angry, but, as he and Nazarian had hoped and surmised, this meeting was about refrigerator boxes. Not battered women. "I don't know what happened. I woke up with Eli. The only think I can think of is Rohypnol."

"Rohypnol. The date-rape drug?"

124

"That's all I can think of," repeated Melvin.

"You guys dating?"

Hogue watched the duo endure his humor. "You guys were together last night?"

"All of us went to celebrate over at the Grill." Melvin looked over at Nazarian.

Nazarian nodded. "We had a couple of drinks, everybody did. And that's all I remember."

Melvin looked at Hogue and asshole. The shared account of the evening had just departed from the truth. Yes, they'd had a drink.

In fact, three. Four. Then Nazarian had cornered him. "Hey, Melvin."

Melvin nodded. If he didn't know better, Nazarian had huffed a few lines of coke in the men's room. A genial bonhomie had pervaded the group of afternoon millionaires. "Whazzup, Eli?" Melvin smiled, but Eli would pay for the golden gun in his face.

"You know the chick in the Wells-Fargo commercial?"

"You mean Rhonda Carling." One of Hogue's twenty-eight. "The one who looks like Catherine Deneuve."

"She sure does." But taller, bigger tits, and no brains. Better than Deneuve. "What about her?"

"Maybe she could be a part of *Gumshoe*. I'd like to get to know her a little bit."

Melvin could imagine a thousand ways the director might get to know her. Nine hundred and fifty of them with her legs in the air. And what had he heard about Nazarian? That he hurt people. Paid them off. But maybe that was all bullshit. He certainly didn't take much shit on the set. Heather Hill, moron. Motivation, blow job.

He checked his watch. It wasn't seven thirty. Officially, Rhonda was free that night. It was Mandy's night. Rhonda was Hogue free. Statistically, she was on only one day a month. The lunar cycle. That fit. A pack of bitches. Didn't they all bleed at the same time? What had he read about that?

He looked at the Armenian. With that fat check in his pocket. If the

Armenian had huffed enough coke for that fixed, circular, cocaine thinking to begin, only Rhonda would do.

He looked into the director's eyes. "Let me give her a call, see if she's loose."

"Great."

"But she's expensive."

"How expensive?"

"Five grand."

"That is expensive. She's made of gold?"

"Yes. She is." Because she belonged to the emperor. "Anything she wants," said Nazarian, waving his hand.

Of course, she was loose. It's Eli Nazarian, he had explained. The director. He's looking to put someone in *Gumshoe*. The girl who had the part had been shit-canned.

"But he wants to fuck me first," reasoned Rhonda.

"That part is up to you, Rhonda," he had said.

"He wants pussy, I want twenty-five hundred," said Rhonda. "I just did Wells-Fargo."

"I know you did. He saw it. He liked it."

"Fine, Melvin. Make a deal. And have an eightball sent over right now."

"Okay."

"I love showbiz."

"Showbiz is your life."

"And what a life."

Melvin hung up, smiled. It would be a profitable evening.

"Where do I get five grand cash this time of night?"

Melvin saw more white residue on asshole's lip. "If she's too expensive for your tastes, Eli, there's always Hollywood Boulevard." He shrugged. "You want prime, virgin pussy . . ."

Nazarian had to grin. "Did you say *virgin* pussy?"

"Well, almost virgin." Melvin's turn to smile. "Maybe you can't be first, but you could be next." He leaned quietly into to the director. "She never let *me* in."

Melvin accepted asshole's personal check.

"She never let you in?"

"No."

No. But he'd bartered his way in a half-dozen times. A little of this, a little of that. Some of that fine, flaky, Peruvian marching powder. Some of that Persian heroin. When Melvin delivered, he delivered. And never a Moses.

"What's a Moses?" Rhonda had asked as the small, green hill of heroin disappeared up her nose.

He'd grabbed those big titties, thumbed her nipple through the silk. "A Moses is getting *to* the promised land, but never getting in. With me, you get *into* the promised land."

But first, a tonsil wash. He pushed her head down into his lap.

"So you guys remember nothing past The Grill?" Hogue tapped his pencil.

"Nothing," said Melvin.

Nazarian spoke up. "Look, Howard. Everyone knows I like to party. Yesterday you gave me one hell of a bump. My intention was wine, women, and song."

"And you woke up with Melvin."

"Yeah. I woke up with fucking Melvin."

Melvin, annoyed, hooked his thumb at the director. "The way I look at it, Howard, I woke up with him."

Hogue worked a sesame seed out from between his teeth. "You didn't shoot anyone with your golden gun, did you, Eli?"

The golden gun. He'd completely forgotten about it. Until this moment. Where the fuck was it? Nazarian shook his head. "The way I feel, though, I might shoot someone tonight. But I didn't shoot anyone yesterday." And his check? What in fuck's name had he done with that?

"You okay, Eli?" asked Hogue.

Stay on course, you Armenian asshole, thought Melvin.

Nazarian put a hand to his forehead. "I'm having trouble putting things together. Until you mentioned the gun, I hadn't even thought of it."

"Well, you better think of it. The silencer makes it illegal in California."

"By the way, Howard"—Nazarian paused for sincerity—"thanks again for the gun. It's a unique gift. Tremendous. I'll treasure it always. Thank you."

Hogue studied his pair of highly paid liars. Of course, they'd just laid a pile on him. It was their nature. Like snakes bit. "Rohypnol's no accident. If that's what it was. Someone either wanted to fuck you up for shits and grins—or fuck you up for fun and profit."

"*Blackmail,*" said Melvin, pretending to struggle for understanding.

"That's right. We need to find out the rest of what happened last night. Ivanhoe doesn't do blackmail. I'll bring Chuck Hames in." Hogue stood up, turned, looked out the window. "By the way, getting you released from Hollywood Precinct, anonymously, cost thirty grand. You guys will make immediate arrangements to pay Huntington Derian that amount. That clear?"

Hogue watched Nazarian and Shea depart. Chuck Hames had heard and seen everything via the top-notch surveillance system. There was no doubt. The two men were liars.

"You heard all that?" asked Hogue.

Hames nodded, sat. "There's more to that story."

"A lot more."

"What are your priorities, sir?" Always call the boss *sir*. Never, his whole career, had the practice served him badly. From the marines to Blackwater to Ivanhoe. Though he'd gotten a little rambunctious in the Sand Kingdom. Twisted a few towels a little too hard. But those evolutions had led right here. To a plum gig. At six times his previous salary. Hogue paid well. Hames would not question his outrageous fortune.

"What do you think of the Rohypnol theory, Mr. Hames?"

"Usually it's the girl who gets it." Hames allowed his perfectly bland expression to communicate his skepticism. "But I can go to The Grill and ask a few questions. That's where they began to waffle."

"I agree."

"But first I'll swing by Dunkin' Donuts. They run videotape 24/7. Obviously, the gentlemen didn't choose to arrive in a refrigerator box. Maybe the tape will tell me something. Was there a police report?"

Hogue smiled. "There *was*." But Huntington Derian had seen to that.

Hames stood up. "I'll get started immediately, sir."

"Fine." Hogue watched him go. Good man.

TWENTY-FOUR

A Regiment of Dummies

In life, there is no small accommodation of evil. You accept it—or you don't. And though I felt I'd acted with relative decorum over the last twenty-four hours, I could see that a prosecutorial mind could see things differently. Assault. *Melvin*. Kidnapping. *Both assholes*. Grand theft. *The golden Smith & Wesson*.

And since I was no longer paid by the county to solve crimes, I would have to add blackmail to the list if I wanted to be paid for my time and effort.

Terminal Velocity—Eli Nazarian—from Howard Hogue. The gun was worth money.

Hogue would pay to keep it from becoming bad publicity for Ivanhoe.

Nazarian would pay more to keep the incident from Hogue's attention. And police attention.

But Melvin would pay the most. His position wasn't based on demonstrated talent. If Hogue learned that Melvin had procured Rhonda for Nazarian, Melvin's days on the gravy train were over. Emperors did not share their concubines. No matter how many they possessed. The golden gun would also give Melvin vantage over Nazarian.

Yes, there was money to be made. But did I want to make my money that way, assisting evil men to escape justice?

I'd have to think about it.

• • •

The Cadillac growled up the Kirkwood incline from the Country Store. Devi looked over at me. "You alright, Dick?"

"Yeah." But not really. Rhonda and the contemplation of the day's events had chastened my natural liking for Devi. She had accommodated evil. Evil was not always the slippery slope of legend, sometimes it was the gentle downward path into shadow.

We got back to the house, I put on a pot of coffee. She picked up her keys from the kitchen table.

"Where are you going?" I asked.

She shrugged. "I don't know. Home. Where else?"

"Home isn't safe yet, Devi."

"*Jesus,* Dick."

"What?" Her eyes were full. "What? What's with you?"

She set her keys down. "I'm embarrassed. I'm fucking embarrassed."

"Why?"

"The nature of my, uh . . . life's work."

"Be embarrassed. But going back to your house isn't safe. Some bad people are very angry at you."

"I need to feed my cat."

"Feed him later."

"You don't know how I feel."

"Tell me."

"It's like, suppose you helped a woman who dropped her groceries outside the market."

"And?"

"And then you found out that she was a shoplifter."

"You're a shoplifter?"

"Damn you. I'll tell you what I am. I'm somebody who's been looking the other way. I'm no better than Melvin."

"Moral relativism."

"Call it whatever you want."

"But you're not Melvin. You take care of people. You do take care of the girls. Someone has to take care of them."

"Yeah. Somebody." She ran her fingers back through her hair. "What's my job? My job is to ensure that a regiment of dummies is always ready for Howard Hogue to bang 'em in the can."

Well, okay. That was pretty much what I'd been thinking. But something about her choice of words, the *regiment of dummies,* attacked my funny bone. Fibissedah face showed everything.

"You think *that's funny?*" she demanded, her lip in an Elvis curl.

"Not at all," I deadpanned. I tried to breathe evenly and deeply, calmly, like a Beverly Hills yogi, but my facade cracked and I stood there quivering, eyes narrowed with effort, desperately trying to restrain my mirth. Devi stared at me, *if looks could kill,* but then she started to laugh, too.

Maybe it was the release of tension from all we'd been through. Maybe it was the poetry of the moment. But we laughed and laughed and laughed. We sank into our chairs, slapped the tabletop, spluttered until we were sore and tears ran down our faces. I hadn't laughed like that since Lynette in Ojai, where I'd been proven a clueless musical bankrupt.

Finally we arrived at a delicate silence. We eyed one another suspiciously. My mood had changed. I appraised Devi with open friendliness. She got up from her chair.

"Where are you going? I asked her.

She looked stern, but then a smile broke across her face. It was a beautiful thing to see. She walked around the table.

"I'm going to sit in your lap, Dick." So she did.

Later, when she was asleep, Rojas checked in. He apologized. "Look, dude, I didn't mean to cause a sensation. I guess it's been all over the news. Man, I got to thinking one place was as good as another. I should've called you, but I wanted those dudes shamed. *Shamed.* The gun in the *coño* did it to me. Struck close to home."

"I see." Did Rojas's actions change anything? Not specifically. Only in the way that everything that happens now affects everything that happens later. Rojas was a longstanding friend and colleague. He had done what I might have if our positions had been reversed. Better absolution than permission. "Look. Just tell me next time. So I can stay on top of things."

"Sorry."

"No problem." Something struck me. "But the dog. Where'd you get the dead dog?"

"I bought him, dude."

TWENTY-FIVE

Wells-Fargo

Melvin, in pain, hurried across the lot to his office. It was nowhere near Hogue's. It was in the lot's oldest office building. A losers' warren, if truth be told. Eddie Sanderson had blown his brains out in Melvin's office. But who remembered Eddie Sanderson?

He hurt all over. Getting beat up on television was one thing. You got up, fought on, the folks watched a commercial, when they came back you were fine. You were laughing. In real life a punch hurt for a month. Put things out of whack. Kneebone connected to the thighbone. It felt as if your skeleton had been reassembled by amateurs. No wonder boxers mumbled. And the son-of-a-bitch who clocked him—dead man walking.

And the asshole. From fucking Armenia. Hadn't wanted to talk about reimbursing Derian. Well, fuck him if he thought Melvin Shea was going to pay. Melvin Shea wasn't going to pay shit. Melvin Shea needed another line of cocaine.

Mary, his secretary, pasty-faced poster girl of mediocrity, looked up from her desk through smudged glasses. How the fuck did she see? She was a great, woozy blob of cells. Held together by forces only God understood. Feet the size of baguettes. "You just had a call, Melvin."

"I'll get to it later." He needed that line.

"You better get to it now."

"Devi Stanton?"

"No. Mr. Hogue."

Hogue. Hogue. *Hogue.* Had Hogue seen through the pitiful charade he and Nazarian had mounted? Ro-fucking-hypnol. He should stuff the Armenian full of Rohypnol and set a herd of goats to fuck him in the ass. Death by congo-bongo.

He shut his door behind him. Alone. At last. Freed from the wounded-animal syndrome of pretending everything was fine. He sagged into his chair, reached into drawer, pulled out his cocaine apparati, made it right. That golden light slowly kindled inside him. He'd . . . get through this.

Now Hogue.

"Howard Hogue's office."

He slipped into his cheerful, Boy Wonder persona. "Hi, Helena, Melvin, for the boss."

"One moment."

He had waited ten minutes at this juncture on prior occasions. Was Melvin Shea a lapdog? But you didn't hang up on the emperor.

"You're on with Howard," intoned Helena in her best professional contralto.

Boy Wonder. "What can I do for you, Mr. Hogue?"

"Two things, Melvin. I'm, uh, running a little low. On supplies." Hogue paused.

Running low. On Starlet Fuck Powder. "Supplies. I'll take care of that."

"Great."

"And something else, sir?"

"Yes. I've decided on the young ladies I'd like to see next."

"Who and when, sir?"

"Tonight I'd like to see Michelle d'Orsay."

"Michelle d'Orsay."

"Yes. And tomorrow . . . tomorrow night . . . I'd like to see . . . uh, the Wells-Fargo girl."

"The Wells-Fargo girl?" Had Hogue actually said those words?

"The Wells-Fargo girl, Melvin. Uh, Rhoda, Rinda . . ."

"Rhonda Carling?" No. Please, no.

"Yes. That's the one. Couldn't remember her name for the life of me. That's why I call them *darling*."

Then Hogue was gone.

Melvin hung up the phone. He was fucked. Dead. Ruined.

Smashed. They would feed him to the pigs. He was naked on the anvil of bad decisions, the hammer of fate about to fall upon him.

He picked up his landline, jabbed for Mary.

"Yes?"

"Absolutely no visitors."

"No visitors."

"None. Nobody. Nada."

"No visitors."

He hung up. Her stupid loavish feet.

He reached into his desk again. Pulled out the cocaine, in the powdery ziploc. Pulled out the vial of Persian heroin, that lovely and subtle shade of green, mint-cream. Jackie, who operated out of that pool room above Pla-Boy Liquor, always had the best.

Fuck it. Fuck Hogue. He chopped up a little green line for himself. Mixed in some flake. A few seconds later it slipped through the blood-brain barrier.

Jesus God. The up of the coke, the down of the heroin. There was no more sublime feeling this side of paradise. Ask Belushi.

He began to mix Hogue's cocktail. He would get through this. When the powders were proportioned and mixed properly, he cut four six-inch squares from the thick paper of the centerfold of a *Hustler* magazine. Brandy Dafoe was airbrushed perfection. And, for the right price, he, Melvin Shea, could blow a wad down her throat *tonight*. Undoubtedly she espoused world peace and the ethical treatment of animals. He would get through all this.

Each of the paper squares he folded into a little envelope, a bindle; each bindle would contain an eighth ounce of heaven.

The bindles were put into an envelope. The envelope was sealed, folded, inserted into a larger envelope. That envelope was put into a cardboard shipping tube. The tube was taped thoroughly. He shook it. There was no audible clue as to the contents. Just something moving up and down.

He jabbed for Mary, handed her the tube when she entered. "To Helena. Only. Her hand. Got it?"

"Yes," said Mary. "Her hand."

TWENTY SIX

Dick Rings
the Coincidence Bell

Hames had rung Derian and Derian had told him to just come on by.
He'd picked up the surveillance from Dunkin' Donuts. It wasn't raw, live
feed, just a silent snapshot every fifteen seconds. From 2:00 a.m. until
8:00 in the morning.

That particular Dunkin' Donuts had its toe in East Hollywood, and its
clientele reflected its location. A raft of ratty losers, some drunk teenag-
ers from nearby Hancock Park. And some faces that stood out from the
crowd. Hames didn't know all the faces around Los Angeles, but he could
detect backgrounds from body language. Military or law enforcement
personnel had a particular posture. The individuals who stood out he
would show to Derian. Otherwise there wasn't very much. A general rush
outside around ten of six. Some laughing faces returning to their dough-
nuts, their egg sandwiches. Later, flashing lights and police.

Derian had asked him about Blackwater operations in Iraq and Hames
told him some tales. Well, some lies. Bales of cash, bricks of hashish,
camel spiders the size of wolves eating children by the side of the road.
The spiders went right for the eyes.

He fast-forwarded through the tape to the people of interest. At
02:37:345, Derian raised a hand. "Hold up."

"Recognize this guy?"

Derian smiled. "That's Dick Henry." Henry was holding two cups of coffee.

"Who's he?"

"He's the Shortcut Man."

"The Shortcut Man? Don't know him."

"I do. He's an ex-cop. Shot some people."

"He's got a different vibe from the riffraff. What does he do now?"

"He's a freelance opportunist. Gets things done."

"This kinda thing?"

"I don't know what this kind of thing *is*. Yet. But it rings the coincidence bell. Him being right there, obviously waiting around, right before the shit goes down."

"Where's the money in it?"

"I don't know. Yet."

Hames had learned nothing at the Grill. Shea and Nazarian had left in reasonable shape, not even too drunk. "You bailed 'em out of Hollywood Precinct?"

"*Bail* is a legally precise word."

"You secured their release."

"Yes. And I delivered them to Dr. Wolf."

"Beverly Hills Wolf?"

"Our man from Berlin."

Over the course of the conversation, Derian had assessed Hames. Every idea man needed muscle. Hames had whacked some civilians in Baghdad. Theoretical civilians.

He would teach Hames some of what was what and Hames would be grateful. "Wolf is Ivanhoe's in-house physician. For things and procedures that shouldn't go public. If you know what I mean."

Hames had become Ivanhoe's security chief forty days before. Derian was a good man to know. He would cultivate the relationship. "Do we show the tape to Mr. Hogue?"

We. Derian appreciated the *we.* And of course they would show the tape. A monarch should always be made aware of potential enemies. Those who stood for and against him. Derian smiled at Hames. "We'll visit Mr. Hogue tomorrow."

Tomorrow, because if you moved too soon, the monarch might think your job was easy and he was paying you too well. "Tomorrow afternoon, then," said Hames, standing to depart.

TWENTY-SEVEN

Impound Blues

The endless day continued. Then Hogue requesting Rhonda Carling. Didn't even know her name. He was in a bad movie with many reels to go before the end. Did they have reels anymore? Yes. In Lhasa. The cocaine and heroin were providing less and less respite with each whack. He wanted to hibernate for a thousand years. But the endless day wore on.

First, Rhonda. Obviously, she was in no shape for Hogue's alimentary predilections. A story was needed. A tale.

Uh, she was out with a date—no. A girlfriend, yes . . . in Hollywood. No, downtown L.A. No, North Hollywood. *North Hollywood*. The little theater district that backed up to the barrio. That was it. Perfect. Lots of dangerous mongos. With guns. Drugs. Drug problems. Meth. Drug of the week. Hanging with performers after the show. One thing lead to another. Fuck, it was 2:00 a.m. Ten feet from the stage door—two assholes. Knives. Flashing in the light. *Three* assholes. Next thing she knows, darkness—then Dr. Wolf. Good ole Dr. Wolf. And Fairfax Convalescent.

Good. A scenario. It would have to work. Dr. Wolf would be on board for that. Where did the doctor meet her? She, uh, she, uh, she . . . managed to get back to the El Royale. That would work. She just managed.

That took care of Rhonda and the Nazi. Now, Nazarian.

Simple. And too bad. Because the North Hollywood pulp fiction took the Armenian a-hole off the hook. A freebie for the assault that threatened everything. Information that could never get out. Shea on the scrap heap of history. No, the truth could never get out. Luckily, it was not in Nazarian's interest for the truth to get out, either.

But what to do with the Armenian? What Nazarian hadn't done was come to him and apologized for the disaster. Begged his forgiveness, his forbearance, acknowledged his unpayable debt.

Yes, Armenian Asshole, you fucked with the wrong dude. You messed with Melvin Shea and terrible and long-lasting will be my—

Well, it would be. When he could give some time to working out the details.

And the lesser details. Devi. And the dude who hit him. Devi couldn't hide forever. He'd put the squeeze on her and she'd give up Mystery Man.

Christ. It all might work.

But before all that. His Beemer. He'd left it near the El Royale. It had been towed. Mary had found it. The impound yard on Fuller, south of Santa Monica.

The cab was twenty bucks. The yard was full. Every hour new hostages arrived. People who'd lost their cars for one bad reason or another.

There it was. Lonely and forlorn. But looked in good shape. Then he saw the vehicle next to it. A Bentley. Nazarian's? Same model. License plate: Naz. Well, well, well. No one was watching. He drew back his foot, put a big dent in the driver's door. Take that, Asshole from Armenia.

In the cluttered office, radios on the blare, the impound lady presented her bill. $187.50. A rip. The usual Hollywood rip. This would go to the Armenian's account. Too bad Nazarian's car had been damaged at the yard. The yard would hire anyone.

The Beemer rolled smoothly over the wretched, potholed Melrose pavement, turned south on Fairfax. Melvin checked his watch. 7:37 p.m.

There it was. Fairfax Convalescent.

• • •

In the forty-two years of his existence, Eli Nazarian had never considered, even for one moment, the concept of liquid food. Walgreen's sold a variety. It came in any flavor you liked as long as you liked grainy vanilla. Like the early Ford Motor Company philosophy: any color you want as long as it was black.

The bitch had broken his jaw. She must have hit him with a rock.

He'd slept like a dog all afternoon, after the humiliating reprimand, then he'd awoken famished. With his jaws wired shut. Now, with incredible longing, he recalled Fritos corn chips. And pretzels. He relived the crisp snap of celery slathered with chunky peanut butter. He reinhabited the warm, false resilience of a Chicken McNugget.

And he'd *hated* all of those foods. But *now,* Christ.

He looked at the carton. Resource 2.0 Medical Food Complete Liquid Nutrition Vanilla 27-Pack. He sucked a mouthful through a fat straw. He wanted to scream, but screaming vibrated his teeth and that was—it was unspeakable.

How would he direct? Well, quietly. All those crew assholes would love it. Mimicking him behind his back.

He crushed up a pain pill with the end of a table knife into a spoon. It had to be very finely ground. Then he filled the spoon with vanilla shit and sucked the mixture out of the spoon.

Something was wrong. He was forgetting something. At the periphery of his mind. Then he remembered.

The gun.

Where was it?

In fact, he didn't remember much about the previous evening at all. Drinking with the celebrants, talking to Melvin the Pimp about the raspy-voiced, Wells-Fargo bimbo.

He looked out the kitchen window, down at the million lights of the San Fernando Valley. Seven million half-wits. Waiting for the right TV show. So they wouldn't have to think.

The gun. He barely remembered getting to the woman's apartment.

High up. The woman disappointed him. How many times had he forgotten an actress is only as smart as her lines? She was as dumb as a geranium. Or was it a perineum? Wanted to talk about *motion pictures*. Thought he might hire her for *Gumshoe*. Fat chance.

His memories after that point . . . were gone. But no golden glint from the gun.

Then it had to be *here,* at the house.

He started in the living room. The drawers in his desk. Nothing. The drawers in the various built-ins. Nothing. On the Steinway. Nothing. In the Steinway. Nothing. He visualized it again. Lying in that velvet case. Where had he put it? With the separate silencer attachment.

Then he knew where it was. He remembered it—at the bar at the Grill. He remembered its weight of the case as he waited for the valet to bring the Bentley around. He'd put it in the trunk. It was in the trunk.

He rushed out, through the kitchen, to the garage.

The Bentley was not there.

Nazarian's assistant, Marco Calvi, answered on the third ring. "What can I do for you, Mr. Nazarian?"

Marco was Nazarian's fifth personal assistant in the last two years. Marco had known that going in. Nazarian was a total asshole, and cheap, to boot. But work was work.

"I need you to track down the Bentley. I may have left it Hollywood last night."

Marco located the Azure in the impound yard on Fuller. $212.70. Wait a minute. There was a large dent in the driver's door. Mr. Nazarian wasn't going to like that. What to do? Fuck it. He drove his heel hard into the rear door. Twins. Perfect.

Nazarian heard Marco drive in an hour and a half later. Occupationally, Marco wasn't going to last all that long. Next time he would hire a gay man. A gay man could do flowers, food, funerals, and could purchase stylish clothes when needed.

Marco approached Nazarian with trouble across his face.

"What?" Talking through your teeth required lots of lip action.

"Your car, Mr. Nazarian."

"What about it?" The boss was talking funny.

"Two dents. Driver's door and rear door."

Nazarian examined the damage. Some do-nothing, have-nothing jealous toilet serpent had kicked in the panels. But he was too tired to explode. He'd peel someone's skin later. He looked at Marco. "You can go."

Marco walked back down the driveway, to Mulholland, called a cab for himself. Not even the *offer* of a ride. Asshole's mouth was wired shut. *Too bad*.

Nazarian drove the Bentley into its customary place in the garage, then pulled the little handle that opened the trunk. This would be the perfect time for the cable to break. It didn't.

He raised the lid, peered in. Some legal accordion folders, some shitty scripts he'd promised to read but wouldn't, golf clubs, a leather coat. Under the coat? Yes!

He grabbed the box, relief flowing through him, cool water.

Back in the kitchen he laid it on the table. The box was a beautiful mahogany. Classy. Hogue always got the best. Pimp Melvin. Shying away when he'd pointed it at him.

He carefully pushed the two brass hooks out of the eyes, snapped open the clasp.

He opened the box.

It was empty.

TWENTY-EIGHT

Rhonda Redux

Melvin didn't recognize the Filipina at the reception desk. He'd been here before, but it had been a while, with . . . Tricia. Tricia Hornsby. Fell off the roof of her garage. Drunk. After a visit from Hogue. Where did they ship her? Idaho. Idaho, somewhere.

"Can I help you?"

Boy Wonder. "I'm Dr. Franchetti. Dr. Wolf sent me. To look in on Rhonda Carling?"

Josie Liman checked her list. There it was. Carling. "Room 156, doctor, to your right, toward the end."

"Thank you, miss," said Boy Wonder.

He passed twenty rooms of misery as he approached the end of the hall. There was no good way to die, but fast was better than slow.

He entered 156 quietly. Rhonda was the only occupant. He looked down on her. Christ. Nazarian had really done a job. She looked like meat. Grotesque, swollen. Yellow, black, and green. Deneuve was gone.

"Rhonda. It's Melvin."

The unrecognizable creature opened one eye. A lurid red one. "I knew you'd show up."

"Well, here I am."

"Did she tell you?"

"Did who tell me what?"

"You assholes."

"I don't know what you're talking about, Rhonda."

"Of course, you don't."

What had he expected? A tick of anger tightened his gut. Anger at Rhonda, at Nazarian, at Devi, at Mystery Man. At Hogue.

"Look. I'm sorry all this went down."

"He's hurt people before."

"I didn't know that."

"Liar."

"I didn't do this to you."

"Fuck you. Did she tell you my number?"

"I don't know what you're talking about, Rhonda. I'm trying to help you."

"I want a million dollars."

"A million dollars."

"That's right. That's what I told her."

"Told who?"

"Told Devi."

"Devi was here?"

"Like you don't know."

"I didn't know."

"Liar."

"When was she here?"

"Fuck you, Melvin. Devi doesn't talk to Little Melvin? On her knees? I did."

"I'm not here to talk about Little Melvin."

"I want a million fucking dollars. Look at my face. Look! It's ruined. Ruined!"

"You'll get better. I'll take care of everything."

"Fuck that. I want the money. Or I go to the police, to the *L.A. Times*, to CNN, to everybody. I go every-fucking-where people will listen to me. 'Cause I got a really good story to tell."

147

Now there was an iron band around his gut and he felt his face tightening and hurting. He tried to breathe deeply. That hurt, too. He walked toward the door.

"You leaving, asshole?"

"No." He shut the door. "I don't want the world sharing our business."

"I do. Unless I get what I want."

"Let's discuss what you *really* want."

"I told you what I really want. I want a million fucking dollars. Howard's got it. You get it for me. Or I bring the house down."

The iron band grew cold. "You'll bring the house down."

"That's right, Melvin. The whole evil fucking house. *Down.*"

"Okay."

"Okay? Okay, what?"

"Okay, Rhonda. I get it."

"Look at my face, Melvin."

Melvin nodded. "I see it."

He looked around.

"What are you looking for, Melvin?"

"I'm looking for my camera."

"Camera? You're going to take pictures?"

"So everything will be documented." On the other bed was the camera. It looked just like a pillow. He walked over, picked it up, came back. "You know"—he paused—"you may be right, Rhonda."

"Right about what?"

He looked down at her. "That there's no fixing that face of yours."

"What?"

"Say cheese." He brought the pillow over the railing and down on Rhonda's face. She struggled. He pressed hard, with both hands. The planes of her face visible through the pillow. The forehead. The nose. The chin. Then, after a while, she stopped moving. He pushed down harder, counted to twenty. He needn't've. The struggle was over, the spirit loosed.

He looked down at her face. Out of her misery, dead as Elvis Presley. Long live the king.

All in all, it had been a quiet way to go. He removed the slipcase from the pillow, tossed the pillow back on to the other bed. He felt calm, yet energized. He could feel his heart beating in his chest. In his own face, he felt no pain. He had not come to dispatch Rhonda, but like a good golfer, faced with an unpromising lie, he had relied on instinct and boldness. So, he had carried the day.

He looked around the room. He had brought nothing, he would leave with nothing. Except the pillowcase. He folded it five times. Now it would slip into his pocket.

An odd factoid filtered into his mind. Any plane of real matter could only be folded seven times. Hmmm. Sounded like bullshit. He opened the door with the pillowcase. Wiped the exterior handle with it.

No one was in the hall. The fluorescent lights buzzed and flickered, reflected off the linoleum. A TV laugh track was audible down the hall, toward the front desk.

But he would not go out the way he had come in. There had to be an emergency door.

At his end of the hall, thirty feet away, a perpendicular corridor went left. He turned the corner. The emergency door was twenty feet away. Right next to the fire alarm. Perfect. He pulled the fire alarm on the way by.

The red bell clamored its ear-grinding rhythmic cacophony, and then, after a charging, low roar, the sprinklers gave forth in a sibilant rush.

Melvin pushed the bar on the exit door and stepped into the night.

Except he had done none of those things. But, looking into her stupid, swollen face, the face of a woman who could ruin him, *ruin him,* Melvin had found himself calmly capable of killing. He was amazed at how clearly he could see himself putting her out of her misery.

In the abstract, sitting at your grade-school desk, killing seemed utterly impossible, an inconceivable set of circumstances. But now it was a tool that lay on the table, casual, askance, available. Necessary?

How many lines had he crossed such that this line meant so little? That was the thing about crossing lines. Seldom were there real consequences. Usually a negligible expense of energy; lifting the metaphysical foot and crossing over. But the crossing invited the next transit.

It was him. It was that simple. His success was her failure. Her success was his ruin.

That's what made a good screenplay. The opposition of ideas.

So he had agreed with her. Yes, Rhonda, you'll get your million dollars. Yes, I see your point of view. Absolutely justified. Relax, Rhonda. Heal, Rhonda. Be back tomorrow,

Rhonda, with concrete steps toward your goal.

The Beemer started right up. An automobile he couldn't afford if his circumstances changed and his life fell to pieces. If Hogue got wind. He had never considered his life fragile. But it was.

All life was fragile. Everything depended on a million hidden factors, most of which never came into play. It was all a house of cards. In a game that everyone bought into, fought viciously to win. And then you croaked anyway.

He should call the fucking Nazi doctor. But a wave of fatigue and pain rolled over him, pushed him into his seat. He desperately needed sleep. Had he just contemplated *murder*? He wasn't thinking straight.

Sleep.

He'd call Mengele tomorrow.

TWENTY-NINE

Meet Me in St. Louis

Meet Me in St. Louis. That would be it. Best of the best. Musicals. The highest and most sublime expression of American culture. Wolf had studied. He saw and appreciated the unbroken line from Greek plays to Italian opera to *West Side Story*. Tonight he would again savor Esther's dilemma.

What a day it had been. You never knew when a gift, a celestial gift, was sailing down the line. He had digested his day slowly and now smiled at his prospects. Life was a game of applied pressures. He now had Melvin Shea and Eli Nazarian directly under his thumb. The facts had sorted themselves out.

Melvin had trafficked one of Hogue's girls, and Nazarian, that wildly indulged psychopath, had beaten the crap out of her. The golden gun had proved his presence at her apartment. And where he put that gun!

Guilt, seeking silence, equaled money. Simple, sound, historical. His concerns were now mathematical. How much should each man pay for his silence? A lump sum, or money over time? Didn't matter. Acquiescence to his request was the thing. And regardless of term, knowledge never died. Did it?

Bring on Judy Garland. Wait. Maybe he would go modern. *Moulin Rouge* with Nicole Kidman. Or *Chicago*. Catherine Zeta-Jones.

Nicole. Yes. Sweet Nicole.

THIRTY

A Call from On High

Razor in hand, I contemplated my imperfect face.

My life as a shortcut man had not been a considered career choice. One thing had lead to another, to another, to another. What I had was momentum. But I'd put nothing away for a rainy day. Sometimes I was flush, sometimes I ran on empty.

But what does any man do? You go on, day by day, playing your version of the game, until the day comes that you can't. I'd realized a few things. When my number came up, like it certainly would, I wanted to go quick rather than slow.

As long as I could enjoy a sunny day, under my own steam, I'd call that living. I could be that old screw, sitting on the bench in park, watching the delinquents. But I knew, as I reached the end of the line, my beliefs might change. What was unthinkable today might be palatable tomorrow. Would I persevere as I carried around an oxygen cylinder? Dialysis three times a week? Would I be so scared of dying I would tolerate a colostomy bag hanging out of my side?

My greatest fear was Alzheimer's. I'd seen Georgette's aunt Nan. She terrified me, horrified me. If I received such a diagnosis, what would I do?

At some point previous to the diagnosis you'd know something was wrong. How would it feel to forget? Or would the capacity to realize your incapacity recede before and with the disease? Once the disease had real substance did you know you were ill? Was it too late to commit suicide? While you still had the means of free will in your grasp?

I had no religious convictions on the subject. If my life was my own, if free will was the essence of soul, my choice to die could be no sin. No god, if there was one, could judge me. In fact, God might commend me. Certainly, if I had created the human race, I could take no joy in ordered sycophancy.

I looked in the mirror, continued shaving.

The temptation to trade the golden gun had resurfaced. And there was a beautiful stranger in my bed. I wanted to go someplace I'd never been before. Amsterdam, maybe.

The phone rang. "Hello?"

"Hi. Is this Mr. Henry?"

"Maybe. Can I help you?"

"This is Helena Richards . . ." The smooth contralto paused. "From Howard Hogue's office. Is this Dick Henry?"

"What did you say that was, again?" asked Estella. Tavo, sweating profusely, stood just inside the door with a big tree in a very yellow pot.

Tavo extended his hand toward the tree. It had kind of a randy odor that he hadn't noticed when it had been parked out with the Dumpsters. Too late now. He should've just bought some ten-minute carnations from Rite Aid. They lasted for ten minutes after purchase and didn't weigh eighty pounds. "This is a special tree," Tavo lied. "It's an El Dorado ficus. I thought you deserved this."

"Why do I deserve this?" inquired Estella. Her nose twitched. "To honor your beauty," returned Tavo, smoothly, "today, and everyday."

Some smells were so good they turned the corner and were bad, thought Estella. And vice versa. But Poky seemed excited.

Poky was her Chihuahua.

THIRTY-ONE

Acquisition Error

Huntington Derian got in early next morning to see Hogue. Though he was familiar with many aspects of Hogue's life, the man was still, fundamentally, a mystery to him. If you had a billion dollars in your checking account, what would you do?

Because you didn't have to *do anything.* With mortal concerns reduced to the abstract, might you be pushed closer to the realm of spirit? What was the point of the ultimate game?

He read a book by somebody. *The Significance of Putty.* In that book, an angel had explained the purpose of all sentient, self-aware life: to take part eventually in the formation of a multidimensional tapestry of soul that would warm the feet of God.

To warm the feet of God. Well, that was one answer.

"Have a seat, Hunt," said Hogue. "What do you have for me?"

"I met with Chuck Hames yesterday. He got the surveillance tapes from Dunkin' Donuts."

"Hames is a good man."

"Yes, he is."

"People of interest?"

"I think so. What I'm thinking is that we have a case of kidnapping on our hands."

"Kidnapping? Interesting."

"There are two forms. Transportation and asportation."

"What's asportation?"

"Holding someone where you find them."

"I see. So this isn't that."

"No, it's not. But they were held. Somewhere."

"And brought to Dunkin' Donuts."

"Exactly." Derian handed his boss the DVD.

Hogue turned to the console behind him, slipped in the disk. "Who will I see?"

"Guy named Dick Henry."

The blank screen lit up. "Why do I know that name?"

"They call him the Shortcut Man. He's a . . . a problem solver." Derian grinned. "Remember the Art Lewis funeral?"

"The resurrection! The funeral with the resurrection."

"That's the guy."

"He did that?"

"He was involved somehow. I'm not sure which aspect."

"Wish I could've seen that."

Derian slapped his knee. "They had folks running all over the place. Twenty car accidents in the parking lot."

"What happened with all that?"

"Well, the court declared a marriage that happens after death is invalid." Both men laughed.

"On the other hand," said Hogue, "you wouldn't give a shit."

"Beyond the sphere of mortal concern," Derian continued. "And the judge who put the scheme all together, Hangin' Harry What's-his-name, blew his head off."

Hogue snapped his fingers. "I remember now. The judge was married to Ellen Havertine."

"Good-lookin' lady."

"Fine-looking." Hogue reflected. He'd slept with her. Thought he had. Probably did. Must have. But the memory was fuzzy. Maybe she'd just blown him. She *had. Golf ball through the garden hose.* To help get her series off the ground. *Special Counsel.* Yes. And hadn't she sucked some director's dick back when she was twelve or something? Lolita. Nabokov. Practice made perfect.

On the monitor, Dunkin' Donuts flickered to herky-jerky, fifteen-second life in black-and-white. Hogue looked up to view the seedy night parade.

"Henry comes in at about two thirty-five."

Hogue studied the screen. The doughnut business was a good one. Flour, water, and sugar were irresistible adjuncts to the stimulant, coffee. And the coffee, low-end beans. Of course. Not that anyone could tell the difference. Starbucks had sold shit beans at premium prices for a few years awhile back. They had called it an acquisition error. *Right.* And lately, some Ecuadorian beans that had *actually passed through* monkey sphincter were commanding tremendous sums. Actual *shit* beans. What a business.

On-screen, the Shortcut Man appeared in the picture. Derian pointed. "Here he is."

Hogue didn't recognize Dick Henry. But after the fifth or sixth stop-shot he thought he recognized the man Henry was talking to.

A man he hadn't seen for twenty-some years. *A dead man.* Hogue couldn't breathe.

Derian had been watching Hogue. Something was wrong. "Are you alright, Mr. Hogue?"

An artificial grin slithered across Hogue's face and disappeared. He put a hand to his stomach. "Must have been something I ate." Hogue stopped the DVD. "Why don't you leave this with me, Mr. Derian?"

"Fine, sir." Derian maintained his face in neutral. What on the tape had affected Hogue? "I'll get on my way let you get back to business."

Derian would reexamine his copy of the DVD when he got back to his office. No, better yet, he'd run the tape past Lew Peedner, Henry's old partner. Maybe Peedner would see what Hogue had seen. And Peedner had it in for Henry. There was nothing like a little institutional gratitude.

Rules were rules. But gratitude was money in the bank. And sometimes you needed a bank to bend a rule or two.

Hogue was finally alone. He ran the DVD back and found Davis Algren. And ran it back again. And again. It was him. There was no doubt.

Algren was obviously in bad shape. Even in black-and-white the man appeared weathered. That grimy, shiny, reflective ruddiness that only years of alcohol and outdoor living could confer. His features, once stunningly handsome, now thickened, coarsened, scarred.

By himself, Algren would have been a remarkable curiosity. But the presence of Henry changed everything. Was it coincidence that put the two of them talking at a filthy doughnut house in the middle of the night? Hadn't the Henry fellow purchased *two* cups of coffee?

Maybe it was a coincidence. But you couldn't play it that way. No.

Undead Davis Algren was telling tales to the Shortcut Man.

THIRTY-TWO

Angles and Angels

"What else do you know about Howard Hogue?"

Devi looked at me across the kitchen table. I'd let her sleep and sleep and sleep. Looked like it had done her good. "I've told you everything I know. I've never met him. Why?"

I told her about the call from Helena Richards. And the invitation.

She sat there and thought about it. Exhaled her blue smoke slowly. "The only thing I can guess is that he knows something about the Rhonda situation."

"That's all I can figure. So where's the leak?"

"It's not Rhonda, it's not Melvin, it's not Nazarian. Which leaves Wolf." She looked into my eyes. "It's not me."

"Assuming the worst about you, it's not in your interest either."

She shook her head. "It isn't. It doesn't kill me, like it kills Melvin, but it leaves me dirty. Which means getting dropped off at the next corner." She paused. "What about the night guy at the El Royale?"

Winslow Peckman. Winston Peckman. Winston Peckham. That was it. *Winston Peckman*. The junkie with the job. Hell, most junkies had jobs. "Let's see." I thought out loud. "He knows Rhonda. He met you, he met Wolf, he met me, he met Melvin—"

"And he met Rojas and Tavo. Then Wolf went back."

I shook my head. "I know he sure as hell did some heavy-duty wondering. But I don't think anyone left him a card."

"It's got to be Wolf."

"Wait a second. Pecker would know Hogue, too. Hogue rang her bell up there, didn't he?"

"He banged her can," said Devi.

That set both of us off again. I shook a finger at her. "This is serious shit, here."

"It's Wolf, Dick. Night Guy might have known Hogue, but he wouldn't have known about the exact relationship between Hogue and Rhonda. And he'd never call anyway. It's got to be Wolf."

"Okay. Let's say it is Wolf. Why would he rat out Nazarian and Melvin? He knows how they fit into the equation. Perfect for blackmail. Which lasts and lasts. Going to Hogue would be a onetime explosion. Which might come back at him."

There was no ready answer for that one. We settled into silence. She looked at me, smiled. "I slept well last night, Dick."

"Yeah?"

"Yeah."

"Good. I'm happy for you." My appointment with Hogue was at two thirty.

"You know what I'm going to do, Dick?"

"No. What?"

"I'm going to sit on your lap."

Yup. One day the Shortcut Man may be dragging an oxygen cylinder to a dialysis appointment, colostomy bag by his side. Getting off the wrong bus at the wrong stop, wondering what the fuck he's doing at the YMCA. If that occurs, and you see him, drag his cane away and beat him to death with it. Please.

But, today, in the present, where lots are cast, I'm following a beautiful girl to my bedroom.

Sufficient unto the day is the evil thereof.

The girl is laughing. Can you hear her?

THIRTY-THREE

Himmler Calls

Melvin woke from a dark and dreamless sleep to the sound of the phone. He checked the screen. Wolf.

Wolf. Perfect. Rhonda. "Hello?"

"Melvin, this is Dr. Wolf."

"Hold on for a second, Doc." He put the phone down. Tylenol with codeine. Where was it? His face felt worse today then yesterday. Like the Nazi had told him it would. There it was. On the dresser. He opened up the vial, shook himself out two, put them in his mouth, looked around for water.

In the bathroom he cupped his hand, washed them down. And why not a piss while Speer was waiting?

He got back to the phone. Wolf was still holding. "I'm back, Doc. Had to take a piss." That would tighten him up.

"How are we this morning, Melvin?"

Melvin was immediately and deeply suspicious. Wolf had the bedside manner of a tarantula. "How are *we* this morning? *I'm* sore as hell. Like you told me I would be. You want to give me a massage or something?" Had something happened to Rhonda? "What's up?"

A silence. Melvin looked at his phone. Still connected. "Actually, I'm calling about my bill. I mean, *your* bill, Melvin."

"Your bill? You're on salary as far as I know."

"Salary is for normal conditions."

"What conditions are you talking about?"

The doctor sighed. "I guess I'd be happy to talk to Mr. Hogue about my concerns."

Surprise, surprise. Himmler was trying to blackmail him. You could annoy a man with a true grasp of human nature, but you couldn't disappoint him. Melvin smiled. It was no way to treat a future partner. He'd play along. For a while. "What are you talking about, Dr. Wolf?" he asked in a small, frightened voice.

"I'm talking about a thousand dollars a week, every week, Melvin. Or a flat fee of fifty thousand dollars." The doctor's voice was triumphant. "You see, Melvin, I saw the golden gun."

Well, well, well. The doctor had seen the golden gun. Undoubtedly, at Rhonda's. Why hadn't he seen the gun? Because Devi, that bitch, moved it before he came. Aha. Devi was seriously in the game, as well. And the Mystery Man? Was he in on it, too?

"Melvin, are you there?"

"You're *blackmailing* me." Melvin scratched his balls. He was aghast, *aghast*. Round up the usual suspects. "That's ag-gainst the law, D-doctor." He filled his voice with fear.

"I'll want that money this week. Or arrangements made."

"Fine. I'll be right over."

"*What?*"

"I said, fine. I'll be right over. I know where you live." Melvin hung up the phone. He wasn't going to pay Goebbels a nickel. Wait a second. Could Goebbels pay him?

He stepped into the shower. Everything would work out. In time.

THIRTY-FOUR

For the Benefit
of Smokin' Jack

At Irv's Burgers, corner of Santa Monica and Sweetzer, Lt. Lew Peedner waited for Huntington Derian. It would be hard to remain inconspicuous in the company of a fat man in a red suit. Except at Christmas. So he'd set the meeting right across, kitty-corner, from the West Hollywood City Hall.

Then he saw Derian exit City Hall and start across the street. Then wait for the second signal. Finally he arrived.

"Hi, Lew," said the attorney, patting his head with a monogrammed handkerchief.

"Hi, Hunt," said the lieutenant.

"What's good here?"

"You've never been?"

"Been past a thousand times."

"They don't make what they can't do. They deliver on everything they promise. I'm having the cheeseburger special."

"Then I'll have that, too."

The burgers were excellent as long as you didn't consider what hamburgers everywhere were made of. Diseased, hormoned, overmedicated cattle staggering gratefully to the sledgehammer. *WHONK!* But the ser-

163

vice at Irv's was superb and personal, including, on each paper plate, a hand-drawn caricature of every customer.

Lew looked at his illustration. Intentionally or not, the illustration had captured his sad fatigue. He glanced at the attorney's plate. A generic, jovial fatman. But a resemblance.

"What's up, Hunt?" he began.

"You heard the news yesterday. The bigwigs in the refrigerator box."

"With the dead animals."

"Animal, *singular*. A dead dog."

"I'm not familiar with the particulars. Fill me in."

"The bigwigs were brought to Dunkin' Donuts. Obviously, against their will. We don't want to embarrass the department."

Lew wasn't seeing where this was going. "What department?"

"LAPD."

What the fuck, here. "Am I your straight man, Hunt? Give it to me all at once."

Derian shot his cuffs, smiled. How many people in the world had the luxury of wearing a red suit everyday? Besides himself? And those cardinals boinking the altar boys. Derian had seven identical suits. North Indian silk. He handed Peedner a DVD. "This is from surveillance tapes at Dunkin' Donuts. It may be a coincidence, a huge coincidence, but your old pal was hanging round and round just before the shit came down."

And Derian was a poet, as well. Lew was not going to play straight man. He just stared at Derian, waiting.

"Your old pal, Dick Henry."

"*Dick?*"

"Aka the Shortcut Man."

"Dick is no longer part of the department."

"A difference without distinction as far as the public is concerned. Wouldn't you say?"

"Your bigwigs are okay last I heard. What do you get out of this?"

"The pleasure of serving our community and being responsible corporate citizens."

That couldn't be all.

"And perhaps, the opportunity to rehabilitate Jack Wilton—rather than incarcerate him."

"Ahh. Smokin' Jack." Jack Wilton was a rising star on the Ivanhoe slate. With an appetite for heroin, cocaine, and underage quiff. Unluckily, he'd purchased some tar from an undercover officer behind the Clown Room. Smokin' Jack was looking at significant time in county if proper channels weren't properly greased. "He's working on *Gumshoe*, am I right, Hunt?" Of course, channels would be greased.

"You are indeed. Lot of money riding on him." Derian paused. "And upon young Jack's shoulders, the lawful hopes and dreams of many upstanding citizens."

Hmmm. The opportunity to whack Dick Henry around. Could Dick be involved in a kidnapping? Couldn't be. But . . . he wouldn't put it *entirely* past him. If the fee was right.

Had to be a story with Shea and Nazarian. Wonder what it was.

THIRTY-FIVE

A Rare Honor

I was waved onto the Ivanhoe lot at ten past two. I put my temporary permit on the dashboard and looked for a parking place. I'd been on every lot in the L.A. area and liked them all. Stars of old beamed down from large murals, tough as nails, sweet as pie. After a while, you thought you knew them. Fred, Ginger, Lana, Clark.

Hogue's office was in a newer building, adjacent to an English village set. A beautiful, buxom redhead graced a bench, did her nails, smiled as I went by. I was in no hurry. I turned back, inquired if I was close to Mr. Hogue's office.

Yes, I was. In fact, his office was that very large window looking down on us right up there. She stretched largely, languidly. I thanked her and went on my way.

The office of Hogue's secretary, Helena, was larger than my house. And better furnished. Ten minutes after my appointment time, I was informed that Mr. Hogue would see me now.

Hogue's office was as large as a department store. You couldn't ski and you couldn't surf, but everything else was a possibility. I was unsure of where exactly to proceed but then I was hailed by a man in a forest.

Actually, it was a ficus grove.

Ficus trees had been imported to Los Angeles in the seventies for their swift growth, their graceful appearance, their capacity to thrive on neglect. They responded to their welcome by uprooting sidewalks and impeding sewers and drains all over the city. Plumbers and street maintenance men rejoiced.

Hogue's grove was still adolescent and under control. Hogue rose from a comfortable leather chair and extended a hand.

"Welcome, Mr. Henry."

"Mr. Hogue."

Finally. I'd shaken the hand of a billionaire. And one of America's most prolific can-bangers. A rare honor. He bade me sit and I did.

"How's business?" asked Hogue.

I tipped my head, looked around. "I think I'm in the wrong business."

He laughed. "I heard you had something to do with the Art Lewis funeral."

"I was *there*. It didn't go so well."

"So I'm told."

I waited for him to segue into the Rhonda Carling matter.

"What does a shortcut man do?" he inquired.

I shrugged. "A little bit of this, a little bit of that. Solving various problems. By various means. But I won't be hired for a strictly criminal enterprise."

"The Art Lewis matter was legal?"

"At its core, I believe I was on the side of righteousness."

"Says who?"

"Says me. The buck stops here."

He turned to a low table, teak, opened a leather register. Carefully he tore out a completed check, handed it to me.

Pay to the order of Dick Henry. $5,000.00

"What's this for?"

"For your time this afternoon. My time is valuable. I assume yours is, too."

I placed the check on the table in front of me. "My time *is* valuable. Why am I here?"

Hogue leaned back, studied me. "Are you a man of discretion, Mr. Henry?"

"I'm not the law, and I'm under no obligation to apprise anyone of anything."

"I have a question for you."

"Shoot."

"Have you ever heard of a man named Davis Algren?"

"No."

"No?"

"No."

He pushed the check toward me. "You've never met the man, Davis Algren?"

"No."

He took the check back. Opened his register, removed another one, slid it over.

Pay to the order of Dick Henry. $10,000.00

"You don't know Davis Algren."

I looked at the check. Then back at Hogue. "I don't."

He took back the check for the ten, put a check for twenty-five in its place.

Pay to the order of Dick Henry. $25,000.00

"A last time, Mr. Henry. Have you ever talked to Davis Algren?"

Twenty-five grand. Which I could put to very good use. I shook my head. "I sure wish I had. But to my knowledge I haven't."

Hogue nodded, sat back, spread his hands, *what can you do*.

"Is this all you wanted to talk to me about, Mr. Hogue?"

"I thought this might be the beginning of a fruitful relationship."

"But I don't know Davis Algren."

"You *say* you don't know Davis Algren."

I stood up. "I'm sorry, Mr. Hogue. You've really confused me. I'll be pushing on."

"Wait."

"What?"

"Take one of those checks."

"I can't. I wouldn't know what I was taking it for."

"Your time is valuable."

"Look. Why don't *you* tell me who Algren is? Then we'll both know and we'll have something to talk about."

Hogue stared at me. "Thank you, Mr. Henry."

"Thank you, Mr. Hogue."

I left him, bemused, in his ficus grove.

THIRTY-SIX

Partners

Melvin rolled through West Hollywood on Sunset, finally passed into Beverly Hills. Alta Drive was one of the first few streets, there it was. He made a left, recognized Wolf's residence.

Melvin had left his house in good spirits, but contemplation of Wolf's demand started steaming him up. The evil Kraut must consider him a kunt, ready to lie on his back, pull up his knees, and get schlorked by a Nazi.

Behind every great fortune is a great crime.

A precept of universal acceptance after three drinks at the party. Then you named names and the innuendos began to fly in earnest. Getty. Kennedy. Rothschild. Gates. Though Gates had apparently nerded his way to the top. His crime had been a stiffie and pimples. But the world had paid dearly for his humiliations.

Wolf did not possess a great fortune, obviously, but he had secrets. Melvin Shea would ferret them out. By the time he rang the doorbell he was coldly furious.

A young, pretty Hispanic woman opened the heavy door six inches, inquired as to his business.

"I'm Melvin Shea. I'm here to speak with Dr. Wolf."

"Let me see if the doctor is available, sir."

"He's not available?" Of course the Nazi was available. He'd just tried so shake him down for fifty grand.

"Let me see, sir."

Melvin grabbed the door, pulled it out of her fingers, then shoved it back violently, a six-inch throw. The door hit the woman square in the forehead. *Bonk.* Down she went. Melvin stepped in, stepped over her, looked back. The woman, moaning, tried to sit up, rubbing her head. "INS, darling. You better get your ass back to Culican." Wherever that was. If it indeed existed.

Melvin walked into the house. "Dr. Wolf? Dr. Wolf? It's Mel-vin." Singsong. Like Nicholson in *The Shining.*

He wandered into the kitchen. "Dr. Wolf?" No one in the kitchen. A door led outside. Melvin looked out. There was the good Nazi himself, sitting down by the pool, under an umbrella, writing in a notebook. And wouldn't that be a funny title for a film? *The Good Nazi.*

The good Nazi didn't realize he had visitors until Melvin was ten steps from the table. He stood up hurriedly, alarmed, off-balance.

Melvin put two hands into the doctor's chest and pushed him into the pool.

Wolf splashed under, spluttered to the surface, flapped around.

Melvin peered at him. "Sure hope you can swim, Doc." On the table was a hard cheese, some salami, sour sourdough bread, and a silver knife. He sliced off some cheese, salami. Good stuff.

At the edge, Wolf moved hand over hand to the shallow end, then pushed through the water to exit at the steps.

Melvin held up the salami knife as the enraged Nazi approached. "Think this could go into your belly? Fuck up something important?"

Wolf paused, eyes on the knife. "This changes nothing. Did you bring my money?"

Melvin smiled. "You bring *my* money?"

"You're going to pay me fifty thousand dollars."

"Be happy to. Right after I receive your fifty thousand."

"I'll take ten thousand today."

"Fine. Right after I receive *your* ten thousand today."

The Hispanic woman who had answered the door walked out from the kitchen, pointed a finger at Melvin.

"What *happened*, Paulita?"

The doc sounded really concerned. *Duh.* He was doing a little push in the bush.

Paulita looked at Melvin. "He hit me with the door."

The doctor turned. *"You hit her with a door?"*

Melvin nodded, sliced off another piece of cheese. "The front door. It was either that, Adolf, or send her to the gas chamber." Melvin lowered his voice, whispered, "I think she may be *illegal*." He smiled. "She said she didn't know if you were in. Imagine. Lying—for a blackmailer."

His presumed power over Melvin had totally dissipated, evaporated. Something had happened. He wondered if Paulita noticed his clothes were soaked. "Go lie down in your room, Paulita. I'll be up to check on you."

Paulita looked up at the doctor reproachfully, turned abruptly on her heel, and went back inside.

Melvin waggled the blade. "Wife know you're getting some of that south-of-the-border poontang, Doc?"

Wolf shot a glance toward the house.

Melvin laughed. "Guess not." Maybe he'd like to dip his wick south of the border, too. Or just take a dip in the pool. Or just piss in it. He gestured toward one of the doctor's other chairs. "Why don't you sit down, *partner,* and I'll tell you what's gone down."

Wolf sat, regarded the grinning pimp. His natural enemy. *Partners.* Something had gone very wrong. Melvin would pay. Wolf would out-wait him. And then . . .

"We have a problem," began Melvin.

"We?"

"We. We have a problem. Rhonda Carling."

"Why is Rhonda a problem? *My* problem?"

"She wants a million dollars. I don't have that kind of money lying around. Do you?"

"Of course not."

"Then we have a problem."

"Explain."

"Rhonda wants to blab. She wants to bring the house down on us. On Narzarian, you, me, Devi."

"Me? How?"

"It's been two days since Nazarian fucked her up. Why haven't you informed Hogue?"

"Because I didn't know anything."

Melvin let his eye wander around the grounds. "You got a nice place here."

"What are you saying, Melvin?"

"I'm saying you had an opportunity to do things right, to talk to Hogue. But your stupid blackmail used up your little window. Now you're one of us."

Wolf felt sick. The pimp was right. Hogue could think he was in on it. Then it all could go. The swimming pool, the built-in barbecue area, the pergola hung with vines. His whole life.

Because he had seen the golden gun and gotten greedy. *Fool. Imbecile.* Now he had inherited a set of low, vile companions. The grinning pimp was right. There was no way out. He would sink with them all.

Unless.

A serpent, dormant and nearly forgotten, stirred in its lightless, frigid lair. "Do you have a plan, Mr. Shea?"

Mr. Shea. Melvin nodded at the doctor. The doc was now seeing things his way.

THIRTY-SEVEN

Dead Certain

Hogue had summoned Hames right after Dick Henry left. "What do you think?" he asked. He was back behind his desk.

"I saw the exchange, Mr. Hogue, but I'm not familiar with the situation."

"Was he telling the truth?"

Hames had seen the meeting go down live. Dick Henry. The same man he had isolated on the surveillance video from Dunkin' Donuts. How much credit had Derian claimed in the matter?

"By the way, Mr. Derian expressed great confidence in your abilities."

"Very kind of him." He thought a second. When a person lied, if he were untrained, he gave himself away a million different ways. But those ways were specific to the person and the situation. He didn't know Henry, he couldn't really tell for certain. "Generally, I would say, Henry gives no obvious signs that he's lying. But I don't know him well enough to know. However, because we have real-time video of him, that video can be slowed down and examined for micro-expressions when the specific questions are being asked."

Hogue nodded. Could he trust Hames? Could he trust anyone?

"The one good thing you've done, sir, is asking him the same question repeatedly. Our database won't be deep, but it'll be wide."

A silence commenced. And expanded.

Hames, sensing opportunity, stepped into the vacuum. "Is there something I could accomplish for you, sir?"

Hogue's resources, vast as they were, did nothing directly for him now. He was helpless. "There, uh, there may be something."

Hames studied the billionaire. Hogue had offered Henry twenty-five grand to instigate a conversation. Henry had claimed ignorance. Hogue had not believed him.

"Let me say one thing, Mr. Hogue. A man does not achieve what you have achieved by luck. Though accidents do happen. But it is not my job to make right what fortune has allowed. Life happens. Shit happens. I look forward. Not back. And my only loyalty is to you. Consider me completely at your service."

Hogue had read Hames's service record. And his further adventures in Iraq. He was a man who followed orders, didn't ask questions later.

Hogue leaned forward. "There's a man named Davis Algren, who played a peripheral part in a Hollywood incident of thirty years ago. Mr. Algren, erroneously, believes that certain things happened, believes that certain people are responsible. The weight of this knowledge has caused . . . has caused Mr. Algren to crumple under the pressures of life. He's now a homeless alcoholic."

Hames summarized. "Davis Algren has information you think he has shared with Dick Henry."

"That's right."

"I take it this is still sensitive information."

"Exactly right."

"In the worst case, we have to assume this information has already been shared."

"Agreed. Yes."

"So our purpose is to neutralize Dick Henry—to stop him from using this information. For what he may perceive to be good or evil."

"That's right."

"If an accident befell Mr. Henry—you could live with the pain."

"I could."

"And if I could hire Mr. Henry to help us protect the innocent, as we know the facts, you could live with that?"

"Yes, I could."

"Yet Mr. Henry claims he does not know Mr. Algren."

"That's what he says."

"He's a liar, sir?"

"Yes."

"You're *certain* he's lying?"

"Dead certain."

THIRTY-EIGHT

Davis Algren

I walked out of Hogue's office amazed. I'd been ready to talk about Rhonda Carling, he had not even mentioned her name. I called Devi, she didn't pick up.

Turning down large sums of money was no way to do business. But I had no idea who the billionaire was talking about. I'd never heard of Davis Algren, had no real idea where to begin. But I knew who would.

Fifteen minutes later I entered the Hollywood Professional Building. Again I heard the One Tenor, demonstrating his la-la-las. I sympathized with him.

Being a teacher required specialized knowledge and awareness. I had dropped in on Martine's second-grade class down at Christ the King. There I was reacquainted with the attorney's maxim: Never ask a question to which you don't know the answer. I found it applied to teachers, too.

Miss Hatton was twenty-three, a recent graduate from teacher's college. Underpaid, overwhelmed, and inundated by visiting parents, Miss Hatton had called upon Andrew Lee.

"Andrew Lee, give me a word that starts with B," ordered a perspiring Miss Hatton.

Andrew Lee rose from his seat and achieved fame. "Booger," said Andrew Lee.

I still recall the gratified shout of laughter that greeted young Lee's correct answer. Unjustly, I still believe, Andrew Lee was banished to the hallway.

I arrived on the fourth floor and knocked at Myron Ealing's office.

As always, he was happy to see me. "Brother Dick, come right in," he boomed. I followed him back to the inner sanctum, took a seat at his desk. He dug into his de rigueur tin of Christmas corn and put a huge handful into his mouth. He washed it down with his life's only beverage, Diet Dr Pepper.

Diet Coke I could handle, it was okay. Diet Pepsi was a face-shriveling river of poison. But Diet Dr Pepper was embalming fluid once removed.

"What can I do you for?" inquired Myron.

"Another name."

Myron was always pleased to encounter a challenge. "Any luck with Ellen Arden, by the way?"

Luck? My search for Ellen Arden had led me to Devi, and through Devi to battery, theft, kidnapping, convalescent homes, meeting billionaires with peculiar fixations. And it all had begun, I guess, here at Myron's office. Luck? I decided to go simple. "Actually, Myron, no luck at all."

The big man smiled. "Like Albert King."

If it weren't for bad luck, wouldn't have no luck at all.

Albert King, along with Freddie and B.B., were the three kings of the blues. For most of his life, Albert had made his living as bulldozer operator. An occupation he was proud of. Supposedly he was so good with the big machine he could knit with it. And who could forget *Born Under a Bad Sign*? Or *Crosscut Saw*, for that matter? Pearly King, my friend, occupied a lesser pedestal.

"Have you ever heard of Davis Algren?"

"Davis Algren." Myron leaned back, stared at the ceiling, cogitated. After a bit he raised a finger. "I've heard the name. I've heard the name." Then he snapped his fingers. "Got it. He's an actor. Seventies. Eighties."

An actor. In Hollywood. *Duh.*

Myron was putting it together. "Handsome guy, very handsome, but never really got it together. Noir movies." Myron's huge fingers danced on the keys of his computer.

Myron's database on underground Hollywood was huge. "Here he is," said Myron, fingers dancing on the keys.

I walked around the desk. I didn't recognize the man on the screen. It was one of those suave, look-over-the-shoulder shots. "When was this?"

"Twenty-five years ago, thereabouts. He's about thirty-some, here."

I'd never seen him before in my life. "Is he still in Hollywood?"

But Myron was thinking. "I take it back."

"You take what back?"

"I said he never really got it together. That isn't true, exactly. He had it going for a while. Low-level stuff. Third hat in the room. Then something happened. He was in the hospital or something. Maybe the bing."

"The bing?"

"The nut house."

"Then?"

"I dunno, he disappeared. I thought he was dead. What happened that you're asking about him?"

Of course, I couldn't give Myron the 411. Didn't want to lead him into harm's way. Curiosity kills the cat. "A very important man in this town called me in. Asked me if I knew him."

"Knew him. Not knew *of* him."

"Did I *know* him."

"Then he must be alive."

"Who is this important man?"

"I can't tell you. Yet."

Myron shook his head. "I'm a big boy, Dick, but okay. What did you tell this important man who's name you can't reveal?"

"I told him the truth. He repeated the question three times. He was very serious. Each time upping the ante. At the end, I walked away from twenty-five grand."

Myron turned to his computer, entered a small blizzard of data. Something came up on the screen and he pointed a jumbo finger at me. "You were in Howard Hogue's office."

Fibissedah face couldn't hold his cards.

Myron was jubilant. "It was in Hogue's office, wasn't it? How do I know?" Myron pointed at the screen. "Because Algren did most of his work for Hogue." Then Myron tuned in on a distant beam. "Wait a second. I remember hearing something about a screenplay. That Algren wrote." Myron's giant brain churned in parallel through the petabytes. "I think it was Algren."

"What was it about, great sage?"

"About a Hollywood party that went bad." Myron reached for more Christmas corn. "It was a little too real."

"Too real?"

"People took it as blackmail."

"And Algren was never heard from again."

Myron shrugged his mountainous shoulders. "That kinda makes sense."

I needed two things. To know what Algren looked like today. And to find his screenplay. If it existed. What was it that had gone down? That was enough to worry a billionaire? And why was Hogue so sure I knew Algren? "Who carries old scripts, stuff like that?"

"No one's going to have that. Especially if it really was blackmail. It'd be all over the Internet right now. Conspiracy theories and all that shit."

He was right. I stood up. "Thanks, bud."

Myron rose, ponderously, extended his huge hand. He could crush ball bearings. "Come back soon. Missed you."

"Missed you, too."

Once you were in with Myron, you were in. His door was open, his window was open, his heart was open. A real friend. And, of course, he knew and loved Enrique Montalvo Rojas. And Bosto Ket as well. The three of them would play mau-mau and drink deep into the night, their laughter reverberating off the walls, spliffs waving in the air.

As I made my way down the stairs of the Hollywood Professional

Building, I heard the One Tenor again. More la-la-las, then a venomous shriek. Poor guy. Maybe he was a genius. But even noble Plato's reception in Hollywood would probably not have been august and respectful. What did he know about shadows and light?

Another shriek. I stepped out onto Hollywood Boulevard.

Andrew Lee, tell me a word that begins with B.

THIRTY-NINE

Burying the Hatchet

Peedner hadn't talked to Henry since he cut him loose in the Violet Brown murder. What was there to say? If he, and not Dick, had shot Elton Reese four times, the results would have been the same, his career ruined, but at least he would have been responsible for his own fate. As it was, the tincture of victim had stuck with him for years. Bad Luck Lew.

And it had crept into his own soul, too. He expected to be ripped off at Coke machines. Washing machines to fail a week after the warranty had run out. To buy a winning lottery ticket and lose it.

There was one unalloyed pleasure in his life. Kristy. His one hostage to fortune. No bad luck there. Or with her mother. Marilyn brought him some coffee, the smell of her good cooking in the air. "You find Dick yet?"

He was running through the DVD. Perhaps there were other faces he would recognize. Derian had paid him $1,500 cash to check it out.

"I think we might get Kristy's ears checked," said Marilyn.

"Her hearing's perfect," said Peedner. Dick was supposed to come up around 2:35 a.m.

"Perhaps you should find out what she learned at school today."

School was the ruin of children. Until the time they went, they were truly yours. They reflected the things you taught them, in the manner you taught them. After enrollment, you could never defend them adequately. Ideas came from everywhere, like viruses. Maybe ideas *were* viruses. Like grafitti was a footprint. Everyone liked leaving footprints. *Kilroy was here.* Lew looked at his wife. "What did she hear at school?"

"About President Lincoln."

Lincoln? Why were they teaching a seven-year-old about Lincoln? What could she really internalize? Though, all in all, it was a mild stupidity, not like passing out condoms to first graders. You put this on your *what?*

Kristy entered defiantly. "My hearing is perfect."

Lew nodded. "Of course, it is. Now what did Mrs. Nichols teach you today?"

"President Lincoln treed the slaves," stated Kristy.

Marilyn smiled in a sunny manner.

"*What?* You mean he *freed* the slaves."

"That's what Mommy said. You're wrong, too. He *treed* the slaves."

"No, dear. He *freed* the slaves."

His daughter regarded him with a cold, reptilian patience. "Fine, Dad. But he treed them first."

Lew looked at his daughter. Someday she would be married. He considered the young man. Singled out by fate. A young man presently chewing a wad of gum and rattling a skateboard down the sidewalk. Would he have bitten off more than he could chew?

Perhaps. The question was—was he good enough for an angel?

In that moment Lew decided he would visit Dick Henry.

I hadn't expected any communication from Lew Peedner, so I was a little wary when he rang. "*Lew?* What's up? You alright?"

"I'm fine."

"What can I do for you?"

There was a pause.

"Guess it's been awhile."

"It has."

"I was wondering if I could stop by for a few minutes."

"Unofficially?"

"Unofficially."

Something was up. It wasn't a matter of counting the toes I'd stepped on recently. I step on toes for a living. "Uh, sure. When?"

"Tonight sometime?"

"Come now. Know where I live?"

"Yup. See you in twenty."

Devi walked in. "What's up?"

"My old partner is stopping by." I guess I looked furtive.

"You mean your ex?"

I hadn't explained Georgette and the crew to Devi. It wasn't her business. I guess she'd seen the pictures on the wall. "My ex-partner from LAPD."

"That's nice."

Maybe.

"I've heard that's like a marriage," she said.

"It's better than marriage."

"Better? Why?"

"No sex."

"No *sex*?"

"And you don't argue about money."

"What do you argue about?"

"Everything else." Yeah. Lew. We were brothers. And we fought like brothers. Loved like brothers. Shared a million greasy Hollywood pizzas and a million dirty jokes. And we'd taken some righteous assholes off the streets of Los Angeles. Then I gave Elton Reese the quadruple ventilator. I missed Lew.

Twenty minutes to Lew meant an hour to anyone else. He wasn't late like Lynette had been, constant and outrageous, but there was only one Lynette.

I heard a car stop in front of my house. I felt a little nervous. I looked out the window. It was Lew.

I opened up and waited. He opened the gate, walked up the brickway, climbed the three stairs to the porch.

He looked at me. I detected no anger in him. "Hey, Dick."

I was still wary. "Hey. Come on in."

In the living room, I gestured him into the couch. "Can I get you a beer?"

"Still drinking Coors?"

"Of course."

"Good. I'll have one."

He sipped it with satisfaction, looked around. "Nice place."

"Thanks."

"How's Georgette?"

"I don't know specifically. Guess she's fine." She'd been bugging me lately about a serious conversation. Which could be good or bad. "I'm supposed to have dinner with her tomorrow."

There had to be a reason Lew was here. I guess I'd have to wait until he told me. "How's Marilyn? And the little one? Kristy, right?"

"She's not so little anymore. She's studying Lincoln. Marilyn's alright, too."

"Good." A pause turned into a silence. "This is like our first date, Lew. Why are you here?"

My tall, gaunt ex-partner let his hands fall into his lap. "What do you know about the Hollywood bigwigs?"

"Which Hollywood bigwigs? I party with them all."

"Like always. I'm talking about Nazarian and Shea. The refrigerator-boxers."

"Why are you mixing me up in all this?"

"Don't bullshit me, Dick. I saw the surveillance DVD from Dunkin' Donuts. And there, plain as day, in the middle of the night, was Dick Henry. I'm thinking, that's no coincidence."

Devi entered from the kitchen. "I can explain."

Just what I didn't want. I pointed a rigid finger at her. "You're not going to explain a thing. Go out on the back porch and read a book or something."

Devi's face went red, but she left.

"The next question is obvious," said Lew.

"She's a friend of mine."

"What does she want to explain?"

"She's a lamb in this whole thing. Well, pretty much a lamb. Half a lamb."

"Rack of lamb."

Lew knew I loved rack of lamb. Though the name was more formidable than the dish itself. Anticipating my first Rack of Lamb I thought I might need an ax. Instead, I could've used tweezers. "Look, Lew. I'll tell you everything about her if you really need to know. But first let's deal with what's up."

"Fine. What is up?"

I studied my former partner. "I don't want to put my head in a noose, Lew."

"Have you done anything nooseworthy?"

"No."

"Then let's talk," Lew said.

"Off the record."

"Off the record."

"I mean really off the record."

"Fine."

"Shea, Melvin Shea, is Howard Hogue's dog robber. Shea decided to pimp out one of Howard's girls out to Eli Nazarian."

"The director."

"Him, yeah. Well, Nazarian rearranged her face, shoved a gun up her snatch. Fucked her up. The girl called Hogue's girl scout leader—"

"Girl scout leader?"

"Hogue's got thirty girlfriends. Stashed all over town."

"Girl scout leader. Got it." Lew pointed to the kitchen. "That's her?"

"That's her."

"She goes over there to help, didn't know Nazarian was still there. He decides he's going to kick her ass, too. But she's an ex-Marine and things didn't go down as he planned. In fact, she thought she'd killed him. That's when she called me. I'd met her earlier that night."

Lew shook his head, smiled.

"What?"

"You never change."

Lew was right. I attracted trouble like better men attracted women. "I don't try to get into these situations, Lew. I'm thrust into them."

"I like the ex-Marine factor."

It was my turn to smile. "So do I."

"When did this happen?"

"Early yesterday morning." Jesus. It felt like years ago.

"Ask me if I've missed your drama."

"I know you have." I was just being me, but I had a sudden intuition Lew wasn't angry at me any more. Where had that thought come from?

"You know what," Lew paused, as if putting a thought together, "I'm not . . . I'm not . . . *pissed* at you anymore."

"You crazy? You got grounds."

"Maybe I have. And maybe I am."

I grinned and he grinned and we left it at that.

Once, during my time in the Navy, probably in the vicinity of hops and a fattie, a shipmate and I declared we were each other's best friend. Which ruined everything. Whatever being best friends entailed, it meant different things to both parties, and was as rife with misunderstanding as the concept of love. Soon we detested one another.

Lew and I went back to business. But I was feeling—I was feeling *sunny*.

"You've explained Nazarian," continued Lew. "What about Shea?"

"I'm not sure how Shea got there, I think the doctor called—"

"What doctor?"

"Girl scout doctor."

Lew just shook his head.

"So when Shea knocked at the door, I, uh, uh . . ."

"You what?"

"I hid in the closet with the director. Who wasn't as dead as I'd been led to believe."

"Jesus, Dick."

"And when Shea opened up the closet door, I, uh, I knocked him out."

Lew squinted, trying to stuff the facts into a single sack. "Do you know how they ended up at Dunkin' Donuts?"

"I called for transportation and the transportation crew improvised. Next thing I know, I'm listening to local news and thinking, this is one hell of a happy ending."

"Take off someone's pants, add a dead dog, it's always a happy ending."

"What do *you* know about Nazarian, Lew?"

Lew shook his head. "He always makes money. And every so often he hurts someone. Big cash pay-outs."

"How many times?"

"Three, four times over the years."

"Who turned you on to the surveillance tape?"

"One of the Ivanhoe shysters. They're talking kidnapping."

"That's bullshit."

"They know it's bullshit. They want some quid pro quo. To drop possession charges against Jack Wilton."

"What's he into?"

"H."

"Too bad."

"Yeah."

"So, anything on the surveillance DVD?"

"No. Just you. Talking."

Of course there was nothing. I had just sat and waited. Then Lew's words hit me. "What did you just say about the surveillance DVD?"

"Nothing. There was nothing on it."

"You said something else."

"What did I say? Buncha night crawlers and then you, sitting there. Talking."

"Talking?"

I didn't remember talking to anyone. I did remember Hogue's question: *Had I ever talked to Davis Algren?*

"Can we take a look at that DVD, Lew?"

Lew took the DVD out of his pocket.

Lew fast-forwarded, and then, there I was. Talking. To the bum. With whatever he had wrapped in the white blanket. The bum turned directly into the monitor. And suddenly I saw the face under the face. Davis Algren.

"What did you just see, Dick?"

"I thought I recognized one of the night crawlers."

"Did you or didn't you?

"No."

Lew gave me his famous I-detect-bullshit squint. But he didn't push it. "This Nazarian character bothers me."

"He should. He's going to kill somebody. One of these days."

"What's the difference between a sociopath and psychopath?"

I'd read something. But a long time ago. But a few crumbs came back. "Nazarian is . . . he's a psychopath. They're smooth, socially, they have manners, they can mimic the emotions of others. But they have no conscience . . . about what they do, or lying about it later. These people are often very intelligent and they get along in society."

"That sounds like our boy. Will the woman he hurt file?"

"No. She wants money."

"That's pragmatic."

"A million dollars."

"That's dangerous money."

"Sure is."

"She better wise up."

Lew picked up his keys. "Keep me informed about Nazarian."

"He could use a little justice."

Lew grinned. "But your girl kicked his ass?"

In all honesty she wasn't my girl. And she probably was listening. "She's her own girl, Lew. But she did break his jaw."

"Broke the man's jaw. You gotta like that."

Lew got to his feet, all six foot four of him. "I ever tell you the one about the dude farmer?"

"Yes, you did."

"And his prize mare?"

"Yes, Lew, I've enjoyed that particular joke many times."

"With the shroud?"

"The shroud that turns into a handkerchief. Yes, you've told me. Funny then, funny now."

"So you don't want to hear it again?"

I grinned. "I do, but I'm restraining myself."

And that was that.

We parted, for the first time in years, in friendly fashion. I was smiling from deep inside.

Devi had come in, angry, as soon as Lew was gone. "Thanks for humiliating me in front of your friend."

"He's more than a friend. He's a cop. You don't talk to cops."

"Sorry."

There are eight million ways to enunciate "sorry." Giving rise to many millions of interpretations. And misunderstandings. It was my impression she wasn't sorry at all.

"*You* talked to him, Dick."

"After I found out it was going to be private."

"Man to man."

"Yeah."

"*Man to man*. What bullshit."

190

She was right. The term *man to man* usually meant tell me now and later I'll screw you later for your own good.

But she didn't know Lew.

Her phone rang. She examined the incoming ID, shrugged in my direction, answered. "Hello?" She stepped into the kitchen.

Davis Algren. What did he know? Obviously, something Hogue feared he would tell me. That's why Hogue had offered me twenty-five thousand dollars. I'd copied Lew's DVD. I ran it again, studied Algren.

He wasn't worth a hundred bucks, lock, stock and barrel. So why hadn't Hogue taken care of the Algren problem beforehand? Because he didn't know he was around. I'd inadvertently brought him to Hogue's attention, and the billionaire had assumed that chance was plan. Why? Because Hogue was guilty. Of something. Something he was still afraid people would find out. Maybe Hogue was protecting someone.

All in all, Algren's life was worth far, far less than a hundred dollars. I'd have to warn him.

Devi came in, looked at me.

"What?"

"That was Rhonda's sister. Rhonda isn't at Fairfax anymore."

"What?"

"She checked herself out."

"That doesn't sound right."

"No, it doesn't. Because it's impossible. They also told her why she was there in the first place."

"I think we know that."

"Exhaustion."

I had a rush of dark feeling. Exhaustion was the Hollywood euphemism for addiction or other bad behavior.

"What do you think, Dick?"

"I think she's in trouble. I think she did some blabbing. Million-dollar blabbing."

"To who?"

"Nazarian and/or Shea? They have the most to lose."

"Melvin's life would collapse completely."

"And Nazarian?"

"Nazarian's movie made two hundred eighty mil domestic. *So far*. That means it'll do equal that in DVD, and half of that in foreign. Which means he'll be forgiven an indiscretion here and there. He might be embarrassed."

"Psychopaths don't get embarrassed."

"I heard you guys talking about them."

"I knew you were listening."

"I couldn't help it. Both you guys are old and deaf. Lew sounds like a nice man."

"He is."

"You guys had a falling-out?"

No, darling, we had more of a falling-in. We fell into a world of shit which I stepped out of and he couldn't.

My phone rang. "Hello?"

"This Dick Henry?"

The voice carried threat. I didn't recognize it. "Maybe. Who's this?"

"This is a friend."

"Yeah? Speak your piece, friend."

"You're playing a dangerous game."

"I don't like threats."

"This isn't a threat. It's an opportunity."

"Get to the point."

"I'm talking about Davis Algren."

"You must work for Howard Hogue."

"I'm talking about Davis Algren. You've got to choose. His side or the other side."

"I don't know Davis Algren."

"You've abandoned the field of opportunity. That's too bad."

"I don't know Davis Algren."

"So be it, Mr. Henry." The connection was broken.

I looked at my watch. I would have to find Algren. Let him know what was up. Get his story. But it was late. And soon Devi would want to sit in my lap.

I'd try to find Algren. Tomorrow.

FORTY

Angel's Gate

The *Hush, My Baby* was a forty-foot motor yacht, a Meridian 391. It congenially offered four berths in two cabins, a large saloon, a galley, and a flybridge with a helm advertised as second only to the starship *Enterprise*.

Of all the things that Ulbrecht Wolf had owned in his lifetime, his yacht was the dearest to his heart. To see it rocking gently, serenely at Cabrillo, in the afternoon sun, was to experience true and profound joy. It was to know that God had forgiven him his sins, approved of his subsequent life, and had rewarded him accordingly.

Wags suggested that a boat owner was only happy two days in his life. The day he bought his craft and the day he sold it. Bullshit. He was happy at least two times a month, sometimes for the duration of a weekend, as he lolled about the boat. With Paulita.

Lovely, enticing Paulita. Had he appeared weak when he had not revenged Melvin's slamming her head with the door? Perhaps. But the pimp would pay. Eventually. And she would know about it. Wolf did not take insults lying down.

Another good thing about the *Hush, My Baby* was Gretchen's seemingly allergic reaction. She would much rather day-spa with her friends at the Hotel. The pink hotel. She'd been down to the boat twice. And that had, apparently, been enough. The perfect wife!

And now, that dismal cargo in the salon. In the long canvas sail bag he and Melvin had carried aboard. Stiffened with a piece of plywood, the bag ushered the mortal remains of Rhonda Carling to her first and final voyage on the *Hush, My Baby.*

Melvin's presence on the boat was an abomination and a defilement. The man oozed filth through every pore. His laugh a grating and humorless bray. His choice of anecdote crude, lewd, and ordinary. And yet, the pimp's presence was required if he were to keep all Wolf had accumulated over a lifetime.

It was true. Things unthinkable in one's twenties became casual articles in one's sixties. When the end was in sight. When nagging pains became conditions. When love had escaped him, when isolation was embraced with cold and reluctant pride.

And then Paulita.

Betty Ann Fowler, the girl of whom he had hoped to forget everything, was now beside him. Invisible and reproachful. Hadn't he promised her that she would be the only one? That never again would he put himself in such a position?

Forgive me, Miss Fowler. But *I* saved *you* from a life of ridicule and pain. From a life of recrimination, rage, and regret. You didn't have to go to that party. With those hungry men. No, you didn't. You went of your own volition.

Remember the horror in Florida, said Miss Fowler in return. I gave you the opportunity to reclaim your honor, to reclaim your soul, to choose the path of righteousness. But, no. When did the Hippocratic Oath become the Hippocratic Guideline? When did the Ten Commandments lapse into the Ten Suggestions?

When? When that dose of morphine sent Miss Fowler unto whatever reward she was entitled to. But nothing could shut her up. What 500,000 battered women had in common.

When would Miss Carling begin whispering?

He would have to kill Melvin. That was clear. Because the pimp would never let this go. Would never cease reminding him of their gruesome brotherhood. Their deathless entanglement. Miss Fowler was a tragedy. Rhonda Carling was a necessity. Melvin Shea would be a statistic.

The Angel's Gate lighthouse was now passing on his right. Just minutes from open sea. And safety. What crimes had passed silently beneath Angel's Gate? Its nocturnal stab every fifteen seconds.

He and the pimp had argued about the coup de grâce. I am providing the means and opportunity. I won't do everything, he had insisted.

Fine, said the pimp. Gimme the shit. I'll do it. Do I need to find a vein?

It didn't matter. Not with enough Dilaudid it didn't.

Right before their eyes, she had sunk into death. First a small moan, then a general relaxing of the frame and the face. As her cares, his cares, and Melvin's cares slipped away. Her breath became shallow, shallower. The power of a butterfly's wing. And then . . . then that infinitely delicate magic switch was thrown, that most subtle gradient passed, and the spirit that was Rhonda Carling passed out of the physical universe.

Of course, Melvin would have by now turned his thoughts to his host's demise. Murder all over his ugly face. Filling with a smirking glee.

Melvin stood at the prow, smoking his cigarette into the wind. He had grasped the power of life and death. And nothing would ever come close. The god that was Melvin Shea.

It was a clear and gorgeous night under a canopy of diamonds. Again, like that night so many years ago, the body was wrapped in anchor chain. Secured, in these modern times, with plastic tie wraps. They had removed her clothes. Less to identify.

"She had a nice rack, you have to give her that."

What could you expect of him? A last, pimpish benediction. But those breasts. Plainly artificial. Meaning someday, someday far below, they would be released, their serial numbers stamped in eternity. Was silicone lighter than water?

Some craft in the harbor. Whale watching or harbor tour. Hey! Look at that! A pair of tits!

The eyes and other soft tissue would last four hours. Then, for a while, she'd be her own little reef.

He got her shoulders, Melvin got the feet. Heavy. One. Two. Three, and . . . that soft splash. The slight, diminishing musical clinking of the chain. Then the slap of waves on the hull.

FORTY-ONE

Sullivan's Troubles

The next day I had shortcut work, small stuff, and accomplished it. That night, about eleven, I got down to Dunkin' Donuts, started showing a still I'd culled from the DVD.

There were three types of responses. The first, a casual glance and dismissal. *Nah. Never seen him.* Then there were those who didn't even look. *Nah.* All involvement with *the man* lead to trouble. Been there done that.

The third type was the most interesting. Body language suggested Algren was recognized, the viewer was startled, the viewer looked at me with a combination of fear and anger, then turned away from me.

After a while, a group of third types, both men and women, had gathered in the parking lot, looking in at me, gesturing.

I went outside, walked toward them. The knot dissolved, reassembled in a ragged half-circle.

"What do you want with Dave, man?" The speaker was a younger man, thirties, bearded. And angry.

"I need to talk to him."

"Yeah?"

Never answer rhetorical questions. "I need to talk to Mr. Algren. It's urgent. Anybody know where he is?"

They looked at one another. Almost like a comedy routine. Except nothing was funny.

"Why do you need to talk to him, man?" The bearded man stared at me.

I felt that tingle in my fist. "If this was your business, friend, I'd've sent you a letter. But it isn't." I tamped the tingle.

I addressed the group. "But I'll tell you all anyway. I ran into Dave three nights ago. Right here. I didn't know his name. But someone saw me talking to him and that person thought Mr. Algren told me something I shouldn't be knowing. I think Mr. Algren might be in danger."

Again, the group members looked at each other. A woman stepped forward. I put her in her mid-forties. She'd been pretty once. Had the bone structure.

"Yes, ma'am?"

"You're a little late."

"I'm a little late?"

Nods around the quorum.

"Dave is dead," said the woman.

The woman's name was Hannah. Algren had been found on Cosmo Street with his throat cut.

When did this happen?

Last night. Around two in the morning.

Good sweet Christ. While I was in Devi's arms. I felt sick. Sick and guilty.

Hannah and I found Jack in the Box, across from Amoeba Music. I bought her a cup of coffee. She had green eyes.

"What was your relationship to Mr. Algren?"

"I was his wife."

"His *wife*?" I don't know why I was surprised. I hadn't meant to be rude.

"Well, not legally, of course." She extended her hand. There was a slim, plain, silver band on her finger.

"He must have loved you, ma'am."

She smiled. "Oh, he did. We were together ten years." Her eyes were full. "We were married on Vine Street. Under a full moon."

"Where on Vine?"

"Over the star of his favorite director."

"Who was that?"

"Preston Sturges."

"Over near where Molly's Burgers used to be. Near Selma."

"Right there."

"Mr. Algren had good taste."

"And he liked the hot dogs, too."

I laughed and she laughed. "Dave loved *Sullivan's Troubles*. It was his favorite movie by Mr. Sturges."

"*Sullivan's Travels*," I corrected, gently.

"That must be the sequel."

I stepped off the path for a second. "Who was the younger guy, the guy with the beard, the guy who wanted to kick my ass?"

Hannah waved her hand in a flutter. "Someone who never will. He's all talk. His name is Danny. He's a writer, too. Friend of Dave's. They fought all the time. About Bukowski."

Bukowski, the patron saint of the down and out in L.A. If he could make it, from where he came from, from where he placed himself, anyone could. I wasn't much on his poetry, or anybody's poetry, but Bukowski's books were simple and clear, joyful and refreshing. Cold, clear water on a hot day.

He didn't fuck around with big words. As a result there was room for content between the lines. Hilarious content.

His literary opposite, Malcolm Lowry, knew every word in the English language, used each one with painstaking exactitude. His work was dense and heavy—nothing between the lines because everything was *in* the lines. Much as I admired Lowry and his erudition, I preferred Bukowski.

"Tell me about Mr. Algren's writing."

"I never saw him write a word. He wrote *in his head*. I mean, he said he did. People made fun of him; how can you be a writer if you don't write?

But he said he'd put it on paper when the time was right. He said he was writing all the time."

She continued, quietly. "He loved me, Mr. Henry. He really loved me. You know why?"

"Why?"

"Because he did."

Which was the only answer to why we might love someone. Because we do. Period. Nothing more, nothing less.

"Didn't Mr. Algren write some screenplays?"

"Just one."

"You read it?"

"No."

"No?"

"I didn't want to."

"I see." I did see. Hollywood acquaintances had told me of being urged to read friends' work. Finally they gave in. If the work was good, everything was fine. But if it wasn't, the relationship would suffer. The odor of failure and ineptitude would seep in. Like sewer gas.

"Would you like to read his screenplay, Mr. Henry?"

"It exists?"

"I have the only copy. Would you like to read it?"

"Absolutely."

From her Ralphs cart, in a thirty-gallon plastic bag, at the bottom, Hannah retrieved Davis Algren's screenplay. "Maybe, if it's good, you can do something for Dave."

Me? I couldn't do anything for anybody. In that world. "If I can I will, Hannah."

"Thank you, Mr. Henry."

"Thank you, Hannah."

She placed the battered screenplay in my hands. "Take care of this."

"I will."

Her chin began to quiver.

FORTY-TWO

Plop Factor

I rolled the Caddy over to Denny's on Sunset near the 101. I got a booth looking over at Meineke Car Care Center. I recalled the prime directive of the unscrupulous mechanic: *Immobilize the customer*. Hence, the dead-blow hammer.

My waitress brought me coffee and I ordered an Early Bird. I mean Super Bird.

I felt horrible. If only I'd tried to find Algren last night. But I hadn't.

I carefully laid out Algren's manuscript.

I didn't know much about movies. Just little things I'd heard here and there. The screenplay told you the story. The music told you how to feel about the part of the story you were watching.

And I remembered plop factor. Plop factor was related to the weight of the screenplay; the sound it made when dropped flat on to an executive's desk from a height of eighteen inches. One page of a screenplay equaled one minute of screen time. Any screenplay over a hundred and ten, a hundred and twenty pages meant the writer didn't know what he was doing. Write a fat masterpiece and no executive would ever open it. Much less read it.

I raised Algren's work and let it fall. It fell like an anvil. Amateur's work.

Could there be a great 250-page screenplay? Yes. But already, your thinking was skewed. Already, you were thinking like an *artist*.

Movies had been created in the vacuum of dying vaudeville. The sole purpose of movies was to continue the enticement of customers to purchase expensive food and drink in cheap, poorly furnished, dark rooms. What was cheaper than popcorn? All you needed was a hot plate and you served your hostages in a cardboard box. Accompanied by a starving pianist. Then, a forgotten Einstein salted and buttered his popcorn to enhance thirst. Which required more drinks. Which lead to more popcorn. The circularity of it all was a revolution and a bonanza.

The fact that movie stars emerged from this simple, silent formula astounded and delighted its creators. In the great American spirit of hucksterism, academies with wonderful names were created to burnish and glorify the beautiful puppets. And, in a stroke of further genius, once a year, every year, the hucksters gathered to award gold-plated statuettes to the employees who moved the most popcorn. Pretty soon, and on purpose, the lowly origins of the business were hidden and forgotten. The Golden Age of Hollywood had arrived.

Why the nix on the 250-page masterpiece? Popcorn. You sold your popcorn and drinks *before* the curtain. Not during the movie. A six-hour film sold popcorn every six hours. A ninety-minute film sold popcorn every ninety minutes. Hence, your ninety-minute shitbird sold four times the popcorn of your six-hour masterpiece.

My waitress swept in, delivered my shitbird. I sipped my coffee and opened the screenplay. I mean, my waitress delivered my *Super Bird*.

The screenplay was called *The Farmer in the Dell*. I kid you not. I'd read a few screenplays people said were great, like *Chinatown,* for one. Robert Towne, I think. *Chinatown* did what people said great screenplays did. Whetted your immediate interest and continued to induce your hunger. Because the audience only wanted to know one thing. What happened next.

He's your father and *your uncle*. Wait. That wasn't it. That was me addressing my cross-eyed cat.

I'm her mother and *her sister*. That was it.

I detected no such cleverness in *Dell*. It went on and on, from platitude to coincidence. With a few songs sprinkled in for leavening. Then someone robbed a bank. I quit.

I shut it, turned it over, ate my sandwich. A real disappointment. Someone was upset over this? No way. I'd learned nothing. Forty-three pages were all I could take.

SAM
(urgently)

Stick 'em up.

After the Super Bird was done for, I flipped through the pages. Then something caught my attention. The font at the end of the script was different from that at the beginning.

The second screenplay was called *San Pedro*. It opened at a mansion in Hancock Park. Home of a famous producer. Hubert Hull. Hollywood stars, important people, servers and servants, whores. Powders, liquids, and compounds.

Then things went dark. A movie star, Hale St. Everly, high on acid, injured one of the pay-to-play girls. She had been disfigured. Disfigured to prove that the movie star possessed the power of healing. Like the biblical hero he had just played. To statuette reviews. St. Everly walked around, bloody hands in the air, rejoicing. The party was ended abruptly, guests sent home ignorant and incurious.

God said to Abraham, kill me a son.

But the movie star's healing power fell short. A doctor was summoned. An Austrian. Ulmer Winz. A meeting was held. The host, the doctor. The star had been put to sleep with an injection. The host explained the logistics of the situation to the doctor. A lot of money rode on the star's continued stardom. Professions, crafts, jobs, table scraps. It trickled down like a fountain. The whore, on the other hand, was unconnected any-where. No family, no agent, no friends. No nothing.

And her face. It had been cut to pieces. The nose severed. An ear sev-ered. A lip bitten off. Deep cuts in a radial pattern around the mouth. Keeping her alive would be cruelty. Her dusky beauty gone forever.

The doctor, left alone with his patient, made a decision. He prepared another injection.

The young woman died easily, vagus, the tenth cranial nerve, slowly losing its power to signal inspiratory neurons in the medulla oblongata. Finally her breathing ceased altogether.

The producer was effusive in his thanks to the physician. But now there was a disposal problem.

Into the guest bedroom walked David Balgren. Balgren's sudden appearance frightened the producer and the doctor as they stood over the corpse. Balgren, a journeyman actor, allayed their fears. He had access to a small craft. Moored in San Pedro. Maybe he could be of assistance.

His offer was taken up. The craft passed the Angel's Gate lighthouse and made its way into open sea. Balgren and Dr. Winz consigned Betty Ann Fowler to the timeless deep.

The movie star awoke the next day in the home of the producer, Hull. St. Everly was naked. He had several cuts on his hands and fingers. He reported a terrible dream. Deep was his relief when he was assured of his innocence. It had been a dream.

Balgren met with the producer the next week. Great gratitude existed, reward was promised. Wait.

When Balgren called the next month, the producer was cordial. But things were still in a holding pattern. Another month passed. He was invited to dinner in Hancock Park. Dr. Winz was also in attendance. At dinner the actor felt drowsy.

He awoke in an unknown hospital. Where he was an involuntary guest. He had threatened important people with violence. A judge had written a commitment letter.

Luckily, electro-convulsive therapy restored his mental equilibrium. After seven years, he had been released from the California State Mental Hospital at Camarillo. With a new suit and two hundred dollars. Cash.

His name escaped him but he thought it might be Dave.

I got home to a quiet house. Devi was asleep on the couch.

I let her be. My mind was wrapped up in the Algren script. There were no good guys in *San Pedro*. If I saw what was meant to be seen. Hubert Hull was Howard Hogue. Dr. Winz was Dr. Wolf. Hale St. Everly was Hale Montgomery. Balgren was Algren.

And if true, it meant America's favorite granddad, Hale Montgomery, was a murderer.

And Algren himself. A tragedy. In the Greek sense of the word. A man brought low through his own weakness. A downward spiral since the night he had offered aid to evil men.

What was I to do with all this knowledge? I didn't know. I had three bottles of single-malt whiskey on my desk. Laphroaig was the only one whose taste I could honestly identify. I sat down, poured myself a shot. Sipped and burned.

I didn't even know that Devi had gotten up.

"You alright, Dick?"

I nodded. "Yeah. Good as ever."

"I've really messed your life up, haven't I?"

Yes. You have. But life brings what it brings. "Well, at least you did it fast."

She snorted. "You were supposed to say *no,* Dick. That I'd made your life better. Maybe paradise on earth."

I looked at her. Into her eyes and down her one, ornate, Chinese arm. The burn had warmed up my gut.

"I know what you want," said Devi.

"You do?"

"Yes. Puss told me."

"*Puss?* Again? Why don't you keep her out of it?"

"She called *me,* Dick."

Devi didn't move and I looked back up into her dark eyes. For a second I thought I was falling right in.

Then she walked around my desk, put her hand on my knee. "Why don't you come to bed, Dick?"

So I did.

FORTY-THREE

Rhonda, Sylvette

Melvin awoke, slammed a few Tylenol with codeine, looked into the mirror. A man's character was measured by the obstacles he faced. Melvin Shea was a giant.

Qualms, second thoughts, regrets, recriminations. They were for losers. The strong went directly into history, revered, or feared, but remembered. Killing a single man was murder, killing millions was the generation of statistics. Ask Stalin, Mao, Pol Pot. Were none of these men afraid of hell? No? Well, neither was he. You did what was necessary.

His immediate problem, still, was Rhonda. Hogue was still planning the funky dunky.

Obviously, Melvin would have to augment his North Hollywood theater-thug confection. That part worked. That got her to Fairfax Convalescent. Now she had to disappear. Thinking, he realized he didn't have to explain much. Because he, too, was *mystified*. After the assault, Rhonda had been admitted to Fairfax Convalescent. But then, a few days later, she'd checked out for parts unknown. She wasn't at home. And nobody, Mr. Hogue, nobody seemed to know where she went.

Back in the real world. Would someone miss her? Badly enough to call the police? Badly enough to insist on action, demanding authorities go up to the El Royale and look around? Blood and shit all over the place. And where was the gun? The golden gun would give him the leverage to straighten out Nazarian. Fucking Devi. He was going to peel her skin. Evidence of her guilt was the nonreturn of his calls.

Devi, later. Hogue, now.

Helena answered. "Mr. Hogue's office."

"Helena, Melvin here. For the boss."

"One second."

Music came up to ease the wait. The Eagles. He loved the Eagles. And hated them, too. They were too perfect. Kurt Cobain. The man who'd singlehandedly ended the reign of the hair bands. Cobain had blown his head off with a shotgun. Heard the Eagles were getting back together.

"Melvin?"

"Good morning, Mr. Hogue. It's Melvin."

"What can I do for you?"

"Got a little news for you, sir."

"Yes?"

"One of the Special Talent girls was injured."

"Oh. That's too bad. Who?"

"Rhonda Carling."

"Rhonda. I recall the name."

"You were going to visit her this week."

"*Rhonda*. I remember."

Of course, you remember, you prick. She was blond, eight feet tall, and had humongous tits. Like the other twenty-seven.

"You say she was injured?"

"That's right, sir, and she—"

"I'm guessing she's on the disabled list."

That would be one way to put it. "Yes, sir, but—"

"Tell you what, Melvin. Did you see *The Schwarzschild Radius*?"

"Uh . . ."

"Five years ago. The sci-fi epic."

That. One of the worst pieces of shit ever made. Of course he hadn't seen it. "I'm told it was very underrated."

"Did you see it?"

"I *think* so. About black holes."

"One of the worst pieces of shit ever made," said Hogue. "With a gigantic Jewish name in the title."

"Yes, sir. So you didn't like the movie."

"Or the title. Especially the title. *The Schwarzschild Radius*. Sounds too educated. Like a movie about chess."

Jews and chess. A box office juggernaut. Where was the master canner going with all this?

"Now, don't we have a girl from that movie in our program? She was one of the ambassador's assistants. Ambassador to Kroglians, or something ridiculous."

Suddenly Melvin remembered. The Kroglians had four arms, two livers, and bad table manners. "I remember the girl. Sylvette Walker."

"That's her. Set up Sylvette for tonight. I feel like changing my luck."

"Sylvette Walker. I'll set that up, sir."

"Fine."

"Wait. Make it tomorrow night, Melvin. Sylvette for tomorrow night."

"Sylvette, tomorrow night."

"Bingo." Hogue hung up.

Sylvette Walker was unique among Hogue's girls. She was black. Well, café au lait. Nine feet tall, gorgeous, built like a '58 Caddy, and wore a blond wig. And she had back. Way back.

So much for Rhonda Carling.

FORTY-FOUR

Hearsay

I'd called Lew that night, told him about Hogue, my mystery call, Algren's death, and the gist of the screenplay. The next day, Lew had asked Captain Dempsey at Hollywood Precinct if he might take a look at the crime scene on Cosmo Street. Fine with Dempsey. The murder of a homeless man in busy Hollywood was a zero priority matter. Those few who cared were leery of the law. Everyone was created equal, true, but some, as always, were more equal than others. In death, Algren had achieved full equality with all those who'd ever lived, great or small.

His body had been stuffed between two Dumpsters. Someone had stolen his shoes. The coroner had concluded that Algren had died of a single, vicious thrust of a sharp object from the side that severed his left carotid artery on the way in and ripped out his trachea on the way out. Algren had lost consciousness in five seconds, had been dead in less than sixty. Just a single moment of pain. In the coroner's opinion, the killing was professional, reminiscent of military methodology. The object was Algren's death, not his suffering.

The coroner had also shown Lew the small bag with Algren's effects. Four dollars and thirteen cents, a pocketknife, an empty wallet with his ID and a library card, and from around his neck, on a faded red ribbon, a strange-looking brass key. If it even was a key.

● ● ●

I awoke the next morning with a headache, pushed through it. I was meeting Lew at the Farmers Market, in the east courtyard. There he was with coffee and a doughnut. A movie director was holding court a few tables off. Maybe it was Mazursky.

"Hey, Lew."

"Hey."

I got the giant glaze and a cup of coffee from Bob's. The doughnut was as big as a personal pizza.

I didn't go for personal pizza. Pizza, to me, was in essence celebratory, meant to be enjoyed with friends. Not furtively, alone, warding off calories, sucking baby aspirins.

I told Lew about my meeting with Hogue and my mystery phone call. How I might have prevented Algren's death.

Lew shrugged off my guilt, moved forward. "Why didn't you tell me you recognized him on the DVD?"

"I hadn't put it all together yet." Of course I was not directly responsible for Algren's death. I was a cog in the machinations of fate. But still. Absolution, eventually, would rise from within, as the emotional color of the incident faded to black-and-white. The fade of emotional color was what made us human. It allowed us to file away and forget, it allowed us to pick up the pieces, allowed us to love again. The direct grant of absolution was one of the few wisdoms of the Roman Catholic Church.

"Tell me about Howard Hogue."

"You mean America's premier can-banger." I couldn't help adding that fact.

"Can-banger?"

I explained Hogue's proclivities. And the extraordinary lengths he went to achieve them.

"Twenty-*eight*?"

"Could be more now. Could be twenty-nine."

A very tall, buxom blonde in black tights sauntered across the courtyard, disappeared in the direction of the souvenirs and candy.

"That was a Hogue girl."

"You *know* her?"

"No. That's his type. And those were size fives, Lew."

Lew stared after her. Stilettos. "How do you know they were size fives?"

"Because you never numerically mention a woman's shoe size if it's higher than five."

"But how do you know those were fives?"

"Because I actually mentioned an integer."

Lew just looked at me. "Fuck you." He shook his head. "Let's start over at the beginning. Hogue called you in to see if you knew Algren."

"Yes."

"And you knew him but you didn't *know* you knew him."

"So I was dismissed. Then I went to see Myron. He found me a picture of Algren from thirty years ago."

"You didn't recognize him."

"No. Then, after you came to visit, and I realized who Algren was, I got the mystery call."

"And yesterday you found Mrs. Algren."

"Yup."

"Tell me about the screenplay."

"Hogue threw a party. Thirty years ago. Hale Montgomery took too much acid and fucked up a whore with a knife. *Really* fucked her up. Hogue's Dr. Feelgood was called. They all decided she was ruined."

"What was her name?"

"I don't know her real name. A black girl. Pretty new in town."

"Then?"

"Then they put her out of her misery. I mean, she was pretty far gone. Her nose was cut off, an ear, I guess. Cut all over her face."

"Hale Montgomery?"

"High on acid. Woke up the next morning with cuts on his fingers. They sedated him that night. He woke up the next day, didn't know what he had done."

"Does he know now?"

"I don't know what he knows. He may *not* know."

"Son-of-a-bitch. What did Algren have to do with all this?"

"He was at the party. Saw the girl's body. Told 'em he had a boat down San Pedro."

"She slept with the fishes."

"She *sleeps* with the fishes."

"Why didn't Algren go to the police?"

"Because this is Tinseltown. The girl was dead. He didn't do it, there was no going back. He saw a ride up the mountain."

"Hogue."

"I guess Hogue agreed to help him."

"What happened?"

"Algren was put off for a while. Then he was invited to Hogue's place for dinner. At the dinner he started feeling bad. Woke up in Camarillo. Didn't get out for seven years."

"After he got out he wrote the screenplay."

"Called *San Pedro*."

"So the screenplay itself was blackmail."

"But the blackmail thing didn't work out."

"Obviously. If he ended up on the streets."

"He never worked again." Not on Myron's radar, anyway.

"They threatened him with something."

"Something worse than another seven years in the bing."

Lew nodded, thought. "So you didn't know the danger Algren was really in until you read the screenplay after he was dead."

"I guess so."

"Then you're hardly responsible for his death."

But still.

"I want to read it, Dick."

"Sure. Come by the house."

We sat there for a while. In the warm sun. A gaggle of pale tourists walked in looking for movie stars. They didn't recognize directors. Or real cops.

"Tell me about his wife."

"Common-law. There were married on Vine Street."

"You don't mean a church on Vine Street, you mean *on* Vine Street."

"That's what I mean."

"That's romantic."

"That's romantic comedy."

I gave a piece of my giant doughnut to a sparrow. Pretty soon I had a cheerful brown brigade bouncing at my feet. I always threw for the ones on the perimeter. The underdogs.

Lew took a little plastic bag out of his pocket, handed it to me. Visible was a brass object.

"What's this?"

"The key from around Algren's neck. Seen one like it?"

I examined it, shook my head. It was heavy in my hand. I slid it back across the table.

"How's the Nazarian girl?" asked Lew.

"I was going to tell you about that. She checked herself out of Fairfax Convalescent."

"*What?*"

"Devi talked to her sister. Her sister called over there. They told her she'd checked in for exhaustion and had checked out under her own power."

"Is that possible?"

"No."

"So nobody knows where she is."

"No." I drained my coffee, saw that cold anger in Lew's eyes. The cold anger of a real cop. "I think she's down in San Pedro, Lew. With the fishes."

FORTY-FIVE

The Pappam and the Cluddum

Heather Hill rechecked her messages. This was the place. Patys on Riverside, Toluca Lake. And this was the time. She'd been waiting seventeen long minutes. The waitress, Belle, was already looking at her funny. Like no one was coming. Pretty soon she have to fake a messaged cancellation.

Animated conversations surrounded her on the patio. People with connections, using those connections. Networking, hooking up, making deals. And there she was, silent in the field of opportunity.

If this were a movie—make it a musical—she would overcome the odds and her fears and stand up and *sing*! Patrons would be horrified, laugh behind their hands, but then the orchestra would come in and by the end of the first chorus, busboys would have tossed their trays aside, ripped off their aprons, and danced! The handsome young man under the corner umbrella would have abandoned his fat lawyer, come across the patio, taken her hands, sunk to his knees and sung about love at first sight. By the end of the song all the patrons would be singing, the lawyer would be nodding, *this girl is a star,* traffic on Riverside Drive would have stopped, transfixed passengers exiting their shiny sedans in happy wonder.

Then a heavy shower of grateful applause and quick cut to the lawyer's office, where he offered his heavy gold pen for her to sign her Hollywood contract. The studio heads argued amongst themselves, *she's mine, she's mine,* and the lawyer waved his arms to restore order and then—

"Miss Hill? Miss Hill?"

The real world resumed and there he was. That nice man. Melvin Shea. "Mr. Shea?" The nice man grinned. He had a lot of teeth. Maybe one of them hurt.

"Call me Melvin, Miss Hill."

Belle came by with that smile and topped off her coffee. "Will you be needing a menu, sir?" Mr. Shea nodded and Belle disappeared. Maybe Belle wasn't so bad.

"How nice you're looking today, Miss Hill."

"Call me Heather."

"Thank you, Heather. I love that name, by the way." Heather was such a common name in Hollywood, it could almost substitute for *darling.* And darling it would be when she was down on her knees. As he guided her by the ears. "So have you decided, Miss Hill? Will you join the Ivanhoe Special Talent Program?"

This was the moment she'd been waiting for. *This* was Opportunity Knocking. She looked Mr. Shea right in the eye. It seemed he was holding his breath. "Yes, Mr. Shea, I want to be part of the Ivanhoe Special Talent Program."

Melvin stretched a smile broadly across his face. The Tylenol with codeine wasn't doing what it had done just yesterday. He'd get the Nazi to write another scrip. Some of those 800mg bombers. "Congratulations, Miss Hill." He extended his hand across the table. "On behalf of Howard Hogue, who will forthwith have his cock up your ass, and the Ivanhoe team, welcome." Except he didn't say exactly that. They shook hands.

The girl began to cry, looking down into her lap, her shoulders heaving. *Jesus Christ.* Every once in a while there was a complete naïf. Came to melodiate, stayed to gargle. *Christ.* At least Mary Poppins knew how to fuck. And how to deal with children. *Stop crying and sing!*

"Thank you so much, Mr. Shea. You don't know what it feels like to meet someone like you." She smiled through moist eyes. "I just have one question, Mr. Shea."

And that would be?

Usually, girls offered a berth in the program talked with their friends about the good news, got a little cautious feedback. Friends who had heard x, y, z. Tit for tat, yin and yang, quid pro quo. There were no questions. "What is your question, Miss Hill?"

"Have you ever heard of Vincent Furnatato?"

"I don't know that name, Miss Hill. Who is he?" Sounded like a repairman.

"He's an actor. A really good actor. He's done some regional theater and some extra work. He was in *The Schwarzschild Radius.*"

"*The Schwarzschild Radius.*" Small world. "Wonderful."

"He was one of the Cluddum."

"The Cluddum. Who were the Cluddum?"

"They were a sect of the Dark Farmers. Opposed to the rule of the Pappam."

"The Pappam." The Pappam and the Cluddum. He was conversing with an imbecile. One of the befuddum. "Tell me about Mr. Furnatato. Is he your boyfriend?"

"Yes. But I'm professionally objective about his talent."

"Of course."

"What I'm wondering is . . ."

Christ the Redeemer. He was going to need more Tylenol before she was finished. Tylenol with heroin.

"What I'm wondering is, might there be a place in the program for Vince?"

Melvin had never heard that question before.

FORTY-SIX

Viking Smoked Salt

The best method for dealing with pain was sleep. Nazarian had slept for almost twenty-four hours. He awoke in agony, but, Christ, he had to be a little better. He swallowed another couple of what the doctor down at Century City Hospital had prescribed. He went to the refrigerator, realized he couldn't open his mouth. He slurged down another disgusting helping of the vanilla nutrition solution. He was ravenous. He'd pay a million dollars for a lousy Denny's Grand Slam.

Which reminded him.

A violet shaft of worry transited his consciousness. The check. And the gun.

His mind was back. He was thinking like himself again. His anger was no longer throbbing and amorphous. It was a thrust, looking for a target and results.

In his office, the phone was blinking. Messages. Maybe clues. He listened to the first of nine.

"Mr. Nazarian, this is Dr. Wolf calling. We need to talk. About the, uh, the special events . . . that occurred over the past days. You've accumulated some significant costs both for yourself . . . and the girl you injured. I'm doing my best to keep everything *hush-hush*—if you know what I mean. But sometimes a *golden gun* speaks for itself. Call me. Good day."

Nazarian hung up the phone, the pain in his tightened jaw flaring to an ice-pick stab. He forced himself to let it go, to relax. The pain subsided back to its normal tide of disquietude. He inhaled, exhaled.

He almost chuckled, but it hurt too much. The Nazi quack was trying to blackmail him. Obviously, the doctor did not know Eli Nazarian.

The Bentley started right up, it'd better; he rolled down Coldwater into Beverly Hills. By the time he reached Sunset his face was on fire. He couldn't keep his growing rage and outrage out of his jaw. *Blackmail.* Fuck it, them, everyone, everything. He would channel every joule of his pain. Into a polite discussion.

He pulled up in front of the address he'd gotten from Marco. The blackmailer lived pretty well, looked like. No wonder.

He rang the bell, heard the chimes through the paneled wooden door.

He could feel his blood pressure rising as he waited. His jaw pincered. A pretty Hispanic woman opened up. She had a misshapen forehead. Probably raised in a mud hut.

"Yes?" said the woman from behind the door.

"I'm here to see Dr. Wolf," he said through clenched teeth. "Is he in?" He tried to smile. A lip smile.

"I see. May I ask who calling?"

She wanted his name. How about his ZIP code? How about his Social Security number? "How about my Social Security number, too?"

"What?" asked Paulita.

Of course, *what.* The little *muchacha* didn't have a Social Security number. He grabbed the edge of the door, pulled it out of her fingers. Then shoved it back, hard, right into Puff's forehead. *Bonk.* Down she went. He stepped over her, into the cool of the house.

At the kitchen table, Dr. Wolf suffered through the sound of Rhonda Carling's chains sinking into the deep and Gretchen's inane small talk about a birthday luncheon for their granddaughter.

"Since they were out of the prime rib," said Gretchen, "which I can't believe—did you know they were out of prime rib last time?—it's unbelievable—what kind of business is that?—anyway I decided on roast beef slices, rare, with Viking Smoked Salt."

The doctor wanted to slap her saggy, rouged, oblivious cheeks. *Whap, whap, whap, whump*. Knock her right on her fat ass. Did she bear any of the weight that he shouldered to sustain their way of life? He desperately wanted to be on the boat with Paulita. Rocking in the sun and salt air. Forgetting everything.

The doorbell rang. A shard of panic pierced him high and low. Head and colon. *The police!*

Eli Nazarian heard sounds from the kitchen, walked back. Aha. The doctor. And his wife. Probably. Wolf got to his feet, confused.

Nazarian stepped up, knocked the doctor to the floor with a backhand slap. The woman shrieked. Nazarian pointed down at her. "One more sound, lady, I'll kill him. Then you. Got it?"

She got it. Strangely, she found no ready connection between her brain and her tongue. It lolled, a fat oyster, behind her teeth. Her legs didn't seem to be her own, either.

Nazarian pulled Wolf to his feet. "Guess what? I'm not paying you a penny. You got balls calling me, you fucking Nazi. Now, where's my gun and where's my check?"

Wolf shook his head. "I don't have the gun."

Nazarian shook him. "Where's the gun? That you mentioned in your call."

"I don't have it."

"Lie—I take an eye."

Wolf shook his head rapidly, side to side, indicated over his shoulder with his thumb. "I saw it at the apartment. The table by the couch."

"And my check?"

"Check?"

Nazarian slapped the doctor again. "Don't disappoint me. My check. Where is it?"

"I don't know anything about a check, I swear to God. I don't know."

Nazarian raised his hand, the doctor cowered. Maybe he hadn't seen the check. Nazarian lowered his hand. "Where're my clothes, Doctor? The clothes I wore here. Where are they?"

Wolf pointed.

Nazarian grabbed his shoulder, shoved him in that direction. "Take me there."

He followed the doctor out of the kitchen, through the garage, through a door into the clinic. Nazarian remembered the clinic. They turned a corner and there was the nurse.

"Remember me? Where're the clothes I wore in here?"

Nurse Stanleigh sensed something wrong. "Doctor, are you alright?"

Nazarian smiled at her coldly. "The doctor *will* be alright if you help us. Where're my clothes?"

Carol looked to the doctor, he nodded, his face burning.

"Your clothes have been dry-cleaned. We were going to call you."

"But you didn't. You go through the pockets?"

"Of course."

"You find anything?"

"Yes."

"What did you do with it?"

"I threw it away."

"You threw it away?"

"I threw away a packet of cocaine, Mr. Nazarian. Haven't you done enough of that shit?"

Nazarian stepped forward, towering over the nurse, a finger in her face. But Carol Stanleigh had seen a lot of bullies in her lifetime and was unafraid.

Nazarian, teeth clenched, was suddenly aware that his jaw was on fire. He turned on his heel, retraced his steps, went out the way he'd come in.

PART THREE

A Sentence

FORTY-SEVEN

In Memory of Betty Ann Fowler

With my contacts downtown, and the dispensation of several honeybees, I checked out the address and background of the Hancock Park mansion where fictional producer Hubert Hull had his fateful party as described by Davis Algren. The address was real.

Tax records indicated the home, at that time, was owned by a company named Frame 24. Twenty-four frames per second was the film speed necessary for human beings to perceive individual photos as a flow, as motion picture, as a movie.

Frame 24 was owned by a variety of partners. The presiding interest was held by the Marjorie Group—one of thirteen entities controlled by Howard Hogue.

But how to trace the girl who'd gone down to San Pedro from a screenplay of phony names?

Lew snapped his fingers. "Maybe her name is *real*. There's no need for disguise."

He was right. The next day we found the one mention of a Betty Ann Fowler in Los Angeles history. An inquiry from her mother in Altoona, Pennsylvania. A month and half after the party. A missing persons report was filed. Nothing ever came of it. Nothing was ever *going* to come of it. She was the wrong kind of victim. Wrong money. Wrong skin color. Wrong everything. Betty Ann's mother, Betilda Rowens, called twice more. And never again.

I looked at Lew, shrugged. We were as close as we were going to get. The screenplay checked out for location and time. Which proved nothing. "Peaches, baby," I said.

He nodded. "Peaches."

Like I told my son about girls. If you want the peaches, you've got to shake the tree. Walking around the tree, looking solemn, looking noble, did nothing but wear out your shoes. And your feelings. You had to employ the direct approach.

"And how do you propose to shake the tree, Dick?"

Thus, the San Pedro Film Company was established in the office under Myron Ealing in the Hollywood Professional Building. It was a two-room suite. A waiting room: a couch, a bookcase, a potted plant, a table, some weekly issues of *Variety* and *The Hollywood Reporter*.

And the office proper through the door. We moved in an old, scarred-up wooden desk, with an ancient wooden swivel chair as its partner. On the desk we put a green-glass banker's lamp we picked up at Staples on Sunset. From the back of the third-floor maintenance closet we borrowed a battered cast-iron safe. It didn't lock. But it looked serious.

We added two tiny cameras that disguised themselves as smoke detectors. Perfect.

We stood back and checked out our work. It looked alright.

Lew sprang doubts. "Who's this going to fool, Dick? Won't they look up San Pedro Film Company on IMDb?"

"Sure they will. And what'll they find?"

"Nothing."

"Exactly. So they'll come here."

"And what does this all mean?"

"We're playing a recognizable hand, that's all. A blackmailer's hand."

Lew shrugged. "Okay."

We'd wiggle the pizza, see what flies it drew, then take their pictures.

Time to break a leg.

FORTY-EIGHT

A Package for America's Favorite Granddad

Holmby Hills was the third of four districts comprising Los Angeles's "Platinum Triangle." Beverly Hills to the east, Westwood to the west, Bel Air to the north, Holmby Hills enjoyed some of the highest real estate prices in the continental United States. On South Mapleton Drive, well back from the street, stood the 11,500-square-foot home of America's favorite granddad.

Hale Montgomery had awoken early that day, ten fifteen, and had already completed a few laps in the pool. Not brisk laps. Brisk laps were fifteen years ago.

In the kitchen, Nessie gave him the special basket from Liquor Locker. "Who's it from?" he asked her.

Nessie shook her head. Her uniform had a stain on it. A reddish stain. "I don't know, Mr. Montgomery. But I think there's a card."

He studied the card. A delivery from Liquor Locker meant somebody was trying to get to him directly, avoiding CAA, avoiding Mort Beider, his useless manager over at Brillstein. It was time to shitcan Beider.

Number Two Bollinger Blanc de Noirs Vieilles Vignes Françaises

1997. Never heard of it. Quite possibly it was shit. He wou
any better. In the dark, statistically, people could barely tel
orange juice.

He pulled out his cell phone and dialed.

"Liquor Locker."

"Hi, this is Hale Montgomery." He always paused right I
his listener time to realize who was on the other end of the
and rejoice. Recognize that burnished baritone. The barite
induced three thousand women to leap out of their panties.

"Mr. Montgomery!" The voice was grateful, excited. "What
you?"

"Well, I just got a nice little delivery from you guys. A bo
ber Two Bollinger Blanc—"

"Blanc de Noirs Vieilles Vignes Françaises 1997. One o
carry."

"Really. How delightful. How much does a bottle of this

"Four hundred a bottle, sir. Retail, six hundred."

"That's a nice round sum."

"Yes, sir. For you, personally, we could do a little better
but, all in all, I think you'll find it a very satisfying beverag
pinot noir grapes. A very good morning libation."

"Of course." If they said so.

"Is there anything else, Mr. Montgomery?"

"No. That'll do it. Thank you."

He hung up before he remembered to ask who it was fr
was the card.

From your friends at the San Pedro Film Company.

He didn't remember any such friends. But the paper was
quality. He opened the envelope.

ANGEL'S GATE

6356 Hollywood Boulevard Suite #317
From the desk of Jack Ireland

Dear Hale,
    Hope this finds you well. We're interested in your thoughts on this script.
For you, as a starring vehicle. We think you can knock this one out of the
park.

                                              Jack

He weighed the script in his hands. Uhhhh . . . ninety-eight pages. He
lipped to the end. 101. Nice. A good professional guess. He still had it.
Of course he did. What was the name of this thing?

San Pedro.

San Pedro. By the San Pedro Film Company. That was a little odd. If
his were San Pedro's first film, fuck 'em. Unless they had a seven-figure
offer. High sevens.

"Nessie?"

"Yes, sir?"

"Chill the champagne for me, bring it to me out by the pool when I
ome down. I'm going to get dressed."

"Yes, sir, Mr. Montgomery." Good. The old man had not noticed the
tain. It was cranberry sauce. But it looked like wine.

FORTY-NINE

Juan Valdez

Luis and Ernesto had arrived at Fairfax Convalescent a little after 9:00 p.m. They parked in the rear, rolled the gurney in. Like their previous delivery, they were only to speak with Moncrief.

Dr. Moncrief, as before, had everything arranged. The woman was off the drip and ready to roll. Luis scrawled something on the release form and they pulled her into the night.

Into the unmarked van she went, everything was secured. Luis told Ernesto to stay in the back. Moncrief said she was heavily medicated, don't let her drown. *Drown?* In her own vomit.

The van started right up, jounced through the alley—sorry, lady—and made a left on Rosewood. Then a right on Fairfax.

Luis, with Ernesto, had picked the woman up from her place over on Rossmore a couple of nights before. She'd taken quite a beating. Looked a little better now. Not that much better.

Luis made a left at Beverly Boulevard. The Grove, and its huge parking structure, would be coming up on his right. Right on Stanley Avenue. There it was.

He turned into the parking structure, took a ticket, circled up to the roof. He wondered where the cameras were up here. Somewhere. Didn't matter. He'd borrowed the license plates from an old Buick. From over to his right, a pair of headlights flashed. He drove over, put his window down.

A man approached from a 700 series BMW. "Luis?"

Luis nodded.

"Park over there," said the man, pointing to the space beside the BMW.

Luis parked, signaled to Ernesto to make ready. Luis exited the van, walked around to the sliding door. "What's your name?" he asked the man.

"That's not your business, Juan Valdez."

Fair enough. It wasn't his business. Who was Juan Valdez? Luis opened up the van. Ernesto had her unstrapped and loose.

"¿Listo?"

Ernesto nodded.

Luis turned to the man who didn't want to give his name. "Open your doors."

The man opened both front and back on the driver's side. Luis leaned in to the van, grabbed her ankles, pulled her legs till they dangled. "Sit her up," he ordered Ernesto.

Once she was up, Luis put his arms around her, stood her up, the drunken kiss position, rotated her to the open rear door of the BMW, let her carefully fall in backward. Except for banging her head, *thunk,* on the doorframe, the procedure went exactly as planned. She never complained. Her skin was warm. She wasn't dead.

Yet.

But her luck had run out. *Fuerte.* Putting her in the hands of the BMW *pinchazo* would do nothing for her health, wealth, or future. The little man obviously cared only for himself.

The man was in a hurry. But he wasn't faster than light. Luis had a clear look at his license plate and memorized it instantly. The car melted off, a big cat disappearing in the night. Luis wrote the number in his book, gave the thumbs-up to Ernesto. Now a call to Dr. Wolf to collect their two thousand dollars. Correction. Ernesto's seven fifty.

• • •

In a small office near Seventh and Alvarado, Luis Torres handed a small piece of paper to the man behind the desk. Seven characters. The man looked at the paper, nodded. *Vuelte sobre una hora.*

Luis returned in an hour, gave the man the sum he had requested. The man held the bill up to the light. Ulysses S. Grant. The bill was legitimate. Probably the only legitimate document on the whole street. Perhaps in the whole MacArthur Park district.

The man reflected. What had the American hero, MacArthur, said? That was it. *I shall return.* And that was what he, Mario Topa, ensured; that his countrymen would return, from deportation, from desperation, from the Aztlán diaspora; singly, by the platoon, by the regiment, by the army. And Mario would further ensure, that this time, with the documents he would manufacture, for a modest profit, these men would stay to father many children and eventually take back the land stolen from their ancestors. Democracy was a numbers game. And the numbers were on his side. Success, eventually, was a certainty. Democracy was a wonderful thing. Though you could take it too far.

Luis stepped into the sun, looked down at what he had paid fifty dollars for. A name and a phone number.

Ten minutes later, from the Grand Central Market, Luis placed a call.

"This is Melvin," said the voice.

"*Buenos dias,* Melvin," returned Luis, cheerfully. "How the hell are you? And how's that girl?"

There was a pause.

"Who is this?"

"This is Juan Valdez."

FIFTY

Last Supper, Interrupted

That stupid shit Wolf. Hiring two clowns for serious work. That was what invariably ruined perfect crimes. The coincidence, the loose end, the irresponsible agent.

Now he was being blackmailed by a couple of wetbacks who'd dropped out of school in the fourth grade. Then the perfect solution came to him.

"*Juan Valdez?* Geez, dude, I was hoping you'd call."

"Well, here I am, Melvin. We need to talk."

"Of course, we do. We need you guys back."

"You need us *back?*"

"Pronto. *Rapeedo.* You need to pick up the girl. Take her back to Fairfax Convalescent."

"Take her back?"

"Take her back, dude. To Fairfax. She's a lot better. You have to come get her."

"Where are you?"

"Cabrillo Marina."

"Where is it?"

"San Pedro."

"What's the address?"

"I'm not a fuckin' taxi driver, *ameego*. Cabrillo Marina in San Pedro. At the end of the Harbor Freeway. The 110. Come to slip 814. Big white motor yacht. It's called *Hush, My Baby*."

Melvin checked his watch. He could do it this afternoon. He had found and stolen the extra key to the Nazi's yacht. Just in case he might need to get back on it for something or other. Because the Nazi didn't like him. And now this. Perfect. "Come around three. Call me when you get here. I'll come out and meet you."

"Same money. We want same money. Cash."

"Fine."

And that was that.

And how appropriate. *Hush, My Baby*. Hush, hush, my Rhonda. Like those melodious fags in their straw hats, the Beach Boys.

He arrived just after two. He loved the salt air. He brought a couple of sacks of Mexican food and the smell filled the enclosed salon. He laid a plastic tarp on the floor.

The wetbacks arrived at a quarter to three. Prepared by their call, he'd waved them in to visitor parking, led them down to the boat.

He shook both their hands, smiled warmly. He apologized for his behavior on their last get-together. "I had a lot of shit on my mind, dudes, no time to get it all done. Know what I mean?"

Luis and Ernesto seemed to be alright with that. Melvin led them past some beautiful boats and finally gestured them aboard the *Hush, My Baby*.

"This the doctor's boat?" asked Luis, stepping on.

"Sure is, brother." Melvin shrugged. "He makes money hand over fist—and he's stingy as an old woman. *Tacaño*. Cheap. He makes money on the poor folks. Crazy money."

Melvin watched Luis and Ernesto appreciate the craft. Eveything was white, chrome, teak, polished brass, and gleaming. They had learned the art of seeming to be unimpressed by the things they would never own. Things that would remain, for their lifetimes, hopelessly out of their grasp, in the hands of rich gringos. *Stupid* gringos. It was funny, when you met a few, how dumb they were. How ordinary. *Estúpidos.*

But food was another matter. He saw Ernesto inhale and hunger.

"You dudes hungry?"

Ernesto looked to Luis. But Luis had smelled it by now, too.

Melvin knew he had them. "Come on below. I ordered up some chow. Maybe you dudes can do some other work for me, too."

Down the quay, a belt sander started up. Fantastic. A hundred forty decibels of noise. *Come on, feel the noise.* Noise ordained by the God Who Wasn't There. The scream of teak. "Down in the salon, guys." Again, the grand gesture.

He followed the duo down the ladder into the quiet. The food was laid out on the table. A small cooler with some Dos Equis on ice.

Ernesto reached for a taquito, Luis for a cold one. Luis turned to thank him but by that time Melvin pulled his revolver from under a stack of folded laundry. Leaving it wrapped in a thick towel, he shot Luis in the balls and watched him crumple to the floor. Ernesto turned. Right between the eyes.

He could hear the belt sander.

Back to the writhing Luis. "So, motherfucker. How does it feel? You were gonna blackmail me? You and your crude, wetback shit? No, man. Not in this world. This is the white man's world. And you know what I'm going to do?"

He pointed the gun inches from Luis's face.

"Fuck you, *cabrón,*" gasped Luis.

"I'm going to recycle you. Round midnight tonight, those San Pedro bay crabs'll be eating your fucking eyes." Melvin grinned. "And you won't feel a thing. You'll be holding hands with Rhonda."

Melvin put a bullet through Luis's knee. It had to hurt. *Had to hurt.* And an elbow shot for radial symmetry. Symmetry was important. Balance.

Good and evil. Light and dark. Up and down. Sick and well. Rise and fall. In and out. Yin and yang. Life and death.

He was a god. He put the weapon to Luis's forehead. Then sent him on his way. It would be nice if God was Caucasian. And He was. Had to be.

He locked up the boat, used Luis's key to start up their white van. Fifteen minutes later, across the two big bridges, he was in Long Beach. In North Long Beach, he parked the van, wiped down the steering wheel and abandoned the vehicle, keys in the ignition, windows down, door unlocked. It wouldn't last twenty minutes. *Bon voyage,* Bait Car.

He took a taxi back to Cabrillo, hopped into the Beemer, rolled for Hollywood. Mission accomplished.

FIFTY-ONE

Ion Winds at the Edge of Time

And now for that quality morning libation. Montgomery checked his watch. Morning had passed. Still, it felt early. Nessie had arranged champagne and ice water, with slices of fruit, cheese, and sourdough bread. Under his large Spanish umbrella by the pool.

He sat down in his woven wicker chaise longue and achieved a perfect recumbency. A bird tweeted and he entertained the thought of a nap, a brief nap, but, no—first the business at hand. He sipped the champagne and reached for the screenplay. Good champagne after all. Dry.

A good screenplay was good on page one. A bad screenplay was bad on page one. Soon he would know what he was holding. He settled in and began.

San Pedro . . . by A. Davis.

By page five he was uneasy. By page twelve he was horrified. At page thirty, he thrust it away, and rose, an old man. His respiration was quick and shallow, his limbs enervated and trembling, his scalp damp and hot.

The impossible had occurred. His most private nightmare had been twisted into black and white, flesh and blood. Into a story of drugged, bestial homicide.

This is Owsley, someone had said, the ultimate concoction from the ultimate chemist. This was how the Beatles had dreamed up Sgt. Pepper. Peter Max, Claes Oldenburg, Roy Lichtenstein—that's where they came from, right? And so he'd swallowed the little red barrels.

At first they'd done nothing. Duds. So he took two more. Suddenly he realized he could see around corners. That he could levitate if he chose to do so. In fact, simply bringing his attention to bear created what he wished to contemplate. He. Was. God. And he always had been.

His hearing was *granular,* precisely aware of even the subtlest contributory vibration. He could travel through space and time, on and with any frequency he chose to entertain or augment. He. Was. Music.

Then he saw the most beautiful woman he'd ever seen. Her skin was light brown, a living duskiness that invited his fingers to *feel.* He wanted to fill her with his god-seed. Looking down upon his member, he saw that though it was part of him, it also had independent life. He summoned it to steel. It rose, by degrees, with every beat of his heart. Steel. Bursting with vertical energy, flag-bearer of indomitable spirit.

He sought her flesh and she willowed beneath him. They were one. They were timeless. They were eternal, born in the heat of the new universe to fly before the shock wave of creation. Then she had summoned forth his seed and he gave her every atom he possessed, turning inside out and disappearing into her completely and forever.

And the beat of her heart was the drum of high music and he was reborn in her light. But that he was reborn *in it,* meant that he was separate *from it,* and a great sadness rose within him, and flung him, like a great wind across the infinite field, and he knew that one day she would die. That her death agonies not be prolonged for eternities he took up a large clear stone and smashed it into her temple and she lay still.

Then with a blade that appeared in his hand for that purpose, he began to disassemble her, that he might restore her to perfection, that they would again ride the ion winds to the edges of time.

He'd awoken the next morning at Hogue's house. Stark naked, with five or six cuts on his fingers and hands. Did I hurt someone, he asked Hogue.

Hogue had smiled. Of course not. You got pretty high and we found you playing with a knife. With no clothes on. You didn't cut your cock off, did you?

He looked down. There it was. Docile and complacent. He reached his fingers into his pubic hair, then smelled them. Smelled like a woman. He'd been with a woman. Who was I with? he asked.

Who weren't you with, returned Hogue, grinning.

Not boys, I hope?

No. Hogue laughed. But that was the only thing that could kill a career, he said. A dead girl or a live boy.

A great relief swept through Montgomery. For half a second he remembered the glint of a blade and a brown-skinned girl lying on a huge bed. It was all a dream. Thank God.

It was all a dream. They told him it was a dream. Hogue had told him. Dr. Wolf had told him. That young actor had told him. The young actor who'd ended up at Camarillo.

And he had so desperately wanted to believe them that he had. But the screenplay said different. Said the girl, Betty Ann Fowler, had been euthanized and dumped in the sea off San Pedro. That Hunt St. Everly, rising star, had been too valuable to punish. That too many people had been attached, one way or the other, to the career of St. Everly.

His heart thumped in his chest. The screenplay was the truth. The mask with which he had hidden from himself for thirty years was ripped from his soul.

He heard the screen door shut and Nessie appeared poolside. Her dark brown skin and white teeth. "Phone call, Mr. Montgomery. Entertainment Tonight. Your interview."

Instinctively, he stood up to go in. He took three dead steps toward the house and realized he couldn't leave the screenplay out there. Lying around. Maybe Nessie, who'd never read a single word of print in their acquaintance, would pick it up. Get engrossed. And the world would fall in.

Nessie saw something was wrong. "You okay, Mr. Montgomery?" Man looked like he'd aged twenty years in twenty minutes.

Montgomery picked up the phone in his office, listened. A woman was happily babbling. He understood nothing, remembered nothing. It was if he had forgotten their common tongue. Oliver Sacks had recounted the results of a stroke in a certain part of the brain. With that location damaged, listeners could no longer detect where one word ended and another began. Had he had a stroke?

"Mrmontgomery?" the woman said. "Mrmontgomeryareyoualright?" Even the phone, in his hand, looked like a foreign object. Which end did you speak into? Finally, he spoke at it. "I can't talk to you now," he said, "goodbye."

He sat down in the chair behind his desk. Nessie appeared.

"Mrmontgomeryareyousureyou'realright?"

He couldn't understand her.

Nessie dialed 911.

Montgomery had recovered somewhat by the time emergency services arrived. He posed for pictures with the EMTs, signed a few articles. He was perfectly fine, he assured them, he had received some surprising news, felt an irregularity in his chest. But everything was A-OK now. The ambulance rolled off.

Nessie was mortified. "I thought you was really sick, Mr. Montgomery. I woulda never called."

"You did what you thought was necessary, Nessie. And I appreciate that." He went upstairs. Slowly.

Nessie looked after him. There was something wrong. Clearly. She'd have to watch him.

He reached the bedroom suite, sat in his old leather chair, looked out the window into the garden. A breeze riffled the jacaranda and sent a cloud of lavender to the ground.

The autumnal season of all living things. The beauty time lent to life by the brevity of its passing. The flowering and the fall. Making room for the new.

He reached for his phone, called Howard Hogue.

"Howard Hogue's office."

He recognized the voice. "Hello, Helena. This is Hale Montgomery."

"Mr. Montgomery! How are you, sir? Are you well?"

Instinct reasserted itself. "I'm fine, thank you." He spoke in movie-star cadence, automatically pitching his voice a little low. "And you?"

"Oh, you know. Busy, busy, busy. Every day a blur. Let me see if Howard's in."

Of course Howard would be in for one of the grand points of light in the Ivanhoe firmament. Then the voice of the billionaire.

"Hale, is that you?"

"Hi, Howard."

"You know what I saw last night? In Blu-Ray? *Three Nights in New Orleans*. I forgot how good that was. How good you were. That was a real piece of work."

"Thanks."

"It made me think. Maybe we should reprise that character. Bring him up to date."

"Stash Rockland."

Stash had been a violent, woman-chasing, live-for-the-moment motorcycle cocaine cowboy. Until the fire in the French Quarter and the discovery of a daughter he didn't know he had.

Only Hale Montgomery's movie-star aura allowed the character to be perceived as real. Millions and millions flocked to the multiplexes. Purchased chemically flavored popcorn by the boxcar. By the boatload. By the landfill.

And now to think, during all that high living and self-congratulation, he had been nothing more than a drugged-out killer, unaware of the damage he had done. A puppet, mindlessly dancing for the man behind the curtain. And what other things had he trampled and destroyed? In his ignorance and enthusiasm.

He felt sick.

"So, whaddaya say, Stash?"

He could feel his mind twisting for the sun. Any actor's reaction in the presence of cash money. "We should talk about it. Can we get Bill Staton to write?" Staton had gone on to bigger and better things after Stash Rockland, but then his ego burst. He fell from heaven to heroin in a year. Now, ten years later, his name had recently tickled the trades.

Hogue mused. "I hear he's writing again." Staton would come cheap. And he was good if he was reasonably sober. "And he may be grateful for a little something to do. Not a bad idea, Hale. I'll have someone give him a call."

The conversation, having reintroduced its constituents, stepped to higher gear. "What can I do for you, Hale? Things alright?"

"I had a screenplay delivered to me today. From Liquor Locker. With a bottle of champagne."

Hogue chuckled. "They say that still works."

Montgomery saw the green bottle on the table by pool. Warm and flat. "It's called *San Pedro*."

"*San Pedro.*"

"Produced by the San Pedro Film Company."

"Never heard of 'em. What's it about?"

"About a party thrown by a producer who lived in Hancock Park in the eighties. Hubert Hull."

Hogue felt his day lurch sideways. Below his desk he hit the switch that started the digital recorder. "What happened next?" The only question any theatrical audience was interested in.

"A girl was killed and thrown into the sea. Off San Pedro."

Hogue bit his lip. However Hames had handled the assignment, he'd fucked it up. The ancient script would be blackmail. A script he had bought and paid for twenty-five years ago. He had destroyed it himself. And the single carbon copy.

"Where are you, Hale?"

"At home."

"I'll send someone over to pick it up right now. And we'll get to the bottom of this."

Get to the bottom of it. Where the body lay. Still. "You'll get to the bottom of what, Howard?"

"What are you asking me?"

"I'm asking IF I DID THOSE THINGS," he shouted. Some interior part of him had broken off, fallen off, had been twisted off. It slammed around his chest, a billiard ball with unlimited rotational energy, bouncing from rail to rail, bone to bone, *thud, thud, thud,* never stopping.

"No, you didn't, Hale. You *didn't*. You got high but you didn't hurt anyone."

"You swear to Christ? *Swear to Christ?*"

"I don't have to swear to Christ. I was there. You didn't hurt anyone."

"But someone *was* hurt."

"That's none of your business. That's *my* business."

"I want to know."

"*Hale*. It's none of your business. Take me at my word and leave it at that. I'm sending someone over right now to pick that thing up. We're being blackmailed, Hale. Let me rephrase that. I'm being blackmailed— *through* you. Someone sent that to you knowing you'd make the phone call you just made."

Hogue wiped his forehead. He needed to think.

"Straighten up and fly right. It sounds like someone kicked you in the cunt." *Jesus Christ.* "But you don't have a cunt. This is just hardball. Get your cup on and stand tall. I'm sending someone over there right now."

Montgomery looked at his phone. Hogue had clicked off. He tossed the phone on the bed. Where, that afternoon, Hilary Bangwell, porn star, was to pay a discreet visit. He felt his cock.

Flaccid, shrunken, without confidence, tired, old, useless. Every single man on Earth eventually had his last screw. Unknowingly, of course. Montgomery looked at the old man in the mirror.

At the kitchen table, Nessie was reading *Essence* magazine. For some reason, the editors had assumed she'd be interested in an article about Rihanna and her vacant thug. The horror! The bite marks! The repercussions!

What did fascinate her was the blank unawareness of the participants. Did they not realize stardom was perishable? A beautiful fruit that eventually sank into rot?

So don't fuck up, children, what won't be yours long anyway. *Shit.* These people weren't stars. They were pimples.

Whitney. Poor Whitney. Now, honey, Whitney was a star. Nessie heard laughter from upstairs. It sounded wrong. She shut her magazine. The laughter went on and on.

And on.

FIFTY-TWO

An Olfactory Event

Henderson and Son was not a criminal enterprise but they had taken a particularly hard edge on a certain business matter. The Hendersons were in retail jewelry and had agreed to reproduce, in gold, a family ring with crest and motto for a thousand dollars. To be given her son on his eighteenth birthday, my client had also provided to the Hendersons her late husband's ring to be used as a model. Summoned to the establishment with the good news that her item was complete, she arrived to the less good news that the ring's cost had risen to $1,817.69.

But that's not what you said.

I'm sorry, we underestimated our costs.

But you guaranteed it.

I'm sorry, ma'am. Our costs went up.

I want the ring at the price you promised me.

I'm sorry, ma'am.

I want my husband's ring.

I'm sorry, ma'am, we'll be holding that against our costs.

You're holding my ring hostage?

That's not how we see it, ma'am.

At this point Annie Black called me, the Shortcut Man. I'd known Annie a long time, she'd been a friend of Georgette's. I could feel her embarrassment over the phone.

"I can't pay eighteen hundred dollars for that thing. I don't have that kind of money. A thousand was stretching it. But I wanted to give it to Carl. Remind him who he is."

Now I remembered. She'd been having a little trouble with Carl. Nothing too serious, yet.

Henderson and Son occupied a choice location on the first floor of the Westside Pavilion. Their display cases were a feast of scintillating eye candy. I called them from across the concourse, explained my concern. They remained intransigent in the face of logic and goodwill.

Fine. I inquired about the half-yearly sales extravaganza I had seen advertised in their window. This they were happy and gratified to explain. It was Saturday coming. From ten till closing. Please stop in for some real bargains. Bargains they wouldn't even pass on to their mothers. But to me? Come on down! In conclusion, they were sorry they could do nothing for Miss Black. Costs had risen. We parted cordially.

Fine. I had given them every opportunity to see reason. My next call was to Rutland Atwater.

That Saturday, two hours after the sales extravaganza had begun, a large man entered and sat down on the couch. The couch where patient men waited for their wives and girlfriends to make their choices.

Horace Henderson Jr. was walking toward the potential client when a horrible odor attacked him. Young Henderson had studied a little physics in junior college. Unlike the eye and ear, and their modest apprehension of wave phenomena, an olfactory event meant particles were *in your nose*. In *his* nose. Young Henderson went down on one knee and violently offloaded the Persian food he had obtained in the Food Court.

Darla, the curvesome blond sales assistant, had gone to assist her boss's son when she too was afflicted. Up dyno-burbled her breakfast burrito.

From the back room, sensing something was wrong, Henderson Sr. motated into the fray just in time to see a brace of potential customers turn from his establishment and run away.

The odor was so vast it took the entire shop in its grasp. From across the room the fat man on the client couch was smiling and waving. Could he not smell?

Of course he couldn't smell. Rutland Atwater's olfactory glands were inoperative. Hence his vocation. He rose and walked toward the shop's proprietor, extending a hand. "I'm Rutland Atwater," he boomed. "Nice place you got here."

Henderson Sr.'s eyes had begun to water copiously. He removed his spectacles and wiped his eyes with a handkerchief. Woozily he realized the odor was affecting his powers of ratiocination. What did this big stink bomb want? "What do you want? What do you want, sir?"

From a downwind bench in Plummer Park, Rutland laid out the lines of his victory. I smiled at him. He had indeed proved to be a man of value. He had transformed his life. He was dressed in a fine suit, he drove a fine European sedan, cheerfully confessed to cultivating the pleasant company of fine European whores. Maarika was from Talinn. He was thinking of writing a book.

Me, I was grateful he now bathed twice a day. Whether he needed it or not. I paid him his fee, the difference between Annie Black's thousand dollars and the more modest sum the gracious Mr. Henderson had agreed to accept for his services. Along with his heartfelt apology.

"So, Rutland, tell me. Is there any other talent in your family?"

"I guess you don't know my brother."

"Didn't know you had a brother."

"Two of them. Each unusual men."

"No doubt."

"Evan is a philographer."

"What's that?"

"He deals in rare documents."

"You mean forgery?"

Rutland smiled. "Not quite. In his business it's called enhancement."

"Here in L.A.?"

"You bet."

Another document man. Besides Carl F. Hodgekiss. That was good to know. "And the last brother?"

"That would be Perry. He's a lock and key savant."

"A savant?"

"The best lock and key man in L.A. Hands down."

"How come I never heard of him before?"

"Because he's been working out of Chicago."

A lock and key savant. I thought of Lew and the odd brass key from Davis Algren's neck. And the wounded Mrs. Algren.

Rutland continued. "But Evan says Perry's got a problem."

"What kind of problem?"

"With cologne."

"How is cologne a problem?" How *was* cologne a problem?

Rutland shrugged, smiled. "I wouldn't know, Dick. I just wouldn't know."

Had smiling *cucaracha* Tavo Gonzales not been a card-carrying gang member, capable of cutting him into small pieces, Herman Mantillo would not have felt compelled to purchase the *diablo* ficus in the yellow pot for forty dollars. Luckily, Velma, his wife, would not be home for four days. He had time.

FIFTY-THREE

Lesbians
and Communists

Devi had not paid much attention to Dick Henry's various cautions and remonstrances. Felonius Monk, the cat, had to be fed. All twelve, lovable, orange-striped pounds of him. So, every day since the day after Rhonda-day, she'd paid a quick visit.

She was in the same jam everyone was at Ivanhoe. The sweet sticki-ness of being very, very well paid eventually was revealed as something she couldn't seem to get her feet out of. What line wouldn't she cross to keep the game going?

Dick had said something she really hadn't wanted to hear. The myth of moral neutrality. If you parsed your bullshit far enough, you got down to right or wrong. No in between.

And, if there were no in between, shit, well her job was—it was wrong. She couldn't put the truth on an application form. Previous job: whore-mistress.

But wasn't Dick's job wrong, too? Beside the point.

But someone had to do her job, didn't they? No. But someone *would* do it.

She had her house. She had her Lexus. She had a closet full of shoes. Imelda's dream.

What would she do now? If she were a free woman. Her old dream of being an actress. Too late now.

And her long-ago desire to be an actress wasn't pure to begin with. Because she didn't love acting. She hadn't shed blood doing little theater in North Hollywood for audiences of three drunks and a child molester. Statisically, one of them would not speak English.

You couldn't pay people to go to the theater in Los Angeles. And no wonder. All the theater companies subsisted on grants, gifts, and guilty ransoms. In return, the companies put on leaden, meaningful plays about lesbians and communists. And dutifully hired parolees to mop a floor here and there and smoke cigarettes in the parking lot. Subscription theater guaranteed an audience of sullen, disinterested seat-fillers.

No, she was no actress. She had just seen the beautiful women on screen and thought *I'm smart enough to do that*. And she was. But fate hadn't singled her out.

What did she love? Animals. Painting. Music. *Shoes*. Helping people.

People did come to her, lay their problems at her feet. Go home with the burden a little lighter. Maybe she'd be a nurse. She had enough money put away for tuition.

Nurses made good money, good enough. Not like she was making now, but good. And they could find work anywhere in the world. Even on those big ships. Cruise ships. Like the *Queen Mary II*. A yearlong *QM* cruise around the world cost $250,000. But a nurse would be paid to cruise.

But today, in the meantime, she would talk to Hogue's latest recruit. Heather Hill.

She'd finally talked with Melvin. Over the phone. He was pissed, but not steaming like he had been. She explained what had taken place. She'd thought Nazarian was dead, had called for help. Then he, Melvin, had intruded. Then had gone on to threaten the cleanup man. She didn't know the clean-up man would clean Melvin's clock, but the cleanup man wasn't the type of a guy you fucked with.

"What's his name?"

"I'm not going to tell you that, Melvin."

"Your relationship to him is worth more than your relationship to me?"

"Just let it go, Melvin. You're okay and you probably would've done just what he did."

"Where's the golden gun?"

Shit. "What golden gun?"

"You know what the fuck I'm talking about."

"No, I don't."

"Wolf saw it. So you saw it. Where is it?"

"I didn't see it." She should have anticipated his question and formulated a strategic reply. Now she was committed to a lie.

"Fuck you, Dev. We'll talk about it later." She was lying. He'd find the gun. When he made her tell the truth. Then Nazarian would pay through the nose. "You ready for Heather Hill?"

"Yes. She talk to Little Melvin?"

"She was too stupid to realize where advantage lay."

"In the backseat. In your Levi's."

"I don't wear Levi's. I wear Brioni. And she didn't get it."

"She'll get something else."

Melvin had to laugh. "She certainly will."

FIFTY-FOUR

Brown-Skinned Woman

In the bathroom, Paulita looked in the mirror. Usually she was pleased with what she saw. But not today. How many times had she been told, warned?

No married man leaves his wife for his mistress. They'll talk about love, they'll give you things, but in the end they'll betray you. Even if they didn't set out to do that. But they will. They'll betray you. Lastly, you dolt, said Lupe, who bore the scars to prove her point, the doctor is a European white man—and you are a brown-skinned woman.

So *what*? He loves me.

He may, dear. But when push comes to shove down, you'll go. You need a man of your own kind. Who'll understand you. And you'll understand him.

You're talking about your nephew.

Tavo would be perfect for you.

Except I don't like him.

That's beside the point.

Paulita studied the lump on her forehead. She looked like a moron. The two lumps. A lump on top of a lump. From those two assholes. White assholes.

In the first case, with the scrawny little man, the doctor had done

253

nothing to defend her honor. He had actually sat down and talked with the man! Tylenol with codeine did nothing for her soul. How dare Ulli talk about love after that insult! A man with Latin blood would have set things right. Quickly. Then talked. If necessary. If Scrawny was capable of speech.

Then the second man. The beast. She had bounded to her feet just in time to see what happened in the kitchen. Where Mrs. Wolf had left a yellow puddle under her chair. Where the doctor had been slapped three times across the face. And had just sat there!

In that moment, Paulita had realized she did not know Dr. Ulli Wolf. She had perceived his wealth: his home, his cars, his practice, his boat down at Cabrillo. She had perceived his wealth and interpreted that perception as power. Obviously, personally, he had none. In truth, demonstrated truth, the doctor was a coward. Well dressed, educated, sophisticated. And cowardly.

The scales fell from her eyes. He would never get rid of his dull cow. He would never marry her. And even if he was in the position to propose, how could she respect such a man? In fact, she felt pity for him. And pity ruled out love.

So she had not told him about the second time the front door had whacked her in the brains. She already had Tylenol with codeine.

She adjusted her uniform, pushed a dark tress of hair over her ear, walked back into the kitchen.

Dr. Wolf sat in the dark and dim of his library. In every way he had been bruised and abraded. He basted in a hot broth of humiliation. His wife, his mistress, and his nurse had all seen him cowed and abject, his buttocks presented high in the air, ready for alpha cock.

The scene played out in his mind over and over, on heavy rewind. From experience, he knew it was the vibrant color of emotion that made the scene so painful to contemplate. With time, the incident would fade to black-and-white and he would be able to file it away and forget about it.

But for now, put what twist he might on the affair, he looked and felt like the personification of soft, runny weakness. He had tried out his *I only did it for you* defense, but only after a halfhearted run at the *strategic restraint* explanation.

Gretchen looked at him with hard eyes.

As bad as Gretchen's stare made him feel, Paulita's downcast eyes, never looking into his own, made him feel absolutely wretched. She was embarrassed to look at him. Who knows what she might have seen? But she had to have seen something.

And, as far as an involved explanation went, she would be a potted plant. His English was good, if accented. Hers was accented and poor. Her German and his Spanish were nonexistent. Their communication, heretofore, had relied on emotion rather than precise understanding. Which meant it was beyond his power to precisely communicate *strategic restraint*. What about admitting fear, fear for Paulita's welfare? It hadn't worked with Gretchen, but that was because she knew him. It was his only chance with Paulita.

There was a knock at the door. He searched for a cheerful, confident smile but couldn't find one. He settled for *extremely busy*. "Come in."

Paulita poked her head in, eyes flitting across his face. "Mr. Shea calling, sir." She shut the door behind her. Not the slightest sign of the profound feelings that had existed so recently between them. *What had she seen?* He was going to lose her. Forever. Fuck Melvin Shea.

He leapt up, hurried around his desk, opened the library door. "Paulita."

Down the hallway, she turned around.

"Paulita, I need to see you. Right now." Fuck Gretchen. Wherever she was. Gretchen suspected nothing. Probably cared less. But even if she were in the kitchen, so be it.

The phone was blinking. Melvin. He picked it up. "Melvin, I'll have to call you right back. Five minutes." He hung up. Paulita walked back to the door of the library, hung back. "Come in, Paulita."

She entered, he shut the door behind her. She looked at him, alarmed. He closed their distance, grabbed her head, kissed her on the lips until she responded. Then he pushed her away, holding her arms.

"You've seen me at my worst, Paulita. But you don't know why I had to do what I did. I had to eat shit for *you*. *For you*. So you wouldn't be hurt. And now you won't look at me. *Look at me*." He looked into the utter mystery of her brown eyes.

"The truth is, I love you more than anyone or anything in this world. Do you understand me?"

She nodded.

From the front of the house the doorbell rang. They both jumped.

"I answer the door," she said.

"Okay." *The police*. The woman had floated to surface. Lipless, eyeless, nippleless.

Paulita returned a minute later, a basket in her hand. "Delivery," she said. She handed to him. In the basket, a manila envelope and bottle of champagne. What was *this*?

Paulita backed toward the door, he reached for her wrist. "I'll talk to you later. We'll do something." Maybe they'd go down to Cabrillo. Unwind.

Paulita exited.

Good. Maybe he could fix things. He could. He *would*. He remembered something he had heard in his twenties. *Most men never marry the woman they love the most*. Why is that, he recalled thinking. Now he knew. The hard surfaces of life pushed emotion to the periphery, where it conformed to available space. *Gott in Himmel*. How he loved Paulita.

Now what the fuck was this basket about. Hmmm. From Liquor Locker.

FIFTY-FIVE

Impervious

Devi pulled into the parking lot behind City National. The City National Tower was the last structure on the north side of Sunset Boulevard in West Hollywood before Beverly Hills began. Across the street was Hamburger Hamlet, her destination. She stopped, put the Lexus in park, handed her car over to the illegal immigrant in the red jacket. "Treat my baby, right, eh?" She smiled.

"Yes, missus." He handed her a ticket. Carlos never displayed humor with white people. He never knew exactly what they were talking about. Or their intentions. "How long gon' be, missus?"

"That's none of your business. Just park the car."

Devi crossed the street, looked back at her car. She hadn't meant to be rude to Pablo or whatever his name was. The Lexus rolled into the garage, disappeared. But this particular City National valet service, or at least this location, had an amusing story associated with it.

It the mid-nineties, some enterprising criminals had hatched a good and simple idea. When the white people valeted their expensive cars here, appropriate cars would be immediately rolled out the rear exit to commit felonies. Armed robbery, house invasion, drug delivery. No one suspected a Porsche Carrera or a Lamborghini coming to call. Hence the innocuous question, *how long gon' be, missus*? In other words, how long do we have to use your vehicle in a criminal enterprise before you return?

257

Devi entered the cool of the Hamlet. She hadn't met Heather Hill but she knew what the woman would look like. All Hogue girls looked the same.

There she was. Blond, ten feet tall, gazongas the size of basketballs. Devi extended her hand. "Heather?"

Heather stood up, reached for the woman's hand.

They both ordered salad. After a bit, conversation was the only alternative. "So what brought you to Hollywood, Heather?"

Her love for the theater.

How was the campaign going?

What campaign?

I meant your career. How were things going?

Well, she got thrown off *Gumshoe* the other day.

Really.

She was really messed up about it. But then realized God only shuts one door in order to open another.

I see. Would that second door be the Ivanhoe Special Talent Program?

Yes. She was so excited.

That's wonderful.

She couldn't wait to meet Howard Hogue.

I'm sure he feels the same way.

She'd asked Melvin a question the other day. He never answered.

What did you ask him?

Could her boyfriend get in the program, too? If he auditioned?

That would be some audition. Devi would pay to see that. The program is usually for girls, Heather.

Could there be an exception? In an exceptional case?

Uh, maybe. Though Devi couldn't imagine Howard performing the Rusty Trombone.

She took dancing lessons when she was younger.

Oh. Excellent. We'll build from there.

Melvin was right. The girl was amazing. She'd left her brains with the orthodontist, back in Lewiston, Pennsylvania. She had perfect white teeth. Suddenly Devi didn't feel like playing the game any longer.

"Heather. Can I ask you a question?"

"I wish you would. The answer is *Pretty Woman*."

"What was the question?" Now Devi was puzzled.

"What made me decide to become an actress."

"That wasn't my question."

"Oh. Well, go ahead. Ask away."

"What's your opinion of anal sex?"

"*Anal sex?* Do you mean—"

"I mean Howard Hogue's dick up your ass. How would you feel about that?"

The girl's eyes went wide and her mouth dropped open. "You're disgusting!" But then her expression slowly changed. She tipped her head to one side, studied Devi. "You're just testing me. Trying to freak me out. That's what you're doing, aren't you? Well, I can't be freaked out that easy. I want into the program. I want *in*."

Devi threw up her hands. The girl was impervious. Devi reached across the table, hand outstretched. Heather took it. "Welcome to the program, Heather. You're in."

Heather whooped. Other patrons of the Hamlet turned to see. "Thank you, girlfriend," said Heather, "thank you!"

"Now, listen. Howard will visit from time to time. He'll want to dance with you."

"To see how my lessons are going, right?"

"Uh . . . yes. And you'll also have to dress up the way he likes."

"Checking my style sense?"

"Uh . . . yes. He'll want to see you in a little black dress and green silk panties."

"Oh." Now Heather understood. "He likes to play Las Vegas. Like

259

Michelle Pfeiffer in the *The Fabulous Baker Boys*." Heather smiled. "I can play piano, too."

How about the skin flute? Devi gave up. Heather was a force of nature. A veggie-force. But a force nevertheless.

FIFTY-SIX

The Presence of God

From your friends at the San Pedro Film Company

Wolf didn't remember any friends there. In fact, he'd never heard of them. But he hadn't heard of a lot of people. He opened the envelope.

From the desk of Jack Ireland

Dear Dr. Wolf,

   Hope this finds you well. We're interested in your thoughts on this script. From a medical point of view, we'd love to have you as part of what we think will be a great team. Thank you for considering this.

Jack

Wolf opened the script. *San Pedro.* A. Davis.

His phone rang. *Melvin Shea.* He'd forgotten to call the bastard back. "This is Dr. Wolf."

"Hi, Doc. This is Melvin."

"What can I do for you, Melvin?"

"Nice day, today. Really nice day."

"Yes?"

"Fantastic day."

"Yes?"

261

"Such a good day that I thought, hey, I'll call up my old pal, Wolfie, and see what's up."

"Nothing is up." Did Melvin think that he was now his friend?

"What I was thinking was that we might take the old boat out for a spin. On the bay. Whaddaya say?"

Take the boat out? For the slimy pimp? "I'm afraid that's impossible, Melvin. Don't call again except for business. Goodbye." Was that emphatic enough? Good *Gott*. He settled into the screenplay.

Ten minutes later his reading creaked to a stop. He was ill. This was no screenplay. This was blackmail. His heart felt weak and pulpy in his chest. He wandered away from the pool, suddenly chundered his breakfast into the cactus garden.

His life . . . was falling apart. Piece by piece. What to do? *What to do?*

He had to think. He had to *think*. This strike at him—wasn't it also a strike at Hogue? Of course, it was. Had to be. In fact, it was aimed at Hogue, *through* him. He would call Hogue, lay it at his feet. Fucking Hogue. That's why he did what he did. Because Hogue, fucking Hogue, had asked.

He looked around. He couldn't stay here. Not here. Not right now. He needed to think. Where thinking was possible. Cabrillo. He'd have Paulita come down. That's what he'd do. *Hush, My Baby* was oceanworthy. Maybe a jaunt down to Ensenada.

He went back in the house. Paulita was in the kitchen. "Come to the library. I need to talk to you."

In the library, after the door was quietly closed, he again grabbed her arms. "What I want you to do now, right now, is take the rest of the day off, *with pay,* and get in your car and drive down to Cabrillo and wait for me. I have to make a few calls, but I'll be right behind you. Understand me?"

"Yes, sir."

"Yes, *who?*"

"Yes, sir.

"Don't call me *sir*."

"Yes, sir."

Christ. "Look. Get your car and go to Cabrillo. Right this second."

"What about your wife?"

"Forget about her. *You* go to Cabrillo. I'll be right behind you."

"Right now?"

"Right now."

"Okay."

His heart soared with her two syllables and he kissed her. "Go."

He opened the door, she stepped through, he shut the door.

One thing at a time. One thing at a time.

Hogue. He had to call Hogue.

Hogue put down the phone slowly. Montgomery and now Wolf. What did it mean? Bottom line, of course, was the bottom line. Money. Sooner or later, someone would stand up and present a bill. Montgomery and Wolf were affluent, true, but he was *resplendent*. Thus, these missiles were meant for him.

And where did Hames fit in? Maybe he had trusted the man too soon. All the trouble had begun after his employment.

Betty Ann. He remembered her as if it were yesterday. They had briefly stood side by side at his party long ago. Each had taken a flute of champagne from the gorgeous boy with the tray. She had looked from him to Montgomery, climbing the stairs, and back. "So . . . you're the man behind the man," she purred.

"That's me," he had agreed.

He was. Hale Montgomery was tall, and wonderfully handsome. Black hair. White teeth. His voice low, with an appealing gruffness. Women tottered when he smiled, melted when he laughed. The natural inclination was to add intelligence to his visible qualities. But that addition would be erroneous. Montgomery wasn't a moron. He was a twenty-watt bulb. Like Elvis, he would have made a fine truck driver or a janitor. A contented janitor. A cheerful trucker with a ready joke. But fate had decreed differently.

He had watched Betty Ann follow the Big Cluck up the stairs. From the landing she had winked at him. And he had winked back.

Then the horrifying revelation. Naked Montgomery, bloody hands raised in the air. How lucky he had been to clear the party as quickly as he had. Then Davis Algren walking in on him. As he stood with the doctor, looking down on the ruined Betty Ann.

But what did one do? Ruin the lives and livelihoods of many in exchange for the ruined life of one? So he had acted like the leader he was.

Leaders made decisions. Right or wrong. They made decisions. That's what *made* them leaders. You did your best and things played out from there.

The girl hadn't suffered. Not any more than she had already suffered. Slowly, very slowly, as the drug entered her bloodstream, the soft lights went dimmer and dimmer. Then there was no light.

Maybe she entered the presence of God.

FIFTY-SEVEN

All the Way to the Bing

At St. John's Hospital in Santa Monica, Odell Wallis waited at the back steps with the wheelchair. This was the celebrity entrance. Soon he'd be wheeling some rich lunatic motherfucker to the bing. Exhaustion.

Hi. I'm Smokin' Jack Wilton and I've been sober for fifteen minutes.

That had been the last one. Just yesterday. Except Wilton had been huffin' and puffin' in the limousine and had arrived blazingly high. Didn't matter. The two-week miracle cure began with wheels on premises. Odell helped Smokin' Jack into the wheelchair and rolled him right into the elevator, up the tower, and directly into the bing. *Exhaustion.*

CLANG went the steel door. Another sponge in recovery.

Ten minutes later, on his union break, out by the Dumpsters, Odell had called the *Hollywood TattleTale* and made a clean hundred bucks. Every job had its perks. And then there was LaShauna in Ultrasound. Who needed the Odell-stick every now and again. Craved it.

Now another limousine approached. Two or three every day. On average. Who would it be this time? All exhausted and shit. The limousine rolled to a stop. The driver exited, came around to open the door.

God damn. God *damn.* It was Stash Rockland. Well, it looked like

Stash Rockland. 'Cept this dude was crying. Oh, no . . . Stash wasn't a pussy, was he?

Pussy sobbed all the way to the bing.

CLANG.

Ten minutes later Odell was another hundred dollars richer.

FIFTY-EIGHT

Negative Buoyancy

The pace of the 405 South did nothing for his BP. His conversation with Hogue had lasted longer than he'd anticipated. He was thirty-five minutes behind Paulita.

Hogue was sending someone to pick up the script. He'd arranged to have it collected from his mailbox. He'd had a feeling Hogue wasn't as surprised as he pretended. Maybe Hale Montgomery had received a similar script.

Hale looked like a senator now. With the brains of a mailman.

Melvin should have been a mailman. Bitter and stupid, crouching under a sack, puling about sick pay. How odd, his phone call. Wanting to go on the boat. What could he have possibly been thinking? *Wait a second.* Wolf's heart went pulpy again. Maybe Melvin *needed* to go out on the boat.

What had he done to deserve this?

Like it was five minutes ago, he felt the resistance of the syringe's plunger as he pushed the morphine into the black girl's left arm. Blood made its complete circuit of the body in one minute. She'd been dead thirty seconds when Davis Algren walked in. It had been the only humane thing to do. Hadn't it?

He redialed Melvin.

"Hey, Doc," said Melvin, full of cheer. "Whazzup? I knew you'd call me back."

"Melvin. Why do you want to go out on the boat?"

"Doc! You cagey sumbitchy. Have I actually managed to get your attention?"

"Why do you want to go out on the boat *God damn it?*"

"Because we need to, Doc. We *need* to."

Wolf felt his colon gurgle. "We *need* to take the boat out." More dead people? "Are you saying what I think you're saying?"

"This is your fault, Doc."

"What is my fault?"

"You hired those two Mexicans. They called me. They wanted money."

"God damn it, Melvin. *Who* called you?"

"Luis and Ernesto."

"Luis?"

"Yeah. Luis and Ernesto. They were worried about Rhonda. They wanted to establish a health fund for her. They suggested cash."

"Cash?"

"That's what they wanted. That's why they're waiting on your boat."

"Waiting on my boat?" He was suddenly in the grip of a klong.

"Yeah, Doc. They're waiting on your boat. But don't worry. They're very patient. Real patient, in fact. Get it?"

A klong was a sudden rush of shit to the heart. Horns blared as Wolf drifted across the lane marker. He was having trouble catching his breath.

"So, like I said, call me back later. When you've got a time figured out. Best late at night. Like the other night."

The pimp clicked off.

Silence.

A driver in a red, boxy vehicle passed him, flipped him the bird.

Good *God*. Paulita would arrive at Cabrillo—in fifteen minutes. And if the hatch wasn't locked, she'd discover two dead countrymen in the salon. Which would go over big.

He couldn't let her do that. See that. He fast-dialed her.

"Hello?"

Jesus. Her voice sounded horrible. Maybe she'd already seen the slaughter.

"Darling, it's Ulli. Are you alright?"

"What *darling* are you talking to, Ulli?" said Gretchen, acid dripping from her tongue. Her faithless asshole husband hadn't been using that Cialis with her. Not that she cared. Been there, done that. "Paulita quit. Left her phone here on the counter."

No. No. No. Nooooo. *He'd called his wife?* What could he say? Jesus, what could he say? Whatever it might be, he couldn't think of it now. He hung up.

Drive, baby, drive.

Paulita finally fought her way to Cabrillo. She'd been crying the whole time. She parked too fast and scraped the bottom of her Toyota on the concrete parking bar. She looked in the rearview mirror. A smeary-eyed stranger with a bulging forehead stared back at her.

She hurried down the floating walkway to the boat. A group of people were standing around. The boat was gone.

The Harbor Freeway ended at Gaffey Street. He was two minutes away from the dock. His phone rang. It would be Paulita, staring at the dead men. "Hello?"

"Is this Dr. Wolf?" asked an unknown voice.

"Who's this?"

"This *is* Dr. Wolf?"

"Yes. Now who's this?"

"This is John Elston. Dockmaster at Cabrillo Marina."

Christ. They'd found bodies. "What can I do for you, sir?"

"I've got bad news, doctor."

Bodies. Police. Listeners. Recorders. He'd have to act surprised. "What kind of bad news?"

"I'm sorry, Doctor. Your boat has sunk at the pier."

FIFTY-NINE

Glastonbury

Perry Atwater had journeyed eighteen hundred miles from Chicago to Los Angeles. Once in Los Angeles, he rented office space in the old Desmond's building. Exactly beneath the offices of Nevil Jonson. I could hear Jonson's tasseled loafers above me as Atwater ushered me in.

Perry bore no resemblance to his brother Rutland. He was tall as a telephone pole, thin as a rail. Then there was the cologne. Undoubtedly he bathed in it. From a discount vat at a Rite Aid desert warehouse. It occurred to me the scent might also be efficacious as moth repellant. No holes in Perry Atwater's wool.

But he was immensely likable and bubbled over with good cheer. The weather had driven him west. At a certain point, you just couldn't take those Chicago winters. He thanked me profoundly for the change in his brother Rutland. A miracle turnaround. What had I said to him?

A man can only change from within, at the time of his own choosing. Rutland was ready to turn over a new leaf, I had merely, uh, provided the rake.

Then I showed him the key. A smile broke over his face. "I haven't seen one of these for a long time." He hefted the key. "These were the days. Extraordinary workmanship."

"What is it?"

"This key is made by the Bauer A.G. Company. Zurich, in the twenties."

"What's it for?"

"It's a customer key for a safe deposit box. Not many of those boxes still in service."

"Anyplace around here?"

"Just one place, if my information is right. Bank of America. In Echo Park. Happens to be the longest continuing-service bank branch in Los Angeles."

"How do you know that?"

Perry was pleased with himself. "Because that's the kind of thing I find fascinating. That branch has been open since 1942."

"And they have this kind of lock."

"Yes."

I picked up the key. It had a four-digit number on the handle, 1376. "This key'll get me in?"

Perry shook his head. "Not even. If I'm thinking of the right mechanism, it takes two keys. One key that's yours, a key the bank retains, and a four-letter combination. It's a key and combination *combination,* if you get me. If I'm right. You'll have to go see."

Mr. Glastonbury, one of the branch's oldest employees, studied the handle of Algren's key. "Thirteen seventy-six," he rasped. "Yes, that box is here."

He led me to a room in the rear of the bank. It was clean, had that old-metal smell. "This is thirteen seventy-six." He pointed to a box at eye level. Then he studied me. "This is not a procedure that requires identification. You either know your part or you don't."

"Well, I don't."

Glastonbury shrugged. "Then it'll be right here when you do."

I explained briefly. A man died with the key around his neck. Maybe important stuff was in the box.

"It's not that I don't want to open it for you. For any number of good causes. It's that I can't. It's a two-man operation."

"Can you explain how that works?"

"I'd be most happy to."

I had a feeling that Glastonbury's expertise had not been found as necessary as it once had been. The old man straightened his tie. Thin and red. "Excuse me for a second."

He returned with a key. Like Perry Atwater had surmised. "Look at your key," he said. "It has seven blades."

I studied my own. Yes. It had seven.

"I take my key," he began, "insert it in the mechanism, turn it clockwise half a turn. Turning my key moves the top three levers and one bolt lever. Then I leave the room with my key. Then you set your alphabetic dials to your secret code and insert your key. Setting the code allows you to turn your key another quarter turn. That quarter turn moves the bottom four levers and the remaining bolt lever. Then you scramble your secret code. So the banker can't see it. After you scramble your code, you're able to turn your key the final quarter turn, opening your box." Mr. Glastonbury smiled at me, proud to have been of service. "And that's what you do. And that alphabetical lock has 234,256 possible letter sequences."

"So your customer is totally secure."

"Exactly," said Mr. Glastonbury, with gravity, "so the customer is totally secure."

In other words, unless I got brilliant, which was unlikely, the oldest continuing-service bank branch in Los Angeles would crumble into dust before that safe deposit box was opened.

"Thank you, Mr. Glastonbury," I said, "you're a credit to your profession."

"No trouble at all, sir," returned the redoubtable Glastonbury, standing a little taller. "Always pleased to serve."

I left the branch chastened by his excellence. A last holdout from an earlier, simpler, perhaps better America.

God bless you, Mr. Glastonbury.

SIXTY

Where You Draw the Line

Chuck Hames had retrieved the script from Hale Montgomery's house. *San Pedro*. He stopped in Brentwood for an iced coffee, flipped through it. Instantly, he'd understood Hogue's interest and concern. The thinly disguised script was blackmail pure and simple.

Hogue, Montgomery, and Dr. Wolf were murderers. Davis Algren was an accomplice after the fact. Though Algren's account was now closed. He had seen to that.

He entered Hogue's offices and stopped at Helena's desk. Stopped at her desk out of courtesy. Helena was the gatekeeper. He had to keep her on his good side, not for himself—he could just walk right in—but for others he might find reason to send.

"Hi, Helena. Boss called me. Is he ready?"

Helena smiled up at him. "Let me see." Helena dialed, spoke softly, put the phone down. "He's ready."

He thanked her, entered. Now where was the emperor? Not at his desk. Not in the forest, not on the green—ah, at the conference table.

"Got it?" asked Hogue.

Hames put it down on the table. "Here it is."

"Did you read it?"

"Of course. It's blackmail."

"Exactly." Hogue studied his security chief. You could never trust anyone absolutely. But while their interests coincided with your own, you were pretty safe. "Sit down, Mr. Hames. What do you see next?"

Hames took a seat. "I think I pay a visit to the San Pedro Film Company. See what I can squeeze out. We know the bottom line."

"Money."

"Exactly. Have you had a call?"

"No."

"It's coming. Where do you draw the line?"

"Money. I draw the line at money. I don't pay. If you pay, you go on paying."

"Agreed." Hames did agree, but nothing was set in stone. Sometimes a little cash greased the skids. It depended on the point of view of the blackmailer. Sometimes the demand was a real, half-justifiable cry for justice.

Hogue's phone rang. Hames rose but Hogue gestured him to stay.

"This is Howard."

Hames watched the billionaire. Hogue cocked his head, then spoke. "Listen, Ulli, I'm in the middle of something right now. I'll call you back in five."

Hogue disconnected, looked at Hames. "That was Dr. Wolf. Guess what he just received?"

"A script. Should I go get it?"

"Yes. Then let me know what you find at San Pedro."

"I'll go by this afternoon. Recon. Then I'll go back tonight and look around."

Hogue nodded. "Sounds good, Mr. Hames."

Hogue watched Hames exit. *As long as their interests coincided.*

SIXTY-ONE

Prick Cop

Nazarian looked into the mirror. He was feeling a little better. Smokin' Jack Wilton. He felt like killing him. *Gumshoe* on hiatus. Until Smokin' Jack was rehabbed enough to continue.

Of course, that was why he loved Wilton. Hiatus would give him time to recover somewhat. The wires in his face would be gone by the time production resumed.

He needed another twenty-six days of shooting. *Gumshoe* would be in the can. Jack could go back to his crack. Or whatever the fuck.

The call from Lieutenant Peedner would have threatened the average man. But Eli Nazarian wasn't the average man. He knew the average man because he wasn't one of them. One of Gödel's incompleteness theorems: *No system could explain itself*. Hence arithmetic could not explain the workings of arithmetic, language required a metalanguage to define itself: noun, verb, gerund, participle, adverb.

Peedner said he could come into the station or they could meet informally.

Informally, of course. Why put himself into an unnecessary box?

Peedner climbed Coldwater from the valley, made a right on to Mulholland. He knew a number of things:

Nazarian had brutalized Rhonda Carling.

Rhonda Carling had been checked into Fairfax Convalescent by Dr. Wolf. Wolf had been assisted by two Hispanics.

Rhonda had supposedly checked out of Fairfax Convalescent under her own name.

Rhonda's current whereabouts were unknown.

Wolf, with Montgomery and Hogue, had previously disposed of an inconvenient woman. At sea.

Wolf owned a yacht currently moored at the Cabrillo Marina.

Like he and Dick had agreed, there was no perfect justice in the world of men. A world of wealth and influence. Betty Ann Fowler was at the bottom of the sea and nothing besides an admission would convict the men who did it. The screenplay was hearsay, nothing more. But maybe the information it contained could help Rhonda's case. Her *case*. Rhonda herself, he had the feeling, was beyond help.

Nazarian had suggested the Glen Centre, right off Mulholland, where the heavenly smells of the Beverly Glen Deli were now killing him by degrees. *Liquid nutrition*. "What's this about?" he asked the hard-eyed cop after introductions.

"It's about Rhonda Carling. You know her?"

Nazarian had played out this conversation in his mind.

Denying he knew her was outright falsehood. Detectives were smart. They dealt with liars every day. Not as good a liar as he was, but still. "Yeah, I know her."

"How do you know her?"

"As an actress."

"She's been in your movies?"

"No. But I thought perhaps I could use her."

"Use her for what?"

"A part in *Gumshoe*."

"With Jack Wilton."

"Fucker's in rehab now."

"You're on hiatus?"

"Yes."

"Did you visit Miss Carling?"

"Yes."

"What did you do over there?"

"We read her part in the script."

"Were you going to hire her?"

Nazarian saw a glint of opportunity, used it. "I didn't think so."

"Did Miss Carling have any other visitors during the time you were there?"

"No. Well, not to my knowledge."

"When did you leave Miss Carling's?"

"Sometime after a lousy fuck."

"But what time was it?"

"I don't know."

"You don't know?"

"I don't know what happened. I was drugged. Assaulted. I woke up at Dunkin' Donuts in a cardboard box."

"With Mr. Shea?"

"Yes. He was in the box, too."

"You had not seen him at Miss Carling's residence."

"No."

Nazarian had a huge ego, Peedner could see it. He decided he'd tweak it. "You say you were assaulted. Sexually assaulted?"

"No. Common assault." He tapped his jaw. It was beginning to ache again. "My jaw's wired shut."

"Sorry to hear that." Real sorry. "Have you heard from Miss Carling since?"

"No. Why?"

"Well, apparently she was assaulted as well. She ended up at Fairfax Convalescent."

"I see."

"You *see*? You didn't know?"

The cop was trying to trap him. Stick to the truth as closely as possible. "No. I didn't know."

"You haven't called around to see what may have happened that night?"

"Look here, Lieutenant. Let me be clear. I'm a selfish prick. I don't give a shit about anybody else but me. If you drove off Mulholland on your way home, I wouldn't care. It would be your problem. Your life—your problem. Rhonda Carling fucked up that night? Didn't know about it. Haven't called about it. Don't care about it. See?"

"So you never cared to find out what really happened to you that night."

Prick cop. "Come on, Lieutenant. You know what Rhonda Carling's about. Maybe she sensed her reading wasn't good and decided to fuck me up. What else happened—I don't give a damn."

Nazarian sat back. "My jaw is broken. And it's healing. I have a star in rehab. That's as complicated as I want things to get right now. Okay?"

Peedner stared at the liar, said nothing. "Not quite okay, but it'll have to do, I guess. For now. The problem is Miss Carling. She was admitted to Fairfax Convalescent in the early morning after your visit. Yesterday she checked out. Nobody's seen her since."

"Just gone."

"Yup. Just gone."

"And?"

"The injuries she suffered that night would have prevented her from just signing out. So where did she go?"

"She checked out under her own power?"

"Supposedly."

"No one's filed a missing persons report?"

"Not yet."

"Then I don't see how this is your business."

"Officially, it isn't. Unofficially, it is. Like our conversation right now."

"Well, good luck with it."

"Thank you, Mr. Nazarian." He slid his card across to the director, trotted out his TV dialogue line. From *Dragnet* to *NCIS*. "If you remember anything else, Mr. Nazarian, please give me a call."

Prick cop.

"And, of course," added Peedner, "we'll be looking more closely into the events of the night in question."

"You do that."

"We will, Mr. Nazarian. Our job is to protect and serve."

Nazarian watched him go, tried not to inhale through his nose. It was the corned beef that was torturing his soul. Fucking prick cop.

SIXTY-TWO

Melvin Points a Gun

He rang Melvin. Went to message.

Fucking prick cops. The golden gun. He'd had little flecks of memory. Dancing around with it. Waving it in the air. The gun would place him at the scene. But it wouldn't prove anything. He'd told Peedner that he'd been there. But it could make things sticky.

Howard would be suspicious. Suspicion would roll downhill. First, on top of the blackmail Nazi, who'd gotten her admitted to Fairfax. Second, on top of Melvin. Melvin, on the way out, would lash out, create a shit storm. Then the doctor would roll over, tell all he knew, and Howard would make sure his golden director never worked in this town again.

He rang Melvin again.

"This is Melvin."

"Melvin, this is Eli. It's been hard to get a hold of you."

"I've been busy, dude. Whazzup?"

"What's up is I need to get in over at the El Royale."

"That might be dangerous. They might be looking for Rhonda."

"Who gives a shit? No missing persons report has been filed yet."

"How do you know?"

"Because I just talked to a cop on the case." His jaw was starting to ache again. "I gotta get in over there. Right now."

"I'm a little busy, Eli."

"If I go down, you go down, Melvin. Don't be stupid. You got keys?"

"Uh . . . yes."

"Then meet me over there. I don't want to have to talk to Hogue."

"Hogue? Are you *blackmailing me*?"

"Easy, Melvin. I don't want to go to Hogue and tell him I lost the golden gun, that's all. That story could get involved."

Fucking asshole Armenian. Hadn't even begun to appreciate all that had been done for him. "Okay, okay. Meet me over there in half an hour."

"Fine."

The locks had not been changed. Melvin's key turned. They stepped into the late-afternoon shuttered dimness and listened. It was absolutely quiet. The smell wasn't good.

Nazarian walked directly to the table by the couch. Nothing, top or bottom. Nothing under the couch itself, nothing behind or under the pillows.

Nothing on the bookshelves. And nothing in the cabinets under them. Melvin looked at Asshole. "Where else were you? Were you in the bedroom?"

"Probably. I was all over the place." Nothing in the big drawers of the rolltop desk. "God *damn* it."

"Why'd you bring the gun here?"

"Why? I don't know. It must have seemed a good idea at the time."

"You don't remember much."

"Fuck you." Melvin was a flunky and he didn't like flunkies. "Can you look in the kitchen?"

"There's nothing in the kitchen."

"How do you know?" Nazarian stared at Melvin.

"Uh . . ."

Nazarian was in his face in a second. "You know there's nothing in the kitchen because you were here that night." He grabbed the flunky's shirt. "When I was out cold, you son-of-a-bitch. You know where the gun is, don't you?"

"N-never saw it."

Nazarian twisted the fabric of Melvin's shirt. "Where's the fucking gun?"

Melvin shoved Nazarian away from him. "Keep your hands to yourself, motherfucker."

"Where's the fucking gun, Melvin?"

"I said I never saw it."

"Then what did you see?"

Melvin saw red and it all came out. "I'll tell you what I saw, you asshole. I saw the girl you beat the shit out of. Saw her lying on the couch, her face smashed. Her tits burned. Blood all over the fucking place. You should see the kitchen, motherfucker. You'd be proud of yourself."

Nazarian's hand rose from his side, fast as a snake, slapped the flunky's face. WHACK.

Melvin went down. Nazarian kicked him in the ass, stared down at him. "Don't you dare judge me. *You?* You're a pimp! A drug dealer! A fucking nothing. A handy-boy for that rich pig. I bet he fucks your ass, too. Don't ever judge me. Don't you *ever* judge me."

Melvin found all fours, got to his feet.

"Now where's the gun, Melvin? Where's my fucking gun?"

Melvin's face was numb from the slap. "I have the gun," he said.

Cold delight filled Nazarian's face. "Where is it?"

Melvin reached into his coat, pulled out the 9mm that had sent Luis and Ernesto to their eternal reward. "It's right here, Eli. You Armenian pig."

Melvin extended his arm, pointed the gun at Nazarian's mouth. "I don't know where you came from. Your mother must have been an animal, too. You're barely human. I set you up with a beautiful woman and you ruin her. And threaten fifty other lives with your incredible carelessness, your self-centered-ness. Who are you? *Who are you?*"

Nazarian took a step backward. Melvin followed, smiling. "You know what happened to Rhonda? You pig. You know what happened? We had to put her down. Put her out of her misery. And you know what we did it with? That's right. Your golden gun, baby. Your golden gun. With her blood and fluids all over it and your fingerprints right there. We were careful not to disturb them. *Thank you, Mr. Hogue, for this beautiful gun. I'll treasure it always.* Why didn't you just suck his cock while you were at it? You owe me big-time. I should blow your worm-infested head off."

Oh, flunky, flunky. I have you now. You're mine. *I should blow your worm-infested head off.* You flunky cunt. *Should blow.* Nazarian took a step forward. "Don't wave that thing around, Melvin. Shoot me." He took another step toward the gun. "Shoot me, Melvin. Right here." He opened his mouth, pointed at it. "Shoot me, Melvin. If you've got the guts."

Melvin took a step back, kept his aim. Killing Rhonda and the boys was one thing. Executing the Armenian Pig, a moment of exquisite sweetness, justified ten times over—what it really meant was the end of everything in life he'd come to enjoy. Prison or no prison, Hogue would sunder him like a gangrenous limb.

"Shoot me, Melvin," urged the pig.

Melvin saw the blue hole in Nazarian's forehead and watched him topple backward, dead before he hit the ground. He lowered the Glock. The Pig wasn't worth his life. "You're not worth it, Eli."

Nazarian leapt forward in that second, wrenched the weapon from Melvin's fingers, threw his right elbow into the pimp's face, hitting him between the eyes. Down went the pimp.

An endorphin cocktail of satisfaction physically rolled over Nazarian's body. Almost like an orgasm. He was filled with twisted joy. Nazarian cocked the gun, stepped over his adversary. "That's the difference between you and me, Melvin. I *will* kill you."

Melvin held up his hand, squirmed away. Nazarian leaned down, pushed the barrel against the pimp's expensive teeth. "Suck the gun, Melvin. Suck it."

Melvin's mouth worked independently of his will. It was in the back of his throat, gunpowder bitter, metallic, nauseating. He sucked the gun.

Nazarian watched his total domination of another human being. He pulled the gun out, dragged Melvin to his knees by his hair. "Time to suck something else, Melvin."

Melvin, eyes on the floor, did nothing. Nazarian slapped him round-house, again, knocked him down again. Raised him by the hair again. "Open up for Eli, Melvin." The pain in Nazarian's face had completely disappeared. "Open up." He was running on high-octane savage bliss. Zzzzzip.

Melvin closed his eyes. Opened his mouth.

Nazarian left him in the darkness of the apartment. After a bit Melvin got up. He thought he would be instinctively sick but he wasn't.

He remembered the taunt from school days. What do you call a man who's only sucked one tiny little dick in his whole life? *Cocksucker.*

Certainly, he had participated in the same act a thousand times. Albeit from the different point of view. He had never felt that he had visited an indelible shame on those who pleasured him. It was not abnormal or disgusting. And all those acts had been consensual, more or less.

More or less.

Millions of men had done what he had just done. Thousands would do it this very night. In Los Angeles. In Greater Los Angeles. For the same reasons a woman might. Love, thrill, money, gratitude, inebriation, barter, betrayal, revenge, force. He had been no different.

Then he smelled his own breath and relived the hand knotted in his hair and the bestial gruntings above him. He ran to the bathroom and was sick.

He rose, saw the mirror in front of him, stared into the dead eyes and tangled hair of his reflection. *Cocksucker.*

The enzymes and compounds and molecules of hatred suffused him, flooded into his brain, and he went down on one knee and retched.

In the medicine cabinet was a bottle of green mouthwash. He drank out of the bottle, gargled until he couldn't stand the burn. He blew it all over the mirror. It ran down, puddled on the sink.

Nazarian.

Nazarian would die. Nazarian would die. Slowly. Bleeding from the balls that were no longer there.

But how.

How? With the golden gun, of course.

The golden gun would lure him like shit called flies. Then Nazarian, begging, would pay the ultimate price. Melvin Shea, master of life and death, merciless, would be cleansed. Purified in blood.

Who had the gun? Well, the Nazi had seen it. So Devi had it. Or had let the Mystery Man take it. It was that simple.

He'd been easy on Devi. Allowing some of his rage and pain to fade in the rip and roar of life.

But, yea, verily, his attention was distracted no more.

Devi.

The gun.

But how would he get hold of Devi?

Then the solution hit him. Sylvette.

SIXTY-THREE

The Purview
of His Expertise

For one aspect of the San Pedro Film Company office setup, I had turned to Myron Ealing for advice. I explained my scenario, that the opening of the safe would trigger surveillance photography. Who did I need, and how much did he cost?

Myron smiled and spread his hands. "I'm your man, Dick, *I'm* your man. Because what you need is a pyrotechnician."

"*You?* You're a pyrotech?"

"You bet I am."

Myron went on to describe his career in amateur munitions. Slight of build, then, and unprepossessing by nature, he would've been shunted aside in the social milieu at Hollywood High had not he displayed his explosionary skills. After lifting a St. Vincent de Paul box eight hundred feet straight up into the sweet night air during a track meet, he settled in as a popular and necessary man about campus.

"It sounded like God Himself," chortled Myron. "All I forgot were the Ten Commandments."

"Sounds like you used a little too much power."

The big man wiped his eyes. "Earn as you learn, baby." Then, brow furrowed, he directed his genius to the current situation. "What we need is flash powder," said Myron, pencil in a scramble. "Six parts potassium permagnate, two parts sulfer, one part powdered aluminum."

Where do you get these things?

Simple. The nursery and the paint store.

How much do you need?

A couple of tablespoons, altogether. And a sparking device. Frictive or electric.

Myon would go electric, with a nine-volt battery trailing two leads. One lead was attached to the safe door. Opening the door would drag one exposed lead over the stationary exposed lead in the safe, completing the circuit in the flash powder. The mixture would produce more light than sound. There would be some smoke. If there were indeed an intruder, a clear photograph could be obtained.

"Can you assure me this won't kill anybody, Myron?"

"Look. I'm well within the purview of my expertise." Myron dug into his barrel of stale cheese-corn.

"Okay," I said.

SIXTY-FOUR

Fifty Pieces of Silver

Chuck Hames's call to the Hollywood Professional Building had led to a message carousel. Hames didn't leave messages. He made a short recon visit, went to the office itself, 317, it was locked. Fine. He would visit later that night.

The building was on the corner of Cahuenga and Hollywood Boulevard, across the street from World Book & News. After hours it was locked, though you could ring upstairs. If you knew someone and wanted to announce yourself. Hames hung around the book stand to see what foot traffic on the boulevard was about. Not too many, not too few. He decided to go in. The entry lock, as he had noted earlier in the afternoon, was a Schlage.

Hames checked his watch, broke out his picks, and began. He was in just inside of eighteen seconds. Public safety was a private joke. The common door lock served only to keep out those who didn't want to come in.

He silently climbed the stairs in his toed, thin-soled boots, placing the heel first, rolling forward on the outside of the foot. Step and wait. Step and wait.

Reduced lighting on, but no people seen or heard. He reached 317. Another stupid Schlage. Thirteen seconds. He was in.

• • •

"I'm not a cop," said the man. "I'm looking for Mr. Algren for a good reason."

"Then why aren't you here in broad daylight?"

"Because I won't find Mr. Algren during daylight hours."

Which Danny James had to admit was the truth. Dave could be anywhere during the day. But, semireliably, at night, he could be found behind Crowned Heads, a club on Cosmo Street south of Hollywood Boulevard.

The man had approached him with a picture to look at. Danny had shaken his head. "I don't look at pictures for less than five dollars. My time's important." The man had given him ten. And had readily interpreted his reaction to Davis Algren's photo. Dave was short for *Davis*. Who would have known?

"So where could I find Mr. Algren?" said the man.

The man was well dressed and physically imposing. Though not by size. Sinuous, latent power. "You're not a cop?" Danny had asked, though he knew the man wasn't. He was something else.

He was not a cop. He was here for a good reason. If Davis Algren was the Davis Algren he was looking for, Mr. Algren's homeless days were over.

"Dave's come into money?" Danny was happy and envious. You always hoped for deliverance. The shot out of the blue. The deus ex machina in real life that would be abhorred in your fiction.

He and Dave had a long-standing argument. Could a story about deus ex machinas utilize a deus ex machina to extract a character from peril? Dave had known all of the theories of writing, though he had shown Danny nothing of his work.

Danny's own work had sent him straight to the meth pipe. When that particular, diabolical sublimate was inhaled, his novel, possibly the Great American Novel, appeared softly before the eye of his mind in golden light. Spare, terse, complete, brilliant. There for the taking.

Yet how sneakily the second hit crept up on him. The second hit wished not to work, it wished to celebrate that which, in all ways but one, was already complete. The third hit realized the hard work would be done on the morrow, when hard work would be more appropriate. Today was joy in the moment.

The man smiled at him. From his pocket he withdrew fifty dollars and put it in Danny's hand. "Take me to Mr. Algren."

So he had walked the man to Cosmo Street and pointed him down to the Crowned Heads.

Fifty dollars! That meant a vial of pleasure that would last and last. As long as he didn't share it with those grasping, ambitionless shitheads who'd never worked a day in their fucking lives.

His novel announced itself as he hurried to Pla-Boy Liquor. Spanish Eddie always had the good rock. His novel, *at last*. It would be called *Arc of the Rainbow*.

Later that night he'd heard the terrible news. Dave had been killed. Out behind the Crowned Heads. His throat ripped out. Danny had almost thrown out the little bit that remained of Spanish Eddie's rock. Eddie had ripped him off. Anyway.

But there was no getting around the facts. He had judased Dave. Fifty pieces of silver. His friends, outraged, drunk, sorrowful, raged on and on. They didn't recognize Judas in their midst.

Only the sublimate drove out the guilt, but that was on hit five, when the novel had diminished to a distant speck.

Finally a solution presented itself. How had Judas died? He consulted the Bible and found that Judas had died in two different, incompatible ways. In Matthew he had hung himself. In Acts he had fallen headlong and burst asunder, his bowels gushing out.

Maybe humankind was built better today; forty generations later, he'd never heard of anyone bursting.

He considered hanging himself. It was cheap, it was simple. A hook, a rope, a chair. But hanging took time. And most people who hung them-selves apparently had second thoughts, clawing at their ropes, going pur-ple. Eyes bulging, their last thought clearly visible: *What the fuck did I do this for?*

He needed technology. Instantaneous deliverance. A bullet. Okay. Death by cop or his own hand. Maybe. He possessed no gun.

Defenestration. One of his favorite words. No. He was afraid of heights. At thirty-two feet per second per second. Poison. No. Agonizing. He wasn't into agony.

Electrocution. No. Wasn't sure how to do that. You didn't want to blow your balls off and live to tell about it. As you sang soprano in the soup-kitchen Christmas chorale.

But then, as he stood on Hollywood Boulevard, it came to him. In a rush of dieseled air. In the draft of the 217.

The bus. One step and BANGO—the next life. Instantaneous, irrevo-cable, foolproof. For the next few days, every time he would look to see what bus was running, it would be the 217.

That was no coincidence. The 217 it would be.

He missed Dave terribly. Their long talks about Bukowski, Fante, *Factotum, Women, Ask the Dust.* If Bukowski had brought it home, while brav-ing three hundred hangovers a year, why couldn't they? They could! They could! The gray vapor traveled the glass pipe and Cosmo Street wasn't so bad after all.

The night of his prospective journey approached, then arrived. He was ready. Spiritually, physically, mentally. He mingled with his friends, looked at them, to remember them, to celebrate them.

He walked slowly up toward Hollywood Boulevard. He listened to the cheerful cacophony spilling out of Amoeba Music. He crossed Sun-set, smelled the two-for-a-buck tacos at Jack in the Box, of course they weren't made of meat. Not even rat meat. *Rattus rattus.* He listened to a busker on the corner with his out-of-tune guitar. Couldn't play, couldn't sing. Probably make a fortune.

At Selma he crossed against the light, waved silently at the Spotlight across the street. Cocksmokers. Not his thing, but whatever gets you through the night, ye merry gentlemen. Life is short.

A Rolls-Royce passed, he hoisted the bird. Fuck Thurston Howell III and his liver pâté. At least the rich did not live significantly longer than the poor. Sure, they got another fifteen at the bitter end, in their plaid pants and soft loafers, wearing adult diapers and hearing aids, but they didn't get an additional, healthful, forty or fifty. The class of '67 would all pass by 2042 or thereabouts. No way around it. Unless you put your hand on the tiller.

Like he was going to do. He arrived at the bus bench early. The 217 wasn't due for ten minutes. If life was foreordained, had the final tumbler fallen into place when he sat down? On this particular bench? It was a warm night. He reached into his pocket, removed the three-by-five card.

I killed Dave Algren. I'm sorry.

When they found him, what was left of him, they'd find the card. And his sin would be expiated.

Hames, with his LED penlight, moved silently around the outer office. It was a setup. There was nothing here. It was a waiting room. A table, a couch, a bookcase, a small stack of trades. Old ones. But no new ones. Maybe from World Book & News. Leftover product they couldn't move.

The inner office was as spare as the waiting room. And old desk and chair, a safe. A single folder lay on the desk, closed.

Hames opened it. In it was an official police photograph. The man he had terminated sprawled between two Dumpsters. He felt his heartbeat in his eyes. Certainly, it was no coincidence that this one photo should be here. What was the purpose of the San Pedro Film Company? How did they know *he* was coming? *Did* they know he was coming?

The San Pedro Film Company knew a lot of things. What they had put together was debatable. They knew where the script came from. They knew the true identities of the characters inside. They knew that Algren had been killed because of someone's fear of exposure. They would know of Hale Montgomery's hospitalization. They would know of Wolf's meltdown at Cabrillo. The fact that he, Hames was here, proved that their opponent was the last man standing—Howard Hogue. What was his own picture here to tell him? He was probably being filmed. There were two smoke detectors on the ceiling. Were they phonies?

This wasn't a real office. There were none of the signs of human habitation. No CDs, no cigarette butts, no trash, no loose pens and pencils. It was a purposeful setup.

He searched the desk. There were five more copies of the incriminating script. He took them though he knew it didn't matter. The script, by now, existed electronically, available to download when the situation decreed. Hogue would have to make some kind of deal. There was no way around it.

He turned to the safe. Its squat, cast-iron heaviness sang its song to him. It was the chosen endpoint of the entire evolution. What was in the safe?

He studied it. The safe would be open because they wanted him to have what was inside.

But should he open it? How would he explain to Hogue that he had come all this way and *not* opened it.

He reached for the handle, trying to feel its aura with the open palm of his hand.

His hand rested on the handle. He lifted, it moved, he pulled the door—

When the transit wire crossed the stationary wire, the circuit was closed and the flash powder ignited. Myron, in his office directly overhead, knew instantly he'd again underestimated the power of his materials.

• • •

First Hames was blind, then he was deaf, then he was burned, finally the door almost tore off his hand. But to Hames, everything had occurred at once. He was blown back over the desk to the floor.

Instinct guided him to his feet. Distantly he knew, from combat experience, that he was now undergoing an acute stress reaction. Though his critical thinking would be cloudy, and his ability to prioritize disabled, an abundance of catecholamines at his neuroreceptor sites would facilitate spontaneous or intuitive behaviors. Don't think. Act.

His eyes had been burned. He could see in excruciating periphery, but directly ahead he was blind.

Get out.

He was breathing, coughing in the smoke. His right hand was useless. He wondered, in the darkness, if it was still there. His left hand probed forward, felt the rippled, undulating glass of the door's interior. He found the door handle, turned it, stepped into the hall. Cool as heaven.

The world was silent, but the light in the hall was overpowering. Shutting his eyes was to scrape burned corneas; instead he shaded his pupils with his numb right hand. Feeling the wall with his left hand, he negotiated the corridor. The stairs were here somewhere.

His foot tried to find the left side of the staircase and his left hand found the rail. In that manner he descended from the third floor to the second. Again, he sought the top stair with his left foot. This time he miscalculated, slipped. He rolled down the staircase, landing heavily in the building's entryway. A knee was damaged, some ribs had cracked.

Get out. Get out.

He rose to his feet, tottered. Keep going. Keep going. Never stop. Don't rest. He found the door, opened it, stepped into the night.

The concussion and the flash of light reminded Danny James that he had not seen all that was to be seen in this world. The 217 would be coming by directly. He was ready. He spun and stared up, hearing the shrill cry of the smoke alarm.

A bomb. A bomb in Hollywood. Islamists. Islamists in Hollywood.

The door to the Hollywood Professional Building opened and a man staggered out. Dude was in bad shape. Danny went over. Dude's face looked toasted.

But through the toast Danny realized he was looking at the man who'd been asking about Dave. The man who *murdered* Dave.

Jesus Christ. No question. It was him. Didn't seem like the dude could see very well.

Down the street came the 217. Epiphany. Danny reached into his pocket, took out the three-by-five card, put the card in the man's coat pocket. Keep walking, dude, he said to the man. Keep moving. Dude smelled like gunpowder. Dude *couldn't see.*

At the wheel of the 217, listening to Marvin Gaye, Lucius Connor decided he could make the light. From the shadows down from the corner two men hurried toward the street.

Stay back, fools. You already done missed your bus.

Connor slammed on the brakes, but twenty-five thousand pounds traveling at forty miles an hour was a force that could not be mitigated.

Chuck Hames was thrown across Cahuenga in a line drive, landed on the sidewalk in front of Popeye's Chicken.

Odell Wallis had just departed World Book & News when he heard the flat thud of collision and turned to see a flying man. *"Damn,"* said Odell.

Odell hurried to the corner and looked down on the man. Nope. No one he recognized. This was just plain, garden-variety, ordinary death. Man versus bus. The numbers weren't with you.

No case for the *TattleTale.*

SIXTY-FIVE

Magic Jack

Hale Montgomery had cried every waking second for twenty-four hours. Then awoke with mind and purpose clear, tears dry. He gathered his clothes, his effects, walked out of the hospital. No Randle McMurphy for him.

A taxi from the queue rolled up. Montgomery slipped in, met the cabbie's eyes in the rearview mirror. A Paki. Somewhere over there. Down there. Whatever. He watched the *where to?* die on the tip of the dark man's grateful tongue. Hale Montgomery was his passenger! He acknowledged the cabbie's awe with a lordly tip of the head. "Twenty-second Street Landing, San Pedro. Can we do that?"

The cabbie nodded. Always say yes to the customer. No matter what the question or who he was. Or how condescending the question. Even if he didn't know where it was. He could find it.

The man in the backseat. His face was familiar. TV. A TV huckster-wallah. That's *right*. The guy who sold the Magic Jack.

Huckster-wallah's tip was meager. Which meant the Magic Jack was bullshit. You didn't tip like a weasel unless you made weasel-money.

Hale Montgomery was going whale watching. If he hurried, he was told, he could make the next run. He hurried.

He took deep drafts of the ocean breeze. It was foggy and cool but it would burn off in early afternoon. The other passengers recognized him, like they always did—looking down when he lifted his gaze. After a few minutes, when the shyness wore off and they realized they were on the same boat with Hale Montgomery, they waved and he would wave back. Youngsters too small to have seen his work achieved awe once removed by way of their elders. Eyes wide, the little people waved and giggled, then retreated back into the safety of their friends.

But not Becky Thompson, age five. "I know who you are," she said defiantly, to his face.

"Who am I?"

"You're Magic Jack."

Magic Jack. He hadn't heard that one. Did it involve a beanstalk? Maybe it was a modern fairy tale. Magic Jack was a kid with two dads. "Who's Magic Jack?" he asked the little black-haired girl.

"He's cheap," said Becky. "He's cheap all year."

Montgomery tapped his chest, infinitesimally insulted—but insulted nevertheless. "I'm not Magic Jack. I'm Hale."

"I know."

"You know what?"

"I know who you are," said Becky.

"Who am I?" asked Montgomery.

"You're Magic Jack."

Arguing with this little girl was like arguing with his ex-wife. There was no point. You couldn't win. Not that logic wasn't on your side. But you couldn't win. When you're in a hole, stop digging.

All girls were wise for their age. Girls were born women, boys were born boys. Then the boys grew up and cleverly insisted on making their important decisions in the dark.

He pulled one shoe off, then the other. Then both socks. He grinned at the kids, waggled his toes. Then he unzipped his windbreaker, dropped it onto the seat.

By the time he had unbuttoned his shirt, an older lady had tapped the helmsman. "I think Mr. What's-his-name is going for a swim."

"A *swim?* Who?"

The woman pointed. Hale pulled off his slacks.

"Whoah, mister," said the helmsman. No shit, Sherlock, they'd blame him for this lunatic. Like they blamed him for everything else.

Montgomery looked down at his boxers. *SpongeBob?* He'd grabbed them in the dark. Another bad decision. Who'd bought these things? The children were giggling and pointing.

"Goodbye, children," he said formally, with a bow. The helmsman was coming.

But too late.

Hale dived into the cold water.

He swam down and down and down. Like Martin Eden. But for a different purpose. Always loved Jack London. He felt strong and powerful and in no need of air.

Maybe fear and panic came with measuring your distance from the surface. No measurement here.

Down and down. Smooth. Strong.

And, then, there she was. Like no time had passed. She'd been waiting for him.

They communicated outside the crude medium of spoken language.

Have you been waiting for me, Betty?

Yes.

I didn't know.

How could you have known?

You're as beautiful as the day I last saw you.

Yes. Yes, I am.

You're completely healed.

I am reassembled.

That's what you wanted, isn't it?

Yes. Time had scattered me. You healed me.

We'll never be parted, right?

Never. Are you ready?
Yes.

She opened her arms. He moved into her embrace, surrendered his individuality, his distinctions, his parameters. He was flow, it was confluence, all was well.

SIXTY-SIX

All in the Wind

Dr. Wolf stood by the slip and looked down. The bridge clearance on *Hush, My Baby* was twenty-four feet exactly. The radar mast, a top-of-the-line Raymarine, stood up an additional four feet, eight inches. Which meant that the marina was twenty-eight feet, four inches deep in this particular channel berth. Because only a four-inch white plastic twig stood above the water. The only unrefracted visible aspect of his treasured craft. Which had cost him a million dollars cash and a sizable trade.

Until he had looked into the water himself, he had hoped against hope that a jest of celestial proportion was being visited upon him.

But it was no joke. God had raised his voice against him and against God there was no defense. His particular acts of evil he had long since put into the balance with the good he might have done. Betty Ann Fowler, Rhonda Carling, and numerous tiny souls never brought to term. Were those murder, too?

And all the good he had done! He'd saved lives. He had treated indigent people for nothing. Well, next to nothing. He had donated money to worthy causes, as urged by his tax lawyers, or Hogue. He had purchased medical supplies for needy communities. He had outfitted ball teams. And did God now disremember his donations for Katrina?

But it was all in the wind. The vectors of fortune had changed. Odious Melvin, the dead men who lay with his boat, Nazarian, and through Nazarian the realization of his weakness, Gretchen and her contempt, Paulita and her disappointment. He could barely stand the sight of himself in his own mirror. The fallen chest. The expanding white softness at the belt-line. But those beautiful, resourceful, intelligent blue eyes.

To hell with it, with everything. He had done what he had done, played the game of life as he had come to believe it should be played.

His plan had gathered form on the ride down the Harbor Freeway. He called his broker and initiated his emergency plan, cashing out every investment he had. That he would die, violently, in a foreign land, unlamented and alone, was his foregone conclusion. He was seeking his own death now, and he would meet it, and his creator, without complaint.

He was going to Mexico. Where a man with ready cash could get things done.

"Ulli?" said a frightened voice. He turned. Paulita. "Paulita!" He grasped her by the shoulders, pulled her close. Her dark eyes were full of fear.

"What happened your boat, Ulli?"

He shook his head. "The boat doesn't matter. You're here. That's what matters. Are you ready to go?"

She would never love him like he loved her. She would never know who he was, what he had done, why he had done those things. She would leave him when he needed her most. She would choose a lesser man in his stead and he would watch them go, red lights diminishing in the night, two points red on black. Then silence and the sigh of a dying wind.

But tonight she would be his.

SIXTY-SEVEN

A Damn Shame

The doctor answered on the third ring.

"It's Melvin, Doc."

"You sound like a Melvin."

"I did what I had to do, Doc."

"No. You went beyond the call of duty. Far beyond."

"You've been to Cabrillo?"

"Yes."

"What time are we going out?"

Wolf checked his watch. He had just passed through the Otay Mesa Port of Entry. He was in Mexico. Never to return. "Be at the boat in an hour."

The boat was gone. First Melvin wondered if he were on the wrong pier. No, he was channelside, where the big boats were.

Where toupeed millionaires wore captain hats to impress paid companions. What was a trophy wife but a paid companion? You traded in your original, whom gravity had condemned, purchased a new model. Tight skin, high boobs. All your old stories new. Her laughter bouncing around the cabin.

The boat was gone. Overhead lighting reflected off the dark water. Unlike the doc to do something like this on his own. One of the millionaires approached. In his captain hat.

Captain-hat looked into the empty slip, nodded his head. "It's a shame. It's a damn shame."

What was a shame? Melvin nodded his head in agreement. What had happened? "What happened?"

"Nobody really knows."

Melvin remained mystified. "Uh, what do *you* think happened?"

"Well, these things don't happen naturally. It was scuttled. That's what I say."

Scuttled? He wasn't sure what that meant.

"Probably behind on his payments." Captain-hat peered down into the water. "Ten, fifteen thousand a month. Got to get out from under that."

What was the old fool looking at? Then he saw it. It was right there. Just a few feet under the water. *"He sank his boat?"*

"That's what I think," said captain-hat. "Opened up a drain cock. Or put a hole in the bottom, turn off the bilge pumps. A one-inch hole, five-foot draft, say, uh, forty gallons a minute. It was settling by the time we saw it. We were too late."

But the doc had a home, a wife, a mistress, investments. He had a life. Could he really cut it all loose?

Melvin turned to the man. "When will they raise this thing?"

"That's the owner's problem. The marina won't do anything as long you pay your slip fees."

Which meant the fish would get to Luis and Ernesto before the authorities did. Which meant he, Melvin, was out of it. Two dead, fish-eaten corpses with holes in their heads on Himmler's boat. Things didn't get much more convenient than that.

"For the sake of the craft, of course," continued captain-hat, "the sooner the better."

Melvin walked back up the pier, disbelieving. On a grand scale, God was wiping the slate clean.

Now for Nazarian.

SIXTY-EIGHT

Last Man Standing

Lew and I met that night at Canter's. Reubens and matzo ball soup. Heinekens.

The San Pedro Film Company had been lethally effective. Hale Montgomery had committed suicide. Dr. Ulbrecht Wolf had disappeared. Chuck Hames, head of Ivanhoe security, had broken into San Pedro Film, seen the scripts and photos of Davis Algren, and apparently been overcome with remorse. Had thrown himself in front of the eastbound 217. With the strange, sweaty, wrinkled three-by-five card in his pocket. *I killed Dave Algren. I'm sorry.*

Myron Ealing had been on scene in a hurry. Turned off the smoke alarm. Didn't see anything.

The cameras had worked perfectly, though the images were overexposed. Chuck Andrew Hames. Had Hames executed Davis Algren? It made sense. Montgomery, Wolf, Hogue, Hames.

With a picture of Hames, I made another midnight run to Dunkin' Donut Hole. Got a lot of hits on the picture from Hannah and the gang. Yes, this guy had been asking about Dave. Everyone was cooperative except Danny Smart-ass, who'd supposedly been Dave's writer friend. He hadn't seen a goddamn thing and who was Dick to say he had?

All in all, Lew and I concluded the Algren script was true. Which didn't mean we could prove it in a court of law.

• • •

Hogue was the last man standing. With a ten-figure bank account. Which didn't mean we couldn't talk to him. Grind him a little bit. Let him know that we knew. Maybe he'd want to confess. Funnier things had happened.

But before we'd worked out a strategy to talk to Hogue, Hogue contacted me. Again.

I was invited for a return visit to Hogue's office. It seemed too public a place to die of unnatural causes.

I accepted the invitation.

SIXTY-NINE

Palmettos in a 7-D

The endgame was where masters revealed themselves. Melvin briskly dispatched a two-inch line of cocaine and a tiny mound of Persian green. The plan had come to Melvin with absolute clarity. It had imagination, dimension, specificity, and a good chance of success. An excellent chance. Maybe one more little, precisely little line, and just a dot of green.

He picked up his phone, called Sylvette Walker.

"Hi, Melvin," she purred.

"I'm going to be in West Hollywood tonight. Why don't you meet me at Bambi's?"

"What do you have in mind?"

"I'll explain when you get there."

"I want that apartment."

"Well, maybe you'll get it."

"What time?"

"Seven."

"I'll see you there."

Perfect. He gathered his things. Cigarettes. Lighters. Duct tape. Rope. Knife. The gun that had dispatched Luis and Ernesto to the Promised Land.

Where was Wolf? Eating beans in Sinaloa. *¿Donde está la baño, señora?*

He was glad he hadn't De Niro'ed the Glock, discarding a piece here and there, as he had planned, in Dumpsters all over town. He would need it tonight. To send the Mystery Man and Nazarian to their just rewards. Everything was playing out like clockwork. Don't fuck with Melvin Shea.

He valeted his car at the Chateau Marmont and walked down to Bambi's old place with his briefcase.

Bambi's mess had been cleaned up by the Kahlo Squad, an organization of his own founding. The squad was a loose group of incurious, silent Hispanic women, instructed not only to clean up but to remove every last article from the premises. What they did with those articles was up to the women themselves. Clothes, shoes, books, food, minor appliances, minor furniture, CDs, DVDs, all tidily disappeared. The squad was always anxious to work.

The place looked good. He would slip Beatriz a couple of extra fifties. Though the kitchen needed more work.

The evolution would go down in the living room. He rearranged the furniture as necessary. He could already hear the sounds of Sunset Boulevard. They'd grow louder as the night progressed. Cars turned at De Longpre, the geometrical array of headlight and shadow climbing up the wall and moving across the sprayed stucco ceiling.

Melvin sat in the cool and the dark and breathed deeply. A breeze eddied through the room. What food wasn't represented up on Sunset? Italian, Japanese, Chinese, Korean, Middle Eastern. Steaks, chops, barbecue.

The phone rang. *Sylvette.* Good. "Hello?"

"Melvin, it's me."

"Ring at the front, I'll buzz you up."

He met her at door, welcomed her in, a kiss on her cheek.

"Aren't you the gentleman."

"Aren't I always the gentleman?"

"I guess."

She was looking around.

"Want a tour?"

"I'd love one. I always loved this place. What happened to Bambi?"

Bye-bye, Bambi. He shrugged, flipped on the lights. The front door opened into a hallway that ran right and left to the bedrooms, went forward past an open kitchen and bar, further forward into the large living room that expanded mostly to the right and looked down, through big, operable windows, onto the street.

"Big place, eh?" He could see with every passing second she wanted it more. And he wasn't going to ask her to sell her soul. Just part of it.

"Can I take off my shoes?"

"You can take off anything you like."

She squinched her toes into the carpet. The carpet was deep, the pile dense. The place smelled good. Cool night flowed in with the lights and sounds of West Hollywood. It beat the place, admittedly a nice place, that she occupied on Wilshire. Wilshire wasn't what it used to be. Not that she'd ever seen it in its heyday.

The living room was furnished in white leather. Big couch, chairs. She sat down on the couch. She looked at Melvin.

"Okay, Melvin. What do you want?"

He laughed.

She opened the top button of her blouse, then the second button. Beneath her flawless face, lips slightly parted, the heavy swell of her breasts, contiguous with size, adrenalized his desire. Her nipples would be dark and hard. Her scented, long-fingered hands, nails in crimson, would gently support his balls, lifting them. Then one hand would grasp and squeeze his cock, thumb riding up just below the glans. *Christ*. He would feel her breath. He *could* feel her breath. More than anything in the world he wanted to send jet after jet down her throat, then thrust her away and look down upon her heaving, heavy-lidded beauty. She would smile. Wipe her mouth with her wrist. As she stared up at him.

But not tonight. *Christ*.

Tonight he was playing by fighter's rules, tonight he would conserve his testosterone until he had accomplished what he had sworn to accomplish.

"Well, Melvin?"

So much for the testosterone bank. He had deliriously squandered his day's inheritance. His body had triumphed over mind and now he wanted every sensation he could acquire. A nice hit of good fragrant green, a nice fat rail of coke, then another one, then a little green Persian chaser. Then he would lay back, adrift in perfect satisfaction, and listen to the sounds of the night.

But, no. This moment required discipline. Because discipline led to victory.

"I want you to do one other thing, Sylvette."

She looked up at him. Men. There was always one more thing. A finger-wave. "What?"

"I want you to make a call."

The fucker wanted pizza. "Who?"

"Devi."

"Devi?"

"Yeah, Devi. I want you to call her. Tell her to come over here."

"You want to do a three-way?"

"No. *Shit.* I need you to get her over here. Now."

"Why am I calling? Why not you?"

"Because she and I are not getting along, right now. If that's any of your business."

"But you want her over here to see *you.*"

"Yeah. That's what I want."

Sylvette looked at Melvin. Melvin wasn't a nice guy. She'd always known that. But hadn't dealt with him on any significant, personal matter. Whatever he wanted Devi for, it couldn't be good. Wouldn't be good. Period.

He watched her thinking. She had reservations. Too bad. If she wanted this apartment, she would call. No, fuck that. If she wanted to stay in the program, she would call.

Otherwise, he'd give Howard the sad news.

Sylvette's quit the program.

Who?

Sylvette Walker. From *The Schwarzschild Radius.*

The black one.

Yeah. Sylvette. She's going back to Gainesville.

Or wherever she came from. Down where the cockroaches were as big as shoes. So big you called them other names so you could avoid disgusting yourself for putting up with them. Palmetto bugs. Gimme some palmettos in a 7D. Wait. Those black girls had big feet. Gimme some them palmettoes in an 11E.

Palmettos could run fifty body lengths in a second. Like a human running 210 miles per hour. Then you dive into a crack and wiggle your feelers.

Why had she coveted this apartment? Strings attached, strings attached, strings attached everywhere. Nothing straight up and honest. Everything curvy and twisty, knotted. But maybe there was a middle way. Like those Buddhists down the hall were always talking about. The middle way. Course, you walk the middle way on Wilshire Boulevard you get run over and killed. Flattened. "You gonna hurt her?"

"Fuck no. I need to talk to her and she's fucking mad at me. You'd be doing her a favor. 'Cause she and I, we *need* to talk."

"If you can swear to me you're not going to hurt her, I'll make the call."

"I swear I won't hurt her." Christ. He was talking to a whore about moral issues.

"And you'll give me this place."

Melvin spread his hands. Always be magnanimous in victory.

"You had this place already. Howard loves you."

Sylvette dug through her purse, found her phone. "Alright. I'll call her." The carpet felt good under her toes.

SEVENTY

If the House Came Down

I had started to believe Rhonda Carling and Betty Ann Fowler were sisters. Sisters of solitude, sisters blown into Los Angeles on winds of dream and ambition, sisters whose disappearances had aroused mild curiosities back home. Sisters of misfortune. Sisters, somehow, of mine.

I remembered Rhonda at Fairfax. Demanding a million dollars. Or she would *bring the whole house down*. Now I was thinking; who would the house fall on?

Nazarian had just made a very, very successful picture. He'd hurt other people before. He paid them off. Would Nazarian kill Rhonda over her demand? No. He might kill in the heat of the moment, but otherwise, given time, he'd think his way out. And if things went public? He'd just made a very successful picture. He'd suffer, but he'd survive. Too many careers were invested in his. Hogue himself would laugh it off. For a four-hundred-million-dollar payday.

Conclusion: the house could fall on Nazarian, but it wouldn't kill him.

What about Devi? I remembered the conversation between Melvin Shea and Devi I'd heard from the closet, Nazarian at my feet. Shea and Devi were essentially in the same boat. Both had known Hogue's stable of women were not devoted to Hogue alone. I recalled my surprise when I'd asked Devi how much money she was making from her unique position.

Thirty-two fifty a week. That was good money. Great money. It had bought her a home in Beachwood Canyon. Had financed her Lexus and other things. But, unless I was a complete fool, which I'd certainly been before, Devi was incapable of killing.

Conclusion: if the house fell, Devi would suffer injury, but not death. Therefore, Devi wouldn't kill Rhonda.

Wolf and Shea.

Wolf could kill because he'd killed before. Why had he killed before? Essentially, for money. For things he could get. For influence and favors. From Hogue. What had he acquired?

I'd called my contacts downtown, spread some honeybees around. The Doc lived very well. Big house in Beverly Hills. Ranch near San Luis Obispo. Nice new Bentley, new Mercedes coupe for the wife. Trips to Europe every year. Stocks and bonds. A yacht at Cabrillo.

Well, well, well. A yacht at Cabrillo. That gave him the means. And a method he was familiar with.

I finished the paperwork check. The Doc was indeed living well. His California income tax reported earnings of close to two million dollars that year. Deductions and losses up the yingyang. A rich man's carefully woven fabric of hyperbole. I felt strongly the Doc was running hard, close to the wind, couldn't afford to slow down.

Now I thought specifically. The fact that Hogue, in our meeting, had not yet learned about Rhonda meant Dr. Wolf had not told him. Why not? Undoubtedly it would have been his duty to do so. Somehow, it was in his interest to keep his mouth shut. What commanded his interest? Money. A man in his position could always use a little more.

I tried to put myself in Wolf's head. He's called out in the middle of the night to attend one of the emperor's women. Did he know who did what? Well, *I'd* seen the golden gun. Chances were Wolf had seen it, too. Who would Wolf lean on? He'd lean on Nazarian. And he'd threaten Melvin.

Then what?

Then I saw it.

In not making a timely report to Hogue, he had made himself into a conspirator. Which meant that Rhonda's revelations would bring the house down on him, too. Conclusion: the Doc could kill Rhonda. To save the life he'd created for himself. Means, opportunity, motive.

I started to get excited. But I had to run Melvin Shea through the process before I put my pen down.

I'd also gone downtown on Shea. He owned an expensive condo, an expensive car, and his California tax return indicated Ivanhoe paid him a huge amount of money. But the little I'd heard from the closet made me think he was a chiseler, financially treading water. Like Wolf, he probably couldn't afford to stop running. And, if caught betraying his master, his Hollywood life was over. Period.

Conclusion: if the house came down, Melvin would die under it.

Question: Could Melvin and Wolf have been working together? No. That partnership wasn't natural. They were not birds of a feather.

The phone rang.

It was Lew. Guess what?

What?

Lew smiled over the phone. He thought Wolf was on the lam. And he'd just gotten a call from Harbor Division. Wolf's boat had sunk at the pier in Cabrillo.

SEVENTY-ONE

Two Hispanics

It came to me in a flash. Wolf had killed Rhonda, left her on the boat, sunk it, and run. Depending on marina protocol, that could give him weeks. "You know who's on that boat, Lew?"

I guess Lew had been analyzing things as well. "Sure I do. Rhonda Carling."

That's why Lew and I had been successful partners. Until the day I'd air-conditioned Elton Reese.

We arrived at Cabrillo within the hour. It was eight o'clock and dark. Tom Pike, Harbor Division Master Diver, was already in his wetsuit. He checked his watertight flashlight, climbed backward down the ladder into the water. Waving, he disappeared.

Lew lit up a Kool. "You think Wolf is down there, too?" I shook my head. "Nah. He's not going to roll over now. He didn't with Betty Ann."

Lew smoked his cigarette and we waited.

Tom Pike resurfaced. Treading water, he put his mask up, made the peace sign. "Two. Two of 'em down there."

Lew turned to me in surprise, turned back to Pike. "Man and a woman?"

"No," said Tom. "Two Hispanic males."

• • •

314

Lew and I met at the morgue the next morning, talked with the coroner, Ellen Myers.

The bodies of the two men been lying on the floor of the sunken *Hush, My Baby*'s salon. The bodies were at ocean temperature, 67 degrees Fahrenheit. The fact that the bodies were at the bottom meant insufficient putrefactive gases had formed to raise the bodies. Interior gassing took two to three days. The fact that the bodies were at ocean temperature meant the bodies had been submerged for at least six hours. Bodies in water cooled at 5 degrees F per hour.

The men, Luis Torres and Ernesto Reyes, were in their late twenties. Reyes had been shot once through the heart from the back. Torres had been shot four times—in the balls, in the left knee, in the right elbow, and finally, point blank through the forehead.

"You're saying he was tortured?" asked Lew.

"Yes. The other shots came first, of course. You don't shoot a corpse. Mr. Torres knew he was going to die."

Marina personnel stated that the vessel had sunk in the early-morning hours yesterday.

"The men were killed aboard the boat, gentlemen," said Ms. Myers.

Lew looked at me. "And I bet the bullets sank the boat. These guys might be the guys who did the drop-off and pick-up at Fairfax Convalescent."

Lew had learned of a pair of Hispanics from a terse and suspicious Dr. Moncrief at Fairfax.

Moncrief, purposefully vacant, seemed to remember a white van. Maybe gray. He'd only seen it at night. Make? Probably American. How old was the van? Not that old, not that new, kind of shiny. Did the men make both delivery and pickup? Maybe. He didn't look that closely. Hispanic men? Probably. Could have been off-brand Asian. Off-brand? Laotian. Burmese. Dr. Wolf had signed Rhonda in? Yes. You countersigned? Yes. But she'd checked out by herself? Yes. She walked right out, under her own power? No, she rolled out. At her own insistence. You counter-signed? Yes. Could Lew see the document? Get a warrant.

We were putting all facts into the Rhonda Carling bag, see if they fit. After all, there were only two Hispanics *in* the story. Both with ties to Wolf. And now two dead Hispanics on his boat.

Maybe the men had come back for another taste. Blackmail. Which made them loose ends. What to do with loose ends? Cut them off. It seemed to fit.

Lew looked up at the ceiling. Would the doctor fire bullets inside his own yacht? No.

It did seem rash. "You're thinking Melvin."

"Yup," said Lew. "I'm thinking Melvin."

I considered a partnership of necessity between Shea and Wolf. It was a possibility. Both had everything to lose.

John Elston, dockmaster, had seen the doctor after his craft had sunk. His demeanor? Like he was in shock.

Then Wolf disappeared. Had never gone home.

We went back to a logistics question. How had Luis and Ernesto gotten to Cabrillo?

Lew put out a query for a white van and got a hit. Earlier that day, in North Long Beach, two adolescents had been arrested for joyriding. In a white van. With a gurney in the back. Bingo. The joyriders admitted they'd had the van for two days.

We hammered out a provisional theory. Luis and Ernesto had been invited down to the boat and executed. By Melvin. How did Melvin know about the yacht? Because he and the doctor had disposed of Rhonda. Prompting the threatened Melvin to invite Luis and Ernesto to Cabrillo. So their bodies, like Rhonda, like Betty Ann Fowler, could be dumped at sea. But Melvin had sunk the doctor's boat accidentally. The doctor had come down to the marina. He had seen his boat and knew what was in it. So he ran.

Maybe.

SEVENTY-TWO

Copycat

Melvin smiled into the mirror. If flight was indeed a sign of guilt, Wolf's flight to Mexico was his godsend. And tonight he would finalize his business with Devi, the asshole from Armenia, and the Mystery Man.

The pieces of his plan fit exactly, like a jigsaw puzzle. The wooden, expensive kind. He felt in harmony with celestial forces. To the bold belonged the world.

Sylvette had summoned Devi. Then Sylvette had split, leaving the front door unlocked. Devi would enter and he would clock her. Like Mystery Man had clocked him.

When Devi got to feeling a little cooperative, he'd have her call Mystery Man. Requesting the golden gun. Because Mystery Man had the gun. Who else? The deal was simple. Golden gun delivered—or Devi's life.

And the Mystery Dude would deliver the gun. His last good deed on earth. Actually, his last deed. Because Melvin would kill him. In front of a terrified, gagged Devi.

Then, when Devi thought it couldn't get worse, he would do to her exactly what that cunt Nazarian had done to Rhonda.

Exactly. Exactly like he'd seen it.

He'd break her nose. Blacken her eyes. Knock out some teeth. Put a cigarette to her right nipple.

Then, and only then, he would call fucking Nazarian. Come get your golden gun, Eli. I've got it right here.

He would greet Nazarian at the door, lead him in. Then, in sight of Devi, he'd whack Nazarian in the head. Hard. Knock him out. Then, using the golden gun, he'd put Devi out of her misery. Right between the eyes. Lastly, using Nazarian's phone, he would call the police and confess. As Nazarian.

Then Melvin would slip out the door, go home, lay out a few sharp lines of Jackie's fine cocaine. And a chaser of that superlative Persian green.

You don't fuck with Melvin Shea.

SEVENTY-THREE

Dinner with Georgette

I suppose I always thought I'd end up back with Georgette. We'd been sailing over the dull seas of matrimony at three knots, until I'd started a fire and sunk the ship. But, looking back, it had been comfortable and regular and I dearly missed my interaction with Randy and Martine. Twelve and seven, now. Wow. Quick. My darling little people.

They said all sorts of good things about marriage. The pancreas secreted better enzymes. The spleen was serene. The liver was more efficient and cooperative. The reproductive system was exercised more frequently, if at a lower level of endorphination. Put that all together, I guess you lived longer.

And ended up wearing paper underpants and playing Uncle Wiggly with other Alzheimer half-wits at Rainbow's End. Right next to Fairfax Convalescent. Not for me. I wanted to go out Rockefeller-style. With a bang. In the arms of a paid companion. If necessary.

Georgette had been messaging me lately. With some degree of urgency. I couldn't figure out why. My payments were up-to-date, the appliances were in good order, we had nothing to bicker about. Which meant it could only be one thing. She wanted to get back together.

And maybe I was ready. Maybe it was time to let that home-cooked slop congeal around my waist. That was the wrong thing to say. What I meant was, perhaps I could sample some calorie-rich, home-crafted cuisine in the presence of my children.

Because things with Devi seemed to be reaching a natural conclusion. Like my relationships with friends on my submarine so many years ago. Some relationships stood on their own. They were rare. Most stood in their juxtaposition to work and duty. And when those exigencies faded, so did the friendship. Devi's vivid sense of danger from Melvin and Nazarian had paled when nothing had materialized.

Caring for Hogue's girls had looked stupid and frivolous for a while. But passing time had restored the allure of thirty-two fifty a week. Heather Hill had been brought into the fold.

And I knew she'd been going back to her house more and more. Feed the cat, et cetera. Relax in a known environment; you knew where the scissors were, there was a jar to put your pocket change, another for pens and pencils, your station on the radio.

But Melvin was still serious bad news. I counseled her not to put herself in a vulnerable position with him. But my cautions were wearing thin. Human nature at work.

So, at this moment, I was rolling toward Santa Monica and the Galley on Main Street. Georgette's choice.

The Galley was small and dark, with ropes and chains in a nautical theme. Surf 'n' turf, good drinks. Georgette and I had always used the place for conversations of substance. That was another reason I knew she wanted to get back together.

My mood lifted when I saw her. She was a big, good-looking woman. Big arms, big legs, big ass—not too big—big boobs. Big.

"You're lookin' good tonight, Georgie."

She smiled, pleased. "Thank you, Dick."

Yeah. She wanted me back. I leaned back, stretched, sipped my Bloody Mary. "There's a lot less of you," I lied, pleasantly.

"What do you mean?"

"You've lost ten pounds."

"No, I haven't."

"Five pounds. I can see it." Ten pounds had been overdoing it a bit.

"Actually, Dick, I've gained seven."

The unwritten, ironclad rules of war dictated a man never acknowledge a woman's claim of gained weight. There was no conceivable benefit to such acquiescence. I shook my head, spread my hands, *seven pounds?*

We settled in to a good meal. Again I found myself wondering what I really liked, lobster or butter. But I was feeling good, it didn't matter. She put down her fork, asked me if I had an extra six hundred and thirty-nine thousand dollars.

"That's a highly specific sum. Looking at a new house?"

"No. You remember Francine?"

Of course I remembered her. Platonically, thank you very much. Again, the rules were ironclad. "Francine? Francine who?"

"My friend Francine. She married Carl?"

"Parents of Randy's best friend in first grade."

Georgette nodded. "Remember she had a little girl, Teresa?"

"Something was wrong with her?"

"Well, they've found out what it is. Refractory epilepsy."

"What's that?"

"Seizures in one hemisphere of the brain are transmitted to the other hemisphere, causing massive seizures. That's the refractory part, the one side to the other. Poor little thing passes out on her feet, falls, smashes her head."

"So, buy her a helmet."

Georgette's eyes flashed and her fork stopped in midair. "That's not funny, Dick."

"Sorry." It wasn't funny. "What do they do for her?"

"There's an operation. A corpus callosotomy," she said carefully, emphasis on the third syllable.

"When are they going to do it?"

"When Francine can come up with—"

"Six hundred thirty-nine thousand dollars."

"Jesus, Dick. I feel so bad for her."

"The insurance companies—"

"Consider it experimental surgery."

"Assholes. What's the operation? What do they do?"

"They go into the brain, cut most of the fiber bundle that connects each side of the brain to the other."

"Sounds radical."

"It is radical. But it cuts the seizure rate by ninety percent. And cuts the severity."

"What about side effects?"

"It does weird stuff. You recognize objects but you can't name them. Stuff like that. But Teresa is still young."

"And her brain could rewire."

"It could. And anything's better than what's happening."

Christ. That was one thing kids could never understand. Until they became parents themselves. A child in the world meant you never slept again. Because you always had one eye open. Praying, hoping, trying to believe that the accidents that happened to others would never happen to yours.

Seizures. Watching your child overwhelmed by some malignant mystery force. Occluding their beauty, their potential for greatness. Knowing you had long since squandered your own potential, trading it for transitory pleasures.

Christ. Seizures so horrific you grasped at the opportunity to cut your child's brain in half. Solomonic. And then the insurance companies pointing to a subchapter in their defrauding manuals, telling you they couldn't help. You were on your own. Sorry.

God damn them all. Pearly's "If There Is No God" rolled through my mind.

if there is no god who will forgive me? if there is no god who will believe me? if there is no god who's gonna save me?

I looked at Georgie. "I'm sorry, dear. I don't have six hundred and thirty-nine thousand." I finished off my Bloody Mary.

Why had she suggested dinner this evening? Not for this . . . utter tragedy.

"Dick," said Georgette, "I wanted to talk to you tonight."

At last. Our conversation lurched around the corner. To the future. Getting back together. I had to admit, she'd maneuvered things very nicely. Francine's tribulations pointed up the value of family. I surrendered, prepared myself for meat loaf and lima beans. "What's up, Georgie?"

"It's about something serious."

"Let's have it." I slipped on my devil-may-care grin. Here came bologna and deviled eggs, mac and cheese.

"Dick. I'm seeing someone."

"You're seeing—*what did you say?*"

"I've met someone."

"Met someone?" The first requirement of communication is common language.

"His name is Hartley Marvel."

"Hartley Marvel?" The second requirement of communication is the desire to understand.

"He's a CPA over at Paramount."

My hemispheres were miscommunicating. "Wait a second," I demanded. "Anyone named Harvey Marvel's gotta be gay." I hadn't meant to talk so loudly. And as far as sexual orientation went, whatever gets you through the night. But that name, Hartley Marvel.

Georgette's eyes glinted in cold triumph. Over the small man who had been her husband. "Hartley's not gay, Dick, believe me. He's a CPA. Over at Paramount."

The restaurant had grown very quiet. Everyone seemed to be eying me.

Our nice waitress, now stony, floated out of the darkness. "Check, please," I said, scraping together my dignity.

In the public parking lot behind the Galley, where my '69 Cadillac Coupe de Ville convertible awaited me, Georgette pulled up next to me in her new, white Mustang. The window whispered down.

"You'll like Harvey when you meet him, Dick."

"Sure, I will." Fat chance.

"You know what he fixed for me?"

It'd better be the garbage disposal. "What did he fix?"

"He reinstalled Windows and put in Quicken."

"*Chicken?* He baked a chicken?" My hearing was good, is good.

"*Quicken*. It's an accounting program."

"Sounds like a handy guy."

"You'll like him."

"Sure."

The hazel eyes that once looked into my soul now looked me over. "Goodbye, Dick."

Off she drove.

SEVENTY-FOUR

Whirlwind

Devi was in Beachwood Market when the call came. She was in the act of purchasing twenty cans of Friskies cat food, Felonius Monk's favorite. Ten cans/five bucks. Felonius had rejected her last offering, raking his orange paw over a house brand from Ralphs that claimed a relationship to liver pâté. The relationship had not fooled the careful cat.

She slid her card through the slot. Cash back? The phone rang. *Sylvette W.*

"Hello?"

"Devi? It's Sylvette."

Sylvette didn't sound good. "Hi, Syl. You alright?"

"I'm over in West Hollywood. In Bambi's old place. Melvin's letting me move in. But I found something. You have to come *over*."

Melvin had moved Sylvette? News to her. "What did you find?"

"I can't *tell you*. Not over the phone." Sylvette sounded agonized. "Please come. Please, please come." Sylvette drew breath. *"Please."*

The last emergency call had been Rhonda. Dick thought Rhonda was dead. But maybe she was back in Florida. Slinging mojitos at the beach. Well, slinging them after she got better. Slinging them after she got her face fixed. Slinging mojitos from under a paper bag.

"Okay. I'll be right over."

"Thank you. I'll leave the door unlocked. *Thank you,* Devi."

What could Sylvette had found? She'd just heard a macabre, frightening report on the radio. Two fetuses, wrapped in yellowed newspaper from the 1930s, had been found in a closet, in a box, in an apartment near MacArthur Park. Two tiny souls who hadn't made it. Maybe they haunted the park.

Devi found a rare parking place on Fountain, walked a block, turned up Harper Avenue. She looked up at Bambi's place. It was dark.

I rolled into my driveway. I'd grown a little tired of Pearly and had just listened to David Lindley's *Win This Record,* in its entirety. One of the best albums ever made. Great musicians, great songs, great arrangements.

Lindley deserved his place in the pantheon. Hopefully on a pedestal. God had blessed him with many gifts, but height was not one of them. Maybe genius only needed a small package.

My phone rang. It was Devi. She didn't sound right.

"What's wrong?"

"I'm at 1350 North Harper Avenue. In West Hollywood. Apartment 3C."

I instinctively wrote down the address. "Why are you there?"

"I'm here with someone."

"Who?"

"Hold on."

A new voice came on the line. "Mr. Henry?"

"Who is this?"

"This is Melvin Shea. You have something I want." He paused. "I want Nazarian's golden gun, Mr. Henry. And Devi here says you got it. If you don't bring it over, right now, I'm gonna kill her. That simple. You know I don't bluff, right?"

"How do I know you won't kill her anyway?"

"You don't. You take your chances. But don't bring it and she's dead. Bring me the gun."

Melvin seemed to have all the cards. "Okay. I'll bring it."

"Now, you haven't disturbed the gun, have you?"

"If you mean, did I clean the blood and shit off it, no, I didn't."

"Good. See you very soon."

I thought about the situation I was about to walk into. Where a desperate man held a gun to a woman's head. A man who had reasons to want me dead.

And the golden gun. Obviously to blackmail Nazarian.

All in all, I realized, it was Melvin's big day. The gun, the girl who set him up for the knockout, the man who threw the punch. The trifecta.

Then, a furthering skein of thought played though my mind; why not, at least for the sake of efficiency, why wouldn't Melvin conclude his *all* his business *all* at once? Michael Corleone at the baptism.

Kill Devi and me, blame Nazarian.

Devi and I would be shot with the golden gun.

Why didn't I let Devi fend for herself in a situation that she had created by her own actions? Why didn't I call the authorities? With their armored trucks, armored vests, bullhorns, snipers, and flash bombs? Why? Because I'm the Shortcut Man and a woman I knew was in there with a stone killer. Because I'm the Shortcut Man and didn't want to go to a funeral and hear somebody say that God called our sister, Devi, home early. Because He loved her. While I sat there. Behind yellow tape. Because I'm the Shortcut Man and Devi, playing her last card, had bet on the Shortcut Man.

I had a plan. Not much of one. Everything would have to go my way. He wanted something I had and that gave me a tiny advantage. It was all I had.

I crossed Sunset at Laurel, at the Comedy Store. Bob Saget was marqueed. On Fountain I turned right. In the second block I saw a copper Lexus. Looked like Devi's. There were no parking spaces. Fine. I backed in, backed up, pushed a silver Acura back into a red zone by a hydrant. I got my briefcase, walked toward Harper. I called Devi.

"Hello?" Her voice weak and shallow.

"Tell him I'm here."

I heard her tell him. He took the phone. "Be careful, man. Be real careful." He snapped off.

1350 was one of the nice older places in West Hollywood. I rang 3C, got buzzed in, walked up to the third floor, stood in front of 3C. I took a deep breath. There was no room for error.

I tapped quietly at the door.

The door clicked open in front of me. Into darkness. I heard a voice from inside. "Shut the door behind you, Mr. Henry."

I shut the door behind me, felt something tied around the handle. The place was very dark, my adrenaline surged, my skin crawled. Around the handle was a string. The door had been *pulled open*. From some distance away.

"Come forward," said Melvin, from far darkness.

"Prove she's alive, man."

I heard him talk to her. "Prove you're alive, Devi."

"I'm . . . I'm alive, Dick."

"Sing, Devi."

"S-sing?"

"Sing."

"What the fuck?" said Melvin.

"As long as I hear her, I know she's alright, Melvin. Devi, where's his gun right now?"

"R-right at my head."

"Good. Start singing. And as long as that gun is at your head you're alright—keep singing."

"W-what shall I s-sing?"

"Let's get the fuck on with this." Melvin's voice was rabbity, showing stress.

"Sing me some David Lindley."

Devi started humming. I recognized it. "Turning Point." Good.

"You understand our bargain, Melvin?"

"What are you talking about?"

"If she stops singing I'm going to shoot you."

"Then she's dead, Mr. Henry."

"Then, for both our sakes, keep her singing." A silence opened up. I stepped in. "Okay, Melvin. What next?"

"Come forward. Through the kitchen, into the living room. I'm at the far end on the right."

"Forward, through the kitchen, into the living room."

"You got it. And hold what you're bringing me in front of you."

"Hold the gun out in front of me," I repeated.

"Hold it out, with both hands, and move real slow. And hold it smart."

My eyes grew accustomed to the darkness. I was standing in the open section of the kitchen. I set my briefcase on a counter.

"What was that?" asked Melvin.

"Just set down my briefcase. With the gun in it. I don't have the case." I unzipped the case, removed the weapon. I didn't have the case but I did have the suppressor, attached. Everything was contained in a clear plastic vegetable bag from the supermarket. Now I held the gun, through the bag, in my right hand.

"Nice and slow," said Melvin, from the living room. Ahead of me, in deep shadow.

Devi's singing was going weak. "Keep singing, Devi." She sounded hurt, tremulous.

"I hope she's alright, Melvin."

"Oh, she's alright. A little fucked up. Didn't really want to help me. But we came to an agreement."

"Keep singing, girl," I said.

Devi kept singing.

"You fuck up, Mr. Henry, I kill her. Got it?"

Oh, I got it, friend. "Got it." I stepped into the living room, turned to the right. There were low shadows at the end of the room. Light rolled across the ceiling from the cars navigating Harper. Or turning at De Longpre.

Devi was tied to a kitchen chair. One eye was swollen shut. Her nose was bleeding. Her shirt was open. Grinning Melvin knelt beside her, pistol to her temple.

"I only had to burn her once, Mr. Henry. She didn't want to call you. She wanted to protect you." His eyes moved over the golden gun, held perpendicular to our lines of vision, my index finger, right hand, through the bag, on the trigger. The suppressor lay across my open left palm. "That thing loaded?" he asked.

"How bad you want to find out?"

"Put the gun down on the ground, Henry. Then I'll take mine down from her head."

"No. Put yours down first." My life and Devi's life teetered on a 300 millisecond reaction-time advantage. His or mine.

We paused, breathed. At the brink. At the precipice. I needed milliseconds. Needed to distract him.

Anger might work. Sting his pride, tweak his masculinity. Three hundred milliseconds. "Come on, cocksucker, put the gun down, let's get on with it."

His eyes narrowed, the gun sagged minutely from her temple. There it was.

I pulled the trigger, put a bullet right between his eyes. He dropped like a puppet with his strings cut, his gun by Devi's feet.

The suppressor had rendered the shot a cough. I cut Devi loose. "Jesus, Dick. *Jesus.*"

Melvin was leaking badly in crimson.

Devi buttoned up, grabbed her purse. "We better hurry. Nazarian is on his way. Melvin called him right after he buzzed you up."

"Put your purse in the kitchen, help me move Melvin."

Devi was starting to freak out. "What are you thinking, Dick?"

"Stop thinking, Devi. Just do what I tell you."

We dragged Melvin into a bedroom, set him down. A dead body is always heavier than it looks. His lolling head banged the floor. Maybe I'd separated his corpus callosum. Which meant his hemispheres wouldn't be communicating properly. An amateur callosotomy. Or whatever it was.

Then we waited. Waiting was a bitch. For the plumber, for the man, for anything. To wait with dead Melvin was agony. Seconds crept by like centuries. Then the phone rang. I picked it up. "Yes?"

"It's me."

"Come on up," I whispered, buzzing him in. I hung up and we waited some more. Then we heard a soft knock at the door.

I went over, looked through the observation lens. It was Nazarian. I opened the door a few inches.

He stepped in. I shut the door behind him. I'd kept the lights low. He was edgy and suspicious. "Who the fuck are you?"

"I'm Melvin's dude. I'm the guy who has your check. And your gun. Come on." I led him into the living room. "Melvin had to go. He left something real special for you. He said it'd make things alright."

But his eyes had already played over the dark-headed girl tied to the chair. "Melvin told me about her," I sniggered. "This bitch kicked your ass?"

Nazarian saw Melvin's blood on the floor, added two and two and made five: the girl's blood. "I hope you didn't kill her, because I want to do that." He strode across the room, alive in hate, drawing back his fist and—

Then the tied-up girl slipped her bonds and threw an utterly vicious straight right. Nazarian fell to his knees and Devi's left hook hit him high on the cheekbone and conveyed him sideways to the floor. *All tumped over* as my Southern friends might say.

Then Nazarian reaped the whirlwind. Hard, furious, cold, professional punches rained down on him. A deluge. Where Noah, in generous comparison, had experienced heavy mist. Nazarian's eyebrows split right and left and his nose was hammered flat. His teeth were knocked right out of his head. His jaw was a sack of jelly beans.

She wasn't human. I had to stop her before she killed him. Finally I dragged her off. USMC, baby.

One last thing. I pressed the golden gun into Nazarian's hand, wrapped it in my coat, put a single bullet up into the ceiling. And the invisible gases passed into the tissues of his hand.

Then a second last thing. I searched Nazarian, found his phone, dialed a number.

"Peedner."

"Murder," I croaked, "murder. 1350 North Harper Avenue. Apartment 3C."

Then Devi and I got the hell out of there.

SEVENTY-FIVE

To Confess and Repent

"Mr. Hogue will see you now," said the lady.

I rose from my seat. I'd been reading the weekly edition of *Variety*. An obituary and remembrance of Hale Montgomery. America's favorite granddad had perished by misadventure, falling off a whale-watching boat in San Pedro. He'd lived a long and noteworthy life. He'd married four times, divorced four times. Creative differences. He'd had four children, none of them now in the arts. He'd been a Catholic Big Brother, he'd jogged for breast cancer, danced for AIDS, sung for the United Electrical Workers, swum for undocumented immigrants. He would be sorely, sorely missed. Goodbye and fare thee well, Stash Rockland.

The lady was holding the door open to Hogue's office. "Will I need a guide?" I asked her.

"A guide?"

"The man's got a big office. Is he in the forest, on the green, at his desk, or in the media center?" There could've been a river, too. With piranha.

I guess the lady didn't think I was very funny. She looked in, then back at me. "He's at his desk."

His desk was huge. He sat behind it, in front of huge windows looking out onto the English village. "Have a seat, Mr. Henry," said the mighty Hogue.

I sat.

We looked at one another.

"So," he finally began, "tell me what you know about the San Pedro Film Company."

"I am the San Pedro Film Company."

"That's honest."

"Let's be honest."

"Okay." He leaned forward. "Both Hale Montgomery and Dr. Wolf forwarded their scripts to me. Which, undoubtedly, you expected. How do you expect me to react to hearsay? Because that's what that script it, hearsay."

"I'm not in the blackmail business."

"You're not? What business are you in?"

"I'm a shortcut man. I get things done. And, had it not been for your insistence, I'd've never known who Davis Algren was."

"I thought we were being honest."

"I am being honest. When you asked me about Mr. Algren, I had no idea who he was."

"There's a picture of you in the doughnut place holding two cups of coffee. You were bringing a cup of coffee to someone you don't know?"

"Mixing a cup of high-test with a cup of decaf makes half-caf. It was two in the morning."

"Your being at Dunkin' Donuts was a coincidence."

"No. I was at Dunkin' Donuts for a reason."

"What reason?"

"One of your girls who lived nearby had been knocked around. I was asked to look in."

"One of my girls?"

"I thought we were being honest."

"How much do you know about my affairs?"

"I know one thing. Which has twenty-eight or twenty-nine parts. But that's none of my business."

Hogue sat back. "Do you have any idea what it is to be rich?"

"No, I don't."

"Money has gravity. After a certain point it has you, you don't have it. *The Schwarszchild Radius.*"

"*The Schwarzschild Radius*? You saw it?"

"It's a movie?"

"Worst movie ever made, Mr. Henry."

"I didn't know it was a movie. I know some casual science. The Schwarzschild Radius is the point of no return, gravitationally speaking, for black holes. Pass over it, you can't escape falling in."

"Because to escape you'd need to accelerate faster than the speed of light. Which can't be done." Hogue spread his hands.

"That's right. I think."

The billionaire considered. "Well, money's like that. It has me. I have so much money I can't trust a soul. No one's honest with me. Everybody has an angle. So love, for example, is out."

"You could divest."

"Give everything away."

"Yes. Start again."

Hogue shook his head. "I'm not strong enough to do that. I've thought about it. Can't do it." He studied me. "How'd you like to work for me, Mr. Henry?"

I shook my head. "You pay too well. I'd never get out." I paused. "And you kill people. You think you're above the law."

"That's because I am above the law."

"You really think that."

"It's the truth, Mr. Henry." He leaned back. "I didn't start out that way. But now, that's the way it is."

"Please explain."

"You know how many people depend on me? Directly and indirectly? Thousands. Men and women, their husbands and wives, their children, their charities, their expensive schools, their this, their that. It goes on and on. All the way to the roach coach parked outside the lot. If I fall, for whatever reason, they all go down, too. Like dominoes. So I'm confident I'll be judged by a higher authority. Who'll understand me better than you can."

"You think you can't be replaced?"

"Just like a hole in the ocean. Of course I can be replaced. But that takes time. And how much time do we all have? My empire fails, like the Roman Empire failed, and we have our own Dark Ages. There's a lot of rich men on this lot. Supposedly rich. But how many of them could stand idle, monetarily, for two or three years? Not many. And all sorts of well-made plans, for good and laudable things, will come crashing down. And I'm part of it, too. Despots don't retire, there's no clear line of succession. They die. They're assassinated. And that's what will happen to me."

"And the sanctity of human life?"

"Like Betty Ann Fowler?"

"Exactly like Betty Ann Fowler."

The billionaire sighed. "I don't expect you to believe this but I think about her every day. Why? Because we made a tiny personal connection. She wasn't afraid of me. She didn't talk at my money. She talked to *me*. And I saw her walk upstairs with that ignorant cowhand, and I thought to myself, I'll talk to her later. But there was no later. She had been utterly ruined, destroyed. And I weighed the entirety of everything and made my decision. That's what officers and emperors do. They make decisions. And that decision led to the next decision and the next. And now here we are. Me and the Shortcut Man."

We looked at one another. In a strange way he made sense. I'd never talked to a king before. I didn't envy him.

"Are you sure, Mr. Henry, that I can't hire you? I need a new head of security."

I shook my head. "No, thank you. I'd get stuck."

Hogue shrugged. "Fine. So, tell me, Mr. Henry." He knit his fingers together. "I don't want the San Pedro script hanging over my head. Even though, in the long run, it'd just be an annoyance. What do I have to do to make you go away?"

"I'm not here for blackmail. But I would remind you of something."

"Shoot."

"Though the mills of the gods grind slowly, they grind exceeding fine." Pretty heavy for the Shortcut Man, I must admit.

Hogue nodded, brushed off the heaviness. "You know, I've heard that. I think cowhand Montgomery said that in one of his epics. One of *my* epics. What does it mean?"

I found myself laughing. "It means if you're liable, you'll pay sooner or later."

"That'd be only fair." He stood up, turned, looked into his English village. Then he turned back. "Last chance. *San Pedro.* What do you want?"

We looked at one another. "*San Pedro* going once, going twice—

Then it occurred to me. "There is something I want."

"Of course there is." He smiled. "What is it?"

"Six hundred and thirty-nine thousand dollars. I want six hundred and thirty-nine thousand dollars."

SEVENTY-SIX

Hope

I couldn't get Davis Algren's wife, Hannah, out of my mind. The pain I had seen in her eyes. And I kept wondering about his safe deposit box key. Why keep a key for a box with nothing in it?

And though I'd forgotten Glastonbury's exact possible-solution number, I knew it was somewhere around two hundred thousand possibilities. Four dials, twenty-two letters apiece, each excluding I, Q, X, and Y. Eventually, whatever was in there would revert to the State of California. Hannah would get nothing.

I examined Algren's scripts closely. Beside the scripts themselves, adding to two hundred forty-some pages, there were the backsides of those one-sided pages, some of them full with notes and scribblings. I went though every page, every note.

Like the drunk searching for his keys under the streetlight, when he might have left them anywhere in town, my reasoning was, though Algren could have left the combination anywhere, the only place I might find it was somewhere in or on his screenplays, the only documents remaining from his life.

In the second hour, when I felt that my eyes had finally crossed, permanently, I found a tiny notation:

gave comb to Hannah 071705

It was the second time I'd run across it, having started through a second time, but this time it occurred to me that perhaps *comb* actually meant *combination*.

I caught up with Hannah the next evening at Dunkin' Donuts. I'd been drinking bad coffee for an hour and it was late and I was ready to go home. But then she came in.

I bought her a croissant sandwich and coffee, then asked her had anything special occurred on July 17, 2005. A big smile lit up her face and she extended her hand with the silver ring. "July 17, 2005? Of course, I remember that. That was the day we were married," she said, "the best day of my life."

"Did he ever give you a comb?"

"A comb?" She was mystified. "I didn't have any hair. I'd been sick."

"I didn't know that. I'm sorry."

Her eyes filled with tears. "I miss him. I miss him."

"And he didn't give you a combination, or a number to remember, did he?"

She shook her head. A long time ago she'd been pretty. "The only thing Dave ever gave me was this." Again she extended her hand, showed me her plain silver ring. "On our wedding day."

Something struck me. "Would you mind if I looked at your ring?"

With suspicion, and with difficulty, she twisted it off her finger, handed it to me. "I've never taken it off. What about it?"

It was a plain silver ring, battered, dented, scuffed, worth ten bucks. But inside, very faintly, were four letters.

Mr. Glastonbury, though grave, expressed pleasure at my return to the Bank of America. "Do you have the code, sir?"

"I believe I do."

"Right this way."

Mr. Glastonbury inserted his key, turned it half a turn clockwise, removed it. "Now I leave the room," he said. "Put in your code, insert your key, turn it clockwise, it'll go a quarter turn. Then scramble your code. Then turn your key and open the box." With that, Mr. Glastonbury disappeared.

I went over to the box, turned each dial to what I hoped was the combination.

H   O   P   E

I could feel my heart beating. I inserted the key. Now or never. The key turned a quarter turn and a rush ran through me. I scrambled the dials. I turned the key the final quarter turn. I opened the box.

The box was wide, shallow, and flat. There was a lot of cash. Why had he chosen to live on the streets? I'd heard of other cases like this, had never been truly able to understand. Penniless grandmother, subsisting on ramen, with $1,000,000 in the mattress. Minimum-wage security guard dies with a $5,000,000 portfolio. Were they crazy or did they foresee a torrential rain?

In this case, Davis Algren, as evidenced by the writings in the box, was round the bend. Aliens had infiltrated the government at all levels. They were augmenting human DNA in search of an interstellar hybrid to conquer both the future and the past. Meanwhile they were living in vast underwater cities, hives really, on the bottom of the ocean. They possessed astounding capabilities. They could raise the dead if their attentions could be turned to your particular situation. There was a seven-day window of opportunity. So don't be too quick in disposing of the deceased.

There was a sheaf of illustrations to accompany the ravings. Kabbalistic diagrams. It must have made sense to him.

There was also a letter to Hannah. A love letter, a thank-you letter. It started well. But Algren had become distracted. What had started simply and directly had veered into reptile people and their strange diets. Page two gave instructions for recognizing the reptile people. Remember

Jim Morrison and the Lizard King? No accident. And if you knew what to look for, there it was. Page three turned to anger at her skepticism. Page four detailed what would be her dire, well-deserved punishment. She couldn't say she wasn't warned.

I counted the money. $27,320. There was no mention of where it might have come from.

Okay, then. I knew what I had to do. And then I knew how to do it. I smiled. It was fate. I knew the Atwater brothers.

SEVENTY-SEVEN

Ellen Arden

When I think of all the things in this world that go wrong, it's pretty much a miracle when things go right. But miracles do happen.

Take Lew Peedner. Screwed to the bone when I punched Elton Reese's ticket. Officially destined to be a lieutenant the rest of his days. A good man with no future.

Then, after the arrest of Eli Nazarian, for the murder of Melvin Shea, suddenly the powers-that-be realize this man, Peedner, is a class-A, number-one, nose-to-the-grindstone, workingman's hero.

They take him up three grades to inspector, he's all over TV, white on rice, he's a Man of the Future. The subject of a Special White Paper Report by Ted Sargent. What this proves, said the chief, is that even the high and mighty are subject to the rule of law. Everything isn't OJ and Robert Blake and the rest of them.

Lew himself, radiating contentment, told me an interesting thing. We were sitting on the patio at Irv's Burgers in West Hollywood. Lew had found some strange prints. Both at Bambi Benton's and Rhonda Carling's. Finally got a match.

"Who?"

"A small time actress. She was in *The Schwarzschild Radius*. One of the worst films ever made," said Lew, authoritatively.

Sonia, the pretty proprietor of Irv's, delivered our burgers with a smile, sliding a paper plate in front of Lew. "For A-number-one police inspector." Lew smiled.

He showed me his plate. I looked at Lew's portrait. It was too accurate to be funny.

It looked like he hadn't slept in three weeks.

"Looks great," I said. I looked at my own. I guess I hadn't slept in four weeks.

Lew looked at my plate, my caricature. "You look like shit, Dick." He took a bite of his burger, savored it. "Best burger in L.A."

"Everybody knows that," I said. In his current frame of mind, Lew would have praised Oki Dog. Pound for pound, Oki Dog delivered your best value penny for penny. Their double-dog chili pastrami cheese burrito could feed a family of four for a week and a half.

But back to the subject at hand. "Lew. You were telling me about the prints you found."

Lew swallowed, nodded, wiped his face with a paper napkin. "Yeah. Prints at both places. From that actress in *Schwarzschild*. She was one of the Cluddum."

"The *Cluddum*?"

"They were a sect of the Dark Farmers. Opposed to the rule of the Pappam."

"God *damn* it, Lew. What was her name?"

I had to wait till he'd finished the last bite of his burger. He licked his thumb. "Her name was Ellen Arden."

"*Ellen Arden?*"

"Yeah. Ellen Arden. What of it?"

Nothing of it. Except she was the girl—who started everything. It took me a while to put the pieces together, but finally they fell into place.

And I had to laugh. Ellen Arden's prints all over the place. It made perfect sense.

Ellen Arden. Of course, I'd always known her as Devi.

Epilogues

Epilogue One

Rutland Atwater was filled with great peace of mind. He'd done Dick Henry a true solid. Introducing him to Perry and Evan, his brothers. And Dick had put them promptly to work. Though he couldn't quite see what Evan would have done for him.

Evan could scribe in the direct penmanship of George Washington. Or Bill Clinton. Or anybody else. He could look, twirl his hand around, and out would come whoever you paid to see.

Adding to Rutland's sense of well-being was his new, black Ford 150. Could carry one helluva payload. And the new truck would drive him to his new apartment out on Hillhurst Avenue near Franklin. Where he could walk to Yuca's Hut. Some of the best Mexican food in Los Angeles. Mexican food had to be cheap. To experience a sixteen-dollar enchilada, like at Pancho's in Manhattan Beach, was to invite a raping of both wallet and gullet.

Rutland exited the hardware store with his purchases. Parked next to his 150 was an older truck, a Toyota. In the back of the truck was a lovely ficus tree in a very large, very yellow pot. Something like that would go well on his patio. His patio overlooking the city. But . . . next paycheck.

The driver of the Toyota nodded at him in friendly fashion. *"Buenos dias, señor,"* said the man.

"I like your tree." Rutland smiled.

Well, well, thought Herman Mantillo, will wonders never cease. He got out of his truck, approached the large gringo. "Allow me, *señor,* to make you a present of this tree." It stank to high heaven, the cats had attacked it, Velma would be home tomorrow, and it was a long drive to the unincorporated section of Los Angeles county where he had planned to roll it out and drive away.

"Oh, I couldn't do that," said Rutland.

"Oh, yes, you could," said Herman.

Epilogue Two

Hannah met me at the Sunset Denny's near the 101. Of course she was wearing her ring. "You know, Dick, I never took the ring off so I never saw what he'd put in there. Hope. I love it. How did you know?"

"Remember the key around his neck?"

"The weird brass key. He called it the key to the future." She tipped her head, studied me. "Was it a real key?"

"Very real. A key to a safe deposit box."

Too many of Hannah's hopes had been crushed flat. She had no optimism left. She looked up at me, almost cringing.

"It took two things to get into the box, dear. A key and a combination. The combination was in your ring."

"H-O-P-E?"

"That's what it was." I slid an envelope across the table. "And this was what was in there."

She opened the envelope with shaking hands. In it was a deposit slip. She read the figure almost uncomprehendingly. "Twenty-seven thousand dollars?"

"Twenty-seven thousand three hundred and twenty. Dave wanted you to have that."

Her head slowly bent toward the tabletop, she took a ragged breath. "Ohhhhh," she said, "ohhhhh." Then she dissolved.

I drank my coffee, looked over at Meineke, across the street. Remembered Bukowski's episode packing brake shoes. Regular, jumbo, or superior. Something like that.

She was back to herself after a while. She looked up at me. "I can't really believe this is really happening. To me. To *me*."

"Well, it is happening. But you need to get your act together. Not that getting it together is a prerequisite. The money's yours under any conditions." I slid a card across the table. It had Devi's name and number. "This lady can help you out. Get things straight. Because this is *your* good fortune. Share it with everybody, everybody will have nothing. And Dave didn't give it to everybody. He gave it to you. But you do what you want."

She reached for my hands across the table. "How do I thank you, Dick?"

"You don't thank me. I didn't do anything. You take care of yourself. And get on with things."

She nodded.

Then I took another envelope from my pocket, slid it across the table. "What's this?"

"A letter from Dave."

She drew it slowly toward her.

"You don't have to read it now, Hannah."

She didn't.

A Letter

Darling Girl,

Loving you was the best thing I ever did. The best thing I ever could have done. You were the light in my darkness, the rain on my thirsty soul, the breeze that cooled me when I was on fire. Looking into your green green eyes was perfect happiness. I'm looking down on you now, right now. And I can see your future. You're going to be happy. You're going to laugh, really laugh. Many wonderful days lie ahead for you, many wonderful days. Find someone and love him like you loved me. And when the wild stars are blowing around heaven and your heart is joy . . . think of me.

Dave

Yeah. The Shortcut Man wrote that.

Don't read anything into it.

THE END

Acknowledgments

Andrew C. Rigrod, Esq., Paul and Polly Pompian, Ryan Harbage, Tom Sturges, and Colin Harrison: thank you all for your support and encouragement.

If There Is No God

if there is no god
who will forgive me
if there is no god
who will receive me
if there is no god
who will laugh with me
if there is no god
who will believe me

if there is no god
who will I wait for
if there is no god
who will defend me
if there is no god
who will speak for me
if there is no god
who's gonna save me

    if there is no god I say
    feed the children anyway
    keep the water blue

don't look to the stars
the old gods are dead
who are the new gods
we are

if there is no god
who will cry murder
if there is no god
who will roll thunder
if there is no god
who gets the money
if there is no god
willya still love me

Words and music by Pearly King (www.pearlykingmusic.com)

About the Author

p.g. sturges was born in Hollywood, California. Punctuated by fitful intervals of school, he has subsequently occupied himself as a submarine sailor, a Christmas tree farmer, a dimensional and optical metrologist, a writer, and a musician.